HITLER'S EYES NARROWED AND SPARKLED AT THE SAME TIME.

With great fervor he initialed the document which would dispatch a homicidal Siegfried toward Roosevelt.

"Let us hope this will be the end of that cripple in the White House," Hitler muttered, withdrawing his pen. Goering was halfway out the door when Hitler, almost as an afterthought, jerked his head up.

"Goering!" he shrieked suddenly.

The Air Minister turned.

"This 'Siegfried' is more crucial than ever. See that he succeeds."

That evening in his radio chamber, four thousand miles to the west, Siegfried rejoiced in the unqualified authorization from Berlin that he had dreamed of for years:

PROCEED!
ADOLF HITLER

FLOWERS FROM BERLIN

NOEL HYND

ZEBRA BOOKS
KENSINGTON PUBLISHING CORP.

ZEBRA BOOKS

are published by

Kensington Publishing Corp.
475 Park Avenue South
New York, NY 10016

First printing: May 1987

Printed in the United States of America

*for
Jeremy's aunt
with love*

—We know of new methods of attack; the Trojan Horse, the Fifth Column that betrays a nation unprepared for treachery. Spies, saboteurs and traitors are the actors in this new tragedy.

> Franklin D. Roosevelt during fireside chat
> to the American people, May 26, 1940

We Americans have always been blessed with great leaders at crucial times.

Washington at our birth. Jefferson at our first age of crisis. Lincoln at the Civil War and Wilson for the first world war.

And then Roosevelt. *What if there had been no Roosevelt?*

> John Gunther
> 1950

Cambridge, Massachusetts

May
1984

PROLOGUE

Memorial Hall, on the fringes of Harvard yard, is the very quintessence of old-guard university architecture. Ivy climbs its aged white columns and red brick walls in abundance. Built in tribute to the Harvard men who perished in wartime, the hall maintains a quiet, timeless dignity amid the bustle and clamor of Cambridge. Yet on the final day of spring term in May of 1984, even Memorial Hall was alive with excitement. Students who might otherwise be on their way to the Cape or to the beaches of the North Shore on an impeccably sunny morning were busy jockeying for seats in the great lecture hall, rousing and crowding out the ghosts of other eras.

Undergraduates had completely packed the sprawling, multitiered amphitheater by 10 A.M. Political Science 217 was concluding for the semester. Today was the final lecture. But it was *the* lecture, the one Dr. William Thomas Cochrane of the Economics Department gave every year. And every year, as the students put it, it was a "sell out." No extra places in the eight-hundred-seat hall, even though the topic was never covered on final exams.

Dr. Cochrane gave the lecture each year because it added that ineffable extra insight into the course. It put things in perspective. Poli Sci 217. American Political Systems in Wartime; 1917-18, 1941-45. Today's topic, "Roosevelt and the World War." Harvard students had their own nickname for the close-out lecture: "Poli Spy 217." Even at age seventy-eight, Bill Cochrane could still pack a house.

Dr. Cochrane entered the lecture hall a few minutes before ten. He was a man comfortable in tweeds and a tie and who wore his age with equal grace. Tall and sturdy, his shoulders were still straight. His hair was thinning and flecked with gray, but surprisingly dark. His one concession to age: reading glasses of a stronger prescription than he'd worn back when he'd worked for the government—just below cabinet level during the Eisenhower and Kennedy years.

There was a woman a few years younger than the lecturer seated at the far left of the first row. Had she opened her mouth to speak, they would have known she was English, though she'd spent the last half century losing the intonations of her birthplace. She was, had anyone looked closely, the paradigm of the patrician English lady of her day. She had a pleasant face and a clear complexion. She wore a dark green cardigan sweater and a wool skirt. A few years earlier, she'd given up the pretense of chasing age from her hair, so now she was very frankly gray. But her hair was arranged in a neat bun and she remained very pretty in an uncommon, aristocratic way. Men who noticed her did not immediately take their eyes off her. It had always been that way.

At 10 A.M., without a cue, the students began to quiet. Copies of *The Harvard Crimson* rustled as they were folded into notebooks. Dr. Cochrane looked up from the lectern—he always spoke without notes—removed his reading glasses, paced a few feet from the front center of the hall, and in his unmistakable yet unassuming way took control of the class.

"Roosevelt and the War," Dr. Cochrane said by way of introduction. He spoke in a clear, concise voice. "You'll allow me, I hope, a bit of historical speculation over the next ninety minutes. You will indulge me, I hope, the opportunity to suggest what *might* have been, in addition to what *was*."

He paced thoughtfully near the front row of students. He felt his audience settling in with him.

"For any of you who are recent transfers from New Haven or any other institution," he digressed momentarily, "we are discussing the *second* Roosevelt. And the *second* world war." A ripple of laughter eased across the amphitheater.

"August 3, 1939," the popular emeritus professor began, recalling his material vividly. He spoke in a bold voice that filled the hall. The students were already entranced. The Englishwoman permitted herself a smile. She remembered also. "Washington, D.C. Ninety-one degrees of city-wide steam bath for the fifth day in a row . . ."

PART ONE

Washington, D.C., and New York
1939

ONE

August 3, 1939. Washington, D.C. Ninety-one degrees of city-wide steam bath for the fifth day in a row. A relentless sun and a humidity unfit for any living, breathing creature. Six more weeks of summer in the American capital and not an evening breeze or a godsent thunderstorm in sight.

The windows were open at the White House and fans whirled in more than a hundred rooms. Fifteen minutes remained before a luncheon meeting between Secretary of State Cordell Hull and the President. Franklin Roosevelt sat in his wheelchair in the Oval Office and studied the disturbing four-page report that he had received that morning. These days the President's mood matched the weather, hot and oppressive. Neither seemed likely for sudden change.

Europe was going to hell. The Nazis had taken Austria and had been given Czechoslovakia. Salazar was entrenched in Lisbon, and Franco had taken Madrid in March. Hitler lunched with Mussolini on a fourth-century A.D. veranda in Rome, and Joseph

15

Stalin, freshly invigorated by the liquidation of his enemies at home, folded his arms on a Kremlin balcony and glared westward. The Red Army, under Stalin's direct command now, was bigger, tougher, and better equipped than ever. But then again, Hitler had more panzer divisions than anyone could count already in place in Bohemia and Moravia.

At his desk, Roosevelt lit a cigarette. As soon as current work could be concluded, the USS *Tuscaloosa,* docked at the Washington Naval Yard, was ready to take FDR and his family to Campobello until September. The President longed for the foggy, misty New Brunswick coastline that he had loved since his boyhood. His sinuses bothered him; so did his arthritis.

Meanwhile, the Republicans imprisoned on Capital Hill sniped daily at Roosevelt. A second Democratic term in Washington had failed to cure a 12 percent unemployment rate. And the 1938 elections had put the taste of FDR's blood in the mouths of the opposition: the Republicans had gained eighty-one seats in the House of Representatives, eight seats in the Senate, and control of thirteen additional statehouses. Suddenly, new presidential prospects were everywhere. Ohio's Senator Taft had won re-election big, as had governors Stassen of Minnesota, and Saltonstall of Massachusetts. New York's racket-busting district attorney, Thomas Dewey, was drawing the largest crowds of any Republican since the President's cousin, Theodore Roosevelt. And the influential eastern press was lining up behind the longest shot of all, Wendell L. Willkie, the president of a utilities company and a former Democrat. All these were added to Michigan Senator Arthur Vandenberg, a paunchy cigar-puffing white-suited gray-haired arch isolationist whom everyone expected to be the candidate and who led Roosevelt in every important poll. Quaintly, Roosevelt referred to Vandenberg, an old-fashioned tubthumping orator, as "the windbag," and the rest of his potential opponents were the "the Neanderthals." But clearly, Roosevelt's private dismissal of his opposition was defensive. Since the midterm elections, he had become increasingly isolated within the White House. And the enemies were everywhere.

Even members of his own party were disgruntled. When would the President announce his own plans? Was he, or was he not, running for a third term? Even Eleanor, who had publicly professed her distaste for another four years in Washington, did not know.

"Eight years is enough for any one man," she had said on June 6 in Chicago. But clearly, on this and most other important matters, the President was keeping his own counsel.

There was no credible successor to carry forward the New Deal. The candidacy of Harry Hopkins was stillborn. John Nance Garner of Texas, the Vice-President and the darling of the increasingly powerful reactionaries within Roosevelt's own party, was already campaigning. So were the six Republicans, equally rock-headed in Roosevelt's opinion.

"Andrew Jackson," Roosevelt was now telling Democratic leaders, "should have picked someone more in sympathy with his policies than Martin Van Buren if he'd wanted his policies continued." The history lesson was meant as a warning. But the party leaders were responding with their own warnings: Roosevelt was the only candidate who could hold together the political coalitions in the North and the West in 1940. Roosevelt, they told him, was the only candidate who could prevent the nation from being turned over to the club-swinging isolationists.

"Would your husband consider a third term in order to further his concept of internationalism and the New Deal?" Eleanor was asked in Penn Station by a New York *Journal-American* reporter in July.

"You'll have to ask *him* that question," she had answered.

"But hasn't he told you?"

"I haven't even asked him," the First Lady replied, stepping briskly into a private railroad car bound for Washington.

That evening in the capital, the pressures and political harassment evidenced themselves for the first time upon the President himself.

"Mr. Roosevelt? Would you even *want* a third term?" Walter Lippmann asked during an impromptu press conference.

"I don't know, Walter," FDR snapped back without a nuance of a smile. "But I'd certainly like a second one."

And so it went.

Whatever his political concerns, no one could doubt the President's equal concern with naval matters. And the report that he read on this sultry August morning before lunch was a classified document from the Department of the Navy.

All his life, Franklin Roosevelt had been fascinated by the sea and in love with ships. As Secretary of the

Navy during the Great War of 1914–18, he had been so successful at securing materiel that President Wilson had once called him to the White House. There, the thirty-four-year-old Roosevelt had been gently reproached for his ardor.

"Mr. Secretary," Wilson had said in his genteel, measured tones, "it seems you have cornered the market on supplies. I'm sorry, but you will have to divide them up with the Army."

By the time Roosevelt had occupied that same office, he had collected no fewer than 9,879 books and pamphlets on naval matters. A few were housed in the library at Hyde Park. Several hundred were at Warm Springs, Georgia. But most were in the White House. When asked by an interviewer during the first term how many volumes he had actually read, Roosevelt replied, "All but one. But that one just arrived last evening."

Roosevelt ran his hand across his brow and reread the U.S. Navy report before him. He was deeply and clearly anguished. The HMS *Wolfe,* two days out of New York, had been ripped in half by an explosive device placed by a saboteur. The *Wolfe* had sunk in ninety minutes. Thirty-nine English merchant seamen had lost their lives, four of the five members of the French purchasing commission had gone down with the ship, and the entire cargo had been lost. All this on a voyage that had been shrouded in the strictest secrecy. A special detail of United States Marine guards had been posted at the Erie Boat Basin in Brooklyn where the HMS *Wolfe* had been docked. But someone had placed an explosive device aboard the ship.

Sabotage on the East Coast, the President concluded as his intercom buzzed, was totally out of hand. The President turned his wheelchair and answered the intercom.

"Mr. Hoover is here," his secretary, Missy LeHand, told him.

"Two minutes," the President answered.

Waiting a few minutes was just what J. Edgar Hoover needed these days, Roosevelt mused. The President eased his wheelchair back behind his desk and neatly placed the Navy's report on his right-hand side. He readied himself for the meeting with the FBI director, a meeting to which Hoover had been summoned just one hour earlier.

Roosevelt disliked and distrusted Hoover. Hoover was a Republican, a Coolidge appointee dating back to 1924. But even worse, in the eyes of the current President, was Hoover's greedy amalgamation of power within the newly formed FBI. Hoover, it was known, had begun a grand collection of fingerprints and files, accessible primarily to himself. And still worse, Hoover seemed intent on building a political power base out of the recent successes of his agency.

Over the last few years, the FBI had, through a combination of hard work, luck, and occasional diligence, captured several of the most notorious—and inappropriately romanticized—outlaws of the era since the stock market crash. One by one, Ma Barker, Baby Face Nelson, Machine Gun Kelly, Pretty Boy Floyd, and Bonnie and Clyde Parker had fallen into the hands of federal authorities. Always, Hoover was there soon after the arrest to link a hand onto the prisoner's elbow and have his picture taken. Even when the FBI hadn't even been in on the capture, Hoover was there to claim credit. When John Dillinger, for example, had been shot to death outside the Biograph movie theater, a grinning Hoover had been in Chicago the next day to have his picture taken with the cadaver.

To Roosevelt, who knew a thing or two about power bases and who vastly preferred to have his own picture taken among boy scouts or WPA camp workers, such behavior was more than a trifle irritating. He had it in mind, in fact, to replace Hoover in another year. But meanwhile Roosevelt and Hoover were stuck with each other.

There was a knock on the door to the Oval Office and Mrs. LeHand was the first to step through. She ushered Hoover into the President's working quarters, glanced disapprovingly at the FBI director, then closed the door as she left.

"Come in, J. Edgar, come in," the President said, not looking up. Roosevelt sat at a desk that was neither very big nor very neat. Papers were in disarray in every direction and a half-empty can of Camels stood on the left-hand edge. Then Roosevelt glanced up, blinked, cocked his large head, and smiled. J. Edgar Hoover stared at what was—with the possible exception of Adolph Hitler's—the most famous face in the world.

To Hoover, Roosevelt looked like a caricature of himself. The President's face was tanned and mobile, his eyes never at rest. When he smiled, his mouth took the shape of a V, his long jaw tilted upward, and two long grave lines bracketed his mouth. His round glasses reflected like windowpanes in the sunlight.

"Do sit down, J. Edgar," F.D.R. said. He motioned to a leather armchair.

Hoover mumbled a good morning and sat down. He consciously tried to keep his eyes off Roosevelt's withered legs, visible through the open front portion of the desk. Then Roosevelt adjusted his glasses slightly, as if to bring his visitor into proper focus.

The corners of Hoover's mouth were turned ferociously downward. His neck was crimson, his collar tight, his eyes afire. Shadows from the window behind Roosevelt darkened Hoover's face, but made him squint at the same time.

"It would seem to me, J. Edgar," the President began, "that there exists a certain gathering importance to this matter of German saboteurs and agents within the United States. Yet your Bureau appears unable to make the appropriate arrests."

Hoover bristled instantly and opened his mouth to speak. Then he stopped. From the President's intonation, Hoover knew there was more. And he knew better than to interrupt.

Back in July, Roosevelt had attempted to revise the Neutrality Act so that the United States might aid the democracies of Western Europe against Nazi aggression. Roosevelt had been defeated in both the House and the Senate. The United States was to remain strictly neutral and send no war materiel to anyone.

Undaunted, and risking impeachment, Roosevelt attempted anyway to assist those whom he considered to be America's friends, particularly England and France. But equally undaunted, a nameless, faceless agent of the Third Reich had very effectively taken matters into his own hands. Roosevelt recited from memory a litany of incidents.

An explosion in a Newark, New Jersey, warehouse had slowed the delivery of five thousand M-1 rifles to anti-Fascist partisans in Greece; a dynamite bomb in a Ford parts plant in Delaware had destroyed production capacity for a specific line of tank gearboxes essential to the French Army; yet another bomb, planted near a furnace in the Frankford Arsenal in Germantown, Pennsylvania, had almost brought down that entire edifice, a disaster which might have set back munitions production in the eastern United States by nine months.

On and on the list went, incident after incident. Hoover squirmed uncomfortably until the President concluded with the plight of HMS *Wolfe.*

"Tell me, Mr. Hoover," Roosevelt asked rhetorically, "how *does* a saboteur, particularly the one whom your Bureau is searching for, creep onto a religiously guarded vessel, plant a bomb, and sneak off again?"

Hoover was about to answer, but Roosevelt kept talking.

"There is a man at large somewhere in America," Roosevelt postulated, "who is both an expert at espionage and high-level explosives. He is costing us lives and he is robbing precious war materiel from the democracies of Europe. But he is an unnaturally clever man. Your FBI cannot arrest him because you do not know whom to arrest. You cannot look for him because no one knows for whom to look. Indeed, the local police departments in the cities and towns of the Northeast cannot be used because we haven't the faintest idea which ones should even be contacted."

Hoover sat in silence. The President looked him up and 'down. "Well, what do you think, J. Edgar?" Roosevelt asked at length. "Have you been struck dumb? You've barely said a word since you walked in here."

"The Bureau," Hoover replied quickly and defensively, "is working on this precise case day and—"

"What has been accomplished?"

Hoover groped. He mentioned a Portuguese network that could be closed down at any moment. And he spoke of a man named Fritz Duquaine who was believed to have entered the country from Vancouver some months earlier and who the FBI had good cause to believe was operating in the Northeast.

"But you have no proof?"

"No, sir."

"And you have no suspects who are so enormously gifted with explosives?"

"No, Mr. President." Hoover verged on mentioning that no fewer than 43,000 immigrants had filtered into the United States from Germany since 1929. Sorting through them for a gifted bomber was not easy. But Roosevelt was speaking again.

"Tell me," said the President. "Do I misunderstand the situation or am I correct? What we need is a face. A name. Or a past. We must find out who this man is, where he came from, and what his background might be. All this is even more important than a current identity because this man would certainly be gifted also at changing identities."

"That's all correct, sir."

Roosevelt continued to lead the conversation. "So what we are talking about is a bit of *detective* work. Identifying this particular man and locating him is the first task, without which any other plans are meaningless. And, of course, this work must proceed without alerting the suspect. Otherwise he will disappear and move elsewhere. Or return to Germany, perhaps."

Mrs. LeHand buzzed the intercom again and notified the President that the secretaries of State and Interior were awaiting the President in the downstairs dining room. Roosevelt selected a fresh cigarette from the tin of Camels on his desk, placed it into a tortoiseshell holder, and slipped the holder between his teeth. Then he shifted uncomfortably in his chair, leaned back slightly, and lit his cigarette.

"Now, Mr. Director," Roosevelt concluded, "who is the best detective in your Federal Bureau of Investigation?"

Hoover considered it for a few seconds. "The best detective within the FBI," answered J. Edgar Hoover, "would be Frank Lerrick. Special Agent Lerrick is director of personnel as well as my own chief assistant. He's currently employed at Bureau headquarters on Constitution Avenue."

Roosevelt pursed his lips and waited impatiently. He glanced downward to the papers on his desk. Hoover shifted his weight slightly in the armchair.

Then Roosevelt looked up again. "Tell me, J. Edgar," the President said, "weren't we successful several months ago in infiltrating a man into Germany? A man who returned some very good intelligence for us? He was a linguist and a financial man of some sort.

Even had explosives training in the United States Army."

"Yes, Mr. President. That's entirely correct."

"I believe he's returned home, has he not?"

"Yes, sir."

Now the President cleared his throat.

"Yes, of course," said Hoover, as if to suddenly remember. "Naturally, the man is still employed by the Bureau. I believe his name is—"

"Cochrane," Roosevelt said. "I happen to recall. William Thomas Cochrane. Where is he?"

"He's currently assigned to Baltimore."

"Baltimore?" The President arched an eyebrow. "Doing what?"

"He's in the Mid-Atlantic States Banking Fraud Division," Hoover said.

Roosevelt added nothing for many seconds. *"Really?"* he finally breathed.

"I can reassign him this afternoon," Hoover volunteered.

The President smiled widely and extinguished his cigarette, carefully removing the stub from the holder. "Very good, J. Edgar," Roosevelt concluded. "I was confident that you would know exactly who should head this investigation."

As if by magic, two Secret Service men appeared and moved to a position behind the President of the United States, preparing to wheel him to the luncheon for which he was already five minutes late. Hoover instinctively rose. The Secret Service agents, employees of the Treasury, ignored him completely.

"I think," Roosevelt said in parting, "that you and I should meet again, J. Edgar. In about a month. I'd like

26

to know how this saboteur has been captured."

Hoover thought his ears were failing. "A month?" he asked.

"Good Christ, Mr. Hoover!" Roosevelt suddenly roared, his chair halting, his face florid. "There's a war breaking out in Europe! You don't think we have all year, do you?"

TWO

I

Franklin Roosevelt and J. Edgar Hoover: the aristocrat from Hyde Park and the ambitious self-made Washingtonian who in 1917 had landed a twenty-five-dollar-a-week job as a file clerk in the crime bureau. They were never the best of friends. Frequently, during the overlapping years of their careers, they were political adversaries of the bitterest sort. Extraordinary events were essential even for the two men to sit cordially in the same room with each other.

But the extraordinary events had already occurred—with no distinct pattern at varying times on two different continents. At their center were three principals: a dedicated spy serving Hitler's Germany, a young Englishwoman, and a widowed American banker in the employ of his own government. Certain of the events reached as far back as two decades. Others were relatively recent.

For example, late in June of 1939, the spy who called

himself Siegfried had again traveled to New York. He had been at Fritz Duquaine's apartment in Manhattan's East Eighties when a third man, one whom both Duquaine and Siegfried expected, knocked on the door. It was just past 11 P.M. Duquaine recognized the knock and admitted his visitor, a naturalized American named Wilhelm Hunsicker. Hunsicker, as Siegfried sat in an armchair and studied him, was a hulking, heavy, thick-browed blue-jowled man who was the head butcher on the passenger liner SS *Panama*. Duquaine often used Hunsicker for special assignments, such as this one. The *Panama* had been in port for twelve hours and would be sailing again that next evening, bound first for Cork, in Ireland, and ultimately Genoa.

But Hunsicker was also a courier and brought with him an urgent message from the Gestapo. Siegfried was no longer to use the old route for messages—the diplomatic dispatch route through the Portuguese Consulate in New York, via Lisbon to Berlin.

"Instead," said Hunsicker in German, reciting without curiosity the message he had memorized in Genoa, "you are to begin radio communication directly with the Third Reich at 1900 hours, Eastern Standard Time, July 15. By that time you will have your receiving set ready. You will listen for the call letters assigned to you."

Hunsicker opened his wallet. He handed Siegfried a coded scramble of letters which had been handwritten on the back of a baggage receipt from the ship. From these letters Siegfried broke down the code and determined the call letters that German intelligence, the Abwehr, had assigned to Siegfried's radio set—

CQDXVW-2. Siegfried would be communicating with radio station AOR-3 in Hamburg.

Siegfried showed no emotion whatsoever. "It's damned well about time," he finally answered. "When you get back to the Reich, Wilhelm, you can ask those incompetents in the Gestapo what took them so long."

Hunsicker was visibly surprised at the reproach. His eyes skipped to Duquaine. But Siegfried held his attention.

"Now," Siegfried said, "you have something else for me, don't you?"

Hunsicker nodded, then handed Siegfried a small green envelope, the type a jeweler might use. Siegfried pocketed it.

A tall, spare man with a cadaverous face, Duquaine stood to one side and watched the transaction. A skilled spymaster, the graying Duquaine had been in the employ of Germany since 1913. Unlike the other two men in the room, he was a Boer, born in the Transvaal in 1890. He harbored a deep hatred for England and America, the two Anglo-Saxon superpowers, and if pressed would explain his passion by citing atrocities inflicted upon his parents by the British Army. He stood near the apartment's sooted fireplace and watched Siegfried finish a cherry brandy. Despite his decades of experience, Duquaine was still perplexed by Siegfried. The man was an enigma.

"There is nothing else, is there?" Siegfried asked the courier, who was strangely silent.

"No," answered Hunsicker, suddenly ill at ease.

"Then Herr Duquaine and I wish to speak privately." Siegfried's eyes indicated the door.

31

Hunsicker wavered for a moment. His eyes flirted expectantly with the bottle of brandy. Then Duquaine interceded.

"Thank you, Wilhelm," Duquaine said. "I will see you tomorrow when we sail."

The huge man glowered for a moment at Siegfried, retrieved his hat, and departed. Then Siegfried reached for a paper bag beside his chair. "Now I have something for you," he said to Duquaine.

He produced a German-language version of the Holy Bible, an edition old enough to have been printed in the last century, which made it several years older than Siegfried.

Siegfried thumbed the book a final time, ran his fingers across the binding, then flicked it closed. The book was ornate and looked much like a family heirloom.

"My gift for those in Hamburg and Berlin," Siegfried announced. He handed the Bible to Duquaine, who accepted it. "How long is the *Panama's* voyage to Europe?"

"Seven days." Duquaine poured himself a brandy and angled the conversation in a different direction. "You're capable of building this transmitter yourself?"

"I've been ready for several years." He glanced at his watch, then raised his eyes to Duquaine again. "You know, Duquaine," Siegfried added, "I can win their whole war for them if only Berlin will let me. You'll tell them that, too." It was more of a statement than a request.

"I will stress your enthusiasm."

Siegfried gave Duquaine a mildly contemptuous look and again changed the subject. "Your ship sails at eight in the evening?"

"Yes."

"You'll be wise to be on it. Your organizations here are filled with traitors and amateurs. It's a wonder any information of any value at all gets back to Berlin. Even through the channels of the Gestapo itself." Siegfried fingered the bottle of brandy, then decided against any more. "If the Lisbon route has been compromised, my dear Duquaine, it's a matter of time before you are, too."

Duquaine pursed his lips and gazed at the younger man. Walking the streets or going to a movie was exactly what he'd planned for the next day, for exactly the reason cited. In three decades of intelligence work on three different continents, he had never seen anything quite the equal of this thirtyish, dark-haired man. Siegfried was brilliant, but excessive beyond words.

"Which leads us to the final question," edged Duquaine. "Berlin insists on a system of contact."

"Of course." Siegfried allowed a silence.

"You have devised one?"

"When you return to America," said Siegfried, "you will go to Battery Park, across from the Statue of Liberty. You will go on Tuesdays and Fridays and appear in front of the Sailor's Monument at noon, when the park is most crowded. You will carry an umbrella and an attaché case in your left arm. In your other hand you will have a tabloid newspaper, folded. You will then go to a bench at the south end of the park and sit for fifteen minutes. Watch the ships in the harbor. If I care to contact you that day, I will find you as you leave the park. For what I am doing, I must be certain that there is no surveillance."

"And I notice that there is no way you wish us to contact you?"

"I can be contacted by radio. From Germany. By the High Command only."

"And this sitting in the park, these orders you are giving me . . . what if it rains?"

Siegfried stood and reached for his own coat and hat. "You're supposed to be brilliant, also, Herr Duquaine. If it rains, use your umbrella."

Duquaine watched Siegfried pull on the overcoat and depart. Duquaine was enough of a professional himself to genuinely understand the danger—and the value—of such a man. Siegfried worked alone, with no immediate allies. He was impossible to control; orders could be issued only as requests. Duquaine wondered if Siegfried could even control himself.

Duquaine, in fact, had been in the espionage game long enough to reduce certain aspects of it to a science. The first thing he wanted to know about a man was his motivation. Why did a man become a spy?

He could answer that question about himself. Hatred of the Anglo-Saxon world. And he could answer it about most of the men he'd encountered over his lifetime. Political zeal. The sense of danger. Anger. Vengeance. Money. Sex. Every man had his motivation. Yet with Siegfried, motivation was invisible. Siegfried, Duquaine had decided one rainy evening long ago, was pursued by certain inner demons. And only heaven and hell knew what they were.

It was well after midnight, but not yet 1 A.M., as

34

Siegfried walked down the three flights of Duquaine's tenement. He paused in the doorway and scanned the street. He lit a Pall Mall and began to walk.

A few restaurants were still open in Yorkville, but the last patrons were starting to emerge. The kitchen staffs and dining-room employees were starting home. A handful of bars remained open, though none were crowded. Much of the joy of the German-American beer halls had disappeared over the last few years. The mood was more somber, even occasionally tense. Some had taken Swiss names as the international situation grew cloudier. The Bremen had changed its name earlier in the year to the Zurich. And the Munchen Bar, the fixture at the northwest corner of Eighty-ninth and Second, was now the Fondue Chalet, for God's sake! Why, Siegfried wondered, didn't anyone in America understand the wonderful things that Adolph Hitler was accomplishing on behalf of the German people? Why did the American press spread such insidious *lies* about the Fuehrer's national socialism?

Siegfried was intoxicated by everything that currently transpired in Germany. The enormous proud rallies! Handsome blond boys in uniforms! Laughing, healthy women! The powerful, fearsome black, red, and white flag everywhere! The degenerates and undesirables finally on the run! Siegfried accepted totally this New Order for the final two thirds of the twentieth century. This was how the world *should* be. . . .

On this particular night in Yorkville, Siegfried could hear his own footsteps. That, of course, suited him perfectly. He preferred to move at this hour. Anyone suicidal enough to follow him would be immediately conspicuous . . . and would suffer the consequences.

Idly, and with some pride. Siegfried recalled the first time he had murdered for the Third Reich.

Siegfried had been in England in the city of Birmingham four years earlier. A coalition of Communist-led unions had shut down every factory in the city and had called for a massive May 1 rally. The strikers—textile, auto, chemical, and electrical workers—congregated at Hockley Circus and on the roads west. Then at 10 A.M. on a Friday, they had moved in a rowdy, rambunctious, singing, cheering legion down Hockley Road, across Great Hampton Street, and toward the center of the city. As they started up Constitution Hill, their voices came together in "The Internationale."

Siegfried, not long out of university, passionately hated that mob of ten thousand. The Marxists were the most vile force in the twentieth century: out to destroy churches, nations, and Aryan culture. It was bad enough that they had taken over peasant Russia and butchered the Czar. Now the industrialized West was their target, and weak-kneed liberal democracies like England and France simply stood by.

Only Adolph Hitler could stop them. And Siegfried—Hitler's loyal, anonymous, brilliant acolyte—was intent on doing his part.

The cheering throng surged into Colmore Circus and filled the mall. Police waited in a long, tense, blue line, not liking what they saw, but just watching. Watching. Like the limp-wristed government of Neville Chamberlain.

At twenty-two minutes after ten, just as the workers moved into St. Chad's Circus, one stick of dynamite—

crudely but securely attached to a cheap Swiss alarm clock—detonated beneath the gas tank of a Triumph four-door. It blew fire and automobile parts toward the head of the crowd. The mob abandoned its flags and slogans and turned back upon itself. Pandemonium reigned, but the marchers could move neither forward nor backward. That's when, at the foot of the mall, Siegfried's second bomb detonated: three sticks of dynamite encased in iron piping and sparked by a remote-control signal. The device blew iron shrapnel out of a trash can for fifty yards in every direction. It was Siegfried's masterpiece.

At the end of the day, in what would become known as the Birmingham May Day Bombing, nine lay dead and forty-seven other marchers were wounded. Some lost fingers and hands; other lost feet or eyes. Those closest were deafened. One policeman was blinded. Siegfried left England two days later while Scotland Yard was still chasing its tail. He traveled on an American passport, of all things, and when he arrived in New York word reached him through Fritz Duquaine that Hitler himself was elated.

Now, America was next. The most dangerous individual bomber in the world, dedicated to his Naziism, was at complete liberty in a slumbering America, intent on changing the course of history.

Intent and confident. All he needed now was the specific orders from Berlin.

II

New York City was peaceful this evening, Siegfried

observed. The contrast with the magnificent bloody scene in Birmingham was never far from his mind. This was a perfect night for thinking or relaxing, even for indulging in a man's simple sexual pleasures, if time permitted. Siegfried liked nights when he could hear his own footsteps. The atmosphere aroused him.

Siegfried walked westward across a darkened Eighty-second Street, then crossed Central Park, strolling near the lamplights. He paused only to light a fresh Pall Mall with the stub of each preceding one. Each time, as he lit, he scanned the area behind him.

Not a soul. Siegfried was endlessly careful about the rudimentary things.

On the west side of the park, Siegfried turned downtown and at West Fifty-seventh Street he checked his watch. He had hours to spare so he doubled back to Park Avenue, turned south again, then twice slipped up and down side streets toward Lexington. The FBI was a pretty amateurish outfit, to his knowledge, led by that clown Hoover. But every once in a while they got lucky.

At Forty-ninth Street Siegfried saw a green and white Checker cab sitting outside the Waldorf Astoria, the driver sleepily peering over a tabloid newspaper. The spy raised his hand.

The driver set aside his newspaper. He moved his cab a few feet up the curb and looked at the passenger's suit, peaked brimmed hat, and expensive raincoat. He took his fare to be a businessman out on the town.

"Just goin' home, mac?" the driver asked amiably as Siegfried slid into the back seat.

"Trying to." Siegfried spoke with a neutral, clipped accent which the driver took to be American.

"Where to?"

"Pennsylvania Station."

"Not many trains at this hour," the driver said as he pulled out onto the empty avenue. "Hope your wife isn't waiting up for you."

"It doesn't bother her, so it shouldn't bother you," the passenger answered.

"Yes, sir."

En route to the station, the cabbie spoke one other time. "You see about that game Hubbell pitched against the Dodgers yesterday?" the driver asked.

"What?"

"Carl Hubbell. The Giant's pitcher. One-hit shutout."

"I don't follow baseball," Siegfried said.

"Oh," the driver said. "Never mind." He glanced at his passenger through the rearview mirror. Siegfried was staring at the driver's hack license, posted near the meter. On the license were the cabbie's name and photograph. The passenger was staring intently, as if to memorize them for later use. A sudden tremor overtook the driver. The quiet man three feet behind him, seated equidistant between the two doors, gave him the creeps. There was something about the man, he suddenly realized, that filled him with fear. That sensation only deepened when, as if by some sixth sense, the passenger raised his eyes to glare back into the rearview mirror.

When they arrived at Pennsylvania Station, the fare was eighty-five cents. The passenger gave the driver a dollar, refused change, and disappeared between the two eagles at the sandstone steps to the terminal.

Within the station, a crew of Negro redcaps, dozing

39

and nodding sleepily near a baggage cart, raised their heads hopefully when Siegfried entered. But they lowered their heads again when they saw that the man had no luggage. Siegfried walked to the baggage-counter at the far end of the lobby and claimed a small brown suitcase.

Then, bag in hand, Siegfried found an open gate leading to a train that would leave for Newark, Trenton, Philadelphia, and Baltimore in another twenty-five minutes.

Perfect, the traveler thought to himself.

Siegfried walked into a nearly vacant car, passed two shabbily dressed men who were snoring in their seats, and entered the washroom. In the cramped quarters, he pulled from the suitcase a complete change of clothing, retaining only his white shirt and underwear. He folded his raincoat into the suitcase and neatly packed his dark suit and his tie. He replaced his neckwear with a sportier, more colorful tie and then donned gray slacks and a dark blazer. His hat he carefully crushed and placed on top of his suit as he closed his luggage.

Then he recombed his hair and put on a pair of glasses. He studied himself in the mirror. He looked rather different. Younger. A trifle sportier. More like an out-of-town businessman than a city-bred executive. He was pleased with the transformation.

Siegfried was off the train in five minutes. At a second checkroom on the lower level of the station, he rid himself of the suitcase once again. Now it was almost 3 A.M.

He went to a telephone and dialed a number in Murray Hill. Siegfried listened. He pictured the small apartment in the East Thirties where the number rang.

40

He envisioned the dark-haired woman sleeping in her bed, rising and walking into her living room. Then she answered.

Siegfried gave her a moment to emerge from sleep. "I'm in town for a few hours," he said softly. "But *only* a few hours."

The woman's name was Marjorie. She recognized the voice of a man she knew to be Mr. Bolton, a manufacturer of inexpensive clocks and timepieces in Meriden, Connecticut. She also knew him to be a wayward husband.

"Tell me, sugar," she said, running a hand through her brown hair, "What do you do earlier in the evenings? Whenever my phone rings past two A.M. it's only one person. You."

"I missed my connecting train back from Atlanta," he said amiably. "But does that mean I should miss my fun?"

"I'll be waiting."

Marjorie lit a cigarette and straightened the three compact rooms of her apartment. Then she took off her night gown, showered quickly, perfumed herself, and changed into a lavender peignoir.

Men, Marjorie knew, had their likes and dislikes. A man's request varied little from one visit to the next. In the five years that she had supported herself in this way, the five years since the collapse of her second marriage, men had ceased to be much of a mystery. They came to her for what they did not get at home. She would serve them and make them comfortable. And Mr. Bolton, her clock manufacturer, was one of her more desirable customers, she thought as she finished with her eyeliner. A true gentleman. A man of breeding, if she

41

was any judge. She looked in the mirror and entertained an idle thought about him. He was exactly the type of man, she had thought many times, that if she were to, well, remarry . . . But she quickly dismissed the notion. No use entertaining the impossible. Besides, her buzzer had just rung.

She kissed the spy on the lips when he stepped through the door. Mr. Bolton had his routine, just like her dozen other regulars. He never went into her bedroom. She led him to the armchair in the living room.

She poured him a scotch and water. She let him sit down and relax. He spoke for many minutes on the state of the clock business—meaningless garble to her. But she didn't know a single businessman who didn't pour out his professional problems before he could fully relax. The doctors, she had observed long ago, were different. They wanted to be in and out in a few minutes.

Mr. Bolton talked of main springs and timing mechanisms and of contracts filled and unfulfilled. He said he was depressed about the nature of the world. America was headed for another war, he feared, and while a mobilization might make him rich making inexpensive watches, he grieved at the prospect of being a war profiteer.

"What do you think about Roosevelt?" he asked her. "Do you think he'll get us into the war?"

"He says he hates war," she answered, surprised at being asked her opinion on anything.

She stifled a mild yawn, but he caught her. Then he looked at her differently. "I know you're sleepy," he said. "You're very kind to entertain me at this hour."

He withdrew his wallet and counted out twenty-five dollars.

"A girl has to keep her boyfriend happy," she answered soothingly. She watched him fold the money and place it on an end table. "Business gets a man all tensed up," she continued. "He can't sleep. A real man has to let go sometimes."

He nodded. She moved closer to him and sat down on the arm of his chair. He smiled and let her lean down to kiss him. He slipped his arm around her waist. Then she let her peignoir tumble open so that he could see her. His hand was within the peignoir a moment later.

"I think this would be the *perfect* time," he said.

She let her clothing slide away completely, then she helped him undress. He reclined in the chair, relaxing completely. She knelt before him. She knew what Mr. Bolton liked.

"You're very kind," he said as she began. "And very gentle."

Men were so predictable, Marjorie thought. Their impulses were so simple. And her Mr. Bolton was not a difficult man to please. Why didn't his wife do the few extra things he asked? What, she wondered, was wrong with his wife, anyway?

It was just past seven when Siegfried returned to Pennsylvania Station. The waiting room and grand lobby were just beginning to come alive with the earliest of the daily commuters. Siegfried studied the dowdy weariness of the men and women who presumably passed this way each morning. He shuddered.

43

At a Union News stand, Siegfried bought a *Herald-Tribune* from a man who appeared to be legally blind. Then Siegfried walked to Gate 15, where the Lackawanna Railroad's first train of the day would take him through northern New Jersey to his home.

"Morning, sir," said a cheerful conductor, recognizing him from many previous trips.

Siegfried fumbled for his ticket. "Never remember where I put the damned thing," he muttered absentmindedly. Then he found it.

"Here we are, Jeffrey," he said, calling the familiar conductor by his name. He handed the man his ticket. "See what the Giants did yesterday?" he asked. "Hubbell was it?"

The conductor's face flashed with surprise. "You bet it was Hubbell!" he said. "One-hitter against the Dodgers. I didn't know you followed baseball, sir."

Siegfried shrugged. "Doesn't everyone?" He flashed his most gracious smile, took back his canceled ticket so that he could doze on the short train ride, and found a seat at the rear of a NO SMOKING car near the door. Hubbell, he thought. The Giants, he thought. Baseball. Americans were so dumb, Siegfried mused. So provincial. So naïve and so painfully easy to fool. And Siegfried was so expert at preying upon the smallest and most precise details.

III

The next morning Siegfried examined and opened the small green envelope placed in his hand by Hunsicker. Out rolled a diamond about the size of a peppercorn. For a moment, Siegfried coldly examined the gem. Somewhere in Germany or Amsterdam, Siegfried knew, some Jew's passage out of Germany had probably been purchased with it. Damn the filthy Jews, Siegfried thought. The parasites of the twentieth century! They had brought upon themselves everything that was now happening to them! But then he closed his hand on the gem and turned away from his personal hatreds.

He traveled to Philadelphia and sold the diamond to a dealer along the 700 block of Sansom Street. Then over the next few days he visited electronics stores at random and acquired the basic parts of a shortwave station. Purchase and assembly would be long, tedious jobs. But he had complete privacy in his home. And he had time.

By July 6 he had completed the receiving unit and had strung a strong coaxial copper wire as an antenna. He switched the unit to the ON position and it leaped to life. As he turned to the construction of his transmitter, he listened for hours to the dots, dashes, and indeterminate blips of international Morse code that shot across the shortwave bands. His fluency with code returned as he worked. It became a language to him. Then he completed his transmitter, equipped it to operate off normal house current, and connected it to the same antenna as his receiver. It was July 10.

Now Siegfried turned to his telegraph key. He worked off a dummy transmitting pattern, listening to his own transmission via headphones. When he began he could send approximately ten words a minute. But by July 14, he could send thirty.

He was ready.

The evening was warm on July 15. At 6:55 P.M., the

sun was setting. In Hamburg, it was nearing 1 A.M. A perfect time for shortwave reception.

Siegfried sat by the dials of his receiver and counted the minutes. Five. Four. Three. Two. One.

It was seven o'clock. Siegfried's frequency was tightly channeled and his receiver was tuned as sharply as possible, his antenna facing Europe. He waited. He could feel sweat begin to form on his hands and on his back. Then his receiver crackled and his scalp crawled with nearly adolescent excitement.

He could hear Hamburg! Not as clearly as he might like, but he could hear his Gestapo counterpart! Hitler's Reich itself!

The message was in uncoded German. Siegfried wrote it down in pencil on a note pad as he measured off the dots and dashes.

REGRET PORTUGUESE CONTACTS SEVERELY COMPROMISED. SEND ONLY ONE TIME PER WEEK. FURNISH DAY YOU EXPECT TO SEND. WE ARE PREPARED 700, 1300, AND 1800 HOURS ALL DAYS. FURNISH SECOND FREQUENCY OUTSIDE AMATEUR BAND. REGARDS.

AOR-3

To which, Siegfried immediately replied:

YOUR SIGNAL VERY WEAK. IMPROVE IT. I WILL SEND WEDNESDAYS AND SUNDAYS 2300 HOURS. WILL LISTEN SATURDAYS, SAME TIME. SUGGEST CODE ON ALL FUTURE TRANSMISSIONS. AWAITING . . .

CQDXVW-2

Siegfried leaned back from his work and removed his hand from his telegraph key. He massaged the cramping muscles of his neck. He stared intently at his receiver, listening to the thin haze of static that encroached on the AOR-3 frequency.

Several long minutes drifted by. He wondered if he should retransmit. What was wrong with those bastards on the other end? Didn't they understand? Were they not pulling in his signal? Why didn't—

In the midst of his curses the frequency came alive again with a simple command:

CODE UNNECESSARY TONIGHT. USE NAVAL CODE IN FUTURE. MESSAGE TONIGHT?

AOR-3

Much more like it, thought Siegfried. With satisfaction, he began his transmission.

LYCOMING AIRCRAFT IN LONG ISLAND HAVE ENGINE DESIGNED TO FIT INTO WINGS OF FIGHTER AIRCRAFT LIKE A SANDWICH. HAVE STOLEN A BLUEPRINT. CONDENSED SAID BLUE-PRINT AND HAVE SENT IT VIA SS PANAMA BOUND IN COVER BINDING OF HOLY BIBLE. ALSO: HMS WOLFE WAS TAKING MUNITIONS AND BOMBSITE CARGO FROM BROOKLYN TO CHERBOURG APRIL FOUR LAST. BOARDED SHIP BEFORE DEPAR-TURE. PLANTED HEAVY FLOWERS FROM BERLIN. MOST LIKELY SUNK WOLFE.

CQDXVW-2

Barely taking his eyes off his receiver or his telegraph

key, Siegfried used his sleeve to mop the sweat rolling down his temples. *Damn this small, cramped room,* he thought. These bloody secretive working conditions! The almost nonexistent light! Being a spy meant working in spaces with the size and charm of an oak casket. Siegfried shuddered.

He waited. *Come on, you morons!* he thought. *Don't you know it's a matter of time before the stupid Roosevelt administration sets up listening and tracking stations? Come on! Respond, damn you!*

Then in another five seconds his receiver was again alive with dots and dashes. Siegfried could "read" the Morse code as it came off his receiver. But he transcribed it onto paper, anyway.

BRAVO, SIEGFRIED!
AOR-3

"Of course, 'Bravo, Siegfried,' you cunts!" he said aloud to himself. "You're safely in Hamburg, I'm here in America, and who do you think is going to win your whole fucking war for you?"

REQUEST NEW ASSIGNMENT.
CQDXVW-2

Siegfried tapped out.

He waited for a moment. This time Hamburg was ready.

BROWNING MUNITIONS CORPORATION OF CHI-
CAGO DEVELOPING LINE OF ANTIAIRCRAFT

GUNS FOR EXPORT TO U.K. MUST KNOW: WEIGHT
OF GUN IN FIRING POSITION—4-LEGGED CROSS-
MOUNTING—CALIBER, WEIGHT OF SHELL,
WEIGHT OF CARTRIDGE, MUZZLE VELOCITY,
HIGHEST ELEVATION, RANGE VERTICALLY AND
HORIZONTALLY, FIRING SPEED, ESTIMATED DE-
LIVERY DATE—

Siegfried angrily broke into the German signal.

STUDY YOUR MAPS! HAVE NO ACCESS TO
BROWNING FACTORY. AM NOWHERE NEAR CHI-
CAGO. SEND ASSIGNMENT IN EASTERN U.S.A. OR
FIND ANOTHER AGENT, YOU HALF-WITS!
CQDXVW-2

Siegfried glared furiously at his equipment. He
reached to a pack of Pall Malls and pulled one out with
his lips. He waited for a response as Hamburg
presumably recoiled from his transmission.

The wait was painful. He smoked two cigarettes. His
anger grew. Then he heard a signal, grabbed his pencil,
and transcribed:

BRITISH VESSEL HMS ADRIANA SAILED TO U.S.A.
UNDER STRICTEST SECURITY. DOCKED AT U.S.
NAVY YARD AT RED BANK, NEW JERSEY. DIS-
COVER: MISSION, CARGO, DESTINATION.
AOR-3

Siegfried smiled. At last they began to understand.
He tapped back:

As his forefinger came to a rest, the spy leaned back in his wooden chair. He blew out a long breath and felt his pulse subside. He glanced at his watch. Seven and a quarter minutes of transmission time. He shook his head. Did Hamburg think he was playing games? Certainly the Americans wouldn't think so if they traced him. He cursed profanely as he took down his antenna.

Piece by piece he sealed his whole station into the walls of his transmission chamber. He replaced the wallboards, panel by panel, using his strong left thumb to push nails into their proper grooves. Siegfried admired the way his nails slipped perfectly in and out of the holes he had bored for them. *If only people behaved as diligently,* he thought.

He looked again at the notations he had made from the messages he had received. Then he crumpled them into an ashtray and set fire to them. He stirred the ashes when the paper was completely consumed. Next, he poured the ashes into a wastebasket that he would empty later that evening.

He tucked his Pall Malls into the breast pocket of his shirt and was finished. His location was so ingenious, Siegfried was convinced, that in a century of searching, only he could find his station. As long as his signal escaped detection and tracking, he would never be caught.

Moments later, the spy was out in the open air, enjoying the peaceful evening. He was quite content with himself, having completed his last assignment with unparalleled brilliance. Now he looked forward to his next mission. The *Adriana,* whatever that was.

He passed someone he knew on a quiet country lane and exchanged a greeting in perfect English. And the spy who would win the war for Adolph Hitler used his most insidious weapon, his anonymity, to disappear quietly into the vast population of middle-class America. For Siegfried on July 15, 1939, everything was just that easy.

PART TWO

Laura Worthington
England and
America
1935-39

THREE

Her earliest memories were of her own room in her father's mansion overlooking Kensington Gardens. She must have been about four years old back then, she one day realized, because her father was just home from the war and that was in 1918.

On the brown uniform of the British Expeditionary Force he'd worn an assortment of ribbons and medallions. They were pretty to a little girl. He'd hoisted her in his arms, and after she had joined her mother in embracing Papa, her fingers had wandered to the bright colors and the gleaming brass and silver. She was fascinated by them.

"Want them?" Major Nigel Worthington asked his daughter.

The little girl nodded excitedly.

He took them off his uniform, to the dismay of his wife, and removed the pointed ends of the pins. Then he placed them in a small ivory box that he had brought back from France for her. He set them on the floor and sat by approvingly. Thus, the Military Cross, the

Distinguished Service Cross, and the Victoria Cross, among others, became favorite toys for little Laura. She would pin them on herself and her dolls. A few days later one of the nursemaids of one of her playmates said that her father must have been very much of a hero to win all of those medals.

"Were you a hero, Papa?" Laura asked her father the next Sunday morning.

"No more than anyone else, Laura," he answered. "Millions of men and women were in France. Almost all of them were very brave."

"Why did they go?" she asked.

Nigel Worthington took a long look at his daughter. Then he picked her up in his strong arms—which she always loved—and carried her to the bay window of the mansion's master bedroom.

Across the street, which was cluttered with carriages and new motorcars, were the gardens. It was a chilly November, so people were all bundled up as they strolled.

"That's why, darling," Nigel Worthington said, indicating an expanse of London beyond his window. "Because I love my country. And because England asked me to serve."

The little girl contemplated her father's words, in the manner that only a girl of four and a half could.

"Can I be a hero, too, someday, Papa?" she asked.

He laughed and hugged her, nuzzling her neck.

"Of course you can, sugarplum," Dr. Worthington said. "Of course you can. Someday you can be a hero, too. *For England.*"

*   *   *

Laura Worthington was the daughter of a mildly eccentric London physician, Nigel Worthington, who had once been a renowned young surgeon on Harley Street, where he, his practice, and his patients all prospered together. Life, in the early part of the century, smiled upon him.

Before establishing his medical practice, he had been a brilliant student at Oxford, where he'd read Modern Languages. He'd taken time out during the Great War to serve with the First London Rifle Brigade and had been an artillery lieutenant at the Somme in July 1916. Nigel Worthington had again been lucky. During the darkest day in British military history—some 21,000 dead and 35,000 wounded during the Fourth Army's futile advance toward German trenches—young Worthington escaped without a scratch. His only wounds, as he saw death all around him, were psychological.

Then a few years later, fate double-crossed him.

In early 1922, when his daughter, Laura, was eight years old, the influenza pandemic swept London. Laura's mother, Victoria Worthington, went from perfect health to a cemetery within ten days. From there on, Nigel Worthington withdrew from the world that he'd known. And he took his daughter with him.

He forswore his surgical practice and moved himself and his daughter to an enchanting, sprawling four-bedroomed Georgian house on the outskirts of Salisbury. Around the house was an acre of garden and around the garden was a high wall. Dr. Worthington kept hours as a general practitioner—he was known in the city as quiet, somewhat moody, but an excellent doctor. Yet he always knew that he could withdraw to his home and dedicate himself to the one thing he still cared about. It was not medicine, and not the comparative study of languages. Rather, he gave himself entirely to the raising of Laura, a beautiful little girl who, day by spectacular day, became an almost ghostly image of her dark-eyed, dark-haired mother. Dr. Worthington hired a governess named Mrs. Frasier, who lived in and who was home when he had office hours or house calls. By now Laura was Nigel Worthington's sole commitment in life.

From her father's own voice and hand, Laura learned an appreciation of music and art, literature and philosophy. Nigel Worthington sat by his daughter's side for hours—sometimes rescheduling patients to do so—to watch her growing fingers glide across the keyboard of a piano, exactly as her mother's once had. He taught her about God and Christianity just as he taught her to respect all other people and their religions. He educated her with humanist values and he instructed her—from his relationship with her mother— what sort of love could form a lasting union. From his experiences as a soldier and a doctor, he taught her that war was mankind's ultimate and most unforgivable evil. And he impressed upon her that human life was sacred.

He taught her to reason and to think. Finally, he taught her integrity to her own values.

Laura then, by age eighteen, had her mother's beauty and her father's intellect. There was little surprise when she passed her A-levels, applied to university, scored highly on her entrance examination, and was accepted as one of thirty-six women of a class of more than seven hundred at the University of Bristol. And it was at Bristol that she met Edward Shawcross, the boy who she quite naturally assumed she would someday marry.

Edward was tall and quiet, wavy-haired, nice-looking, but decidedly tame, and, by Laura's standards, conservative. They were twenty-one when they met and were both in their final year of university.

Edward was the second son of a wealthy spirits importer in Bristol and had designs of his own to augment the family fortune. He had his eye set at an aging sandstone mansion in the city of Bath, just off the Landsdowne Crescent, which he would buy—here his father was of inestimable help—gut, renovate, and convert into the finest inn and restaurant in the county of Somersetshire. Laura was to be, in a highly glorified manner, the innkeeper's wife, serving both her husband and the Shawcross & Company brandies, ports, and sherries.

One day in the spring of 1936, Edward showed Laura the gracious old mansion, his arm neatly tucked around her waist.

"And, of course," he whispered to her with his usual blend of innocence and lechery, "I wouldn't mind having our own household staff of five. Maybe three sons and two daughters. But the sons first, of course."

"Of course," replied Laura. It was not a totally unappealing proposition. The wealthy hotelier's wife. There would be money, a certain middle-class respectability, and even a dab of glamour, if the dining room could maintain a high reputation. Life treated many women to much worse. It was just that . . . well, Laura tried to stifle the feeling, but it was all so clear cut. Early on, she entertained the idea that there was slightly something missing. But she fought the idea. There was nothing really wrong with Edward Shaw-cross and Lord knew that he did not make the difficult physical demands of her that many young men made. Laura also knew that there were several hundred other girls—many of them attractive and from good families—who would claw her out of the way if she didn't appreciate him.

It was just that, well, couldn't life bear her some surprises? Some *adventure?*

Edward owned a new Alvis "open top." They spent Saturdays motoring in Devon when the weather permitted. On a day in late May, not long before final examinations, they drove out to Cornwall for a weekend. One of Edward's aunts owned a cottage near the sea. The aunt was conveniently vacationing in Portugal.

At the cottage, Edward—who was a superior chef already—roasted a rack of lamb, poured unhealthy amounts of his father's best imported claret, and created a supernal raspberry soufflé for dessert.

Afterward, they lit the log in the fireplace—it was still cool in May—and sipped Beaumes de Venise. Toward ten, Edward placed his hand on her knee.

"Tonight?" he asked.

"Yes," she said.

They went upstairs, found a large comfortable bed, and virtually fell into it. Laura lost her virginity with surprising ease and no second thoughts at all—the dividend of too much claret, perhaps—and afterward Edward confessed that it was his first time, too. This, Laura had already guessed.

Their scheduled marriage remained unofficial and at

least a year away. Laura did not know whether or not she was in love with Edward Shawcross. When pressed, she told him that she was. But was she? She wondered. She knew she had grown to like Edward very much. He was always around. And he was good to her. But was that enough?

Their affair continued. Months passed. She went to a discreet doctor in London, gave her name as Mrs. Vincent Thomas of Basingstoke, and purchased a diaphragm. She thought long and hard about her relationship with Edward Shawcross. Things seemed to be happening too quickly.

Home in Salisbury after graduation, Laura spent much time in the Georgian house in which she had been raised. Mrs. Frasier was long since deceased by now and it was just Laura and her father. Nigel Worthington was proud of the beautiful young woman he had raised. But he was under no illusions about her, a woman's needs, and Laura's relationship with Edward.

One night they talked. "I'm expected," she said ruefully, "to make a decision that will affect the rest of my life. It scares me, Papa."

"He's a fine young man," Nigel Worthington said. "He treats you well. He could offer you a good home and a good life. He bestows love upon you."

Laura nodded. "But I don't love him," she heard herself saying.

"Yes. I know," her father answered.

Nigel Worthington had a much older brother who had quit school, moved to America years ago, and successfully gone into the steel business in Pennsylvania. The two branches of the family had remained in touch. The English side had the grace, the education, and the culture. The American side had the money and the informality, both in vast quantities. Nigel suggested that his daughter spend the following summer visiting. There was an exchange of letters. Dr. Worthington had a niece Laura's age who was finishing university at a strangely named place called Bryn Mawr. The niece, Barbara Worthington, whom Laura had met years ago, wrote that she knew dozens of boys from Yale, Princeton, Williams, and Penn. Barbara promised to give Laura an interesting summer.

"You'll probably get yourself involved with some dirty-fingernailed Yank millionaire who does violence with auxiliary verbs," chided her father. "You'll love him and never come home."

"That's not my type, Papa, actually," Laura answered.

"But it might be an excellent time for your trip to America, mightn't it?" her father said. "With what's going on in the world, who knows how long travel will be safe?"

And if a war starts, she thought to herself, *Papa will have me safely tucked away in America, rather than in England, where there could be fighting.*

But Laura's spoken response addressed none of this.

"I suspect you're right," she said. "About the right time to travel, I mean."

"The *Queen Mary* sails every other Thursday for New York," her father said at length. "What would you think of that?"

Laura said she'd think a great deal of that.

One week later, Laura traveled by train to London to

book passage. She was met by a man named Peter Whiteside, a longtime friend of her family.

Whiteside was slightly younger than her father. Laura had known that Peter Whiteside and her father had served together during the Great War. Since then, Whiteside had been in and out of the government, mostly in when the Tories were in power, and out when the Liberals held a majority in Parliament. Right now, the Tories were in and so was Whiteside. "Buried somewhere in the Ministry of Defense," as he himself had put it in March when Laura had seen him last. "But whenever you come to London let me take you to lunch."

Today was "whenever." Whiteside was a tall man, with short hair that was as black as a rook. His face was thinner than the rest of his body, giving an austere, almost gaunt cast to his face. But his eyes were lively and intelligent; they were deep gray and sharp as thorns. He wore a navy suit and his regiment's necktie. He kissed Laura's hand when he met her at the railroad platform.

"Laura. I'm charmed as ever. You look ravishing today."

Peter Whiteside, she thought, was one of the last of the true English gentlemen, along with her father. The dying breed. The Great War had changed everything in all of Europe. No one made men like this anymore.

"Come," he said, taking her arm. "We have a reservation at the Ritz dining room for one o'clock. I've made an appointment for you at the Cunard offices for the afternoon. I'd like to stop by my office first. Something to discuss."

"If you're at all too busy today, Peter," she offered,

"I'll be in London again before I leave."

"Nonsense," he said. They passed through the sooted iron gates of the station. There was a Rolls Royce waiting with a driver. Peter Whiteside ushered Laura toward it. "The 'something to discuss' is between us," he informed her.

"Oh," she said.

London was best seen from the back of a limousine. Or so Laura decided as the chauffeured automobile pulled away from the curb. "Now," Whiteside said at length, "tell me about your impending travels."

She did. And by the time she had finished, the chauffeur had delivered them in front of a sturdy Edwardian town house, nestled on a quiet tree-lined side street. They were in a residential neighborhood bordering Earl's Court and Kensington, and Whiteside leaned forward and opened his door. His driver opened Laura's door and Whiteside ushered her inside, where, upon entering a white rotunda, she began to focus upon the nature of Peter Whiteside's business.

There was a guard in a suit just inside the door. He nodded curtly as Whiteside entered. Directly in front of them was a portrait of His Majesty, George V, and beyond that, a Union Jack stood in its stand, making its own statement.

Whiteside led her down a short hallway. His office was at the end.

He moved behind a polished rosewood desk and seated himself only after Laura did. He leaned back very slightly in a leather swivel-based chair, steepled his fingers in front of him, and assessed Laura for a final time.

"I think you'll enjoy America," he said at length.

"Indeed, I suspect you'll have a wonderful trip."

She looked back at him, appraising also. "Peter," she said very firmly, "would you mind telling me why I'm here?"

His fingers broke their token marriage and he returned his hands to his desk. "No. Not at all," he said. "Certainly I owe you the explanation, whatever you may ultimately think of it." Whiteside's gaze lowered for a moment and he glanced at a pair of papers before him. Then he looked back to her.

"Laura," he said, "this building belongs to the Ministry of Defense. I work here. They are my employer. I need to know if you would be willing to do something for England. Something which might seem very simple, but which is, in actuality, very important."

Laura responded with a very stunned silence for several seconds. "You'd better tell me more before I say anything," she said.

"Laura," Peter Whiteside answered, "as any fool with two eyes could tell you, Europe may soon again be at war. Inevitably, Hitler will draw England in. If this is the case, the intelligence networks which we piece together now—and the information we have access to—may be of vital national interest. Should I go on?"

Laura found herself nodding, and tingling very slightly with excitement.

"This office, the one you are beautifying as we speak, belongs to Military Intelligence 5—intelligence gathering within the United Kingdom. However, it is part of my duty to coordinate operations with M.I. 6, counterintelligence and intelligence gathering abroad. Specifically, operations in the United States and Canada." Here Whiteside glanced at his desk again, double-checking the papers before him. "Your trip comes at a very propitious time. And leads you to an excellent place. For our purposes, that is."

Laura was incredulous. "You want me to become sort of a spy? Against the Americans, is that it?"

Whiteside smiled indulgently. "Not at all," he said. "Or at least, not exactly." He pursed his lips against his fingertips again. He was about to continue when she interrupted.

"I thought the Americans were our friends," Laura said.

"Some of them are," he answered. "Some of them are not. President Roosevelt is definitely a friend of England. The Vice-President, Mr. Jack Garner, definitely is not. But this is precisely the type of thing which we would want you to find out for us. On a lesser scale, of course. One knows all about the American government officials. It's the people, the important families, we wish to know more about. *We need facts, Laura. My office deals in facts.*"

"I'm sorry," Laura said. "I don't understand."

Whiteside smiled consolingly. "Laura, dear," he said, "I've known you since you were this high." One of Whiteside's hands fled the desk and he held an open palm two feet above the floor. "I would never place you in any danger, you must believe me. But, follow—this office engages in two types of intelligence gathering. What we call 'white,' which is the accumulation of information from open sources. Newspapers. Magazines. Conversations with people. And then there is 'covert'—"

"Which is just what it sounds like," said Laura, breaking in.

"I would ask you to work for us in the former category," Whiteside said. "Your situation is absolutely perfect. You are young, beautiful, single. You will have entrée to the families and situations which we wish to know about. I stress, we are not placing you in any danger. We simply wish to put your eyes, ears, and brain to work *for England.*"

Several thoughts shot simultaneously through Laura's mind as she listened to Whiteside: that her earliest memory of Peter Whiteside had been when she was a little girl of approximately five and Peter Whiteside, single, using a cane to brace a hobbling leg, had come along on a trip to Scotland with the Worthington family. That from what she knew about such things, Whiteside must carry a reasonable bit of authority within the M.I. 5 or 6 and that he made his own recruitments. That the rumors that always circulated about flirtatious Peter were probably true— he did like boys *and* girls. And that he was here now in front of her, poised like a spider in his own web, trying to recruit her to work for him.

"So I'm to be a spy," she said in mounting wonder. "Is that it?"

His eyes danced in an absurdly young way. "Hitler has spies," he said with a flicker of a grin. "England gathers intelligence in the interests of her own defense. When were you thinking of sailing?" he asked.

"June the fifth," she said.

Whiteside glanced to a calendar on his wall. Her eyes followed his and she saw the bold figures 1937. *My God,* she thought to herself, *I'm already twenty-three years old.* Calendars began to bother her.

"That would be excellent," he said. "Before you

leave, today in fact, I can submit to you a list of families and individuals whom you could be meeting. Buy a new address book and write these names in among those whom you already know. File a report every two weeks. Anything that strikes you as interesting. Political sympathies are foremost, of course. We must know where pro-British or pro-Nazi sympathies lie in America. If a war comes, American assistance may be critical. For this, we will need public opinion on our side."

There was a pause and Laura was aware of two men arguing in the hallway.

"And how would I correspond with you?" she asked, savoring the conspiratorial aspects of Whiteside's proposal. "A coded telegram? A scribbled message slipped into a stone wall? A rendezvous at three A.M. at the New York waterfront?"

"A simple letter in the English language would suffice," he said. "Address it to me, your Uncle Peter. I will give you a postal box number in London. You will simply discuss your visit to America. And your friends."

There was another long pause as Laura considered everything.

"Well . . . ?" Whiteside finally inquired. "This is, after all, for England." He nudged her along: "I must say, Laura, you came highly recommended for this assignment by a former member of M.I. 6."

"*I* was?" she asked in total surprise. "I didn't know until today that I knew anyone who did this sort of thing."

"You've known at least two. I'm one. The other recommended you."

"Who?" she demanded.

Whiteside chuckled softly and amiably. "I'll tell you over lunch," he said, "and only if you accept."

"I have *already* accepted."

"Then we can continue on to lunch," Whiteside said merrily. He rose but Laura did not. "The Ritz dining room is waiting."

"This young Englishwoman," she said, "does not budge until she receives the promised information."

Whiteside offered his hand to guide her. "Portrait of a retired spy," he began. "Read Modern Language at Oxford in the teens. Joined First London Rifle Brigade, became an intelligence officer, attached to artillery. In 1916 became too valuable to risk at front-line fighting, so was transferred to the War Office in London."

Laura's mouth flew open in amazement. Whiteside continued, "Spent eleven months running spies in and out of France, then volunteered again for the front lines. Returned to his regiment, awarded the Royal Legion of Honor—"

"My father!" she exclaimed in a breathless whisper. "You! The two of you . . . of course . . . !"

"I've always felt, Laura," Whiteside concluded, guiding her to the door, then opening it for her, "that talent, ability, and intelligence are hereditary traits. I think you'll serve His Majesty well in America. Don't you?"

Laura was filled with conflicting emotions when she saw Edward Shawcross again. It was one week later and upon a trip that they had long planned. They drove

69

to London, where Edward had booked rooms on separate floors of the Savoy—Laura's suite overlooking the Thames and the Embankment—and took her to dinner each evening at the Savoy Grill. It was there, during dessert, that Edward set before her a small box from an Amsterdam jeweler.

Laura opened it. An engagement ring with a diamond the size of a small pebble sparkled and winked at her.

"Don't say anything," Edward said. "Wear it if you like it. And you can give me your honest answer when you return from America."

They went up to her chamber, toasted London with French champagne from 1926 and then tumbled into the deliciously sinful Savoy double bed. They made love until Edward fell asleep, still resting on top of her.

At 4 A.M. Laura awakened. There was a stream of soft moonlight from where the curtains were not completely drawn. On her hand Laura saw the glimmer of the diamond. She studied the stone for several minutes. Edward Shawcross, the front of his naked body against her back, snored softly. Then Laura was aware of his arm, tightly around her.

Perhaps she made too much of it. Perhaps the moment was too symbolic to be meaningful. But Laura felt smothered. Their romance had had all the expensive accouterments, but had it any soul? Or was an attractive willing young woman just another item in a wealthy young man's collection of objects?

One voice within her told her she was being unfair. Another voice urged her to flee.

Then, as she stared at the dazzling stone on her finger, the sparkle diffused. There was moisture in her

70

eyes. Tears. She was not in love with Edward Shawcross and now knew she never would be. And she wanted desperately to love the way Victoria and Nigel Worthington had loved. How could she ever tell Edward? He had showered so much upon her. How could she ever summon the courage?

A week later, Edward borrowed his father's chauffeur and Bentley for the day. He motored with Laura from her home in Salisbury to Southampton. Edward obtained a visitor's pass at the Cunard pier and accompanied the woman he loved to her stateroom. There she found four spectacular floral arrangements of his choosing.

He will suffocate me for the rest of my life, she was thinking.

At 11:30 the *Queen Mary*'s thunderous horns blasted twice to signal all visitors ashore. Anchor would be lifted promptly at noon.

"Edward, it's time," she said as gently as possible. He sat in a captain's chair and for one horrifying moment she thought he had booked passage with her.

He didn't move. *God,* she thought, *how I am coming to resent his presence! Why doesn't he get up? Why doesn't he leave?*

"Edward, dear," she said a second time. "I'm sorry. But you *must* go now. We'll see each other in ten weeks."

"Will we?"

There was a hesitation that was too obvious, then she answered, "Yes. Of course."

A long pause followed. So did a gaze that she did not know how to interpret. Then he said, "There's something that I need to know. I know I shouldn't ask.

71

But I'm going to."

She waited.

"That *thing* of yours," he said. And instantly she knew. The proper Victorian, he always referred to her diaphragm as the "thing." "Are you taking it with you?"

All the easy lies occurred to her and danced across her lips. Then all the hurtful implications of honesty also flashed before her. The truth won.

"Yes," she said.

He looked at her in contempt, then anger. He fingered the arm of his chair but looked her directly in the eye. He stood. For one awful moment, she feared that he would strike her.

"You cheap, ungrateful little tart!" he said, with controlled rage, his voice bold but no louder than before. "I should have guessed. Do you know how much I've spent on you?"

"No, Edward, I don't," she replied. "But maybe you can tell me."

His face reddened, and suddenly she overflowed with the urge to destroy this moment, to cry out for forgiveness and explain that what he was thinking was not so. But the *Queen Mary*'s horns blasted another time and Edward moved very quickly toward the door and then through it. Laura didn't follow. The first important romance of her life had ended just that swiftly. Her father had always insisted that the critical moments in life always arrive with astonishing suddenness. Then they are gone. As always, Nigel Worthington had been correct.

There was an eerie silence in her stateroom and her subsequent passage to America was quiet and uneventful. She kept to herself and made no friends. When she saw her own image in the mirror, she noticed that her expression alternated between sadness and relief.

Only one order of business remained: on her first day in New York, she insured Edward's ring and mailed it back to him.

FOUR

"I promised you a *summer*," Barbara Worthington proclaimed soon after Laura's arrival from England. "And I will give you a *summer!*"

Barbara Worthington was true to her word. A tall, blond, pretty large-boned girl of twenty, she blithely prescribed a brisk, adventuresome summer romance for her English cousin. Laura, rebounding from her battered engagement to Edward Shawcross, was in every mood to oblige.

Evenings were spent at Lake Contontic, one of the better-heeled sections of the Poconos. On weekend evenings touring bands came through—the Dorseys, Glenn Miller, Buddy Rogers—fresh from Atlantic City or Philadelphia, and played Contontic's Lakeside Ballroom. There congregated what the social columns of the day's big-city newspapers referred to as "the bright young people." They were the privileged offspring of the correct families in New York and Philadelphia. They had the right clothes, the perfect addresses back in the city, the fastest, most expensive new cars and the unimpeachable pedigrees. Most had been coming to the lake with their families for a generation or more. Peter Whiteside had done his homework well before providing Laura with more than five dozen family names. Many were on his list.

She dutifully reported to him, penning chatty letters at the big old-fashioned oak desk in the Worthington family's cabin. She wrote about the people she had met. *This,* she thought to herself in the midst of a third handwritten letter, *is the strangest, lowest-key "spying" anyone in the world has ever been asked to do.*

But she completed the letter and mailed it. She wrote at least one a week now. But idly, she began to wonder whether Peter wasn't a trifle strange. What difference did it make what these new friends of Laura's thought? Why was Peter wasting government time on this? Or was it government time at all? Was this his own little Peeping Tom game? Or was it something she couldn't comprehend at all?

But, no. She considered Peter and how long she had known him. She thought of the very visible government office and the very clear instructions he had given her.

For England, she recalled him saying. And then for some reason her mind drifted way, way back to her girlhood and another image was keyed: that of her father holding her in the bay window overlooking Kensington Gardens and explaining to a little girl who couldn't comprehend what war was and why he had gone to fight.

For England, he had said.

She drew a breath. It sounded frightfully specious, the whole thing. But she wrote a fourth letter and posted it, like the others, to Whiteside's mailing address in London. Not long afterward she received a letter back.

"So glad you are enjoying yourself, young lady," Peter Whiteside wrote. "Everyone sounds fascinating. I never get to America anymore so you must tell me more, more, more. Facts. I want *facts!*"

She sighed. If she were a spy, she was a strange one. But so be it. *For England.*

Lakeside Ballroom was one of those vast, noisy summer auditoriums. It had gaudy crepe paper strung across the basketball backboards, from one to the next, was illuminated by a dangerous amount of colored candles plunked into the noses of cheap chianti bottles, and was festooned with an explosion of red, yellow, and orange Chinese lanterns. It was also much more fun than it had any reasonable right to be.

Maybe it was the heavy aroma of leisure in the air. Maybe it was the mood of the summertime. Or maybe it was the excitement of the urbane young university crowd to whom Laura had been given entrée by her cousin, who now doubled as her confidante and best friend. For whatever reason, Lakeside had long been a magical place for a summer romance. The girl who did not eventually lose her heart and everything else here at least once, Barbara explained cheerfully, had a hard, cold heart indeed.

"Of course, I don't have to explain such things to *you,* Laura," Barbara said one evening in July, combing out her hair in the front seat of the family Ford. "Husband hunting *is* permitted," she said with a wink, "as long as you're not hunting someone else's. And I don't know what it's like in England, but over here a girl never seals a deal without giving away a few free samples."

Laura and Barbara exchanged a conspiratorial laugh as the conversation ended.

An orchestra in green coats and gold trim was thumping out jazz tunes from the twenties one evening in late June when Laura, Barbara, Barbara's boyfriend Victor, and several friends entered the ballroom. It was only a few minutes later when Stephen Fowler wandered into the ballroom by himself. Laura, seated with Barbara and Victor at their usual corner table, felt herself one of many females watching the young man.

"Who's that?" she asked her cousin, who knew everyone.

"Stay away," said Barbara.

Laura tugged excitedly on Barbara's sleeve. "I want to know," she insisted.

"That's Stephen Fowler," Barbara said. "Stay away unless you're prepared to be a very bad girl this summer."

"Introduce me," answered Laura.

As Stephen scanned the ballroom, he saw Barbara beckon him to a seat at their table. Laura took a much closer look as the orchestra suddenly amused everyone with their version of *Flat Foot Floogie with the Floy Floy*.

Stephen Fowler, tall and thin, with strong shoulders, and neatly trimmed brown hair, glanced at Barbara's cousin and smiled. He liked what he saw. Returning his gaze, then looking away, so did Laura. Her initial impression of him was one of an intelligent, athletic man, perhaps even one of those barbarian Americans who play their strange sort of football game at college. Barbara specialized in such men.

"Stephen," Barbara said coyly, "this is Laura Worthington. She's here for two months only and you're to keep your hands off."

"Impossible," said Stephen Fowler, taking Laura's hand and kissing it in an overly dramatic manner which amused everyone at the table, including Laura.

He is *good-looking,* Laura thought to herself. *Too bad he's so aware of it.*

"Stephen was Victor's residence counselor at Princeton," Barbara said, by way of furthering the introduction.

"I had no life whatsoever before this very moment," said Stephen, holding his gaze upon Laura.

"Oh, brother . . ." moaned Barbara.

"A man *without* a past, in other words," countered Laura. "How *sorry* I am for you, Mr. Fowler," she said with mock formality.

"I'm hardly worthy of your pity," Stephen said, continuing the game. He hung his head in penitence.

"Oh, damn you, Stephen!" Barbara chided merrily. "Would you stop flirting and just ask the poor girl to dance?"

"Would you like to dance?" Stephen Fowler asked.

"I would *love* to dance," is what Laura answered.

He graciously took her by the hand and was aware of her accent for the first time. He had led her only a step or two toward the dance floor when they both heard Barbara calling after them with unwarranted glee.

"Oh, *Steph*-ie!" she sang out. Stephen turned and

79

looked back to where Victor was lighting a cigarette from one of the candles. "Be kind to her," Barbara called. "She's coming off a broken engagement. No dancing out to the sun deck and no offers to show her the boathouse."

From somewhere a mischievous smile crossed Stephen's face. "I'll have her back in ten minutes," he promised. "Or not at all."

Then he took Laura in his arms and did not surprise her by being an excellent dancer.

Laura, after a moment or two of small talk to the accompaniment of a tango beat, took Stephen to be handsome, wealthy, flagrantly intelligent, and exactly the type of self-possessed American male she had already learned to dislike. She quickly sensed, however, as he next eased her into a smooth foxtrot, that she would not learn to dislike Stephen Fowler.

He was also older—thirty—and he wore his maturity well. He had gone to Princeton as an undergraduate and had earned his bachelor's degree in the midst of the Depression. His father had lost about 80 percent of everything in the stock market in 1929 and the Fowler family of Bala-Cynwyd had maintained the role that vanquished dukes played in Europe after the Great War—aristocracy without money. Yet the family had recovered well in the latter years of the Depression, held onto their home and their social ranking, and were, in a small sense, forging something of a quiet multimillion-dollar comeback.

For his part, Stephen had done a little bit of a lot: some political study here, some economic study there; a job at Girard Trust for several months in Philadelphia; two summers with a Protestant missionary group in Nova Scotia; a strange stint as a merchant seaman to the Caribbean and back ("So that I could afford to see the place," he explained), and even a bit of travel to England and the Continent, of which he now spoke little. ("I was sick from the water in England and from the cheese in France," he complained at the time, "and came home early.")

Thereafter, Tigertown had taken him back. His stock at Old Nassau had remained high and Princeton offered him a job in 1935 as an instructor of political science and residence counselor at $1,150 a year , plus meals and board. All of which, of course, was how he knew Victor and how he knew Barbara. And how he met Laura. That, and the fact that in the tight, cozy summer society at Lake Contontic, every "good" family knew every other "good" family.

"You were engaged?" he finally asked. "I didn't see a ring."

"I sent it back."

"Where's the shattered young man? Or did he shoot himself?"

"Back in England," she answered, as members of the band sang the chorus of "Chicago, Chicago!" "And I'm certain that he's doing well, thank you."

"What made him let you out of his sight?" he asked. "I doubt if I would have under the circumstances."

"You are an excessive flatterer, Stephen," she reproached him. "Barbara should have warned me."

"I'm not flattering. I'm telling you the truth. If I were engaged to you, I'd never let you out of my sight."

"He didn't, either," Laura answered. "That's why I broke it off."

For the first time, she'd outpointed him. Stephen

Fowler was not certain of how next to proceed.

Laura was no stranger to men who made the bold approach. She was quite capable of discouraging them or putting them completely off. But only when she cared to, which was not this evening. There was something about the way Stephen Fowler held her as they danced, something about the way he glided her around the hardwood dance floor, something even just right about the American jazz, the trumpets, the saxophones, the ersatz Hawaiian wall hangings and the breezes which wafted through the screened window onto the dance floor. Yes, Barbara had warned her about this place. But there was even something about the way Stephen lightly cuffed his palm at the small of her back as they danced. This was, Laura knew quickly, the type of thing that she might even like to see get a little out of hand.

"It was my idea to break the engagement," she answered. "At first, I thought it would be a good idea to get away from each other. To see if the relationship was . . ."

"Real," he said.

"Yes."

"Were you in love with him?"

"That's actually none of your—"

"In other words, you weren't."

"You're very sure of yourself," she retorted.

"It's not hard to figure out," he said. "If you went away and aren't desperate to go back and see him, you weren't in love. It's that simple."

Suddenly she felt a surge of sympathy for Edward Shawcross and wanted to defend him. "He meant a lot to me," she said indignantly. "I liked him very much. And—"

"And you tried to be in love with him, but couldn't," Stephen said. "Happens all the time, you know."

"I guess you're an expert," Laura said as the music stopped. There was polite applause from around the ballroom.

"Not an expert," he said, retreating in tone. "I made a few lucky guesses."

"We should be going back to Barbara's table." Laura began to move, but Stephen firmly held her hand.

"One more dance. Please?" She agreed and it turned into a slow waltz. Now Barbara was on the dance floor, too, with Victor, and once when Laura looked over Stephen's shoulder she saw Barbara giving her a naughty smile. She could also see, by the way Victor held her, that Barbara and her boyfriend were lovers.

Stephen Fowler led their waltz beautifully and the ballroom itself was soon swimming with reflected lights off the mirrored ball at its center. Stephen possessed her very capably in his strong arms, and Laura, for the first time that evening, began to wonder if she was a goner.

"You taught Victor at Princeton?" she asked.

"I hope so," he answered within Victor's earshot.

"I've never been to Princeton," she said. "I hear it's very pretty."

"Would you like to see it?"

"Someday, of course."

"What about next weekend?"

She drew an extra inch apart from him and gazed steadily into his eyes. "What?" she asked.

"As long as you're no longer engaged . . . and as long as you were never in love to start with, we can drive down next Saturday. I'll show you the town and the university. The whole area, in fact."

"For the day?"

"For the weekend." Stephen smiled.

"Mr. Fowler," she reproached with undue formality, "I met you two minutes ago."

"But I think we like each other."

"Do we? *That* much? I know all about weekend invitations." Fleetingly, she thought of Edward and wondered how her declaration had sounded.

"I'm sure you do," he said. When her eyes narrowed, he grinned again.

"I don't know the first thing about you," she said as they continued to dance. "Aside from your name and that Barbara once mentioned you to me."

"What would you like to know?" he challenged.

"Do you have a job?"

"No."

"What do you do?"

"I play tennis, swim, and sail," he answered.

"In the fall then?" she asked. "What will you do for a living?"

"You won't believe me."

"Try me, then."

"I'm accepted into divinity school," he said. "I'm entering Yale University this fall."

She missed a step and her feet tangled slightly. *"Divinity* school? You? To become a parson?"

"A Lutheran minister, actually."

She took another look at him, tall, strong, and handsome, owning a face that should have been in movies and a self-assurance that she knew had probably broken many hearts. She stepped away from him one pace and in her incredulity began to laugh.

"A *minister!*" she exclaimed. "You're joking!"

"No," he said, standing before her as those who waltzed past them watched the intrigue. "I'm *not* joking." And he wasn't smiling now, either. So she knew. He was serious.

He held his hand out to lead her back into the waltz. "You don't act much like a minister," she said.

"You don't act much like a woman shattered by a broken engagement," he answered.

"Who said I was 'shattered'?"

"Barbara."

"Barbara doesn't know."

"Then you're not shattered?" They picked up the cadence of the waltz again.

"No."

"Then come down to Princeton this weekend with me. I have the nicest Nash convertible you've ever seen. We can have lunch at my club and if you want we can spend Sunday at the shore."

"What shore?"

"My family has an oceanfront home in Sea Girt, New Jersey," he said.

This all sounded terribly familiar. "And your aunt is normally there, but she may be away this weekend, right?"

"Wrong," he said. She waited. "My parents are normally there. But they'll *definitely* be away this weekend."

The music stopped and Stephen applauded the band, who rose, bowed, acknowledged the ovation, and began to lay down their instruments for a break. Laura stood with her arms akimbo, assessing Stephen Fowler.

"Well," he said, looking back at her. "It's only an invitation. No one's forcing you. And you can think about it."

"I'd love to go," is what Laura surprised both of them by saying.

"You're sure?"

"I'm very sure," she said.

They walked back to the table holding hands and even Barbara Worthington looked askance.

"See, Barbara," said Stephen. "Back within ten minutes. No damage done and we never left the room."

"Uh-huh," said Barbara, who was scrutinizing her cousin carefully now, as if searching for paw prints.

Stephen Fowler held a chair for Laura and seated her. Then he drew a long sigh and exhaled with too much drama. "I think I'm in love," he announced.

"Oh, brother . . ." Laura, Barbara, and Victor said in unison, and turned their heads away from him in harmlessly overdone contempt. But when Laura turned back to him, it suddenly struck her that, once again, he was not joking. Laura pinched herself and discovered that, yes, this was really happening.

The final touch: the Fowler family of Bala-Cynwyd, particularly Stephen, was on Peter Whiteside's far-flung otherworldly list. Then again, wasn't everyone she met these days?"

All right, Peter, she thought to herself. *This time I'll give you a* detailed *report.*

* * *

It was later that evening, when Barbara and Laura returned to their family's cabin, that Barbara filled in a few of the initial biographical notes on Stephen Fowler.

He had been third in his class at Princeton, a spring track star (not football, as Laura had erringly guessed), captain of the swimming team, treasurer of the Class of 1928, president of the Debating Society, editor of the *Princeton Literary Quarterly* ("He writes well enough to become a professional novelist or essayist," Barbara insisted as she undressed completely and stepped into the shower), and had in fact been accepted for theological study at Yale.

"Him?" Laura asked again, watching Barbara through the open door to the bathroom. Laura lay on her bed, wearing only her slip and bra, one shoe off, the other dangling perilously from a toe as she held her leg out straight.

"Him," confirmed Barbara. "He's unusual."

"I know."

Then Barbara added the final detail as she washed her hair. The Fowler family was old money from the Main Line. Someone named Amos Fowler, two generations back, had owned the tracks upon which the Reading Railroad had conveyed its freight. The Fowlers were millionaires more times over than anyone could count.

"And with all his fortune," Laura asked, "he's chosen to become a minister?"

"Honey," answered Barbara, rinsing off, "with his money, he can *afford* to become a minister."

Laura grew very quiet. Barbara finished her shower, draped a robe over her shoulders, and toweled off.

Then, sensing Laura's mood, Barbara continued in cautious tones.

"I should tell you, I suppose. Stephen's had quite a few girlfriends in his time. Girls from good families, I mean. Girls who don't normally go to bed with men."

"I'm sure," Laura said.

"So you like him?"

Laura returned Barbara's knowing gaze. "He asked me to go away with him next weekend. To Princeton and then to Sea Girt. Can you imagine that? I barely know him."

"And?"

Laura mused upon it. "I might need a new dress or two," she said. "And I definitely need a new bathing suit."

At twenty-three, Laura Worthington was pretty daring, and wise enough to know exactly how to conduct the whirlwind love affair that she now sensed before her.

Only, it became more than a whirlwind. Soon after the weekend in Princeton and Sea Girt, Laura knew she was onto the real thing. She was indeed, as she liked to phrase it, a goner.

Laura wrote a final letter to Edward Shawcross. She felt she owed him that much. In it, she actually said little, only that she would always recall him with kindness no matter how he felt about her. She mentioned that she had met someone new but she spared him the details. She was certain, she wrote, that he would soon find a younger, prettier, altogether better girl than she had been. In no time they would be operating his dreamed-of inn in Bath, complete with household "staff of five." When she sealed the letter, she felt both saddened and relieved.

Then Laura drew another piece of stationery. For the first time, she wrote to Peter Whiteside and revealed the depth of her involvement with Stephen. Always before, she had discreetly mingled word about him into the news of other people she knew at Contontic. And yet Whiteside must have sensed something.

"More about this wonderful young man," he had written back once. "What about the divinity student?" Whiteside had asked on another occasion after Laura had purged any mention of her romance from her correspondence. *What did Whiteside know about love between a young man and a younger woman?* she thought huffily. This *is none of his business.*

"What about the young Fowler fellow?" he'd written a third time.

So now she told him everything. If he didn't like it, she concluded, he could bloody well find another pen pal. She mailed this letter at the same time as the note to Edward and enjoyed a robust sense of accomplishment.

A response from Peter Whiteside came back like a yo-yo.

"Laura," he wrote. "You are very young and very impressionable. I daresay you've had only one other serious romance. Are you certain that this is in your best interests? Peter," he signed it.

She read the letter twice and took it to be both smug and condescending. She crumpled and burned it. Then Laura burned the rest of Peter Whiteside's letters. She felt free of him. Emancipated. But she continued to simmer.

At length, she penned one final correspondence to him, complete with a tone which she took to be the match of his.

"In response to your question," she wrote, "am I certain this is in my best interests? My response, sir, is yes. Very definitely. Laura."

Then she cut off communication with Peter Whiteside. Completely.

Laura Worthington and Stephen Dobbs Fowler were married on August 28, 1937, by the Reverend Adrian McFarlane at the Lawrenceville chapel. Dr. Nigel Worthington came from England for the occasion, was a houseguest of the Fowlers in Bala-Cynwyd, and was more than suitably impressed with both Stephen and his family. For their part, Stephen's parents were absolutely enraptured by the noble English physician and his mild eccentricities.

The wedding was small upon the insistence of Stephen and Laura. Only the immediate families. Stephen's younger brother was the best man and Barbara Worthington was the maid of honor. There were only thirty guests, but Laura was not spared the usual inane remarks which make any wedding complete.

Stephen's brother, in an odd moment to Laura: "You don't have a younger sister back home, do you?"

One of Stephen's aunts? "There's nothing wrong with having a romance with a religious man. I'm sure he didn't make the physical demands upon you before

90

marriage that most men make."

And, of course, from Barbara, with a twinkle in her eye: "Some summer romance! You pick off the most eligible bachelor at Lakeside, then marry him so no other girl can borrow him next summer!"

"Sorry," answered Laura. They exchanged a hug.

"Who says I can't be borrowed?" asked Stephen, overhearing their chatter. He embraced his wife from the back, kissed her on the side of the neck, and, when no one was looking, brushed his hand across her backside.

"I thought you were a gentleman," she chided *sotto voce*.

"Only before marriage," he answered. "An animal ever after." There was champagne on his breath.

"Fabulous," she replied.

"By the way," he asked, "who is Peter Whiteside?"

The name came to her as a surprise, particularly from her husband's lips. For a second she had no response.

"Who's Peter Whiteside?" he repeated. "I want to know."

"*Why* do you want to know?"

"Ah, ah," he chided. "Husband's rights! And I asked you first." His voice was teasing, but she recognized its insistence.

"Peter Whiteside," she said, recovering carefully, "is a divinely charming man with radiant gray eyes who is urbane, handsome, talented, bears a frightfully stunning resemblance to a tall, athletic Noel Coward . . . and who also happens to be my father's age, and an old, old friend of the family."

"Oh," Stephen said. Half a grin crept across his face.

91

"I see. Church, army, and club establishment, right?"

Laura let him easily off the hook. "He served with my father in the war. They've been like this"—two delicate fingers crossed, two polished pink fingernails meeting—"for years."

"I understand," he said.

"Why?"

"He sent flowers," Stephen told his bride of one hour. "And this note."

He handed her a small unopened envelope. Laura slid her finger into it and tore. From it, she drew Peter Whiteside's personal calling card, engraved only with his name. Upon it, in the handwriting Laura knew so well, Whiteside had neatly penned in blue ink:

To Lovely Laura,
With all my affection and sincere wishes for your lasting happiness,

Peter

Laura felt a sensation of warmth toward Peter, something she'd never known she'd entertained for him. She smiled. She looked up to show her husband the kind note from her father's oldest friend. But Stephen had discreetly disappeared to allow her to read the contents in privacy. Then she smiled again. Her husband, it occurred to her, had been *jealous*.

Jealous of fey, middle-aged Peter! The thought greatly amused her and she tucked the card into her wedding gown. Later in the afternoon, she found the greatest, most gorgeous bouquet of flowers—four dozen magnificent long-stemmed red roses—that she had ever seen in her life. It had been confected in New

York, upon wired directions from London. Naturally, it was Peter's.

After the ceremony, they left for Quebec in Stephen's red Nash convertible. They spent their honeymoon night in a small white guesthouse two miles north of Brattleboro, Vermont, and were served breakfast the next morning by a blushing landlady at the inn's table of honor.

So that's what it would have been like to run an inn, Laura thought idly. *Serving breakfast to obvious lovers, both married and illicit.*

In Quebec City, they stayed in a suite in a west tower of the Château Frontenac and spent time walking the Plains of Abraham. Stephen was fascinated by military operations from other centuries and wanted to inspect the precise location where the French had lost North America.

They stood on the ramparts overlooking the St. Lawrence River and the vastness of the province, which spread northward. "The French lost because they underestimated the enemy," Stephen said. "They never believed that the English could attack by ship up a secure river, then successfully scale these cliffs and invade Quebec."

Laura nodded.

"Conclusion?" Stephen demanded, assuming a scholarly tone.

"Never underestimate the British Navy," she said. "The British Navy hasn't lost a decisive sea battle since 1453 at Castillon."

He raised his eyebrows and allowed her point. "A

better conclusion," he demanded. "With modern implications."

"I give up."

"The French are terrible military strategists," he said. "Always planning for the last war, not the next one. Like this Maginot Line they have now. All their fortifications stretched from Luxembourg to Switzerland. Know how you cross it?" he asked.

"How?"

"The same way you now get to England," he said. "You use airplanes."

They lunched and laughed at a splendid little country restaurant in Levis, a ferry ride across the St. Lawrence from Quebec, and toward dessert Laura felt an inexplicable pang of sadness.

Stephen had caused it inadvertently. As she examined her feelings she realized how smug one could be in America over the politics of Europe. Hitler, the hoarse fanatical little tyrant of the MGM newsreels, and his pals Mussolini and Franco, were all firmly in power and flagrantly rearming themselves. Central Europe seemed destined to be carved into pieces and the two democracies of western Europe, France and England, seemed fragile and indecisive. Meanwhile, America slumbered.

Laura thought of England and thought of her father. Both were very distant. Then her thoughts rambled further as she grew very quiet over coffee. She was now thinking of Edward Shawcross.

Married as she was to a different, more *exciting* man, she began to see Edward in perspective for the first time. It was as if she had stumbled across some torn black and white photograph from an old scrapbook.

94

Edward had been a decent man, she decided. Thoroughly decent, but damnably predictable. She viewed a variety of images of him, things she had once seen: Edward neatly assembling his books, tightly knotting his tie, sharply combing the part in his hair, methodically planning their engagement and their life. Edward's orderliness had been his finest quality and his most serious undoing. Personal relationships were like that. Laura would opt for chaos and iconoclasm with a man like Stephen every time. Who ever heard, for example, of a divinity student with a red Nash convertible? Who, indeed? And that was just for starters.

Stephen reached across the table and took her hand. Much in the manner of a medieval courtier, he kissed the back of it and snapped her out of her reverie.

"A penny for your thoughts," he said.

"I was thinking," she answered, "of how much I love you."

FIVE

"It's perfect," Laura said.

"Then we'll take it," Stephen said, turning to the rental agent.

It was the autumn of 1937, and with exactly that much discussion, Laura and Stephen rented a comfortably snug white wooden house on a shady New Haven street five minutes' walk from the Yale campus. There Stephen entered divinity school and continued his studies.

As the semester passed, Laura and Stephen's circle of friends grew. They invited friends in for dinner, visited other couples, and went out to dinners. Hitler's occupation of the Rhineland, the civil war in Spain, and Mussolini's annexation of Ethiopia were far, far away and rarely discussed. The execution of Bruno Hauptmann for the kidnap-slaying of Charles Lindbergh's son was a topic much closer to home.

With her husband, Laura took drives in the New England countryside on resplendent weekend afternoons, and they saw plays previewing in New Haven in advance of Broadway openings. Together they found small French and Italian restaurants in quiet corners of New Haven, and twice Stephen took Laura down to New York for the weekend. They behaved both like newlyweds and newly-in-loves and Stephen even took her to the Yale-Harvard football game, which sold out Yale Bowl in November. By midway through the fourth quarter she vaguely began to understand the rules. Harvard won thirteen to six, which to a girl from Wiltshire, sounded like a pretty wild game of football.

After Thanksgiving, Laura grew restless. Stephen was immersed in his studies and had also become involved in the Christian Political Union at Yale, an extracurricular discussion and lecture group which sought, among other issues, to address a Christian response to fascism and Marxism. The Union met once a week at the outset. Then it was two evenings. Then four. Laura indulged her husband and thought it wise to find an outside activity of her own.

At Christmas, she found one. Upon the suggestion of a faculty wife who had become a close friend, Laura went for an interview at the New Haven Board of Education and applied for a job. When the all-male board heard the tones of Wiltshire in her voice, they figured she was cultured. So they asked her about Shakespeare. When Laura revealed that she knew all about not just Shakespeare, but also Milton, Chaucer, and Keats, they hired her to be the fourth-grade homeroom teacher at the best of the city's elementary schools. American men, Laura pondered upon accepting the appointment, had a strange way of maximizing a woman's abilities.

Meanwhile, Stephen rewrote the position papers that he'd conceived for the Yale Political Union and he drafted them into magazine articles. The first one, entitled *What is Christian Responsibility in 1937?*, he sold to *Christianity Today,* the prestigious publication funded by the United Lutheran Churches. In Stephen's article he deftly argued that Christian responsibility was limited by the realities of the modern world. In Spain in particular, he postulated in his article, there was little that American Christians could—or should—do. In light of the fact that much of the Christian establishment in Spain supported Franco, whose army had already begun to move northward toward Madrid, the views of the apparently conservative young theologian were not terribly surprising. (It was, after all, atheistic Joe Stalin who was supporting the anti-Franco loyalists.) But it was the eloquence of Stephen Fowler's argument that drew attention, eloquence combined with a thorough knowledge of history, political systems, and the scriptures.

Other articles followed. Stephen Fowler was published in *American Mercury* and *Harper's.* Then, as he honed his conservative views more sharply, he wrote a two-part essay in *The Atlantic.* And at age thirty-one, Stephen Fowler was suddenly the lightning rod for a reasoned conservative point of view within the United States. The America First groups contacted him, as did wealthy conservatives and Republicans. Laura, in fact, was stunned by the number of people who contacted her husband. She lost track of who they were or how many there were. Equally, Stephen Fowler was stupefied by the attention. All he wanted to do, he said, was continue his studies.

Then something happened. Laura did not know what it was, because there had been nothing tangible that had caused Stephen to change. But suddenly her husband was strangely quiet and, worse, strangely remote. It lasted for weeks. Having never seen him in such a state previously, Laura did not know. Was her husband's mood a sort of concentration stemming from his work, or was it some inner turmoil? Were the demons personal or professional? When she asked him, he said nothing was wrong.

As the weeks passed, she knew one thing. His change of moods was starting to affect the marriage. He had lost interest in sex. He never initiated anything. She had to be the, well, the aggressor. And even then, there was a preoccupation on his part. He didn't take the time with her that he used to. Sometimes she was convinced that he was simply going through the motions and his passions were elsewhere. It was as if, she almost felt, his orgasm was now enough for both of them.

All right then, Laura finally decided, we'll let it be like this for a while. When his mood changed, when the furor around his publications died away, then things would return to normal. Why wouldn't they? Stephen was still a decent man. And handsome.

But things *didn't* change.

At the political union it was is if he were in mourning for some tragic bereavement of which he never spoke. He seemed to lose his voice, falling oddly mute. He offered no opinions and made only noncommittal responses. Friends—he had many—said that he was perhaps rethinking his previous positions, or maybe working on writings of a weightier sort. (Laura, who knew that he had stopped writing at home, realized this was not the case.) His mood continued through the spring term and into the summer. They went to Lakeside for only two weekends. ("It's really for single people, you know," he said.) And then in the fall he buried himself in his theological work and the Yale library. Friends spotted him roaming the stacks devouring anything that could be found on contemporary European political systems as well as twentieth-century Christian writings.

Laura was going crazy. She wanted back the passionate lover, the vigorous virile young male, whom she had married.

In the evening, she would undress in front of him. She would move to him in the middle of the night, letting a bare breast press snugly against him. Or in the early morning, when she felt his first stirrings, she would reach gently to him as he was half awake and take his penis delicately between her fingers. She would bring it to the hardness that she desired and would allow him no excuse whatsoever.

He would oblige, naturally. But he responded mechanically. She wanted him to come after her in the way he always had before they were married, or in the way he had on their honeymoon night in the Vermont guesthouse when he'd barely been patient enough to allow her to remove her dress, and *hadn't* allowed her time to remove her stockings.

Something was seriously wrong. Laura did not know what it was. Nor did she have anyone she could confide in or whose opinion she could reasonably seek. Stephen had been her best friend in addition to being her husband.

One afternoon in April, midway through his final term in divinity school, Laura stood undressed before a full-length mirror and studied herself. Was she not as attractive as she had been when they married?

This question and darker ones darted through her mind. Then Stephen entered their bedroom and stopped short.

"What are you doing?" he asked.

For some reason, before her husband's malignant stare, she felt like grabbing a sheet and covering herself, as if this man whom she loved and with whom she shared a bed should not see her fully unclothed in daylight.

"Just looking," she said.

"For what?"

There was a pause and next she heard herself saying things she hadn't planned. "I'm trying to see why you don't find me attractive anymore."

Stephen retrieved some papers that he'd left on his night table. "Who says I don't find you attractive?"

"You never want to make love anymore. I practically have to force you." Now she did reach for a robe. She slid into it as he leafed through the papers.

Then her accusation registered. He swept an imaginary hair away from his face and answered, "I'm not sure what you're talking about, Laura," he said evenly. "I've had a lot on my mind." He paused, then: "You know, I have exams coming. I can't be beholden to girlish moods and—"

"These are not moods!" she exploded. "I'm talking about something seriously wrong between us! You are *always* preoccupied! And you act like . . ." Laura fought back a stream of tears as she shouted, "You act like making love to me is a chore!"

"Laura, would you keep your voice down?"

"I will not!"

"Making love to you is not a chore."

"You act as if it is. Eighteen months ago if you'd walked in and found me undressed, you would have grabbed me and thrown me into the bed."

"Laura, it was new then. We've grown up a bit. We're both adults and we have professional obligations."

She controlled herself, but her voice was breaking. "Stephen, I want to be your wife. I want you to love me. What's the matter? Why won't you tell me?" She began to cry.

He stepped to Laura and put an arm around her. It was an arm of comfort, not fully an arm of affection.

"Laura, I don't know what's bothering you, but we can discuss it tonight, if you wish."

"You're going to your damned political union tonight. You won't be home till midnight. You're always going to—"

He stole a glance at his watch and interrupted her. "I have a class in half an hour, Laura," he said. "I'm sorry. I have to go." He walked out of the bedroom and did not return until after she had gone to sleep that evening.

The next morning Laura sat down at the dining table in the house near the Yale campus. Stephen was out already. Laura opened a box of stationery and wrote a long mournful letter to her father. She sealed it. Then she tore it up. It was only when she went to burn it that other burning letters flashed back to her. And she thought of Peter Whiteside again.

103

She took another sheet of paper. On it, she wrote simply,

> Peter,
> I'm not happy.
> Laura.

She wrote her return address on the top left corner of the envelope and she posted it airmail.

The response arrived sixteen days later.

> Dearest Laura,
> England is very beautiful in early summer. We would all cherish seeing you.
>   If I may be of any help . . .
>
>   Peter

Laura read the letter and cried.

Then, a few days thereafter, and just as unpredictably as ever, Stephen broke free from at least some of his invisible restraints. He began writing again, then held the floor at the political union until the early morning hours. He spoke, wrote, and lived like a man possessed.

He had examined every bit of his philosophy, he declared, and had found it entirely lacking. Not in *reason,* but in *compassion.* In human spirit, he said, he had been entirely mistaken about many things.

Spain, for example. Germany, for another example.

"It is the full responsibility of *any* Christian," Stephen declared, first in a political forum at Yale and then in writing in *The American Mercury* and then—addressing different questions, of course—in *The*

Atlantic, "to combat totalitarianism and oppression wherever it is found." He cited the gospels of Mark and John and the teachings of Paul. Examining his own change of spirit, his conversion, as it were, he cited his own "youthful naïveté and a muddled idea of what this world is capable of being." On his own road to Damascus, Stephen had had his own vision. It was now his contention, in complete contradiction to everything he had previously felt, "that any Christian is one of God's soldiers. As in the time of Jesus and as in the time of the Crusades, there is often a time when a moral man must bear armament and fight. The Holy Land," he concluded, "takes different forms to different generations. In this century, the Holy Land may be Spain or Germany or all of Europe. God willing, the tyrants of Western Europe will not push moral men to the point where reaching for a rifle is the only act remaining for a Christian of conscience."

"And what about *you?*" Laura asked Stephen when she had read his manuscript. "Are you going to pick up a rifle and go to Spain? To combat the Fascists?"

His answer surprised her, even in its vagaries. "Perhaps," he said in the library of their home.

"And what should I do while you're off fighting?" she asked tartly. "Wait to see if I'm a widow? Have an affair with some student or professor? Go with you?"

"I don't know, Laura," he answered. "We're entering an era of sacrifices for the good of humanity. Maybe you should examine your own priorities. Your own sense of selfishness, perhaps."

He had that way of always turning a discussion back against her. *Selfishness!* She felt wounded.

Stephen had emerged from his trance and had

reversed his political point of view almost completely. But at home, nothing changed. He was silent in the evenings. They had long since ceased to entertain their friends. And physically, well, she realized, Stephen didn't seem to *want* her anymore. That was all there was to it.

Gradually, it occurred to her. This was what a crumbling marriage was all about. She had to get away. She would go crazy if she didn't.

She had put money away from her teaching salary. Now she dipped a little deeper into each week's paycheck and squirreled away the extra dollar or two when she could. Laura knew exactly where she wanted to go. She knew just who she wanted to see. By mid-May, merely days before Stephen's graduation exercises, she had enough money to visit a travel agent in New Haven.

Stephen returned home in the middle of one afternoon. In his hand he held a letter which he read and reread. He wore an expression bordering upon extreme apprehension.

Stephen found Laura in the living room, waiting for him. She was going to speak first. But he looked up only once and then his eyes settled back to the correspondence. "What's that?" she inquired.

"My appointment," he said. "The Lutheran Council is sending me to New Jersey. After my ordination, of course." His tone was much calmer than she'd heard it in several months. "There's a little parish in a town called Liberty Circle," he said. "Northern New Jersey, I think. Ever heard of it?"

She shook her head.

"I haven't, either." He reread a few more lines. "I'm

to assist an older minister who'll be retiring within two years. I'm to meet his parish and assume some of his duties. I presume I'll then be staying there."

She nodded.

"Why the long face?" he asked. He began to fold the letter. "New Jersey's not so bad. Not even so far from here, is it?" He tucked the letter away.

"I'm going back to England," she said softly.

His face paled, then flushed with an expression she had never seen before, hurt mingled with indignation and confusion. It took him several seconds to absorb her simple announcement.

"When?" he finally said.

"Next week." She said that she'd tried to talk to him a thousand times, but had never been successful. She said it was partly her fault, but definitely not entirely hers. She wanted breathing room, she insisted, if she couldn't be loved, instead. She wanted to see the things that remained eternal for her. England. Her father. The charming, rickety house in Salisbury which he, as a moneyed American, could probably never comprehend. But that was moving into personalities, which she didn't wish to do. Throughout all this, her husband was either expressionless or slightly nodding.

There were other things that went unsaid: all this could have been avoided if maybe once in the last few months he had whispered that he loved her. But he didn't know the phrase anymore. He knew only the church and global politics. She wanted to say that she didn't really want to separate from him, and she wanted Stephen to rush to her, embrace her, and cry that he didn't want this, either.

Instead, he looked at her with growing understanding. And then the nodding was more evident.

"It doesn't have to be permanent," she added toward the end. "But we need to put each other in perspective."

His response stunned her. "I think it's a good idea, Laura," he finally said softly. "For both of us. I'll be honest. I've felt this way for quite some time myself. We need some time apart."

There was little else to add. Only the details. Her ship would sail from New York the following Wednesday. She would miss his graduation. Her transit was already paid. She had purchased one-way fare and the ship was named the SS *Panama*.

"I've never heard of it," Stephen said. "But you're not taking it. Not on that date."

"And why not?"

"You're married to me, Laura," he said. "And that means something. The least you can do, even if you're not happy here, is stay until June. We're moving to New Jersey. I can't do that without you."

Reluctantly, she agreed.

In the weeks that followed, Laura spent a great deal of time on small matters of organization, inventorying their possessions and spending too much time looking at the souvenirs of the days when they were happier.

The move came in mid-June. It went smoothly. Stephen's new parish was situated in an old white church off a quiet square in a small town. Their new home, which greatly resembled the house in New Haven, was across the street. Stephen addressed his new congregation twice that month. He spoke of Christian responses to totalitarianism. The parishioners accepted him quickly. They liked him, in fact. So Laura booked passage to England again, once more on the SS *Panama*.

"At least this time I've heard of it," Stephen observed.

"I don't think that remark is very funny," she snapped back. "I'm leaving you for several weeks. You don't seem to care."

"I didn't ask you to go," he countered. Always, he had that way of turning things back upon her.

In the days that followed, their relationship assumed an odd formality. They slept on separate sides of the same bed, dressed and undressed at differing times, and generally treated each other with the cordiality of roommates or as a couple who had been lovers very briefly long ago.

On the night before her departure, she lay wakefully in bed and toward 3 A.M. was on the threshold of sleep. She felt him move suddenly and his hand was just below her breasts. She turned more toward him. Delirious words were forming in her mouth and she almost spoke.

Then she realized that his hand was still. She shuddered. It was almost inanimate. Mercifully, he thrashed a second time in his sleep—as if disturbed by some formidably chaotic dream—and his hand flew away. He resettled himself facing the other direction and Laura was left alone with her crushed expectations.

All twenty months of her marriage flashed before her in a final fit, off-line and flickering, like an unbalanced film projector gone irretrievably beserk. Then she closed her eyes and clenched her teeth as tightly as she could. She suppressed the fury, the emotion, and the frustration that were within her. After a passage of several minutes, it didn't seem that bad anymore.

The consolation of going home was there, at least, so she managed to sleep. She was comforted greatly by a recurrent vision of her happy girlhood in Wiltshire.

On the next day, a frightfully hot one, Stephen saw her to her ship at the Cunard pier in New York. She had no idea when she would ever see America, or her husband, again. That evening in the ship's dining room, she happened to note the date of her sailing. It was printed at the head of the evening's menu:

July 3, 1939.

PART THREE

William Thomas Cochrane
1934-39

SIX

Like Washington to the south, Baltimore in 1939 sweltered through a dreary, steaming August.

William Cochrane sat studiously in his office and used two fingers to peck at the black Royal typewriter at his desk. His glasses were sloped downward toward the bridge of his nose. He frowned slightly as he peered through them and attempted to finish this second letter. The first one, addressed to the Director of Personnel, Morgan Guaranty Trust Company, New York, was already sealed and stamped. It lay to the right of the typewriter.

Bill Cochrane's suit jacket from Dunhill Tailors hung on the back of his chair. It was past four in the afternoon, and though his necktie was straight—there was a line in the FBI manual about always having one's necktie straight—his white shirt was starting to lose its crispness. The room was warm.

Cochrane's fingers held still for a moment as he chose the proper phraseology. One weighed one's words carefully when writing to J. Edgar Hoover himself.

Oh, what the hell, he finally decided. Might as well just get on with it. No pleasantries. As few final endearments as possible. Just the facts. He typed the final sentences.

> . . . And so it is with reluctance that I submit my resignation from the Federal Bureau of Investigation, effective as of 5 P.M., August 30, 1939. It has been my pleasure to be of service to the Bureau over these past six years. I pray that I have also been of some aid to my country.

He drew a breath and reread. *There,* he thought to himself, *that does it. Just the proper note of humility and patriotism.* He studied the letter from the top to bottom again. Why was this so difficult? he wondered. He had made his decision almost six weeks ago.

There was a knock on his door and his secretary entered. She was a thin, earnest girl named Patricia. For a moment she stood in silence, waiting for Bill Cochrane to lift his attention from the piece of paper before him.

The man she watched for those few seconds, the man she worked for, was thirty-three years old with sandy, blondish hair. His eyes were sharp and his complexion slightly ruddy and sun-beaten, the result of long weekend hikes through the Maryland countryside. He looked younger than his years, however. Dwelling upon the typewriter and sheet of paper before him, he looked like a young professor or maybe a law student.

Then he looked up. His preoccupation broke and from somewhere came a handsome smile. "Yes, Patty?" he asked gently.

"Washington," she said, indicating the telephone. She spoke in a voice not too distant from a whisper. "I think it's Mr. Hoover."

He laughed. "Doubt it," he said. "Unless he's looking for someone to head up a new office in Topeka."

Patricia gave him a smile and rolled her eyes. She pulled the door closed as she left. Cochrane reached to the telephone, picked it up, and leaned back in his swivel chair. Now that his resignation was typed there were few horrors that a direct call from Washington could hold.

Then he brought the tilting chair back down to earth. Patricia had been right. Cochrane recognized the clipped, nasal-pitched voice of the Devil himself. There was something, Hoover told him, that the FBI needed to discuss with him personally. That evening. In Washington.

"I want you to drop whatever you're doing and get the hell down here immediately," Hoover ranted. "I'm having a car sent to take you to the train station."

Cochrane looked at the cracking green paint on the wall of his office. He thought of his current assignment in Baltimore and his previous one in Washington. He smiled ruefully and looked at his letter of resignation.

"You bet," he said. And he was about to add that there were one or two things that he wished to take up with Hoover, too. But by that time, Cochrane was listening to a dial tone.

Twice previously in his life William Thomas Cochrane had addressed a letter to J. Edgar Hoover. The first had been sent in early 1934, about twelve months after an aging Paul von Hindenburg had bestowed the chancellorship of Germany upon a former Austrian house painter. The headlines in the daily newspapers had prompted Cochrane to write.

The letter read:

Dr. Mr. Hoover:
I am a banker and an investigator for the international division of the Georgia National Bank in Atlanta. I speak French and German fluently.
Judging by the course of world events, it seems to me that your FBI will soon need men for specialized jobs in Europe. Do you think you might find a use for me? I'm bored here.

Sincerely,
Wm. T. Cochrane

Hoover admired the sender's nerve in writing directly but had little other reaction to the letter. Plenty of people wrote to him asking for jobs. Half of them were certifiable lunatics.

But Hoover noted the official stationery of the Georgia National Bank. The word "international" did catch his eye. And French and German, he reasoned. Hoover began to think. Washington was buzzing with rumors about America having to get into the espionage game, something the United States had never done in peacetime, either officially or unofficially. Hoover lived and slept with the vision of other investigative agencies being founded, principally at the expense of his own.

So the director's hand stayed for a moment above

the wastebasket. Hoover picked up a mechanical pencil and drew neat script letters upon the upper left corner of the correspondence.

"Frank: See about this," he wrote. Then he sent the letter along to Frank Lerrick, the Bureau's gaunt, short and unsmiling director of personnel, a Hoover crony since the 1920s.

The initial reports concerning William Cochrane returned to the director of the FBI within five weeks. They were decidedly mixed. But Hoover reviewed them with interest.

On the negative side. Cochrane's personal politics were unobtainable, primarily because he never discussed them with anyone. There was little chance, however, that he would turn out to be some crimson-hearted Bolshevik. By family and background, Cochrane appeared to be a conservative, quiet, introspective, softly spoken man, actually more equipped to handle investigations in an office and on paper than out in the field where a misstep could cost an agent his life.

Cochrane's father had been a major during the world war of '14–'18, which was seen as a plus. His mother was a librarian. Cochrane was born and raised in Virginia, where his father had been the editor of the Charlottesville *Eagle* after the war. He was the middle of three brothers. He had gone to college at William & Mary, where he had acquired the finishings of a southern gentleman. There, proctors left the rooms during examinations and, in theory at least, a young man was to learn a sense of honor as well as his academic lessons. Cochrane graduated *magna cum laude* in European history, then obtained a masters

117

degree in business at the University of Pennsylvania, way up north in Philadelphia.

But certain countercurrents caught Hoover's eye. Cochrane had traveled abroad. He had also acted at a theater in Provincetown, Massachusetts. Cochrane had played Sam Evans in Eugene O'Neill's *Strange Interlude* and had even been a favorite of O'Neill himself, who occasionally lurched by for a performance. One of Cochrane's former directors had gone on to bigger things in New York. To an investigating agent, the director had mentioned, "Cochrane's fine gift at impersonation as well as a stellar memory."

Other details stood out. In keeping with family tradition, Bill Cochrane had served in the military, a peaceful stint as an ordnance officer at Fort Bragg, South Carolina. And then there had been the tragedy about his family life. He had married in late 1932 to a young woman named Heather Andrews, the only daughter of a moneyed Atlanta family who traced their roots far back to prerevolutionary Georgia.

"So he's married?" asked Hoover.

"Widowed," said Lerrick. "As of July of last year." They sat in Hoover's office with the report on Cochrane on the desk between them. "A highway accident. Their car was hit head on from the right side by a truck with a drunk driver. Cochrane came out of it badly banged up. But, uh, his wife didn't come out of it at all."

Hoover pursed his lips.

"Some people think he's compensating for the loss of his wife by throwing himself headlong into his work. Know what I mean? Burying himself with work to forget?"

Hoover nodded. "Maybe it's why he wrote to us. New job. Change of location. Helps a man sometimes. Other times it makes him more zealous." Hoover lofted his thin eyebrows, then relaxed them. Zeal didn't bother him if it could be harnessed on behalf of the Bureau. "What else?" he asked.

Lerrick sat by quietly as Hoover rustled through various written accounts concerning Cochrane. The director took his time and concluded a careful reading of the personnel inquiry. Cochrane, he read, had intelligence and an outstanding knowledge of international banking which, when combined with his fluency in two European languages, presented certain special talents to the agency.

But the summary on him concluded:

He has talent and intellect. But there is a serious question as to whether he could take the toughening up and physical discipline needed to become an agent for this Bureau. Similarly, book smarts and acting talent do not call upon the street smarts which would also be essential to this position. His emotional stability is also a question at this time, due to the recent loss of his wife.

"Then what is the conclusion of our inquiry?" Hoover asked.

"His letter should be kept on file. Maybe he'll be needed someday. Maybe not. I, uh, don't think he's material for us. Not right now, anyway."

"Better think again. You had two agents investigating him?"

"Yes. That's correct."

Hoover asked for their names. Lerrick gave them.

"Have them reassigned before they embarrass us again," Hoover said. Then he tossed before Lerrick a second correspondence that he'd received from William Cochrane. With the letter were clipped a series of black and white photographs which Cochrane had shot with a miniature camera concealed in his suit pocket. The photographs showed the two FBI agents who had been following him over the course of two weeks. The note, on the stationery of the Georgia National Bank, read simply:

Mr. Hoover:
   If this is the quality of your surveillance teams, our enemies should be greatly comforted.

Sincerely,
Wm. T. Cochrane

Lerrick took the prints and thumbed them with suppressed anger. "So he's clever. I wonder how tough he is."

"Find out," Hoover requested.

In June of 1934, Bill Cochrane entered the National Police Academy of the Federal Bureau of Investigation. He neared completion of the five months of training that had a dropout rate of 43 percent. He drew excellent marks in all fields: crime scene analysis, visual memory, forensic chemistry, firearms, description, identification, unarmed attack, and self-defense. From his days as a U.S. Army ordnance officer, he knew enough about high-level explosives to practically teach a course himself. He struggled with judo and bordered on mastering it. But one criticism remained.

"You still behave," Alan Farber, the academy's assistant judo instructor remarked sourly to Cochrane one afternoon, "like some goddamned piss-elegant Southern gentleman. Every time you throw somebody you're always saying, 'Sorry'!"

"Is that right?" asked Cochrane.

"You bet it's right, boy. And you can bet your sweet Rhett Butler ass that it'll be in my report on Friday when I write it."

"Which hand do you write with?" Cochrane asked.

"Right. Why? What's it to you?"

"Just wondering. Sorry."

The next day, in a self-defense session, Farber's right hand was broken by an overzealous student who threw the assistant professor nine feet in the air during a drill on knife attacks.

"He's starting," typed Alan Farber in the final report, "to look like an outstanding recruit. Maybe some good hard field work would roughen up a few of the smooth edges. It would also measure how good an agent he might someday become."

So upon graduation, Cochrane was sent to Kansas City, where he was soon going cheek-to-jowl with a gang of railroad-yard thieves. Then he was reassigned to Chicago, where he passed an engaging six weeks. Some Sicilian gorillas were edging into the funeral-home business at the expense of some honest German-American undertakers on the North Side—making substantial contributions to the overall funeral industry at the same time.

In both situations, Cochrane worked under the

command of one Richard Wheeler, known as "Big Dick" throughout the FBI outposts of the Midwest. Wheeler, a big, affable ursine Missourian, was already a rising star of the Bureau and making himself a legend.

Wheeler didn't allow petty legalities to stymie an investigation. Once, at 3 A.M. on a rainy Chicago morning, Wheeler had posted Cochrane as a lookout as Wheeler, bearing a screwdriver in his teeth, had climbed a telephone pole. At the summit, Wheeler joyously invaded a junction box, rearranged things, and for the next two weeks manned a pair of headphones in a nearby apartment that tied into the funeral home of one Vito DeMaria. Previously, in Kansas City, also with Cochrane under his bearish arm, Wheeler demonstrated how two federal agencies could work closely to the greater good of the public: he removed twenty-five dollars a week from Bureau petty cash and passed it along to the mailman who had railroad yards. In this way, Dick Wheeler read his victims' mail every morning before they received it.

"How can you do that?" Cochrane asked, the new boy on the block.

"I can't," said Wheeler. "So I do it anyway." When Cochrane grimaced, Wheeler expanded. "Damned common practice, Bill," Wheeler said. "Look. Those bad guys out there do whatever in hell they want. So I do, too."

"Apparently," Cochrane answered.

"One thing you'll learn if you stay on this job long enough," said Wheeler instructively. "No one argues with results."

"Apparently," Cochrane repeated.

Then Bureau headquarters in Washington sent Cochrane swimming into some deep water indeed. He went to New York posing as a Londonderry gunrunner for the Irish Republican Army. In lower Manhattan and Brooklyn, Cochrane put together a good infiltration effort among the Jewish mobsters along Delancey, Hester, and Canal streets—Meyer Lansky, Waxey Gordon, and Whitey Krackauer—and from the nether side of the Brooklyn Bridge, Lepke Buchalter, Gurrah Shapiro, and Mendy Weiss. These were the presiding experts at running weapons in and out of New York. And there were few shortages of customers. *Everyone,* back in those days, had someone he wanted to shoot. Sometimes, even an entire *group* of people.

While he was at it, Cochrane uncovered and blew the whistle on several middle-range operations associated with the same gangs, mostly *shlom* jobs in the garment centers that had to do with sash weights and lead pipes massaging the skulls of labor organizers.

"There's only one problem with Cochrane," observed the other agents who worked out of the New York FBI office on Cardinal Hayes Place. "He can't keep his nose out of someone else's case."

By mid-1937, the other agents in New York and the jagged-fingernail set along Hester Street received the fulfillment of their most earnest wishes. The need for American agents abroad had reached a crisis point. President Roosevelt himself was concerned about access to information in Europe should the United States be drawn into another world war. The U.S., after all, had never engaged in espionage abroad. There was something inherently unseemly about it. Nonethe-

123

less, the President took two steps.

He asked a Wall Street lawyer and world war hero named William Donovan to travel to Europe and study how an intelligence service might be established. And second, he launched a personal directive to J. Edgar Hoover to establish a foreign branch posthaste.

At the invocation of the word "foreign," J. Edgar Hoover remembered Bill Cochrane's letter of 1934. He abruptly recalled Cochrane to Washington to prepare for European service.

"What's been our success rate so far in Europe?" Cochrane asked Frank Lerrick toward the end of a second week of reorientation.

"Success rate? What do you mean?"

"Other agents?" Cochrane asked. "How are we doing?"

"There, uh, *are* no other agents. You're the first."

There was a long, long silence. "Oh," Cochrane finally said. "Thanks for the honor."

Cochrane traveled by the Polish liner *Pilsudski* from Washington to Bremen, working under the cover of an American businessman sympathetic to Hitler's National Socialist Party. His only orders from the FBI were, "Find out what you can, and don't get caught. More than likely, we won't be able to get you out."

"Any particular set of rules to play by?" Cochrane had asked the day before leaving.

"Spies don't play by rules, young Agent Cochrane," Hoover had snorted. "And that's what you are now. A spy."

"And remember this," Frank Lerrick added, by way of benediction. *"In this line of work, there is no such thing as coincidence. Keep your eyes open. Always."*

"He's quoting from the goddamned manual," Cochrane suffered to realize.

". . . and that's what you are now. A spy," Hoover was concluding. "Use the brains you were born with and the skills this Bureau taught you. If you're exceedingly lucky, that might be enough."

SEVEN

Bill Cochrane's arrival in Berlin from Bremen coincided with a state visit by Mussolini. Cochrane was grateful for the public activity. Better for him to move around the city and become oriented. Better for him to observe.

The old Germany, the one he had read about, was still there. The polite, orderly people, the handsome blond children. There were the quaint, aging gingerbread buildings both from the medieval period and the previous century. And there were the stark iron monuments erected to those who had sacrificed "for the Fatherland" in the Great War.

But then there was the New Germany. Everywhere, particularly upon Il Duce's arrival, there was the new red and black warlike facade. Everywhere Bill Cochrane looked there was a march. Everywhere there were Swastikas, Hitler Youth, evening parades by torchlight, and grandiose, overstated new buildings.

Along the tree-lined main boulevards were a sea of long vertical banners, proudly alternating with the trees and fluttering. On long poles topped by golden eagles waved the red banners of the Third Reich—with a black swastika in a round white field at the center—and these in turn were interspersed with the red, white, and green banners of Fascist Italy. The displays were powerful and impressive, none more so than from the center of Berlin along the Kaiser Wilhelm Strasse leading to Hitler's new Chancellery in pink marble.

The pink glint of the seat of power suggested an incongruous touch to Cochrane's American sensibilities. In the cafes he struck up conversations with Germans and discussed the new Nazi architecture. Twice Cochrane was told what everyone else in Germany seemed to know.

"Hitler likes pink," they told him.

Cochrane pondered this as he found himself an apartment. When he ceased to think about Hitler's predilection for pink, he was struck by the fact that both the United States and Nazi Germany now had an eagle as their symbol. And there, he concluded, the similarities ended.

About a week after his arrival, Cochrane faced certain disaster. There lived on a side street only a few blocks from the Reichstag a large, smiling, bookish bespectacled tailor named Kuri Kurkevics. The tailor, a Latvian, had been on the FBI payroll for the previous six months. But when Cochrane ambled by Kurkevics' home and then his shop, the tailor was nowhere to be found. The home was locked and dark, the shop boarded up. Clearly, Cochrane's contact in Berlin had been uncovered and, most likely, executed.

Cochrane then improvised.

Two weeks later he opened a brokerage house and

spent his free hours lounging around the bar at the Kaiser Wilhelm Hotel. He took into his confidence anyone with whom he fell into conversation, and mentioned that he had inside information on the American stock market. When investors grinned and offered money to him, he at first demurred, then accepted it a few weeks later purely out of his newly-born friendship. Within two months he had cabled a million and a half dollars worth of investments to the United States. Fortunately, most of them turned out well. More business walked in. Cochrane considered his good fortune to be a gift from a providential God. Until he had arrived in Germany, he had never followed the U.S. stock market. He knew virtually nothing about it, other than having overheard a friend from Chestnut Hill, just before leaving Washington, comment that everything would be going up within a year.

The businessmen, industrialists, and speculators whom Cochrane met in Germany kept their hearts close to their bank drafts. But as their American friend was making money for them, they drew him into their circle. Soon Cochrane was being invited to the very offices, factories, and gatherings of which the FBI would eventually want a working knowledge. Cochrane's gentle nature and social graces dispelled any suspicion. The very qualities that the FBI had once nearly used to disqualify him were now paying generous dividends.

German friends, some in the party and some in the government, took him into private offices in buildings on the Tierpitzufer where the supreme intelligence communities were housed. Once he met Himmler and shook hands with him. Another time he was introduced to Admiral Canaris, the head of the Abwehr, or intelligence division. (Canaris, Cochrane quickly learned, was something of a lightning rod for the few remaining anti-Hitler factions within the government.) And on one grand but nerve-shattering occasion, after a performance of *Die Walküre,* the American was in the same ballroom as Hitler and Goering. Cochrane spent the evening studying the two men in their medal-bedecked black uniforms with red bands and sashes. Cochrane once moved close enough to Hitler to smell the overdone Viennese cologne in which the jittery little tyrant bathed. And at another moment in the evening, Cochrane edged near enough to Goering to see the beads of sweat that were ever-present on the man's thick forehead. Cochrane could have, if he had wanted to, brushed away the dandruff that fell like a snowstorm upon the shoulders of the Gestapo's founder.

Always, Cochrane was introduced as a financier willing to do business with Germany. He used his real name and actual passport. Introduced to diplomats and to those with influence within the party, a catch phrase developed. "Our sympathetic American friend," they called him. The diplomats and power brokers would nod, smile, and boast in civilized conversational tones of their plans for a new German empire, a *new world order,* make that, now that the Jews, Socialists, and Communists were on the run and could no longer pollute the Reich.

"I personally praise Hitler for *that* above all," Cochrane would confide to them.

Then Bill Cochrane complicated his life. He fell for a

woman. Her name was Theresia and she said she worked for a prominent man named Otto Mauer in the Interior Ministry.

It was Bill Cochrane's first serious involvement since the death of his wife. He still traveled with a framed picture of Heather and kept the picture visible in his Berlin apartment. He did not yet have the heart to place the photograph in a drawer.

He first met Theresia on an evening in the bustling Rathskeller Kietel, not far from where they both worked. He was already seated when a single woman in her mid-twenties, tall, dark-haired, and with high cheekbones, took the table next to him. She wore a black skirt, a loose pale pink sweater, and around her neck, fastened with a gold pin, was a striking red silk scarf. Bill Cochrane spoke first, admiring the scarf and asking her in German where she had bought it. At first she was reserved, modest, letting him lead the conversation. But the talk blossomed and he joined her at her table.

Two nights later, they attended a cinema, followed by a late coffee. Then they shared a brandy. He walked her home. She admitted that he fascinated her because there were so few Americans left in Berlin. He told her she fascinated him because she was—quite frankly—so very beautiful.

They stopped at the entrance to her apartment building. Bill Cochrane kissed her. She turned her cheek to his lips and they said good night. Cochrane walked home knowing that she was toying with him. So for a week he didn't telephone.

On a Friday he called her to take her to dinner. She answered the door of her flat. As he handed her a bouquet of flowers, she huddled behind the door in the unlit foyer.

"I'm not dressed," Theresia told him. But she was. Partially. She had showered and dried herself. Clinging to her was a nightgown, thin as gauze.

"Please be good. Please wait," she asked.

She motioned to a sitting area off from the foyer, and hurried past him back to her dressing room. As she passed into the light of the doorway of her bedroom, she was silhouetted for an instant. Bill Cochrane caught the first suggestion of what she would look like naked. Then she disappeared.

Bill Cochrane looked at the dressing-room door. It was still open. A moment later he was standing in it, his head cocked appreciatively, as he watched Theresia before a full-length mirror, wearing only a lavender camisole, perfuming and dusting herself. She saw him and stopped.

"I'm not good. And I won't wait," he said.

She pulled her nightgown back to her to cover herself. She turned, but was far from angry.

"Maybe we could make it a late dinner. Toward midnight," he suggested.

"Maybe," she answered. She added that she knew a cabaret where the best show started at one. He approached her and she halted him again, letting the nightgown slip away but reaching to the top drawer of a dressing table.

With a sly smile, she pulled out the long red scarf that had first caught his eye some ten days earlier.

"I'm told no man can resist a red scarf," she said with a laugh. "No matter how a woman wears it." She tied it neatly around her left thigh, three quarters of the way up from her knee toward the top of her perfect leg.

"You're told correctly," he said. He reached behind her and easily unlaced the camisole. It slid down her body and she stepped out of it. In clothing, she had been an extremely attractive woman. Completely undressed, she was breathtakingly beautiful.

She helped him undress and then they were on her bed. He was kissing her on her lips, on her throat, on her breasts, and everywhere else. He had completely taken control, which was exactly what she had wanted since the first night she had seen him at the Rathskeller Kietel.

As lovers, they saw each other regularly, went to a dinner here, a public park there, and the occasional long walk on a Sunday. And always a rendezvous would end in a bedroom, one day his, the next day hers. They even realized that they were acting like a pair of sex-crazed university students embarked on their first affair. Both knew that it was far from that for either. But neither could possibly have cared.

Then, one night about a month and a half after it all began, Theresia spoke out in the middle of the night. It was past 2 A.M. and she couldn't sleep. So she awakened him.

"What would you do if a war broke out?" she asked.

She was smoking, lying naked near him, and he could see her figure and the pale orange glow from her cigarette. His eye began an easy, leisurely journey which began with her full, perfect breasts. It traveled past her flat, trim waist, settled for a few seconds upon her light brown pubic hair, then savored the perfection of her slim legs. Bill Cochrane knew he was in love.

"Stay in Berlin. Sell securities, if I still could," he

answered sleepily. As soon as the sentence was out of his mouth, he realized the impoverishment of his lie.

"Shouldn't you return to America?" she asked.

"I don't know. Why?"

"Because you should," she said. "All my friends think there will be another war. One to correct the injustices of the last war. They say the Americans will be our enemies again. Roosevelt is partially Jewish, Hitler says."

"That's ridiculous, Theresia," he answered too instinctively.

Somewhere in the far distance, from another apartment, perhaps, Cochrane thought he heard someone playing a flute. Theresia changed the subject unexpectedly, as was her habit.

"Do you have a wife in America?" she asked.

"No."

"That's something else you should do," she said. "Marry someday."

"Someday," he agreed.

"My husband is a lieutenant in the Navy," she said. "I haven't seen or heard from him for six months. The last time, he hinted that he was going to South America. I think he is in a submarine. They never tell the family."

Cochrane listened, watching her breathe, watching her chest move gently up and down and following the glow of the cigarette until she snuffed it.

"My husband would kill you if he discovered you to be my lover," she said, turning toward Cochrane and moving into his arms. "And he would kill me if he knew I was in love with you."

"So we won't tell him," Cochrane answered. Then he

134

kissed her and told her that he was in love with her, husband or no husband. They made love again. He waited for tomorrow and wondered idly if he should see a special contact in Berlin. He needed something small, compact, and thirty-two calibre, in case of some funny sort of emergency.

"I never knew you had a husband," he finally said through a veil of drowsiness.

"You never asked," she answered equally.

Through Theresia, Cochrane met Otto Mauer. Mauer was introduced as a coordinator of labor and industry within the Interior Ministry. Cochrane gravitated toward him as well as he could without arousing suspicion.

Mauer was between forty and fifty, with brown hair that was silvering instead of graying and a narrow, unfriendly jaw. He wore thin round glasses and had an air of being midway between a dentist and an aristocrat. Cochrane, after a few meetings, began to like Mauer. He quickly learned that the man's inimical appearance was deceiving. Or perhaps it was for show. Independently wealthy, he had gone into the government because it had once been a respectable thing to do in Germany. He had also been to university and enjoyed sharing a schnitzel lunch with Cochrane or an evening in a beer garden talking Hegel or Schopenhauer and maybe even flirting with some Kierkegaard, if the evening became sufficiently sodden.

"So unusual to even find a man who knows those names anymore," Mauer remarked one evening as they walked through Berlin. "No one going into govern-

135

ment now with any education. Not since the Nazis closed the universities. Difficult to find anyone with more than eight years of schooling."

Cochrane had a suspicion he was being tested. "But the party has rebuilt Germany," he said.

"Yes. Of course," Mauer answered, lacking any conviction. "Wonderful thing, isn't it?"

They strolled through a quiet park and came to a commercial section. Three shops were boarded up that Cochrane remembered from the previous week. A tailor, a watchmaker, and a grocer were gone. There were heavy boards across broken storefront windows and enormous swastikas had been scrawled across the jagged woodwork. They passed the shattered storefronts without comment.

"Germany is in the process of change," said Mauer, given heavily to understatement. "Not everyone is convinced it is for the best."

"Germany has its historical place in the world," Cochrane answered. "As a power in Europe, for example."

"Germany," Mauer replied, "has started and lost too many wars already." He turned toward Cochrane as they walked. The German assessed his American friend thoroughly. "Why don't you come visit my family some weekend? Not in Berlin, but down to the south. We have our permanent residence outside of Munich. I would like you to meet my wife and son."

Cochrane thanked Mauer and accepted. Later, Theresia said something about having to visit an ailing aunt in Baden-Baden, so Bill Cochrane picked the following weekend to be Mauer's houseguest. He caught an express train from the new station in Berlin.

Mauer had preceded him, taking a personal holiday and leaving on Wednesday.

But as the train carried Cochrane southward, he began to notice crated military equipment stacked in increasing volume from one station to the next. At Regensburg, Cochrane stepped off the train during its fifteen-minute stop, ostensibly to smoke a small cigar. It was a damp day, surprisingly chilly for that time of year. Cochrane walked the length of the platform, as if to savor the exercise.

The supplies carried Wehrmacht insignia and were barely concealed. Had Cochrane wished to look more closely, which he did not want to appear to do, he could have learned which battalions were the intended recipients. But he did pass close enough to the crates and their military guards to actually learn some of the contents. It was the precise war equipment—helmets, rifles, blankets, and knapsacks—Cochrane reasoned, necessary to sustain a light-armored or infantry division. A bit farther south, at Freising and at Landshut, Cochrane observed the soldiers who would be using the equipment. By the time Cochrane reached Munich, soldiers were everywhere. But the equipment was nowhere in view and Bill Cochrane knew he had stumbled across a military secret unknown outside the Third Reich. Germany was fortifying itself for an invasion of Austria. There could be no other reason for a buildup of troops in that area. Surely, Austria, Switzerland, and Czechoslovakia were not preparing to invade Germany.

Otto Mauer met Cochrane at the central railway station. Mauer drove a dark blue Mercedes 260D, its top down, since the weather had cleared. Mauer was shown great deference, Cochrane noticed, by the local police. They drove to the chocolate shop in Freising where Natalie Mauer, Otto's wife, was the proprietor and employed a staff of five. Natalie Mauer joined the two men in the car.

Then they drove twenty minutes out of the city to Mauer's estate, an impressive spread of land featuring a rambling stone mansion behind gates and a brick wall. Inappropriately, a new road had been constructed just outside the estate's walls and a small bus stop had been installed, presumably for the Mauer family's staff. Cochrane reasoned correctly that Herr and Frau Mauer had not been on a bus in their adult lives.

Just before dinner, Natalie Mauer changed into a delicate pink and pale blue Chinese kimono. She was ten years younger than her husband and very beautiful in a way typical of German women—tall and strong, with high cheekbones, dark eyes, brown hair, and a perfect smile. Her legs were long and her arms were slim. She introduced her husband's guest to five-year-old Rudy, their son, an angelic blond child with a crown of tousled curly hair. Then a nurse with an Austrian accent guided the boy to his own play area and bedroom.

Dinner followed. Their cook had prepared a spectacular meal of wild boar, roasted apples and potatoes, and diced chard, all complemented by a 1928 Chambolle Musigny from the cellar.

"The last *good* year of the Chambolle Musignys," Mauer lamented with sincerity. He added that he was sadly down to his last two cases.

After dinner there was German brandy, which

138

Cochrane accepted, and cigars which he declined. He might also have declined the drift of the conversation—contemporary Germany politics. But Natalie Mauer sat in rapt attention, studying Cochrane after they had moved from the table to the salon. And Otto Mauer seemed intent upon the subject.

Natalie turned on a radio, which began a broadcast of an evening of Strauss from the philharmonic in Munich.

Meanwhile Mauer pressed his guest. "But *what about* these National Socialists? You've been in the Reich for a year now. Surely you must have an opinion."

"Hitler has restored respect to the German people," Cochrane said. "Where they laughed at Germany in the 1920s, they now fear the might of the new Germany."

There was a silence as Otto Mauer gravely studied his cognac. Natalie Mauer looked Cochrane firmly in the eye from across the room.

"Hitler is a swine," she said. "And so are the murderers who surround him. Educated people realize this."

With those words she returned her glass to the table and left the room. Cochrane, rebuked by the outburst, felt the gaze of Otto Mauer upon him. He turned to his host.

"I'm sorry if my opinion is not welcome," he said.

A smile crossed Mauer's face. He agitated his cognac slightly in the glass, warming it with his palm.

"We take you to be a man of breeding," Mauer began coyly. "My wife spent time in England and the United States in the 1920s. I studied at an American university. We recognize Americans a bit better than most

Germans do. One pays lip service in public these days to the Nazis. One must. But a man of your station, Mr. Cochrane, does not sympathize with criminals. Far from it, I suspect."

And now Cochrane knew. This whole weekend was a test.

"You are an observant man," Mauer continued. "You have noticed that many Germans recognize Hitler's madness. There are influential people in the Reich who would curb his influence. Perhaps through the Abwehr, where there are many who oppose him. But we lack the power now."

Cochrane opened his mouth to interject. But Mauer silenced him with an upraised hand.

"The youth has been raised to worship Hitler," Mauer grumbled. "And the army is partially controlled by the same monsters who control the party. To stage a successful *coup d'etat,* one must have the people on one's side in addition to the army. The opposition to Hitler has neither."

Cochrane was quiet.

Mauer relit his cigar, and for the first time since speaking of the Chambolle Musigny, a legitimately mournful expression crossed his face. He blew out a long cloud of cottony white smoke. "No one in America understands. Hitler did not rise by acclamation in Germany. And all the people did not blindly accept Nazi doctrine. If they had there would have been no need for a Gestapo or an SS. But now all opposition lives in danger of persecution—loss of jobs, labor camps, or worse. As an opposition, we complain a lot in private. But we are passive. Eunuchs. Damn us all!" Mauer concluded. "We are all cowards."

Cochrane was both chagrined and confused. Exactly what sort of test was Mauer giving him? he wondered. Cochrane felt the German's eyes boring in on him during the pauses as Mauer spoke. Yet Cochrane's only fidget was to remove an invisible smudge from the side of the brandy snifter.

"Really, Otto," Cochrane finally said. "I don't know why you talk in such a seditious way. At the very least, Hitler has brought Germany back from economic ruin."

"And at what cost? A nation's destruction? A nation's soul?"

"I can't answer that," Cochrane countered. "I am not German."

"Then I will ask you a question you *can* answer," Mauer said, setting down his brandy with a click on the table. "Come. Follow."

Mauer led Cochrane up a flight of back stairs to the second floor. They followed a hallway and entered a darkened room. Mauer's voice grew soft as he closed the door to maintain the darkness.

"Don't even touch the curtain," Mauer said as he quietly led Cochrane to a window. "Just look between the curtain and the window frame. Your eyes are good? Look down the road fifty meters to the bus stop."

Cochrane looked and saw two men waiting. They wore dark raincoats and sat on the concrete slab that served as a bench.

"Who are those men? What are they doing?" Mauer asked rhetorically. "One carries a walking stick, but he has been there for three hours. Another merely sits and waits. For a bus you think? The buses have passed each fifteen minutes for the past five hours. But still they

141

wait." Mauer stepped away from the window. "Well?"

"I don't know them," said Cochrane.

"Shame on you," Mauer chided sullenly. "You recognize Gestapo as well as I do. Now drop your pretensions and listen to me. There are only three reasons why the Gestapo would be watching this house. You. Me. Or both of us."

Cochrane searched the eyes of Mauer. For a split second he thought he saw something.

"It is essential that you and I trust each other," Mauer said.

"Why is that?"

"Because, my friend," Mauer said, leading his guest back out toward the hallway, "my hunch—and the hunch of those Gestapo out there—is that you are nothing so simple as a securities broker. You are most likely a spy. And I do not work for the Labor Ministry. I work for the Abwehr Section Z and could have you arrested in five minutes."

Cochrane felt a cold tingling running through him. Suddenly Frank Lerrick's words flashed back to him: *"Don't get caught. We won't be able to get you out."*

"You are absolutely mistaken," Cochrane replied indignantly. "I can't even imagine where you would manufacture such an idea."

"Your contact in Berlin was probably a man named Kurkevics. He was tortured to death a week before your arrival. But he did reveal that he expected an agent of the Federal Bureau of Investigation to arrive in Berlin. I began thinking the other day in my office. You arrived in Berlin at exactly that time."

Mauer smiled gamely. "Do you deny that, too?"

"I deny all of this categorically," Cochrane answered

142

sharply. But there had been an uncertainty in his voice, a slight hesitation, a slight shakiness. And they both knew it.

Mauer wrapped his arm around his guest's shoulders and led him down the stairs. Cochrane wondered if he should whirl, blast Mauer in the face, and flee. But Mauer continued to speak in a calm, conciliatory tone. So Cochrane tried a slight change of tactic.

"I don't understand any of this," Cochrane said. "Explain all this to me! Tell me what you want!"

Then they were in the drawing room again and Strauss was still on the radio. Natalie Mauer was refreshing the brandy snifters. She was as beautiful as before, tall and handsome in her kimono. She had placed dark Swiss chocolates in a methodical pile on a silver tray.

"I'm telling you all this because I believe I am right," Mauer said. "And I also believe you are a man of principles, even if you are engaged in espionage." Cochrane took a strategic seat, not far from the door.

"If I am wrong," Mauer continued, "you cannot hurt me because of my family and my position. If you reveal what I have said to you, no one will believe you. But if I am right, you can help me."

"Help you how?" Cochrane asked. Natalie Mauer was now witness to their conversation.

"We wish to leave Germany, Mr. Cochrane," Natalie said in perfect English. "With our son. Before it is too late."

"We will help you considerably in your task," Otto Mauer promised. "But you must also promise to help us."

"Help you how?" Cochrane almost exploded.

"We have been denied permission to obtain passports," Otto Mauer said. "If you are a spy, you can get us American passports."

"I'm sorry! But this is absurd!"

"My grandmother was half Jewish," said Mauer softly. "Therefore I am one-eighth Jewish. My son is one-sixteenth. There are people who will eventually find this out. My world will change then. I don't consider myself Jewish and I don't care much for the Jews either. But I know someday there will be trouble." Mauer's eyes were intense. "There. You know my secret and I know yours. Now perhaps we can talk. Tomorrow. In the morning. I will tell you everything about the Abwehr. But you must promise to get us out of this country."

Across the salon, Natalie Mauer's face was lined with tension. She stared at Bill Cochrane and now so did her husband. It was an odd stare. Part contemptuous, part fearful, part expectant and hopeful.

Cochrane searched their faces. First his, then hers. And then, from his position across the room, he risked his life.

"I'll be happy to listen to whatever you'd like to tell me," he said. "Then if I can help you, I will."

Cochrane could have bottled the sighs of relief that rose from the Mauers. So, sensing himself on steadier ground, he raised his brandy glass to his lips.

"That's a promise," he said gently, before taking a sip. "A promise between gentlemen, right?"

EIGHT

It was September 6, 1938, when Thomas Cochrane took a long walk through the woods surrounding the Mauer estate. And it was the first American penetration of the Abwehr.

"You cannot take any notes, coded or otherwise," Mauer informed Cochrane as they walked. "You'll be the object of searches eventually. Everything has to be committed to memory. *Everything.*"

Cochrane nodded.

"You told me once that you did some acting. At a summer playhouse, was it? Massachusetts?"

"Provincetown."

"Then your memory should be trained for names and places," Mauer said. "If it's not, that's your loss. I'm only going through things once."

"I'm ready when you are," Cochrane said.

They were far from the manor house, and it crossed Cochrane's mind that Mauer might be leading him into a trap. Suppose his two Gestapo babysitters arrived deep in the forest where Mauer, having lured Cochrane into revealing his purposes in Berlin, could hand Cochrane over to them? What had been done to Kurkevics would seem a picnic in comparison.

So Cochrane maintained his guard. He breathed easier when Mauer led them to a shaded area beneath a single tree at the center of a clearing. Mauer was no fool. No one could hear them in this place. Probably no one other than Mauer's dog could even find them. And no one could approach without being seen.

For whatever purpose, Mauer carried his deer rifle. A man could never be too careful, even if venison was long out of season.

They seated themselves under the tree and Cochrane positioned himself in the shade. "Well, then," he finally said. "School's out. Start at the top. Structure. How much do you know?"

"A lot."

"I'm waiting."

"Yes," said Mauer, "I see that you are." And then it all poured out, first in a trickle and then in a flood. Mauer had been in the Section Z of the Abwehr, usually called Abteilung Z. Z was the central administrative department. It held the files and coordinated the work of the four other units.

"Anything not in our files doesn't exist," Mauer said, a trifle boastfully. "We coordinate the work of the other four sections."

"Jesus Christ," Cochrane said to himself.

"Colonel Hans Oster is the head of the division. I'm his assistant. There's nothing that doesn't pass right in front of me. But I'm jumping ahead."

"The other four divisions," Cochrane asked. "Let's start there."

146

Mauer obliged, growing more loquacious as the sun rose in the sky.

"The Abwehr is divided into five sections, or Abteilungs. Abteilung One deals with straight intelligence abroad. It is headed by General Pieckenbrock, a close friend of Admiral Canaris himself.

"Abteilung Two is perhaps the most important—and most powerful—section. It deals with sabotage within Germany and abroad. The titular commander is Colonel von Freytag-Loringhoven. But the genuine power within the section is Brigadeführer Walter Schellenberg. Schellenberg is a Nazi and a close personal friend of Hitler. Of all five sections, Abteilung Two is the tightest run, the most secure."

Mauer's eyes narrowed. For a moment he watched a small flock of meadowlarks that swooped noisily across the clearing and then disappeared across the treetops.

Cochrane offered nothing, preferring to let Mauer talk.

"Abteilung Three is counterintelligence, run capably by Colonel Hans Bentivegni. There has been little real counterintelligence to date. There has been harassment of certain Hebrews and foreign diplomats through A-3," Mauer declared, "but little substantive work. However, the bureau is well prepared and ready. They receive reports from the SS and the Gestapo. They are empowered to act and won't hesitate."

Particularly in cases like mine, Cochrane thought to himself. "Please continue," he urged Mauer.

"Abteilung Four is open intelligence. Exactly as you'd expect. Reports from missions abroad and military attachés. Newspapers and radio reports.

147

Remarkably effective bureau, considering their product is laid cleanly at their feet."

"And Abteilung Five is yourself," Cochrane volunteered. "Section Z. Central administration, coordination of the other four."

Mauer nodded. "The hub upon which the wheel revolves," said Mauer, nodding and reaching for his cigarettes. "Not a bad vantage point, I'd say."

"What about Gestapo and SS?" Cochrane asked. "Abteilung Two, under Schellenberg?"

"Not exactly," Mauer answered. "Gestapo and SS are products of the party. As such, they have remained completely independent of the Abwehr. It's no small difficulty for the non-party members within the intelligence community. Gestapo and SS report solely to Himmler and Goebbels. Abteilung Two has a certain lateral relationship with them, receiving and sending reports. But the truth is, the entire Abwehr attempts to stay clear of them. Nazis, you know. Strong, stupid, and mean—and excellent at following orders."

Cochrane nodded. Then for the next two hours he barely spoke. The entire framework, spirit, and structure of the Abwehr gradually unfolded before him, name by name, place by place, operation by operation.

Mauer opened a bottle of white wine that he'd kept chilled in a canvas sack. He brought forth two cheeses, a loaf of bread and some fruit. The men lunched, Mauer talking and Cochrane trying to memorize. Certain visions stuck:

"Canaris remains the rallying point in the government for all those dissatisfied with Hitler. Hitler needs

Canaris to administer the Abwehr. No one else is capable. But the generals are loyal to Hitler and would just as soon have Canaris shot. . . .

"Counterintelligence is in its infancy, compared particularly to the British, who have its tradition. Hitler relies on terror at home and military might abroad in place of diplomacy. With enough armament, he feels he renders espionage useless. . . ."

Here Mauer and Cochrane exchanged a smile of irony.

"Ribbentrop, the Foreign Minister, and Canaris despise each other. They rarely miss an opportunity to undercut each other's bureau. . . .

"Abteilung Four insists that the Luftwaffe could destroy the British Navy within five weeks, should Chamberlain blunder the English into a war. Accordingly, General Pieckenbrock at A-1 has suggested that three thousand barges be made ready for a Wehrmacht invasion through Sussex. A flotilla of a hundred fifty ships would also be necessary, but these are already commissioned and sailing. I've seen the reports from naval intelligence myself. . . ."

One by one, Cochrane picked grapes from a bunch that lay beside the two men. He felt the moisture on the palm of his hands. He wondered idly how he would ever be able to return such a volume of information to Washington. Would he have to send a written dispatch through a diplomatic courier, say through Geneva or Madrid? Or would he have to bear the torch in his own hand?

"It is Hitler's feeling that America has no real strategic interest in Europe," Mauer related. "The real enemy is Bolshevism, an enemy common to England

and America as well as the Reich. But the Fuehrer understands that Roosevelt is surrounded by advisors who promote pro-English and pro-Jewish positions. So it is conceivable that a European war could again become a world war. Accordingly, Abteilung One has embarked on intelligence-gathering procedures within the United States and England. I know for a certainty that hundreds of agents have been sent out or contracted. Not all of them German, I might add."

"Have they been successful?" Cochrane inquired.

"So far, volume has outweighed quality," Mauer responded. "But really, when one considers espionage, one only hopes that one or two men will be totally successful. One man in the proper place can defeat an army or instigate the collapse of a government. Take yourself, for example."

"I've done neither," Cochrane said.

"But not for lack of trying," Mauer answered without a smile. "Considering the quality of work which you will now be returning to Washington, I would say that you are the most dangerous man in Germany."

"Second most dangerous. After Hitler," said Cochrane.

"Ah, yes. Of course. After Hitler," Mauer repeated. For several seconds, a wall of silence passed between them. A hundred meters away, toward the edge of the woods, a stag stepped from the forest, wandered a few steps toward them, and froze as Mauer put his hand to Cochrane's elbow and motioned. The two men stared at the animal. Then it turned abruptly and, like many other images that day, was gone.

Mauer continued to palpitate Cochrane's heart:

"When general warfare begins in Europe, the Mediterranean will be closed by the Wehrmacht at both ends. Spain will collaborate. Greece and Yugoslavia will be quickly conquered by a Panzer sweep through Bulgaria."

And: "Reichsmarshall Goering, Commander in Chief of the Luftwaffe, personally told me of a new super-long-ranged bomber being developed in Stuttgart. The aircraft will by mid-1942 be capable of bombing New York from Greenland."

Late in the day, Mauer turned to cases closer at hand. His immediate work within Abteilung Z. The work of his friends. Then he drifted. He mentioned career government servants from his university days who had mysteriously lost their jobs. He spoke of others who had disappeared completely, whether to Switzerland or to a labor camp being a matter of speculation.

Then, walking back to the manor toward evening, Mauer was still able to confront Cochrane with the unexpected. "My secretary, Theresia," Mauer inquired pleasantly. "You find her attractive?"

"I do," Cochrane answered.

Mauer half turned his head. "Are you her lover?" he asked, not missing a step.

"Sometimes."

"Do you ever consider taking her back to America after you leave?"

"Sometimes," Cochrane answered a second time. They were passing through the forest again. Mauer followed a path that was invisible to anyone else.

"She has a husband, you know."

"I know." The concept of cuckoldry after prying

151

through state secrets seemed both forlorn and comical to Cochrane. He wished the topic could be avoided. "She told me all about him," he said, watching a furrow growing on Mauer's forehead. "He's a naval man. Been on a submarine for several months, she thinks. Down off South America and so on."

"That's what she told you?"

"Yes."

"Theresia's husband is a captain in the SS," Mauer said. "He has a greater predilection for adolescent boys than for fully matured women. Accordingly, he allows the Gestapo to employ his wife in certain investigative activities. It advances his career." Cochrane felt a sinking feeling within. "Of course, some such assignments are not totally unenjoyable."

They walked several paces and Cochrane saw his entire relationship with Theresia flash before him. The demure response when he first started talking, yet her strategic placement next to him at the restaurant. Her initial shyness, then her virtual backward somersault into bed with him the night he arrived to find her undressed.

All of this had presupposed his own reactions to her behavior.

"And you're telling me that I'm one of those assignments?" Cochrane answered.

"It's not so much that I'm telling you," Mauer concluded. "It's Abteilung Three that is telling *me*. I pulled the report with your name on it. I will spare you the details. But it is a very exacting report. She cannot decide whether or not you are a spy. But there is thorough mention of the uses of a red scarf. Tell me," Mauer concluded as they emerged from the woods and the manor loomed in the dusk a kilometer down a hillside, "for the sake of all of us. When will you be leaving Germany? Soon?"

Cochrane felt something in the depths of his stomach and fell strangely silent. Mauer said nothing further.

Dinner was subdued that evening. Natalie Mauer and her husband retired early. Cochrane sat up late thinking and at one point moved to the small curtained window at the front of the mansion. His baby-sitters were still at the bus stop. But now there were three of them.

Just as Cochrane boarded the train back to Berlin the next morning, Otto Mauer presented him with an envelope containing a photograph of the three members of his family, double the size of a penny postcard and, judging from the size of their son, of fairly recent vintage.

"This is a portrait to remember your friends by," Otto Mauer said lightly. "In case we do not have the opportunity to spend as much time together in the future."

"Of course," Bill Cochrane answered. He embraced Frau Mauer, who allowed him to kiss her on the cheek. Then Cochrane disappeared to his compartment, knowing that he would not see Munich again.

When he returned to Berlin, Cochrane assessed his situation. He had scored a major penetration of the Abwehr, or so he felt. But the Gestapo had him under a microscope. Arrest had to be no more than days away.

He filed no brief concerning Mauer's revelations. Too risky to put anything in writing. Somewhere too

153

much had already gone wrong.

How had the Gestapo, for example, so quickly picked up his scent? How had they uncovered and murdered the tailor Kurkevics—Cochrane's only liaison—even before his arrival? Luck on behalf of the master race? Blundering by the FBI? Magic? Something was missing which precluded Cochrane completely understanding his situation.

Then again, was Mauer an actual defector? Or was he a double? If Mauer was legitimate, Cochrane's information was too valuable to transfer by any means other than in person. If Mauer was a double, Cochrane might expect arrest within hours.

Cochrane filed a single message to Washington. "Have contacted interesting Russian named Count Choulakoff," Cochrane cabled. "If he wishes to travel, you may wish to buy him a ticket. Fascinating man. I will remain in Berlin for some time."

The cable went to Bill Cochrane's "Aunt Marjorie," in New York. Aunt Marjorie lived inside a Box 1014 at the General Post Office in Baltimore, an FBI mail drop for Frank Lerrick's office.

The words returned from his training in Washington and Virginia:

In this line of work there is no such thing as coincidence.

Cochrane searched for the concidence and couldn't find one.

Then, in Berlin, there was Theresia. She was strangely absent from her job. When Cochrane called, he was informed that her work was being done by a temporary replacement. Meanwhile, Cochrane's tripartite shadow continued. Either one, two, or all of them were on his trail twenty-four hours a day now. There could be no dispatches slipped to couriers bound for London or Geneva. And he would have to act as though Mauer had told him nothing.

He wondered idly: could he still make love to Theresia? From his touch, would she know that something was different? *I have never deceived a woman in this way before,* a voice within him said. *But never has one so deceived you, either,* another voice answered.

On Wednesday night, Cochrane bought flowers in a stall near the opera house and walked the seven remaining blocks to Theresia's flat. He always met her at eight. Tonight would be no different. Cochrane's baby-sitters remained downstairs and across the street as he climbed the stairs. When he knocked on her door, there was silence. He reached for the lock and examined it. It was old and rusting and, ominously, showed signs of previous tampering. Cochrane used a small file that he always carried and the lock virtually fainted when it first felt the pressure.

He cautiously pushed the door open. "Theresia?" There was no answer.

He set the flowers on a table and he walked to the bedroom. At first, when he saw the unclothed body, he instinctively thought she was asleep. But he knew she wasn't. Not by the scent of death in the room. And not by the impossible angle at which her neck was twisted.

Cochrane bit hard on his lower lip. Her eyes were wide in terror and her mouth was wide open, as if frozen in a scream. There was no blood of any amount, only various scars and bruises where she had been beaten. A stray cut here. A welt there.

He looked closer. He saw the cigarette burns at her breasts. He saw others at her lower abdomen and between her legs. He considered the pain Theresia had endured. Then he saw how expertly her neck had been broken.

He bolted to the window that overlooked the alley. He threw it open, heaved mightily, and vomited. Not just once. Twice. Bill Cochrane had never before come across the brutalized body of someone he'd loved. And never before had someone been killed on his account.

He steadied himself. He returned to the body. She was cold and stiff. Dead for several days, he concluded, probably since the weekend.

Cochrane returned to the living room, pursued by the ghost of a beautiful laughing woman in a loose sweater and a black skirt.

His first thought was that her killer had been her husband. He had discovered her liaison and would deal with Cochrane next. Then it all shifted into place.

The Gestapo commanders who had ordered her into an affair with Cochrane had come by for an inquisition. Was she falling for the man? They wanted to know. Was she hiding something? Why was she so slow to obtain satisfactory information from this American? Had she betrayed her commander in favor of a satisfying bed? Obviously, they had decided she had.

He thought back to the last time he had held her, the conversation they had had.

Would he be returning to America? Would he someday find a wife? She had been trying to tell him without telling him. Go. Flee. I cannot sign your death warrant, but others will. So leave Germany at once. I can't. You must. Go! Leave! Once again, a woman he

156

had loved was dead.

Bill Cochrane swept his wet eyes with his hands. He sprang to his feet. He could no longer stay in that memory-infested apartment. He left by the front stairs, closing the door the way he had found it, and carrying the flowers. He appeared as if he had knocked at her flat but had never entered.

He opened the door to the street and bumped into his bodyguards. They stood immobile, staring at him, and they smirked. All three were larger than he was. Typical Nazi hoods. Big, strong, and stupid-looking.

But he looked as if he didn't recognize them. "Excuse me, *meine Herren,*" Cochrane said. He stepped by them and walked calmly. When he arrived at the Rathskeller Kietel two minutes later, he ordered a double cognac and sat alone at a table for two.

Cochrane gradually stopped quaking. He ordered another to steady his nerves, and then another and another. He wished that the liquor would make him drunk. But it didn't. He was too shaken. The cognac made him more introspective. Things became clearer, his perceptions sharper.

He had begun to hate.

He understood hatred, but had always intellectualized it in the past. He thought he had hated the Sicilian heavies in Chicago who had muscled into the funeral-home business; he had thought he'd hated the thick-browed musclemen in New York who thrashed union organizers with lead pipes; he had thought he had hated the two-bit hoods who had stolen produce and meat from the railroad freight yards in Kansas City.

But he hadn't hated any of them. He had opposed

them and he had played the game against them. Some he had arrested. Some he had imprisoned. Others slipped away. But it had been nothing personal. A job. An assignment.

This was personal. These murderous lunatics in their brown and black shirts and their steel-heeled boots, goose-stepping around Berlin. *This,* Cochrane now knew, was hatred.

The waitress refilled his glass. She was a blond woman like Theresia. Cochrane could only look at her for a few seconds. He sipped a final brandy as he watched two teenage boys, smiling and as blond as the waitress, walk by in uniforms with armbands.

Was there no way to live honorably? he wondered. Was there no way to combat evil in the world without innocent people being caught in the middle? Did a man have to commit evil to combat evil? There were times when every philosophy failed him completely. Times like right now.

He finished his drink and gripped the lapels of his chesterfield close to him. He left the cafe. The weather outside was now dismal—wet cold rain. A Mercedes taxi passed too near the curb on the Lindenstrasse and Cochrane was soaked.

He cursed all of Germany and fixed the day's date in his mind. He envisioned the Indian summer of the hills of Virginia and he could see the peaks of the Blue Ridge Mountains, yellowing and fading with the October season. As he walked on the sidewalks of this very foreign country, he was suddenly thousands of miles away and decades into the past. He thought of the old men in faded, tattered gray coats, their fragile chests puffed with pride, telling how it was to serve under

Robert E. Lee in what was to them the Great War; he thought of the 1913 World Series, the first one he could remember, and he recalled sitting in his father's office at the Charlottesville *Eagle*, seeing the game come in play by play on the magical telegraph key; and he saw another day that had long vanished when he and his father had sat on the banks of the Rivanna River outside Charlottesville. His father had told him that some very bad people in Europe had sunk an American boat called the *Lusitania*. Soon America would be in the war and soon his father would go to it. And Bill, as a boy, skipped stones into the river and wouldn't look at his father because Bill was nine and crying because he didn't want his father to be killed.

Funny about love and hatred, Cochrane weighed as he turned onto his street in Berlin, passed the woman at the desk, and climbed the stairs. They both could make you cry.

No matter. His usefulness in Germany had ended. It was now important to complete the business at hand.

He entered his apartment. In one of the darkest recesses of his mind he had always known that being a spy would lead him to a day like this. What was that phrase he had toyed with in the cafe? Something about having to commit evil to combat evil?

He closed the door behind him. The first thing he saw was Theresia's red scarf.

The following Friday morning, Cochrane took a noon train from Berlin and arrived in Stuttgart by evening, traveling with one carefully prepared suitcase.

In Stuttgart he took his dinner at the restaurant in the train station. He allowed his trailers ample time. Two followed him while the other presumably searched

159

his hotel room.

When he returned to his hotel he was pleased to see that his suitcase had been searched and carefully repacked. But his visitor had not noted the geometric patterns with which Cochrane had arranged the suitcase's contents—a pen pointing northward, a necktie pointing southeast.

On the next day he visited Heidelberg and twice again he was searched, once as he dined and again as he toured the ruined castle above the city. On Monday he traveled by train to Freiburg and checked into a hotel that was popular among party members.

He walked the streets looking for an appropriate restaurant for lunch, studying carefully the front and back approach. He considered several before lunching on schnitzel and a Rhine wine at the Zum Noedler.

After lunch Cochrane went to a small variety store where he purchased a small 1.5-volt battery and some heavy wire for hanging pictures. Then he asked the proprietor whether he might have an ice pick. The proprietor said he did. Cochrane selected one with a seven-inch blade.

Next, he went to a department store and purchased a new suitcase, an expensive steel and leather one with heavy, sturdy locks.

Cochrane returned to his hotel and set to work, praying that he would not be interrupted. Sweat poured off his face. The game was life and death now.

From around his left leg, he removed four bars of hollow lead pipe, each about six inches long, that he had kept bandaged to his shin since leaving Berlin. From within a narrow sheath within his belt he

160

removed twenty .22-caliber bullets.

He then prepared his suitcase for his next visitors, carefully closing it and leaving it on his bed.

Cochrane used his file to slit open the false side of his old suitcase. He removed a Swiss passport. He slid it into a folio case. He also kept with him the photograph of the Mauer family.

He then donned his topcoat, casually strolled down the hotel stairs, and left his key with the concierge. He walked out the front door. One of his bodyguards followed. *Too bad they won't all be going up to the room,* he thought.

He glanced at his watch. It was ten minutes after seven. He was several minutes behind his schedule. He entered the restaurant he had studied that afternoon.

He darted past the astonished waiters, past the captains, and then out into the kitchen in front of a bewildered staff. He slipped through the back door into a quiet alley. But instead of fleeing, he moved toward the alley's closed end. There he stood, his back flat against the brick wall of the building, until his trailer appeared.

"Mein Herr?" Cochrane inquired. The man whirled, eye to eye with Bill Cochrane from a distance of five meters. "You are following someone?" Cochrane asked in German. Cochrane's adversary was a thick-browed man who stepped closer.

"You stupid fool," the man said in a guttural German that Cochrane fixed as Bremen or Leipzig. "You are playing games with us?"

But Cochrane's hand was extended to the side. "Games?" he asked. "No games. But does this bring

.back a memory?"

His palm opened and he unfurled Theresia's red scarf.

The German took another step. The man was easily four inches taller and four inches wider than Cochrane. "She screamed almost as much as you will," the German said. "It went on for several hours, you know. Maybe four or five before we—"

In one motion, Cochrane placed the scarf back in his pocket and groped for something. The Gestapo agent's hand went beneath his overcoat and Cochrane saw a Luger. He bolted forward and crashed into the larger man, bringing his knee upward, hard toward the man's groin.

The huge German cursed him and pushed off with his forearms. But the lessons of boxing at the National Police Academy remained with Cochrane. *Always stay in close when fighting larger men. Get inside their reach. Then hurt them.*

As the Luger came out, Cochrane smashed the man's wrist with his own left forearm. Then Cochrane's right hand came stabbing upward, thrusting the ice pick in to the German's stomach.

The man bellowed. His eyes went wide with agony. Cochrane pulled back and the men stood eye to eye. The German tried to aim the gun. Cochrane kneed the man again, harder than before. Then he knocked the gun away. He pulled back the ice pick, braced himself, and stabbed upward again, this time toward the heart. The blade of the pick broke off from the force of the blow and the American stepped away.

The Gestapo agent staggered for several feet, then Cochrane hit him hard from the back, knocking him down onto the garbage-strewn alleyway.

The man moaned horribly and cursed as he hit the ground. Cochrane felt his stomach churning and his own heart pounding. The body kicked and spasmed. Cochrane cursed the man a final time and commanded him to die.

The body went still. Cochrane picked up the Luger and tucked it into his belt. Then he stripped the dead man of his Gestapo identification and discarded his own overcoat, which was now covered with blood. He walked to the edge of the alley and moved down an adjoining side street.

He checked his watch: 8:10. He found a taxi and went to the railroad station. At 8:22 he was on the last train leaving Freiburg for Zurich.

But at the same moment as Cochrane's departure, two Gestapo gorillas tired of fussing with the locks on Cochrane's new suitcase. One of them unsheathed a knife and began to force the catches open.

The blade of the knife protruded through the leather case and triggered the electric circuit that Cochrane had wound around the valise. As the case opened, the battery sent a spark throughout the wire, and the four lead pipes exploded simultaneously. The .22-caliber bullets blew out the upper ends of the steel pipes; every round at the same moment. The two agents were hardly in position to appreciate Cochrane's makeshift machine gun. Nor were they capable of wishing they had never laid a calloused finger on Theresia Erdmann.

Two of the bullets caught one agent flush in the face, one shot blowing a hole where his eye had been and continuing through the brain. The other agent caught the force of the blast with his neck and upper chest. The small-caliber bullet tumbled when it shattered his shoulder bone, ricocheting upward and severing the jugular vein. Unlike his cohort, the wounded German did not die instantly. He managed to crawl several feet to the door to scream for help. But he was too weak to open the door, and the door was locked from within.

Police were summoned. Within minutes all trains out of Freiburg—particularly the two that were in transit southbound for Switzerland—were ordered stopped.

Bill Cochrane sat by a window seat in the town of Mullheim, fifteen kilometers north of the frontier at Basel. He saw several dozen Wehrmacht soldiers on the station platform, carrying their automatic rifles at their waists, and knew there would be trouble.

Moments later, the soldiers were going from car to car.

Cochrane slid a hand beneath his coat to the Luger in his belt. He felt his hand wet against the weapon. He knew that if he were discovered he would have no choice but to shoot his way off the train. But he didn't believe for a moment that he could escape.

He knew also that they would be looking for an American. That was in his favor. That and his experience. Then the doors to his first-class compartment flew open and he was faced with two very tall, very strong, but very young soldiers.

"Passports! Identifications!" they demanded. Their eyes drifted across the other faces in the compartment and settled suspiciously upon Cochrane.

Cochrane stared at the two young Germans, gave them a look of condescension, shook his head in irritation, and gazed out the window.

"Tell me, Sergeant," Cochrane asked in flawless German, "how much longer can we waste our time in this stinking little town?"

The corporal stepped to the sergeant's side and glared at Cochrane. "You have the insolence to ask *us* questions?" snapped the sergeant. "Your passport!"

The corporal made a slight gesture with his gun. Three other passengers cringed. Cochrane glared back. Then with a gesture of annoyance, he reached to his passport and tossed it contemptuously onto the floor at the sergeant's feet.

"Damned Bavarian swine!" he snapped to them. "You don't know how to do a job correctly!"

As the corporal covered Cochrane, the sergeant opened the Swiss passport. He stared at the photograph in the passport and raised his eyes to check it against Bill Cochrane. He found a close enough match. But something was wrong with the man before him and the sergeant knew it.

Cochrane's hand went slowly to his breast pocket.

The corporal eyed him.

"At ease, Corporal!" Cochrane muttered sourly.

Cochrane withdrew the Gestapo shield from his breast pocket. The eyes of the two soldiers went wide with terror.

"Now would you kindly hand me back my passport and get your asses moving through this train!"

Cochrane's other hand remained within his coat, the palm pressed against the handle of the pistol, the forefinger on the trigger. The Luger was Cochrane's only remaining hope if the bluff failed. But the two soldiers were frozen.

"Come on, *Sergeant!* Get on with it! Or you'll be at a

garrison on the Polish border within one week."

Only a second more passed.

"Thank you, *sir!*" blurted the sergeant. He fumbled the passport back into Cochrane's hands. The American snatched it furiously and drove the two soldiers from the compartment with a withering stare. Cochrane thanked a beneficent God that the young sergeant had rattled too easily to obey army protocol—checking the name on the Gestapo shield against the passport. Had either soldier taken that simple measure, all three of them would have died.

NINE

I

In Zurich, Cochrane scanned streets before he walked them and searched crowded places for faces he might have seen before. He sat in cafes with one arm to the wall and facing the entrances, and he walked only on sidewalks that could take him down one-way streets against the traffic.

When he was certain that the Gestapo was not on his back, he looked for an address that he had memorized months previously in Washington: a print shop in a prosperous residential neighborhood five minutes' walk from the lake. From the flowers and public gardens still in bloom at lakeside, a man might never suspect that all hell was breaking loose in every neighboring nation. But Cochrane knew that Gestapo agents made regular forays into Switzerland, primarily to snoop on German Jews with foreign bank accounts. Cochrane's sense of being followed had been honed to a gleaming edge over the last weeks. He never ceased to wonder when he would unexpectedly see the same face twice.

It was almost the Eleventh Commandment: *In this line of work, there is no such thing as coincidence.* He knew somewhere they were behind him.

The print shop was on a side street, nestled between an antique dealer and a tailor. The proprietor, according to the window, was a man named Engle. Cochrane entered and found a diminutive man with white hair, wire glasses, and a sallow complexion. The man, he learned upon initial inquiry in German, was Herr Engle. Conveniently, the shop was empty. So Cochrane switched to English.

"I have some friends who wish to travel abroad," Cochrane said, slipping into a prearranged patter.

"But, Mein Herr," Engle replied with a sorrowful smile, "I do not handle travelers. I am an engraver."

"I must be mistaken then." Cochrane smiled, knowing he was not mistaken at all. "My Uncle Edgar tells me he has an account here."

Engle's eyes drifted to the window at the front of the shop. "Your Uncle Edgar is a dear friend of mine," he said softly. "Please have a seat."

Cochrane chose a chair near Engle's desk. Engle went to his door, pulled down the shade, and put a sign in place indicating that he would reopen in an hour.

Then Engle turned. "You are certain you were not followed?"

"Certain," answered Cochrane.

Engle shook his head very slightly. "Today everyone is followed. Not good for a man of my years. Please. You come to the back."

Moments later, Cochrane was in the rear of Engle's

shop, the doors closed for greater security. Cochrane needed three passports made urgently and smuggled back into Germany. Engle sighed. Cochrane informed him that Uncle Edgar in Washington would handle the reimbursement.

"These passports," Engle inquired. "Swiss? Canadian? American? What must they be?"

"Swiss would be excellent."

"I cannot work without photographs."

Cochrane withdrew the portrait of the Mauer family from his inside pocket. With a pair of scissors, he trimmed it into three single photographs. These he handed to Engle.

Cochrane next printed the address of Frau Mauer's chocolate shop in Munich.

"The passports," Cochrane continued, "must be sent by private courier from within the Reich and in an envelope that will appear to be a business correspondence. It should be marked 'Personal Attention of Frau Mauer.' And I should stress," Cochrane concluded, "that there may be a certain urgency to this order."

Engle raised his eyes slightly. "These days, Mein Herr," he said, "there is *always* great urgency. The world rushes headlong with great urgency. And toward what end?" The old man hunched his shoulders. He sighed. "We will do what we can do," he said philosophically. "Nothing more." Engle cocked his white head. "You are in trouble with the Nazis?"

"A bit."

"Gestapo?" asked the old man.

"Maybe."

Engle studied his visitor. "Did you kill one?"

169

"Probably more than one."

Engle arched an eyebrow. For the first time a crafty smile danced across the merchant's face. "I see," he said. "I suppose then, we must give your order top priority."

"I'd appreciate it."

Engle steepled his fingers, then drummed them slightly against each other. "Be very careful, my American friend," he said. "Zurich is alive with Gestapo and SS. Just in the last day or so there has been a marked increase. Normally there is the usual activity. A German expatriate is found dead here, a wealthy Jew disappears there. But right now they seem to be looking for someone." Engle's gaze alighted on Cochrane. "Maybe an American."

"I've spent the last two days covering my back. They haven't found me."

"May an old man give a young man some advice?"

"Feel free," Cochrane said as Engle's eyes glimmered.

"Continue home immediately," said Engle. "Take the circuitous, least predictable route. I will see that your three friends"—and here the old man glanced down to what Cochrane had written—"the Mauer family, is taken care of."

"Thank you, Herr Engle."

Bill Cochrane offered Engle his hand, which turned into a clasp with both of the engraver's hands. "Filthy bloody Nazis," the old man murmured. "Animals."

Cochrane boarded an express for Geneva that afternoon. It was five-thirty when the train pulled away

170

from the station. In the dining car that night, Cochrane's attention focused on an auburn-haired woman of maybe forty dining alone. He took her to be Swiss, and twice when she looked up she saw him watching her, but against his instincts, he decided that amorous pursuits were not worth the trouble. Not this night. So he suffered through the agonizingly bumpy eight hours alone in his sleeping berth, agitated rather than soothed by the churning of the train, and haunted by every footfall in the corridor. He awoke the next morning to notice that the woman had passed the journey just a few berths from him, accompanied indiscreetly by a man who, as Cochrane learned from a casual inspection of the contents of the man's baggage, was a married sales representative for the Renault Corporation, European Division.

In Geneva, Cochrane took the first plane out, which went to Tehran, where the Gestapo crawled in alarming numbers and where he again changed passports, becoming Canadian and using an English-language bookstore as a dead drop for his new identity. He dyed his hair black, acquired glasses, and found an ill-fitting brown suit worthy of the best tailor Calgary might offer. Then he grew a moustache, stuffed himself with figs, dates, and rice, and gained eight pounds in one week, puffing out his cheeks. Then he returned to the airport.

He flew to Palestine and enlisted as a cook's assistant on a British freighter bound to Bermuda. The trip was laborious, encountering the fickle mid-Atlantic weather of the late fall, and the temperatures in the galley reminded him of Calcutta or, worse, Savannah or even Washington in midsummer. But the vessel arrived safely. He presented himself to the United States Consulate in Hamilton and talked a skeptical undersecretary into placing a telephone call to Washington. On the next day, Washington brought him home, telling him that it all had been worth it, even before they learned what it all had been.

It was November 12, 1938. He had been away for fifteen months. For the next six weeks he was debriefed personally by Frank Lerrick, who generally named only topics, allowing Cochrane to guide him through the Abwehr at Cochrane's own pace. A stenographer recorded everything, and on one day two generals from the Joint Chiefs of Staff showed up also, sat quietly, and listened. Cochrane's testimony filled three locked filing cabinets.

By that time, even the dour Frank Lerrick was grinning like a gargoyle. Cochrane was exhausted, of course, both spiritually and physically, and tended toward an unhealthy loquaciousness. But what did it matter? The FBI had scored a staggering intelligence coup, so it seemed, and Bill Cochrane had done it.

"I can see great things for you in this Bureau," Lerrick concluded warmly when all questions had been asked. "What assignment do you want next?"

"What do I want or what can I have?" Cochrane asked, much too smugly.

"Either. Just tell me."

So Cochrane told him. Lerrick paled slightly and shifted the topic to college football.

Bill Cochrane smiled. Again, much too smugly.

"Now you tell me something," Cochrane said.

"If I can," Lerrick answered.

"What happened to Otto Mauer? And his family? I

promised to get them out of Germany."

A long pause and Lerrick's face went colder than a tombstone. Cochrane lost his smile.

"Jesus Christ, Lerrick!" Cochrane snapped. "I've been talking to you for six weeks. Would you answer my one question?"

"They all got out. They're alive."

Bill Cochrane exhaled an enormous sigh. "That's all I asked," he said.

II

A few days into 1939, Cochrane reported for work and awaited a new assignment. No decision had yet been made on his future.

"He's in good health, has a wealth of talent, and his work has greatly impressed the President on behalf of the Bureau," Lerrick had informed Hoover in the director's office one morning in December. "There's only one thing wrong with him."

"If I recall," the chief said, "he's too much of a gentleman."

"Not anymore."

Hoover thought for a moment. "He's queer?"

"No."

Hoover's eyes narrowed. "Communist?"

Lerrick shook his head.

"What, then?" Hoover inquired.

"He's ambitious. He, uh, wants your job."

"*My* job?" J. Edgar Hoover's cheeks flushed.

"And he says that within five years, he'll have it."

"Is that a fact?" Hoover asked ruminatively. "Well,

fuck him!"

Lerrick, director of personnel for the Bureau, did just that. Cochrane was assigned to the top floor of the FBI's wing of the Justice Department building. He was to review a six-month backlog in the files on interstate automobile theft.

"What is this? A joke?" Cochrane asked Lerrick when he literally button-holed him in the lobby on the first Thursday. Cochrane knew it wasn't.

"Well," Lerrick said in lame mollifying tones, "your face and name are known in Chicago, Kansas City, New York, and Berlin. It's not the easiest thing, you know, uh, finding a position for someone with your experience."

"Why don't you create one, goddamn it?"

"I'll get back to you."

Lerrick did *not* get back to him. Cochrane shared a stuffy, cramped top-floor office with a glum, dark-haired, olive-complexioned, gaunt, flatulent little dwarf named Mr. Hay, who hummed to himself, sneezed a lot, and plodded from one file to another. The office had no window and smelled of stale paper, mildew, paint remover, and, naturally, the dwarf. During the initial two weeks at this occupation, Cochrane was spoken to by Mr. Hay only when the latter needed Cochrane's help in removing something from the top rear of one of the files.

Mr. Hay was fortyish, with a face that could appear simultaneously young and old. He was trapped somewhere between boyhood and old age and wore an absurd brownish-gray wig. His teeth were yellow and his socks were checkered. His three suits came from the boys' department at Hamburger's. For Bill Cochrane, this was something new.

But Mr. Adam Hay was more than a sum of his parts. He had curious habits, too, most of which surfaced during the next few days. For no apparent reason, the diminutive archivist would not answer when addressed by his Christian name, which was Adam. He preferred instead to be always summoned by a clipped military "mister." He brought lunch with him, ate it alone on a public park bench, and indulged himself in his one passion at any free moment: horse racing. Mr. Adam Hay was an inveterate handicapper, studying all aspects of a horse race and its factors before driving to Arlington Park in Virginia or Pimlico in Maryland on weekends to place his bets.

Bureau folklore had it that Mr. Hay made tons of money on the races and passed his picks along to J. Edgar Hoover himself, the Bureau's best-known horseplayer. But if there was validity in such rumors, it remained elusive. Adam Hay lived a quiet conjugal existence in a gritty section of Georgetown, surviving from one paycheck to the next. And he and J. Edgar had never been seen "within six furlongs of each other," as Dick Wheeler, the Bureau wit and diplomat, had so impishly phrased it.

Mr. Hay's other foible was of a different color. Normally alone with his files and archives, he had free run of them. If a request came from downstairs for anything for which the Bureau kept records, it was Mr. Hay, who would scuttle along from one file drawer to another and draw out everything on the subject. Next—totally without authorization—he would read

175

the files from start to finish. Then he would send them downstairs.

"You read everything, don't you? I've been watching you." Cochrane inquired as he viewed this procedure on his second Monday morning in Bureau Siberia.

"Bugger off, Cochrane," the dwarf replied, settling down to a file on Langston Hughes and an even thicker one on Albert Einstein. "It's none of your business."

"No, no," said Cochrane, who smiled and shook his head. "I don't care and I won't tell. I'm just amused by the procedure."

"Treat your amusement like your dick. Keep it to yourself."

"You read very quickly, too," Cochrane further observed.

There was a long lapse as Mr. Hay studied Cochrane. "I'm memorizing," Mr. Hay declared.

"Uh-huh," Cochrane answered.

"You don't believe me?"

"Frankly, no."

"I have a photographic memory."

"No such thing."

"Bet?"

"Sure."

"Let's see your money, Cochrane."

Cochrane laid a five-dollar bill on the archive table. Adam Hay matched it. "Pick a file, any file," the smaller man challenged.

Cochrane found one in a bottom drawer in the B section: Patrick C. Barrie, a ringer of race horses who worked for the Capone syndicate in Chicago in the 1920s. He handed the file to Mr. Hay, who flicked through a page a minute, then handed it back to

Cochrane seven minutes later.

Cochrane took it in his hand and opened it. "Page four," he requested.

To which the dwarf recited the page word by word. Then he pocketed Cochrane's five dollars.

"Let's try again," Cochrane said. "Game?" He took out another five. Mr. Hay matched it with the one he had just won.

Cochrane found a file on Carla Tresca, an anti-Fascist newspaper publisher in New York. Thirteen pages. Mr. Hay repeated word for word after ten minutes of study. Then he duplicated the procedure for racketeer Dion O'Banion and for balladeer Woody Guthrie. Cochrane, meanwhile, was four fives poorer.

"Convinced?" the small one finally inquired.

"Convinced," Cochrane said. "My only question is, why?"

"Why what?"

"Why bother?"

Mr. Hay's dark brow furrowed. "You'll laugh," he grumbled.

"I just lost twenty dollars," Cochrane said. "I won't laugh."

Mr. Hay pursed his lips. "I figure," he explained slowly, "that if this fucking place ever burns down, I'll be the most valuable man here. I can become an assistant director. I know *everything,* Cochrane!"

Cochrane blinked. There was eye contact, then Cochrane smirked.

"All right, you fucker!" Mr. Hay exploded. "Laugh if you want, but that's *my* game plan! What the hell's yours?"

"I don't have one," Cochrane admitted, wiping a tear

from his left eye.

"Then fuck off, Cochrane!" howled the Bureau's only potential three-foot-cleven assistant director.

"I shall. I shall."

Thereupon followed a silence that lasted through the third week of Cochrane's sixth-floor exile and into the fourth. Mr. Hay obtained from Requisitions a stepladder, which enabled him to reach any top rear file on the entire floor. "I used to have this whole place to myself," he then pronounced. "And soon again I will."

"I hope so, Adam," Cochrane answered. But Mr. Hay was finished talking to Bill Cochrane. Forever. Or so it seemed. Or so, at least, they both hoped.

For the Bureau itself, it was the best of times and it was the worst of times, depending whose opinion one sought. The desperado bandits and bank robbers of the Depression era were gone, either dead or imprisoned or somewhere in between; Hoover himself had garnered much of the credit. But the gangland fortunes that had been weaned on Prohibition gin and basement beer were placing a stranglehold on the cities from Illinois to New York. The Bureau, to any intelligent observer, seemed outmanned, outgunned, and outmaneuvered. Or just plain outfoxed.

Two foreign agents, personally dispatched by Hoover, had returned from Moscow via Khartoum with no luggage and figurative bullet holes in their hats. Another had been buried in Rome by jubilant Fascisti, and yet another was missing and presumed dead in the Suez. It was a time when Hoover's agents were running into the ground, sometimes literally, all over the globe.

"Innocents abroad, version 1939," Dick Wheeler ruminated angrily over a triple Jack Daniel's one night in his Alexandria home. Most of the American boys, tough as they seemed coming out of the National Police Academy, hadn't known how to play hard ball with the locals.

As for Cochrane's escapade in Berlin and Munich, there were two ways of viewing it:

One: Cochrane had scored a major intelligence coup. Every bit of information checked and double-checked. The FBI had penetrated a foreign spy service for the first time. The mission was a success.

Or, two: Cochrane had left Germany at the speed of light with every contact apparently—*How? Why?*—compromised and scrambling for cover. The mission was, in the end, a disaster.

As for domestic Bureau politics, Hoover had arm-wrestled increasingly plump sums of money out of the congressional coffers. Frank Lerrick had solidified his position as Hoover's top spear carrier and Big Dick Wheeler had come East from the Chicago and Kansas City outposts to act as Hoover's emissary to the rest of the world. This triumvirate—Hoover, Lerrick, and Wheeler—sat firmly astride the Bureau. And rumors, no, the *truth* of the situation, had it that the Democratic Roosevelt would no sooner challenge Hoover's flourishing authority than he would have his photograph taken in his wheelchair. The President had enough problems with his reelection and in choosing a successor.

As for Bill Cochrane, time passed slowly as he engaged in mortal, silent combat with tiny Mr. Hay in the Bureau archives. Cochrane suffered the middle-aged and mid-life agonies of the grounded professional. He went about his work, but entertained debilitating self-doubts. He knew he had done something wrong, but didn't know whether it was a homicide in Berlin or a misplaced adjective during his debriefing. He did know that he had gone to Germany, done his best, become a killer for his country and had left Germany in his socks. And all this was rewarded by six weeks in a stuffy attic with a cranky elf.

The weeks were totally joyless, despite even a passionless quick affair with a bosomy, blond-haired subliterate secretary from Texas. Her name was Mary Sue and she was on the rebound from a bad first marriage and was looking for a second, better one. Bill Cochrane was not. There was now something chilling about his relationship with women. Both the women he had loved were dead. Perhaps passionless affairs were what he deserved, he told himself, as well as what he was doomed to for the rest of his life. Love was much too dangerous. Trouble was, affairs like the one with Mary Sue left him feeling so damned empty.

So he tried to bury himself in his work, as he had done after his wife's death. But work only conjured up images of dusty wooden filing cabinets and the diminutive sourpuss who reigned in the archives. Further, the current image of Frank Lerrick, who could have changed the situation, was of a somber, preoccupied man who shuffled quickly, silently and without raising his eyes from one office of power to another. Dick Wheeler was inaccessible. The prevailing sound of the day was that of doors closing.

Cochrane might have stayed shelved in the Bureau attic forever, except the Bureau had work to do. Good men were eventually needed.

Frank Lerrick finally reassigned Cochrane to the Baltimore office, where First Maryland National Bank had uncovered a chamber of horrors in, of all places, their auditing room. Cochrane's reception by the other agents in Baltimore was downright frosty. It was common currency that Cochrane and Hoover had locked horns over something or other. No one, including Cochrane, knew exactly what. But whatever Cochrane had, none of the other agents wanted it, either.

So as the months passed in Baltimore, Bill Cochrane felt the final days of his youth slipping away. If his services were not appreciated, he could not give other adults lessons in common sense.

He sought a job in private enterprise. He was, after all, a banker by profession, spoke a foreign language or two, and knew he could count on the Bureau to barter him a fine letter of recommendation in exchange for his resignation.

In confidence, he applied for work at three New York banks. Morgan Guaranty made him an outstanding offer. That settled it.

He would move to New York. He would receive a salary that was more than fair. He would find himself a comfortable apartment and, he hoped against hope, a special woman. He would settle down, remarry, acquire an inch or two around the waistline probably, and mind his own business while the rest of the world tumbled sublimely into hell in a Fascist basket.

He had made his contribution. Who could blame him in his position for now settling on a little peace and quiet?

So on a steamy summer afternoon, he typed out his letter of resignation from the Bureau, a chore he'd been putting off for several days.

And it was at that very moment, as luck would have it, that his secretary, Patricia, entered the room with an outlandish suggestion: J. Edgar himself was on the line, beckoning him, summoning him, no, *ordering* him to Washington as soon as humanly possible.

"Fine, indeed," Cochrane thought to himself, setting down the telephone and gazing at the completed letter on his desk. He looked at the calendar and made a mental note. *August 3, 1939.* "I'll deliver my resignation in person."

PART FOUR

August-September
1939

TEN

". . . and captured as soon as he is discovered," J. Edgar Hoover droned on into the night. "This man must be put out of operation quickly and by whatever means possible. We are acting upon the orders of the White House, itself, Mr. Cochrane. This Bureau's very reputation is at stake."

"Meaning," thought Bill Cochrane as he listened to Hoover, "your own reputation." But after seventy-five minutes of briefing around the oak conference table at Bureau headquarters, Cochrane distilled Hoover's rumblings down to their most simple component:

Cochrane was to perform a miracle. He was to catch the most dangerous and elusive of Hitler's spies in America. Period.

Cochrane could feel his letter of resignation sitting heavily in the inside pocket of his suit jacket. It had been his intention to let the Chief have his say, then present the letter.

It was eight o'clock. Cochrane searched the impassive faces of the two other men at the table, one to

185

Hoover's right, the other to his left. He felt his mood darken. Two hours earlier he'd had a great job lined up in New York. Now, *this*.

Directly on Hoover's right, appropriately, was Frank Lerrick, who still carried the lofty title of Assistant Director—Personnel. It was commonly known within official Washington that aside from Clyde Tolson, Hoover's lifelong friend and companion, Lerrick was the man closest to Hoover's ear and heart. Sometimes even literally, as at this moment.

Lerrick, at age fifty, was six years older than Hoover and a product of the ever-bitchy New York office. He was said to be even-tempered—always in a bad mood—and if he had ever laughed, it was by accident and no one caught him. Frank Lerrick was tight, hard, and silent. He played his college football at Loyola of Chicago, had served with General Pershing in both Mexico and Flanders, and had since 1923 been married to a stunningly beautiful former debutante from Manhasset, Long Island, who was ten years his junior. Lerrick and his wife lived in a spacious remodeled farmhouse in Chevy Chase, where they raised their three children.

J. Edgar Hoover loved him; most everyone else in the Bureau hated him, for reasons real and imagined.

The other man in the room, Richard Wheeler, had left a strategically empty chair between himself and the director when he had chosen his own place.

Wheeler was now in charge of budget appropriations within the FBI. He had long held some cryptic title to match, but no one ever knew exactly what it was. Wheeler was the big, rugged, affable, round-shouldered Missourian who had graduated with honors from the

186

Bank Robbery Division of the Indianapolis office seven years earlier and went on to become Cochrane's immediate superior in the fang-and-claw operations in Chicago and Kansas City. And, if Bureau rumor could be believed, it had been Wheeler's recommendation that had dispatched Cochrane to Germany in 1937.

At age forty-two, Wheeler was now in Washington because Hoover had needed a liaison between the Bureau and Capital Hill. Blond, articulate, and conservative, his usual style—a good-ole-boy grin, a slap on the back, and lunch at a chili parlor—masked his needle-sharp intellect. On the Hill he was much loved, a development that had given rise just that previous week to a second title thrust upon him by the director: Coordinator of Domestic and International Security Operations, which meant counterintelligence, which, as everyone knew, the FBI was not involved in.

This second crown upon Wheeler's head was a master stroke: Hoover had put his most popular employee in charge of espionage, then dispatched him to the Hill to drink beer and eat chili with the various chairmen of committees. In one move, Hoover had outflanked any other intelligence service that Roosevelt might create.

But more immediately for Bill Cochrane, Wheeler was again his direct superior—not such a bad development. Wheeler was a fair-minded man whose opinions Hoover actually sought and trusted. Given the proper circumstances, Wheeler was possibly the most important ally a field agent could have.

"You'll be reporting to me each week on your progress, Bill," Wheeler drawled as Hoover paused. "Monday mornings, I'd think. Got to start the week off someway." He shrugged, mustering a belated grin.

"Of course, Bill," interjected Lerrick with malevolent politeness, "you'll have to drop everything you're, uh, doing in Baltimore. Turn the paperwork over to your assistants."

"That won't be difficult, Frank," Cochrane answered without a blink. "I have no assistants. And, uh, I've been given virtually nothing to do."

Lerrick smarted sharply and looked like he'd swallowed a bad piece of poultry, feathers and all. Big Dick Wheeler's grin broadened like a bear's. Meanwhile, Hoover rambled discursively. A bomb at the naval depot in Brooklyn. A fire at the Frankford arsenal in Philadelphia. That devastating bomb that sank the *Wolfe. Yes, yes, yes,* Cochrane thought. He read the newspapers, too.

Then Hoover moved toward a conclusion. The FBI had next to nothing on the bomber. The Bureau had a few theories, but no witnesses and no clues. Nowhere to even start the investigation.

"Originally we thought this man was part of a network headed by a German agent named Duquaine. Fritz Duquaine, I think," Dick Wheeler volunteered politely. "But apparently he is not."

"How do you know?"

"We have every major ring infiltrated, to one degree or another," Wheeler said. "There's no mention of this man anywhere. He'd show up in a rumor somehow if we had something."

Cochrane nodded. It was just like the FBI to tell him who or what the spy wasn't. He thought of the other letter he'd typed that afternoon, the one to Morgan Guaranty. He wondered whether Patricia had mailed it.

At length, Hoover pushed some files together and Lerrick quickly came to his assistance, energetically arranging them in two piles for no visible reason.

"So then," Hoover said in conclusion, "Agent Cochrane, I'm confident that you'll be successful. Quick and successful."

Then Hoover was out the door with not so much as a benedictory parting word. Lerrick was on the director's heels. They left Cochrane alone with Dick Wheeler, who exhaled a long breath, rose slowly, and with some effort buttoned the front of his jacket. His gaze moved slowly across the table to Cochrane and settled there.

"Got a fine one for you, don't we?" said Wheeler.

"Yes. Naturally," Cochrane answered, examining a dozen tattered file folders. "I can keep these?"

"They're yours now. Course, I'll warn you straight off, Bill. There's not much in them. The investigation was completely spotty until the President called the Chief over to the White House. Ever since then, the Chief's been behaving like he's got a hornet in his underwear."

"I thought he always behaved that way."

"Sometimes it's just two hornets." Wheeler smiled, ever the diplomat.

"Just tell me this. Do we know anything *at all* about the man we're looking for?"

"Well," Wheeler allowed, "we're pretty sure he's German."

"Thank God for that much."

Wheeler gave Cochrane a supportive touch on the shoulder as he departed. Cochrane listened to Wheeler's footsteps diminish down the corridor. He looked at his watch. He had two hours before the last train departed for Baltimore. He reached for the files, picked one at random, and began to read.

Bill Cochrane walked slowly down the concrete platform at Union Station. It was a few minutes past eleven. He was grateful to be sprung from the stultifying assignment in Baltimore. It would take only a day or two for indictments there to be drawn up, anyway. It was the type of case that could easily be passed along to others.

Why then, he wondered, was he depressed? Because he had been more set on leaving the Bureau than even he had realized? Because he actually *feared* getting back into the spy game? Because in mid-life he could actually do without this type of thing?

"Damn," he said to himself, looking down the empty tracks. He scrounged a penny from his pocket and bought himself a ball of gum from a machine. The gum refreshed his stale mouth, so he bought two more and chewed them, too.

He strolled down the platform and listened to the sound of his own feet. Then his footsteps were drowned out by a chorus of upraised voices.

A trio of uniformed British sailors appeared on the platform and began to move toward him, singing raucously and off-key. They filled the rafters of the old train with their intoxicated voices. They braced each other with interlocked arms and sang:

> "Twenty-eight bottles of beer
>   on the wall,
>   Twenty-eight bottles of beer . . ."

Their voices grew louder as they weaved in his direction, singing twenty-seven, twenty-six, twenty-five bottles, one insufferably after another, all doomed to slip and fall.

Then they were right next to him. The sailors were little more than boys, fresh-faced and cleanly shaven, the oldest probably being no more than twenty-one. On their caps they wore the markings of the HMS *Adriana*. They grinned at Cochrane.

"I'd buy you all a beer," Cochrane said in return, "but I don't think you need it." They laughed. "Where you all from?" Cochrane asked.

"I'm from the capital of Ireland," said the first sailor.

"We all are," said the younger boy to his left, a rosy-cheeked youth with short brown hair.

"The capital of Ireland!" shouted the third, much too loudly.

"Dublin?" Cochrane asked.

"Liverpool," exclaimed the first. All three broke up and Cochrane laughed with them. The sailors continued down the platform, lurching, supporting each other and occasionally throwing Cochrane an uncaring dumb smile as they continued to sing:

> "If one of the bottles
>   should slip and fall-l-l,
> Twenty-four bottles of
>   beer on the wall-l-l,
> Ooh-h-h . . ."

Cochrane walked a few feet to a newsstand where he read the headline of the final evening edition of the

Washington *News.* Hitler was demanding Danzig now and the Poles were trying to negotiate. Elsewhere there was a suggestion from a Republican senator that the framers of the Constitution definitely would never have approved a third term for any President.

Cochrane turned away. The sailors had lost count of how many bottles were left, mercifully, and were instead burying their fears in a very real pint of brandy. How many more months, Cochrane wondered, before these boys would be at sea? Hitler would have Danzig, just as he had had Austria and Czechoslovakia. If no one gave it to him, he would grab it. Hitler's own words: *Today Germany, tomorrow the world.* When was someone going to stop him?

"The only ones who want America to enter a European war are the Jews, the English, and Franklin Roosevelt," Colonel Charles Lindbergh had told a rally of America First legions at Madison Square Garden earlier that same week.

If only it were that simple, Lindy, Cochrane thought. If only the politics of Europe were as rudimentary and predictable as the six-cylinder engine of a monoplane.

Cochrane suddenly realized: it was *Hoover* who had depressed him. In his usual crafty way, the FBI director had manipulated him into a no-win position. Catch the saboteur, and Hoover would grab the credit. Fail, and Cochrane would take the blame.

"Hey!" thundered one of the sailors from a hundred feet down the platform. "What did the Belgian amputee say to the German farmer's daughter?"

Cochrane tuned them out. Besides, his train was coming now, chugging up from the south end of the track, its lone forelight like a giant Cycloptic eye casting a blinding yellow beam along the two rails.

All right then, Cochrane decided. Just this one final assignment. The people in New York would have to wait for him. National interest and all that. High priority. Totally secret.

This job would be within the borders of America, he told himself. No Gestapo pursuing him into Switzerland, no long boat rides from Palestine to Bermuda. Nobody trailing him or ripping through his luggage.

The things he held dear would count: cleverness; judgment of character; intuition. He would combat the enemy on his own home ground this time, and *that* would make a world of difference.

This time, he reasoned with great confidence, things would be much easier. The assignment was more finite: catch a spy. There would be no murders, he told himself, and he would not get involved with the wrong woman at the wrong time.

The red and gold cars of the Pennsylvania Railroad rolled by as the locomotive chugged past him. Even the voices of the sailors from the *Adriana* were drowned away.

The wheels squealed and the engine wheezed as the long night-train ground laboriously to a halt. Cochrane boarded, his ticket back to Baltimore stuck in his jacket pocket. He found a seat and was secure in his decision.

His spirits were magically lifted. He was back in the spy game for a final time. And now, he concluded foolishly, he would be the master of his own destiny.

ELEVEN

Siegfried was ready for the *Adriana*.

Smoking a Pall Mall, he drove resolutely northward to Boston on U.S. Route 5. The road was a new two-lane highway that wound its way from Connecticut into Massachusetts and onward into northern New England.

The spy carried a Delaware driver's license in the name of Andrew Glover. Siegfried had forged the document himself. It was flawless. To complete the identity, he had decided that he was a schoolteacher from Wilmington, single, and on his way to visit his summer cabin in New Hampshire.

Oddly enough, though he was known in New York as a clock manufacturer in one quarter and as an inordinately gifted, arrogant, and intense spy in another, Siegfried had the habit of easing into whatever role he was playing. His cover identity was both a discipline and something which he maintained a readiness to convert into at any given moment.

On arrival, Siegfried browsed leisurely through

several scientific and optical supply houses until he found a suitable establishment called Lebow Opticals on Reade Street in Cambridge. Siegfried examined Lebow's strongest telescopes until a short balding salesman named Mr. Kiely appeared quietly at his side.

"What I'm looking for," Siegfried explained slowly, assessing a powerful Swiss-made instrument in his hands, "is something that will allow me to peer right into the craters of the moon."

He turned toward the salesman. For a moment the spy towered above the smaller man and glared down at him. The salesman felt a flash of fear that he couldn't explain. Siegfried set down the telescope that he held. The smaller man struggled with his strange reaction to his customer.

Rallying, the salesman said, "If you'll follow me, sir . . ."

Siegfried gave Mr. Kiely the creeps.

But the salesman led his customer to his most expensive line of optical equipment. "I'm not sure how much you intended to spend, sir," said the clerk, now relieved that other salespeople and customers were nearby.

"Price is not a consideration," Siegfried said politely.

"Very good, sir."

The clerk removed from a display case an eighteen-inch-long American-made telescope called the Celestron 1000. It was the latest and most compact device in the store.

Siegfried hefted it in his hand and admired the feel of the instrument. He elongated the scope and examined the crystal at both ends. Then he turned to the clerk.

"May I?" Siegfried asked, motioning gently toward

the front window.

"Of course," Mr. Kiely replied.

Siegfried stood in the front window of Lebow Opticals and tested his telescope. He peered through his left eye down Reade Street. At one hundred yards, on the eyepiece's second adjustment, he could read one-column headlines on the Boston *North American*. He stretched out the scope to its greatest power, leaned forward slightly to give himself the proper angle, and trained the scope on an apartment building that he estimated to be a mile away, rising above several lower buildings.

Siegfried watched moving figures within distant buildings for several seconds. He could discern facial features. He would actually have recognized these people if he had encountered them an hour later. The spy thoughtfully pursed his lips.

He turned to Mr. Kiely and broke into a warm smile. "Perfect," he said. "Just perfect." Mr. Kiely grinned back.

Siegfried added a tripod to his purchase, paid $467 in cash, and an hour later checked into the Ritz-Carlton, again under the identity of the fictitious schoolteacher from Wilmington, Andrew Glover.

Siegfried left his room only once. Grumbling to the doorman at 2 A.M. that he was unable to sleep, Siegfried went out for a brief stroll. Using pliers and a screwdriver, he stole two complete sets of Massachusetts license plates from cars parked along Boston Common. He concealed the plates within his coat, retraced his own path to his room, and slept.

He checked out after breakfast the next morning and drove northeast until he reached a sparsely traveled two-lane highway that wound by the rock-strewn rivers and jagged hills of southern New Hampshire. When he reached an isolated bend in the highway, he pulled over, waited a moment or two, then left the road completely. Concealed by trees, Siegfried placed a stolen set of plates onto his car. Then he continued until he reached a region of the Monadnock Mountains that was busy with both quarries and forestry. Consulting the Yellow Pages in a restaurant, he easily found an establishment that sold dynamite. New Hampshire placed no special regulations upon its use.

The firm was a supply depot located in a single building off Route 9. The clerk was a grizzled, taciturn Yankee who engaged in no unnecessary conversation whatsoever. Idly, Siegfried mentioned that he had a number of tree stumps and boulders to clear from his land. He needed thirty pounds of the most powerful stuff on sale.

The Yankee complied wordlessly. Siegfried also purchased fuses and detonators.

Then Siegfried inquired as to the availability of nitric and sulphuric acids. The Yankee raised his eyes and found himself staring into the cold eyes that had also victimized Mr. Kiely in Boston. But the Yankee stood his ground.

"Would you be wanting glycerine next?" the clerk asked.

"If you have some," the spy answered.

"Yep." The man answered, recognizing full well the three elements of nitroglycerine.

Much later, Siegfried placed his acquisitions in the trunk of his car. He had thirty pounds of Canadian-manufactured "black" TNT. And he had enough potential nitroglycerine to sink a ship.

Two days later, Siegfried materialized in New York. Ironically, he wandered through a neighborhood that Bill Cochrane knew well. Moving serenely among the Jewish shopkeepers and merchants along Hester Street, the spy purchased two used suits off racks from street vendors who accosted him as soon as he fingered their material. He paid cash and also bought several used shirts, a small straw suitcase, one pair of new shoes, and two changes of pants. Everything went into the suitcase. The suitcase went into the trunk of his car. He drove back uptown and left the car in a lot near Lexington Avenue.

He took the trolly across Forty-second Street to Broadway and found a theatrical supply shop across from the Hippodrome vaudeville theater on West Forty-fifth Street. There Siegfried purchased a variety of hair dyes, dye remover, and a makeup pencil. Farther down the street, at a Woolworth's, he purchased two dozen No. 3 Ticonderoga pencils, the type with the softest lead, and a small box of chalk. Then, at an Eighth Avenue hardware store, he purchased a replacement chain for the gears of a bicycle.

He circled back down Sixth Avenue. He stopped at the Horn & Hardart automat at Fortieth Street and pleasurably took in forty-five minutes of young secretaries on their lunch hour. Watching them, appreciating a snug skirt, a flattering blouse, or a nicely stockinged calf, put him in the mood to visit his call girl, Marjorie. But Siegfried kept the impulse in check.

Today he was working.

He made a final shopping visit to a kitchen supply store in the East Thirties. There he purchased a small mortar and pestle, the sort used for pulverizing herbs.

Then Siegfried retrieved his car and drove to Newark. He checked into a modest hotel. He was still Mr. Andrew Glover, the schoolteacher from Wilmington.

He informed the desk clerk that he was representing a textbook firm over the summer. He would not be there every night, as he had relatives in Westchester and Connecticut, but would, of course, always be returning ultimately. Then Siegfried paid for two weeks in advance, which went a long way toward allaying any suspicions.

Siegfried carried his own bag to his room. He arranged his few toiletries above the sink. Then he took from his suitcase the mortar, pestle, and chalk and laid all three on the dresser. He sat down at the room's writing table and opened the two boxes of pencils. With a butcher knife, he cut open a dozen pencils and extracted the soft graphite.

The spy worked very carefully, avoiding mixing even the smallest chip of pencil wood with the graphite. The process took more than half an hour.

Then Siegfried walked to the dresser. He poured the graphite into the mortar. He broke off a piece of chalk and added it.

Then he began to grind them together, standing before the mirror above the dresser as he worked. He studied his face very carefully, from cheekbone to hairline, from the bridge of his nose downward to his jaw. He wore a slight grin. Satisfaction, he assumed, from knowing that everything was on course.

As he worked, he considered scenarios for the next few days. He knew he would have to take chances not paralleled by any he had taken previously.

He firmly pulverized the graphite and the chalk, every so often looking up at the mirror and noticing a new intricacy to the space below his eyes or around his nose and mouth.

He thought of the Reich. He thought of the feeble governments in London, Paris, and Washington. The Western democracies were unable, unwilling, and unprepared to rise to the real threats of the twentieth century.

He thought of the HMS *Adriana*. What in hell was it doing at a United States Navy shipyard at Red Bank, New Jersey? Soon, at least, he would have *that* answer.

He thought of the dozens of sleek new U-boats that Hitler had christened and launched over the last few years. He thought of the *Adriana's* crew of predictably dim-witted English seamen. He grinned again.

Killing them all would be so disgracefully easy.

TWELVE

In the county of Wiltshire, it was the coldest, rainiest summer since 1912. The rain was implacable when Laura arrived at the Salisbury railway terminal and it only heightened when she boarded the public omnibus that took her out to Friars Lane, where her father still resided.

With the rain there was the dense creeping, crawling smoky ground fog that engulfed lorries and automobiles, pedestrians, dogs in the street, the spire of the cathedral, entire sections of the town, and, for that matter, most of Salisbury itself. July of 1939 set hardly an auspicious mood for Laura's homecoming.

She disembarked from the bus at the end of its line. She felt the swamp beneath her feet as she walked past the modest detached houses, each with its own small garden before it, until she came to Friars Lane. She passed a small thatched cottage in which two sisters, Joelle and Pauline Markham, had resided alone since Laura's girlhood. (The dottering Markham sisters were elderly when Laura was young and, as she spotted them through their paned windows, seemed equally elderly now.) Minutes later Laura arrived before the iron gate that she had envisioned so many times over the last year. Oddly, it was slightly ajar. There was no sign and no name: the occupant had a penchant for both privacy and anonymity. Then Laura was before the large front door. The dark blue paint was peeling. Soaking, she sounded the bell.

Nigel Worthington came to the door himself, opened it, and asked, "Yes?" Then recognition was upon him. He gave a start and almost jumped, seeing a ghost of his late Victoria.

"Papa!" Laura said, her beautiful face radiant with a smile.

"Oh, my God! My angel!" he exclaimed, holding open his seventy-year-old arms. They embraced and he lifted her off the ground. It was only moments later when he felt her tremble slightly with what seemed to be a sob, and when he did not see her husband, that he knew something was very wrong.

The lines in Nigel Worthington's face had furrowed more deeply since Laura had last seen him, and he made his way around the house and his office with a mildly arthritic limp. But the three-story house was rich with memories, almost all of them of youth and happiness; so Laura's spirits were greatly buoyed in her first days home. She saw an old friend or two and wore a brave face in public. She visited the antiquarian bookshops—Stennett's and Forsythe's—in Greencroft Street near the cathedral and she spent countless nostalgic hours rummaging through (but not buying at) the print and map shops in High Street. In the afternoons, when the heavens abated the downpour for a few hours, she often stopped by Lumly's Tea Room—the shop with the eternally steamy front window facing Gravesend Place—and consumed jasmine or Irish tea. Very occasionally, she indulged her lingering girlhood passion for Mrs. Lumly's very own home-baked shortbread. From time to time, she thought of her collapsed marriage.

But as the days passed, the specter of Stephen Fowler haunted her. Was his coldness his way of telling her that he did not—*could* not—love her anymore? What had happened to the joyous life of the young newlyweds in New Haven, the divinity student and his wife who had entertained mirthfully, explored the celebration of foliage in the autumn, and attended at least one new musical and one new drama each season in New York?

Where did it fail? And why? The answers were in neither the jasmine nor the Irish tea leaves.

It was all cruelly unjust, yet bitterly ironic. Laura had turned down a man, Edward Shawcross, who surely could have learned to love her, for a man who from all evidence already did. Where one love could have flourished and grown, the other had abruptly asphyxiated itself. It was utterly confounding.

Once Laura went to a public call box, pumped a king's ransom in six-pence and shilling pieces into the machine, and dialed the number of Edward Shawcross in Bristol. She heard him answer. She heard Edward say "Hello" and "Are you there?" three times in his brisk, highly expectant manner. But something caught in Laura's throat. She hung up and did not call back.

She walked home from the center of town and the rains momentarily had mercy upon her.

At home, she cheerfully did her father's laundry and mended the pipe burns in two of his favorite cashmere pullovers. She sorted out his sock drawer, stitched some upholstery that had worn thin, and, in effect, mastered all the simple household tasks that escape the humble capabilities of any man living alone. In the evenings, Laura read or played the piano and her father smoked his pipe and contemplated the evening's programming on the BBC. For ten full days, they stayed carefully away from any serious discussions.

Then Nigel Worthington confronted his daughter's moods. When she pulled the cover over the piano keyboard one evening, having done reasonable justice to a brooding sonata by Franz Liszt, she saw that her father stood in the doorway to the music room. He had probably been there for several minutes, she realized, inclined against the doorframe, puffing his pipe, and watching her with unconcealed affection and admiration.

"I didn't know you were there," she said.

He gently exhaled a long, disintegrating cloud of smoke. "Whenever you're ready to talk about it," he suggested, "I'm ready to listen."

Laura's gaze traveled slowly through the room. "Stephen doesn't love me anymore," she said. Her voice was unwavering. She had rehearsed the line for many days. "In certain respects," she added, "I suspect he never did."

"I cannot believe that, Laura," Nigel Worthington answered.

"Neither can I," she said soberly. And then, over port

from 11 P.M. until two in the morning, she went through the whole embittering story.

For the next two weeks, Laura behaved much in the way that she had in the months after her mother's death. She spent a great deal of time concentrating on little things: tuning the A above high C on the antique piano and seeing that all the edges of the glass windowpanes in her father's study were freshly caulked for winter. Outside, she pulled up the tiny weeds that grew between the flagstones, and one afternoon she put a ladder to the side of the house and removed from the eaves the empty rooks' nest that had hung there all summer.

Her walks in Salisbury took on a strikingly aimless quality. She ignored some of her favorite shops and eschewed her favorite table by the steamy front window of Lumley's. She still took occasional jasmine tea, but only in tea rooms where she was not known. And more of her hours were spent on the bench in the clos before the cathedral or even out on the plain itself where, wearing a bulky French impermeable against the rain (which was again incessant), a heavy tweed sweater against the wind, and boots against the mud, she strolled for the better part of many afternoons. She cut a solitary figure with a walking stick. Sometimes she was slightly bent, as if the weight of some ponderous emotion hung invisibly upon her. From a distance, she appeared to be a woman of twice or even three times her age.

Which she wasn't.

In the home, there was little mystery. Nigel

Worthington knew the sadness of a young woman resigned to falling out of love. He came to her one evening in the parlor and set a firm hand on her shoulder as she buried herself in a newly published volume of T. S. Eliot.

She looked upward from her reading and searched his eyes. Then her own hand drifted to his.

"You know, Laura," he said, "the door to this house is always open to you. But you've a husband and a life somewhere else."

"Do I?" she asked.

Nigel Worthington nodded. "You did once. You will again. A man doesn't fall out of love quite so quickly. Not if there was anything there in the first place."

"Papa," she said. "I don't know if there ever *was* anything."

"Only one way to know for certain, Laura."

Laura was crying quietly now as she avoided her father's gaze, the tears trickling down her rain- and wind-reddened cheeks.

"Go back to Stephen," her father said. "Try to find what was there. Build on it."

Her grasp tightened on her father's hand.

"Do you think a good marriage doesn't take dedication and work?" he asked. "Do you think it just happens? Do you think your mother and I never had a bad moment?"

"I don't know."

"I do," he insisted. "A marriage is something two people build. I want you to go home and try to make it work again. If Stephen Fowler is such a bullheaded, insensitive, *stupid* young man, then you'll find someone else. But try to repair what you have before you

208

look for something new."

The tears were steadier now. She knew her father, as usual, spoke both from reason and experience.

"Is your doddering old Papa making any sense?" he asked.

She nodded, not speaking for fear that her voice would break. Then, in one motion, she was standing and reaching for him, hugging him as if she would never let him get away.

And Dr. Worthington was patting his grown daughter on her shoulders and along the back of her head. He embraced her, saying inconsequential things like, "There, there, my dear," and he let the affection pour out with her tears.

"I love you, Papa," she said.

"I love you, too, angel," he answered.

Although it went unspoken, this was one of those moments in life that was comprised of more emotion than could be fully lived. It occurred to Laura that men like her father did not exist within her own generation. And it further occurred fleetingly to Dr. Worthington that a young man like Fowler who could cause such misery to such a lovely young lady must be carrying something very small and mean at his core, rather than Christian theology.

But then, just as quickly as the thought had been upon him, Worthington dismissed it. He had after all met Laura's husband upon several occasions, knew the young man's family, and instinctively had liked him. Why else would he send his only daughter back to him?

"There's one other item," Nigel Worthington said at length. "I haven't brought it up until now. I didn't think the time was right."

Laura waited.

"Peter Whiteside insists upon seeing you," he said. "Says it's vitally important."

Laura drew a long sigh. "Tell him," she answered, "that he knows where he can find me."

Thirty-six hundred miles away, in the county and city of Baltimore, there was general consternation at the FBI's local outpost. Cochrane's recall papers to Washington had landed with a loud thump. Idle gossip concerning Bureau affairs was definitely against handbook regulations: an employee would have to be mad to murmur even the slightest syllable of hearsay. So naturally, rumors abounded madly concerning why Cochrane, formerly the Bureau's number one leper, had been summoned to grace by none other than the Chief himself. Such drastic turnabouts were never without reason.

The clerical employees held that Cochrane had once been involved in a dodgy operation in New York in which the give and take with local racketeers had included a little too much of both on Bill Cochrane's part. He was subsequently returning to Washington to face a federal indictment.

Among the field agents, however, an entirely different account was common currency. There was a major scandal brewing at Treasury, the stories maintained, and Cochrane was being called in to blow the Democrats out of the White House in November of 1940. What the Roosevelt administration lacked most with an election year coming, the Republican field agents suggested hopefully, was a good Teapot Dome-style scandal, complete with soiled money and soiled laundry.

210

Cochrane eventually heard both rumors and broke out laughing at each. Meanwhile, he spent three days turning over his own investigative work-in-progress to two younger agents.

Late on his final evening in Maryland, Bill Cochrane had two suitcases jammed shut and a third one, nearing completion, on his bed. He had packed the clothing and personal articles he would need on his extended transfer back to the home office. Just before closing the third, his eye settled upon the picture of Heather that rested in its frame on his night table.

It was August again, almost the twentieth. Bill Cochrane's nerves were always steadier after the anniversary of the accident. Each August, more times that he cared to admit, he saw the fuel truck jumping the divider on a dark Tennessee highway. And then there was always the sound and moment of impact. . . .

It was all in the past now, more distant with each day. When she had died, he'd been a simple banker.

Fragments of fantasy conversation came to mind as Heather listened:

I've begun a new career. They sent me to Berlin. . . .

There is another war coming. I think we will all be in it. . . .

I've missed you horribly sometimes . . . but I'm trying to live my life again. . . .

Perhaps all those things, not necessarily in that order. His eyes drifted from the photograph.

He was tired and tried to sleep. Rest, however, came with considerable difficulty.

THIRTEEN

I

Red Bank, and the United States Navy Yard that had been located there since 1933, was fifteen miles due southeast of Newark. For Siegfried, however, the distance was an exasperating drive of thirty miles, through the incessant trafficked clutter of the towns on the New Jersey side of Staten Island. The drive each way took two hours.

Siegfried purchased a detailed road map at a Flying A station along Route One south of Perth Amboy. He filled his car with gasoline for two dollars and studied the map before proceeding. The map told him that Red Bank was located across a one-mile inlet from the Atlantic Ocean. When the spy came to the town of New Monmouth, he left the coastal road and drove directly toward the inlet. He found it easily. He then drove the length of it until he found an area in which he could park his car without causing suspicion. Thereupon, he slung a camera case over his shoulder and set out on foot, across a field which, after a walk of about a mile, led to a promontory overlooking the inlet.

Siegfried stood overlooking a river to which he did not know the name. He scanned in every direction on his side of the water. There were no houses and no parks. He was blessedly unobserved.

Across the river he could easily see the navy yard. The view was invigorating. So much so, that for a few seconds Siegfried lost his concentration. He mused how it might feel to stand above the Rhine or the Danube in a similar vantage point. Thoughts of Germany returned him to earth, and his work.

The spy walked to the southeast along the bluff and made careful note of the path that he had taken. As he walked toward a slightly wooded enclave he realized that he was following an old footpath. He kept his eye to the ground.

The grass had grown on the path in the same manner as the rest of the field. He scanned for evidence of people: discarded soda bottles. Cigarette butts. Gum wrappers. He found none. He concluded that few people came to this particular place. Yes, the view was spectacular, but it was spectacular all along this inlet. And Siegfried had purposely come to the least accessible spot on his side of the water.

He arrived among a clump of trees. He settled onto the ground and waited for several minutes. Convinced that he was alone, he took out his Celestron 1000 telescope and trained it across the water at Red Bank.

On the scope's third adjustment, the navy yard came perfectly into focus. On the fifth adjustment, the spy could move in tightly enough to read the insignias on the uniforms of the sailors.

He scanned, moving the telescope in methodical patterns up and down, left to right. He found a ship flying a Union Jack. The angle at which the vessel was berthed allowed him to read the legend off the ship's stern:

ADRIANA
Sunderland

Siegfried studied the ship. It was, surprisingly, a frigate, probably about 120 meters from bow to stern. It was particularly hefty for a British frigate, he concluded. The *Adriana* was something of a seagoing pit bulldog, anxious to work but not upset over the prospects of a fight, either.

Siegfried closely scrutinized the top deck and found it was packed with especially large guns. Normally, frigates were scaled down for escort duties in convoys. So why not the HMS *Adriana?*

But what puzzled Siegfried most was that the *Adriana* was a frigate at all. He had expected a military cargo ship of some sort. It would have been armed, of course. Everything that ventured beyond sight of native land was armed these days. But why, the spy asked himself as he scanned the decks closely, readjusting his telescope in the process, was a big brawny frigate parked at a U.S. Navy yard in Red Bank, New Jersey? And why were there both British *and* American naval personnel busy aboard the *Adriana?*

Why, indeed? Siegfried reminded himself—that's what he was there to discover.

The spy set his telescope onto the soft grass by his

side. He smoked a Pall Mall and gazed across the river for several minutes, waiting for an explanation to emerge. None did. He smoked another cigarette and took in the view across the river with his naked eye. What in hell was he watching? What the Americans lacked in subtlety, he reminded himself, the British made up in tight-lipped trickiness. Together, what were they up to? Was he witnessing a small piece of a grander picture? If so, what was it?

He raised the spyglass again. The *Adriana* was briskly taking on cargo. Several teams of sailors were conveying crated goods onto the ship. As Siegfried studied the activity, it suddenly was clear to him that the cargo fell into two groups.

One group consisted of hundreds of large wooden coffin-sized crates that had apparently been trucked to the bow end of the ship. These crates, which seemed quite heavy from the way the sailors reacted to them, were in turn being loaded onto smaller trucks and driven into the lower hold of the ship. It took eight sailors to lift a crate onto a truck. Siegfried calculated that each crate must have weighed seven to eight hundred pounds, considering the difficulty the sailors were having.

Why aren't more men assigned to each crate? he wondered instinctively. Then, seeing how quickly the trucks were moving, he realized the answer. The crates were being loaded as quickly as possible.

Why?

There was only one possible answer. Whoever was receiving the cargo was in a hurry.

The second type of cargo was being loaded every bit as quickly. But these crates were much larger, about the size of small shacks. No team of men could possibly handle these. Large, sturdy, mechanized forklifts were busy at the stern of the ship moving these crates onto steel platforms. The platforms were then lifted by derrick and deposited through a deck hatch into the stern hold of the ship.

Siegfried set the telescope aside and calculated. These crates had to contain extremely heavy equipment, perhaps even motor vehicles of some sort.

He looked again. The containers were much too small for tanks or trucks. Generators, maybe? But what would be the urgency for generators? Ammunition? Never. Not packed like that. Not handled like that. Parts for antiaircraft weapons? He studied the crates carefully. Possible, he concluded. But that was merely a guess. He made mental calculations over how long each type of cargo took to be loaded onto the *Adriana*. He wondered if he was seeing the first day of loading or the fifth. Or the last.

The spy searched both sorts of crates for any markings that might identify the contents. There were absolutely none. Whatever the *Adriana* was taking on for transport back to England, she was taking it on in utmost secrecy.

The further question posed itself to Siegfried: did the crew even know what they were loading? Siegfried decided to find out.

Next, Siegfried's attention focused on the navy yard itself. He studied the patterns of work performed by the teams of sailors. He made meticulous mental notes of the ratio of officers to enlisted men. And he carefully studied the activities of the visiting British as opposed to the resident Americans.

217

Then Siegfried studied the main gate. There were two sentries on duty, both with side arms. The gate was open, but could be securely shut if necessary. The spy put his Celestron 1000 on its tripod and lay flat for an hour with the lens aimed at the gate. Siegfried barely breathed as he studied the traffic that came and went from the yard, and the protocol of the main gate.

Then, toward afternoon, he felt he had diagnosed it. Any civilians arriving had to show passes and go through a security check. Men—and a few women—in military uniform passed through with a simple salute. American naval officers came and went with the greatest ease of all.

Siegfried finally sat up. He stretched and by force of habit reached for another Pall Mall. He looked around to make certain that he was still alone. He was. He rubbed his eyes. They were tired from staring through the telescope.

The spy exhaled a long stream of smoke and then withdrew from his camera bag a sandwich, an apple, and a thermos filled with coffee. He lunched calmly and watched the other side of the river with his naked eye until sunset.

II

The old man who called himself Elmer had been a fixture around Reilly's—at least for the past week. He habitually wore an old suit and on his gray head he wore a peaked cap from another era. He was bent slightly and his face was lined. He was unshaven and sometimes had difficulty speaking, as if his back teeth were missing.

Reilly's was the murkily lit watering hole for the sailors who toiled at the Red Bank naval yard. On a busy night when the ships were in, the place jumped. The old man held court at the end of the bar and liked to play darts against the English seamen, who could always beat him. Elmer also gravitated toward young Billy Pritchard, an American ensign. Pritchard was fuzzy-cheeked and quiet, a kid from Ohio away from home for the first time. The Navy had promised him he would see the world, and so far he'd seen South Carolina and New Jersey. To Elmer, Pritchard made somber comments about going AWOL, but the old man always talked sense into him. Besides, unlike the Brits who flocked around Reilly's in astonishing numbers, Billy Pritchard didn't know how to grip a dart before throwing it. Elmer could always beat him.

Buck was the bartender. He was a big porky red-haired guy with a moonish face and a County Cork accent. He had rejoiced in serving booze to thirsty seamen since the bleakest days of Prohibition. Buck owned the joint and liked it when all the ships were docked. But Buck already had the bad news, courtesy of a British warrant officer.

"English sailors'll be pullin' out next week," Buck confided to the old man. "Don't tell no one I told you. All shore leave's canceled August 27."

"The English like it here," Elmer said, his gray brows narrowing with a mischievous glint. "They like the poontang. They ain't going nowhere."

"There's a friggin' war gonna start, old man," Buck said. "These English boys'll be fightin' it."

"Already fought a war," the old man recalled. "Won

it, too."

"There's gonna be another. In Europe, anyway."
Buck blew his breath into a glass and polished the glass
with his apron. He cast a jaundiced eye upon Elmer.
"Lucky you're old," Buck said to him. "You ain't going
to fight."

"Lucky you're middle-aged," Elmer shot back at him
with considerable irritation. "I was in the last one."

Buck took a long look at Elmer's lined, sickly face. A
new enlightenment came over the bartender. "Hey.
Sorry, old-timer," he said with sudden affection. "Let
me draw one for you. On the house."

"Don't mind," the old man said, watching Buck
place a beer mug beneath Elmer's favorite spigot.
"Don't mind at all if I do." Elmer accepted the drink
and turned with new enthusiasm toward the English
sailors behind him. "Not a man in the house can beat
this old man at darts!" he proclaimed boisterously.

"Penny a point, Elmer," said an English sailor who,
like the others, never bothered to collect after
trouncing the aging American. "Think you can afford
to lose again?" More often than not, the Englishmen
bought Elmer a meal instead.

"Never lost yet to you young saps!" Elmer said
gruffly, snatching some darts from a table.

"What about yesterday?" a sailor asked him.

"Don't remember yesterday," Elmer said. "Here!
Show you how it's done." Elmer's first shot hit the
black border on the edge of the target. "That's
practice," he said. "Just warm-up."

"Go get 'em now, Elmer," someone said.

The old man's point total lagged considerably
behind his opponents'. Meanwhile, Elmer caught

snippets of conversation from the English sailors. The place to visit in New Jersey, they said, was Atlantic City, though the older crewmen remembered it as being much grander before the Depression. And two sailors had almost been severely injured or even killed when the gears slid on the derrick loading the crated motorcycles and sidecars from General Motors onto the *Adriana*. Those big crates weighed a ton and a half, complained one sailor, and one of them had tumbled fifty feet across the Two Deck.

The brothels were better in New York than in Philadelphia, the enlisted men reached consensus, but with the latest shipment of cargo, there was no time for extended leave. The *Adriana* was even being loaded on weekends, as fast as the coffin-sized crates could arrive.

Desmond, Baldwin, and Condon had sprained their backs loading those damnable boxes, someone else complained. Why the fuck did Smith & Wesson have to pack fifty machine guns to a crate, anyway?

Elmer threw another dart. It hit the metal rim of the target and ricocheted away. Billy Pritchard, sitting sullenly toward the end of the bar, nearly caught it in the butt. The Englishmen laughed merrily.

Elmer hung around with them a little longer, then repaired to Billy's side when the Brits wanted a more competitive game. Elmer and Billy were about the same size and saw things eye to eye. Billy was slumped over a drink.

"What'sa matter, Billy boy?" Elmer asked.

"Dunno," said the young man. "Thinking about home too much, I guess."

"Why don't you telephone home? Talk to Mom and Pop?"

Pritchard looked at Elmer as if the latter were crazy. "Long distance?"

"Yeah."

"Who's got the money for that?" the ensign asked with irritation.

"I'll treat you. I got a secret telephone. Not tonight. But I'll show you sometime."

Pritchard looked at Elmer in the dim light of Reilly's. "Yeah," he said after several seconds. "A secret telephone. Sure." He glanced at his watch. "Hey, I got to get back to base," Billy said next. Then he stood, paid, and lurched toward the door. Elmer watched him go.

Elmer assumed Billy's place at the end of the bar and ordered a vodka with a chaser. Through the mirror behind Buck, Elmer watched the dart game in progress. He tuned in the conversation.

"Try not to hit me in the ass, mates," Elmer said, exaggerating an English accent. "Who'd you think I am? Hitler?"

"You look more like Uncle Joe Stalin to me," someone answered with a Midlands twang.

"Them's *fighting* words!" Elmer exploded, leaping upward from his barstool, his fists raised like a pair of gnarled potatoes. Two sailors quickly interceded before Elmer split up with laughter. Then the rest of the sailors realized that Elmer's rage had only been a tottering old man's sense of fun.

Someone else paid for his drink and Elmer watched the young men play darts. He fell appreciatively silent for the rest of the evening.

What a funny bunch of people these Brits were, Elmer was thinking. Motorcycles and sidecars from

Detroit. Machine guns from Illinois packed fifty to a crate. The English were bolstering their ground defenses for a possible invasion from Europe. And Roosevelt, in defiance of every tenet of the Neutrality Act of 1937, was sneaking weapons to them.

Two nights later, Elmer told Billy Pritchard more about the secret telephone. It was a public booth located a short walk from Reilly's, up a hill toward the old truck route beyond Red Bank's downtown. The telephone didn't work right and you could call anywhere in American for a pocketful of aluminum slugs. The telephone was near an all-night diner, Elmer said, which had failed when the new truck route was built east of the town.

"I don't believe it," Billy Pritchard answered, disconsolate and half drunk. "It's bullshit."

"I'll show you."

Ensign Pritchard studied the old man, wanting to believe. "Ah, go on . . ." he scoffed a second time.

"All right," grumbled Elmer. "If you don't want to talk to your folks, it's no skin off my ass."

"Okay. Show me the booth," Billy Pritchard said.

They left together and no one missed them.

The old man guided Billy up a steep incline several blocks from Reilly's. The incline followed a back street upon which the lighting was poor. There was no traffic and Elmer was always a step or two ahead. But sure enough, at the crest of the hill there was a telephone booth, standing like a lonely sentry at the edge of a dark parking lot. The diner that Elmer had mentioned was no more than a burned-out skeleton of an enterprise that served its last lukewarm hash before the stock market crash.

Billy Pritchard looked around. They were easily a mile from the old truck route and only a few yards from the wooded end of a public park. The place, Pritchard now noticed, was eerie.

"I still think you're full of shit, old man," Billy Pritchard said hotly. "What are you up to?"

"Do you see a telephone or not?"

"I see a telephone," he admitted. "Does it work?"

"Try it, you young jerk!"

The old man seemed not quite as bent over as he had seemed earlier, and although Pritchard was breathing hard from the climb, Elmer wasn't. Pritchard stared him eye-to-eye and suddenly came away with a queer sensation. Elmer's blue eyes were glaring now and filled with some intense emotion. The youth couldn't recognize it. Anger? Impatience? He didn't know. He only knew that the glare put him off—scared him, almost—and Elmer's hand was in his coat pocket jangling something. Slugs, Pritchard assumed.

"Go ahead! Try it!" Elmer ordered.

The young officer turned, still trying to decipher the look in Elmer's eyes. Then, just as he faced the telephone, Pritchard realized what he had seen.

The eyes were not the glazed eyes of an older man. In the natural light, Pritchard had seen what the dimness of the bar had always hidden. Elmer's eyes were the piercing, intense eyes of a younger man. Much younger. The realization stabbed Pritchard like a stiletto.

Pritchard began to turn, but suddenly the cold rough grasp of a bicycle chain was around his neck and

Siegfried was pulling the young naval officer backward.

The chain had been knotted at the center, forming a murderous chunk of metal that could crush any Adam's apple and throttle any larynx or windpipe. The hands on the chain were powerful and Pritchard knew he would have only a few seconds to fight.

He flailed at his attacker. He kicked and twisted. He was not weak. He landed several blows of the elbow to Siegfried's body. None slowed the killer. Siegfried only clutched more tightly, as if he were trying to snap Billy Pritchard's neck in half. The youth's head was throbbing. His eyes felt as if they would spurt out of his head.

Pritchard managed to twist just enough to face his executioner. From a distance of inches, he saw the firmness and muscle of the flesh. He saw that the gray complexion was from powder of some sort, rubbed deeply into the crevices around the nose, eyes, and mouth. He saw that the lines were from a pencil. The gray hair, he now assumed, was a dye. *Who . . . ?* Pritchard wondered insanely. *Why . . . ?*

With a final spasm of effort, Pritchard hammered at his assailant's ribs, pounded with an elbow, and brought a knee upward toward the man's genitals. But the killer blocked Pritchard's fists with his forearms. He stopped the knee with his thigh. And all the time, the chain tightened like a steel tentacle around the young ensign's throat.

Billy Pritchard's brain coursed with obscenities. His eyes felt as if they would explode. Then everything was fading and Billy felt terribly weak.

He thought of home in Ohio. . . . He fancied he was

on his way there. . . . Then everything was black. . . .

Working by moonlight, Siegfried stripped the young sailor of his uniform, then dragged the corpse fifty feet into a wooded area where he already had prepared a shallow grave. He laid the body in it and covered it with dirt. He dragged several branches and broken brambles into place across the grave.

Siegfried returned to Newark by car. As was usual, he quietly entered his rooming house through a rear door. He was unobserved. He removed the dye from his hair and the makeup from his face. He shaved.

Then he slept, secure in the knowledge that sometimes great sacrifices or odious deeds were necessary in order to perpetuate a far greater good.

It was the state, after all, that was important. Not the individual. Adolph Hitler thought that, preached that, and said that. And Siegfried believed it.

FOURTEEN

A special terror struck Siegfried when he reached the quiet, winding corridor that led to the engine room of the HMS *Adriana*. He stood in Billy Pritchard's white uniform, a black bag in his hand, and he waited, like a sentry frozen in place, to hear the slightest sound of a footfall.

There was none. But the terror convulsed him nonetheless.

How foolish his gambit suddenly seemed! He had no cover story and no weapon. His black bag carried only the evidence of his purpose there. He had only this sizzling anger toward those morons in Berlin.

Discover what you can concerning the Adriana . . . ! The fools. They would take him seriously in the future. Berlin would have no choice.

His shirt was clinging to his ribs. *Come on! Move!* he told himself. *Keep standing in one place and you're nothing but a target.*

He stepped into a large communal toilet room and watched the corridor in the mirror. He calmed slightly.

Everyone was on the top deck or in the yard. One of the last warm days of August, Siegfried mused. Well, if these damned Brit sailors liked heat, wait till they tasted Siegfried's latest device.

When there was no sound or movement in any direction, he crossed six feet of corridor and entered the deserted engine room. Two huge turbines, gray and ponderous and bracketed by all sorts of filthy black pipes, loomed in the center of the chamber. Somewhere in the distant background a large generator hummed, providing the *Adriana*'s alternate power while the ship was docked. The twin turbines were silent.

Just perfect, Siegfried thought to himself. *Now move, damn you. Move! Are you* waiting *for a confrontation? Do you want to be arrested?*

Siegfried stepped between the two turbines and studied them. Yes, he grinned, one good bomb located between them would disable the vessel.

Siegfried looked across the concrete floor. His bomb was about twelve inches long and nine inches thick. He had to leave it somewhere where it would not be found, perhaps for several days. The device was Siegfried's most ingenious. It was keyed with nitroglycerin and would be detonated by combustible heat and the severe rocking motion of the ship once the turbines were working again, and once the *Adriana* was at sea. No one in the engine room, Siegfried mused idly, stood a chance. *But where to place it?* It had to be between the turbines and out of sight. There wasn't anyplace.

Or was there?

Siegfried eyed the area carefully. The hand on the black bag was soaking. His heart pounded.

The two turbines were flush to the concrete floor.

But between them was a sheet of steel, elevated about eighteen inches above the concrete. The steel formed a platform that would boost a man of normal height just enough to reach the top of the turbines. Then Siegfried was on his hands and knees, flush against the floor, peering underneath into the dark crawl space between the steel and the concrete.

A wave of claustrophobia splashed across him. He shuddered. Was there no other place? No, there wasn't.

He removed his cap and tucked it into the black bag. Then he came to another brutalizing realization.

He would have to mount the bomb against the underside of the steel to assure that it would blow directly upward. To do that, he would need to lift his arms. So Siegfried turned onto his back. He edged his way under the steel platform, squirming deeper, farther into the darkness until he had a creeping sense of being in some damnable tomb, estranged from the rest of the world, a steel and concrete coffin.

He edged ten feet, fifteen feet, twenty feet under the platform, pulling his bag along with him. His whole uniform was soaked. And filthy! He hadn't counted on the grime and grease. He could almost taste it. And now the air seemed thin, as if he were suffocating. His heart jumped and all of his fears came back to him. Why did he have to prove himself to Berlin?

A vision of the Reich suddenly was before him. An open-air stadium in Nuremburg. The military marching music. A glorious sky. A thousand flags and fifty thousand uniformed troopers!

He pushed onward. He was where he wanted to be. He gingerly pulled the bomb from the bag and pressed it to the steel nine inches above his face. He pulled a heavy bolt of tape from the bag. *Just a few more seconds and . . .*

Siegfried froze. He heard two male voices in the engine room. *God in heaven!* He heard the door close and the voices drew closer. Siegfried barely breathed.

Now he could feel the sweat running down his temples from his forehead. Footsteps came ever closer, and he heard the brogue of the northern reaches of the British Isles, Cumberland or Scotland, he couldn't be sure. His ear was not good enough on English dialects. And it barely mattered, anyway.

Then, with a tremendous thump, two sailors were on the platform above him. Their feet shuffled and they were inches above his face.

Inches above his device. *If their thumping sets it off prematurely . . .* Siegfried didn't finish the thought. His hand was still on the bomb. He knew what would happen if the device were detonated.

He could feel the ship rocking gently. A panic seized him and he almost wanted to surrender. He would go to jail. Anything! Just get him out of that tomb!

He bit his lower lip. He heard snatches of conversation from above, the unswerving topic of interest for sailors at work.

"So how's she look? She got big ones, does she?"

"I've never seen Janie's friend."

"I want a girl with big ones, you know."

"You'll take what you can get and you'll be fucking happy with it. You're lucky I find a Yank girl for you at all."

"I'll do you the favor and take both of them tonight."

"You fucking arsehole!"

Then there was the sound of playful shoving and

good-natured punches exchanged. The two young men laughed. They scuffled directly above Siegfried's bomb and then set to work. For thirty minutes Siegfried remained motionless in place. Everything in his body throbbed.

"That does it, then," one of the sailors finally said. Then they turned and jumped down from the platform. Siegfried heard them walk away. The door closed.

He waited several more minutes. Then he slowly took his hand off the bomb. It stayed in place, held securely by the adhesive. As he slid back toward his exit, his shirt rode up toward his shoulders. Then he reached a part of the steel that was slightly concave. For a moment in the blackness, his chest was stuck and he was stricken by an overwhelming panic. But then, with a mighty shove, he pushed himself along with his arms. A few seconds later he was free, and a minute thereafter he was out, sitting upright again and feeling his body creak. He breathed hard and told himself that he would never *ever* do this again. *Not even for Hitler personally!*

He stood and was filthy. He stripped his dress shirt from his chest and kept his undershirt on. He saw a pair of coveralls and pulled them on. Then he found a pair of mops and a pail in a corner of the engine room. He filled the pail with soap and water. A sailor on a work patrol would arouse no suspicion. He emerged into the corridor carrying the mops and the buckets.

No one stopped him. When the petty officer took his eyes off the gangplank for a moment, Siegfried abandoned his housekeeping tools against a lifeboat station and walked calmly down the plank. He mingled with the other men in the navy yard and, fifteen minutes later, disappeared through the main gate.

Rev. Stephen Fowler, Laura's onetime husband, was a man capable of radically changing his opinions. But he was only formulating opinions, not changing any, as he sat by the green-shaded desk lamp in his parish house, staring at the blank sheet of paper rolled into his typewriter. It was eight in the evening of the same day that the spy had been an uninvited guest at the Red Bank navy yard. That evening Reverend Fowler felt himself quite incapable of any strong opinion at all.

Perhaps it was an unenviable aspect of being a celebrity cleric. A man's opinion is asked so often that it becomes difficult to have any opinion or ideas left. *Collier's* had asked him to write two thousand words on why a young man from a good family would choose to enter the ministry. What relevance did it have to 1939 and a world perched on the brink of war? And by the way, could he include a clear black and white photograph of himself and his wife?

Christian Century had initiated a monthly symposium of views concerning American involvement in European politics. Their editors, bless them, had found an eloquent, hard-noggined ostrich-headed isolationist, an old Jesuit named Father Quinn, who could warp any of the parables of Christ to his own purposes. Would young Reverend Fowler, the clear-eyed young Lutheran, care to craft a five-thousand-word response?

"Of course," answered Stephen Fowler from his study over the long-distance wire to his editors in Chicago. "I've been a fan of Father Quinn's muddled theology for years. It's about time someone took him

232

on, isn't it?"

Stephen Fowler typed:

Can a Christian sit by, in the safety of his own
home, and watch his neighbor's house in flames?

Displeased, he leaned back and stopped typing.
Other things were slipping into perspective this evening
and they drew his attention away from his writing.

He stared at the framed portrait at the corner of his
desk. He saw himself and Laura, arms entwined during
more agreeable days. The photograph had been taken
on the ramparts of Quebec City during their honeymoon. In the picture, they stood smiling broadly, arms
entwined, possessed of a love that seemed that it would
last two lifetimes. Laura, at age twenty-three, was so
very beautiful.

How had he let his marriage get so out of hand?

He brooded suddenly. He had not heard from her
since she had gone home to England. He wondered if
she still loved him. He told himself that he had only one
person to blame if she did not. Himself.

Reverend Fowler picked up the typewriter and
moved it aside, clearing his desk. Only one unsatisfying
sentence of his current article had been written. He
could get back to it, he told himself.

He drew a piece of personal stationery as well as an
envelope from his desk. He fished in a side drawer for a
ten-cent stamp for airmail to England. Then in the
methodical neat script of his own hand he addressed
the envelope to Laura Worthington Fowler, care of her
father's name and address in Salisbury.

He wrote Laura a short but succinct letter. He said

233

the things that finally needed to be said. He was sorry for his inattentiveness, he wrote. Ideas had swept him away and taken his eyes off what he cherished more than anything: her. Could she come home and forgive him? He wrote that he still loved her and prayed that she loved him.

He sealed the letter. He took it from his study and placed it on the table near the front door. He would be sure to mail it the next morning even if it meant a special trip into town.

He was about to return to his study, when something caught his eye through the window by the front door. He looked again. He was *certain*—or was he?—that he'd seen a man leaving his church.

Stephen Fowler stood very still and stared. The trees between St. Paul's and the parish house obscured his view, particularly when they rustled. He could obtain no clear sight lines, but he watched for several seconds.

Why would someone be at his church at this hour? Though the doors were unlocked, Reverend Fowler was the only one ever to have cause to enter the church in the evening.

He continued to watch. He caught his breath and held it. He felt a certain apprehension and he stared hard, as if intensity might help. He searched and scanned for the ghost of a tall crooked figure in a dark coat that he may or may not have seen.

But the shadow, or whatever it had been, was gone.

He exhaled and the air rushed from his lungs. He breathed again as he relaxed. He was now convinced that he had probably seen a rustle of leaves, an errant configuration of branches, or a stray dog. He admitted to himself how much he had been on edge recently, particularly since his wife had left him. A man could imagine many things under the circumstances and very few of them were any good.

And so what if someone *had* passed by the church? This was Liberty Square, New Jersey, population four thousand gentle souls, established 1759. It was not New York or Philadelphia. A parishioner might have simply wanted to offer an evening prayer, or seek the comfort of the Almighty's presence.

What could be more innocent? Why else were the church's doors always open?

Reverend Fowler watched for another half minute. When no one appeared or emerged from the front doors of his church, he returned to his writing. There was no use in worrying about the unimportant things. Not with his country—and the world—in the state it was in.

FIFTEEN

I

That next evening Siegfried locked the door of his clandestine radio room and pulled the curtains across the single window. He unraveled his antenna and strung it carefully across the floor, up the cream-colored walls, along the bookshelf that held no books, and parallel to the molding where the ceiling met the walls. He positioned the wire for optimum communication with Hamburg. He checked his watch. It was 10:17 on a Wednesday. He had more than enough time.

The spy plugged in his receiver. It hummed as it warmed up. Then he adjusted the tone by tuning into the dots and dashes of various amateur operators in the area. He donned a set of heavy headphones, plugged in his transmitter, and connected his telegraph key. He limbered his fingers, then cut his own power and monitored a dummy transmission of his own steady hand on the key.

Satisfied, he moved his transmitter back to an ON

position, tuned the receiver to the assigned frequency for AOR-3, and raised the volume as high as possible. He listened to static on the frequency as he checked his watch again.

It was 10:48. He was ready. He smoked two Pall Mall cigarettes. His anxiety heightened as he watched the minute hand on his watch edge with painful slowness toward the twelve. Would the hour for transmission *never* come? he wondered.

As a safeguard against his own timekeeping—which he knew to be compulsively precise—he reached to a boxy Dumont table radio that he always kept turned to 660, WRCA in New York, pilot station of the Blue Network. WRCA always had the precise time, a gong right on the hour.

He listened, keeping his headphones slightly ajar. Then it was eleven; 2300 hours on a Wednesday. *Those bastards in Hamburg better be listening!*

He leaned toward his telegraph key and concentrated. He turned off the radio and fixed the headphones perfectly around his ears. He rubbed the moisture off his palms and he tapped out his own call letters to identify himself: C . . . Q . . . D . . . X . . . V . . . W . . . 2.

He waited. When there was no response for a full minute, he tapped out his letters again. And again he waited as utter silence, confusing and forbidding, greeted him through the atmosphere.

Siegfried cursed violently. He had risked his life that previous day for these bastards safely back in the Reich. Why the hell couldn't they be at their receiving station at the proper time?

Angrily, Siegfried repeated his call letters at ninety-second intervals. His face reddened and the moisture on his hands dripped onto the key. It was essential that all messages emanating from North America be quick and methodical. They *had* to comprehend that in Hamburg! Who knew who else was listening? The Americans would eventually set up monitoring stations.

Siegfried tapped out CQDXVW-2 a tenth time. Then his insides jumped. His headphones came alive with a faint but unmistakable signal. Siegfried recognized the call letters of AOR-3 in Hamburg.

Huffily, Siegfried tapped out his greeting:

IT'S ABOUT TIME YOU CUNTS! HAVE BEEN SENDING FOR FIFTEEN MINUTES!

CQDXVW-2

To which Hamburg replied:

REGRET DELAY. PROCEED.

AOR-3

Siegfried drew a breath and glanced with annoyance at his watch. So much precious time had been wasted. It was essential to beat the listeners. Siegfried transmitted in German:

AMERICANS BOARDING PERHAPS AS MANY AS TEN THOUSAND MACHINE GUNS ABOARD ADRIANA. HAVE ALSO SEEN MOTORCYCLES AND SIDECARS, OBVIOUSLY BOUND FOR U.K. CARGO ALMOST COMPLETELY LOADED AND ALL SHORE LEAVE FOR ADRIANA CREW CANCELED AFTER

AUGUST 27. REPEAT: AUGUST TWO-SEVEN. SUS-
PECT DEPARTURE SOON AFTER THAT DATE.

                                    CQDXVW-2

Siegfried reclined slightly, but a faint response flew
through the atmosphere within seconds.

HAS ADRIANA BOARDED ANY ANTIAIRCRAFT
GUNS?

                                         AOR-3

Siegfried responded.

HAVE SEEN NONE. WHEN WILL YOU IMPROVE
YOUR FUCKING SIGNAL? EXTREMELY WEAK.
HAVE YOU NO COMPETENT ENGINEERS?

                                    CQDXVW-2

Now there was a pause of several seconds and
Siegfried cocked his head in response. *Don't disappear
now, you imbeciles!* he thought. Then he heard them
again.

HAVE YOU DISCOVERED MATERIAL ON BROWN-
ING U.S. ANTIAIRCRAFT GUNS?

                                         AOR-3

Siegfried shot back:

HAVE NO ACCESS. HAVE FOCUSED FULL EF-
FORTS UPON ADRIANA. PLANTED ROSES.

                                    CQDXVW-2

240

Hamburg answered. Siegfried then tapped out his closing—smugly, joyfully, and egotistically:

> PLANTED FLOWERS ABOARD ADRIANA. BY MY
> CALCULATIONS, ROSES WILL BLOOM TWO TO
> THREE DAYS OUT OF RED BANK, DEPENDING ON
> WEATHER AND TIDES, DISABLING SHIP. SUG-
> GEST YOU SEND MORE FLOWERS FROM BERLIN.
>   SIEGFRIED

Hamburg digested the message slowly, then replied with obvious enthusiasm.

> BRAVO, SIEGFRIED!
> AOR-3

Of course, "Bravo, Siegfried," thought the spy, glancing at his watch. The communication had taken six full minutes, all of them filled with peril for him, not them. The transmission was much too long, much too dangerous. Siegfried felt his insides set to explode, for the second time in two days. What kind of life *was* this?

Siegfried leaned back and AOR-3 evaporated into the stars. He felt his own pulse racing when he removed his hand from the transmission key. Good thing he had nothing further to do. He could just disappear into the respectable American middle class and think.

He let several minutes pass as he gradually regained his composure. He smoked two more Pall Malls. Then, as his senses returned to earth, he took down his transmission station.

It was only at that moment that he allowed himself to be satisfied with a job well done. And as he descended the long staircase from his radio room, it occurred to him that some sort of reward was in order.

Siegfried grinned. He already knew what he wanted.

II

Marjorie wore her most seductive black dress, the one that plunged low in the front, and her finest jewels. She used less makeup than usual and her hair was washed, brushed, and styled in a less flamboyant manner than usual. She wanted her Mr. Bolton to, well, she wanted him to know that she was more than just a good prostitute. She was a woman, too. And she deserved to have what other women had, if only the right man would notice.

The buzzer rang and she felt a flash of anxiety. She was acting like a schoolgirl. She tried to settle herself. *Imagine!* she thought to herself. *Me! Marjorie Benton of Hoboken, New Jersey, nervous with a man! How many men have I known?* She didn't like to think about it in those terms. She only knew that her clock manufacturer, Mr. Bolton, was special to her. And she wanted to be special to him.

She opened the door. "Hello, sugar," she said when she saw Siegfried. "Missed you."

He accepted the kiss, but did not reciprocate. She locked her arm seductively with his and led him into

242

her living room. She let him sit in his favorite chair and she went to the bar to pour him a scotch. She gave him plenty of opportunity to admire her from the back. Sure, she was thirty-one, she told herself. But she had the figure of a woman ten years younger.

She brought him a drink and noticed that he hadn't said anything. She handed it to him and he accepted it. "Something bothering you, tonight, lover?" she asked.

Siegfried sipped his drink. "Business," he said. "Rough week." He even managed a slight laugh. "That's why I'm here," he said. "I could use some relaxation. Need to unwind, I suppose."

He was always so considerate, she thought. Not like the doctors and lawyers who came to her: cheap and always in a rush. Not like the policemen whom she paid off with sex to keep out of courtrooms: they were rough and inconsiderate.

She studied Mr. Bolton. Indeed, she noticed, he did look as if he'd been under a great deal of stress.

"Well," she cooed softly, "I know how to make a nice man very happy."

She knew *many* ways, she told herself. And they included rooms of the house other than the bedroom. The kitchen, for example. The den. The family room . . .

She pictured herself with a little girl or a little boy.

"You always make me very happy, Marjorie," Mr. Bolton said to her. *"Very."* She sat on the arm of his chair. He reached for her with the hand that did not hold the drink. He pulled her head down to him and he kissed her, a slightly scotch flavor to his kiss. But she gave him a long and impassioned kiss. He deserved it.

She noticed that there was a slight tremor to his touch tonight. Obviously, something major had happened this week for Mr. Bolton. But she knew better than to ask a customer about his personal business.

Plus, it was time. His head had slipped down from her lips and he was kissing her throat. She reached to the zipper behind her back and loosened her dress. Her breasts were freed from their confinement and Mr. Bolton kissed further downward. He unzipped her the rest of the way. Then she stood, removed her dress, and returned to the arm of the chair. And her sensual, handsome Mr. Bolton was kissing her on the nipples now, making them hard and taut, exciting her in the ways that she'd fantasized in the hours she'd spent thinking about him.

He reached between her legs, which surprised her. Normally the next move was for her to kneel before the chair and satisfy him. He *was* different this week. She found his new mood exciting.

"What would you like tonight, sweetie?" she asked. "The loving you *always* want?"

He motioned with his head. "The bedroom," he said. She was surprised. But she took him by the hand and led him, then undressed him.

She had been naked before him many times, but this was the first time he stood fully unclothed before her. He was surprisingly muscular. His body was not one that impressed when covered with the squarish clothes that he wore. But obviously Mr. Bolton took care of himself. He was in *good* shape. Almost like an athlete, she marveled.

Astonishing for a businessman, she pondered as she

reclined on the sheets of her bed. So unusual. Usually businessmen were so repulsively flabby.

But then he was climbing onto her and suddenly her clock manufacturer astonished her once again. He pinned her fiercely to the bed, entered her, and mõved rigidly and methodically between her legs. Marjorie yelped with both the surprise and the pleasure. Unlike with most of her customers, she was not faking. And she kissed him hard on the lips right before he had his explosion inside her.

Afterward, he lay beside her for several minutes, saying nothing. She did not spring to her feet and dress quickly as she would have with other men. Finally, she spoke.

"For all the time you've been coming to me," she said, "there's something I've wanted to ask you."

"What?" he asked.

"Your first name."

Siegfried thought for a moment. "It's Fred," he finally said. "From Fredrick."

She hesitated. "May I . . . call you that?" she asked.

Again, he thought for a moment, wondering where this might be leading. Siegfried had noticed that she was acting differently. Now he was certain.

"Of course," he said. "Why not? Fred."

He rose and went into the bathroom, where he carefully washed himself. Then he returned. Acting more deliberate now as she remained in the bed, he dressed himself. Then she stood, pulling a red print silk robe around her. He reached to his wallet and withdrew a twenty-dollar bill, plus a five, which was her usual tip.

"Fred . . . ?" she asked.

He looked at her, his hand folding the two bank notes.

"I don't want money from you anymore," she said nervously. "You can come visit me anytime you want. But I don't want money." She felt like saying more, like telling him how she really felt and what she would really—eventually—like to have with Mr. Bolton. But there was confusion clearly discernible on his face. The hand with the money had stopped dead still, and he was staring at her.

"What in hell are you talking about?" he asked.

She had rushed things a little, she felt. But then again, he was a gentleman. She had made him happy— she was certain about that—so this was the right time to be honest with him.

"Maybe, if you like what I do for you, if you even like *me* a little," she edged with a nervous laugh, "we could go out to dinner instead of you paying me. Or maybe we could go to a Broadway show together."

His eyes changed again and the confusion on his face was gone. A smile drifted in from somewhere and he started to laugh lightly. He understood. So she laughed, too.

Marjorie was in the midpoint of a laugh when the hand that held the money switched into a firm open palm, reached backward, and then exploded forward like an express train, smacking her from right to left clearly across the face. The impact was so hard and sudden that it sent her reeling backward. She was holding her stinging, stunned cheek and pressing her own hand against the rattled teeth of her upper jaw. And she was fighting back tears.

Siegfried spoke in very measured tones. "You're a whore, Marjorie," he said, dropping the money on her dresser. "Don't ever forget that. And don't ever overstep yourself again. It could cost you your life."

The spy found his coat in the next room and was gone a few seconds later.

SIXTEEN

On Saturday morning, a Bureau driver—a neat young man who said his name was Thomas Jenks—met Cochrane at Union Station and drove him to a green clapboard house on Twenty-sixth Street in Georgetown. The Bureau had owned it for Special Operations—this, quite illegally—since 1934. The house was faded, small and accommodating. It had a front porch that squeaked at the first footfall. This to curtail unexpected company, Cochrane assumed correctly.

Past the entrance foyer was a sitting room, equipped with some blue upholstered chairs, a sofa that matched the chairs in both pattern and wear, two matching oversized pink lamps that more than bracketed the sofa, and—the prize of the room—a large Philco console radio, presumably for tuning in Roosevelt or the Washington Senators, not necessarily in that order. Adjacent to the living room was a small dining room, furnished functionally with an oval mahogany table supported by thick, overdone legs and surrounded by five matching chairs and—Cochrane lamented immediately—one mismatching one. Cochrane sighed. The interior of the house appeared to have been decorated by the Racketeering Division of the Grand Rapids FBI office. Why couldn't they have hired a vivacious young woman, Cochrane wondered, or at least some disgusting old fairy?

"Anything wrong, sir?" young Jenks asked.

"Everything's just fine," Cochrane answered, whereupon Jenks led him to a small kitchen, which Cochrane found to be freshly stocked.

"Tell me, Jenks," Cochrane asked indulgently, "do you know why I'm in Washington?"

"No, sir," said the younger man, breathing heavily through his mouth. "We're under instructions not to have such discussions, sir."

"Whose instructions?"

"Mr. Lerrick's, sir."

Cochrane wandered from the kitchen through the dining room, toward a flight of stairs. Jenks followed. Cochrane answered, after too long a pause. "Maybe you can tell me more about this house, then."

Jenks stammered slightly and as Cochrane listened, he noted the heavy cloth curtains, blocking any view of the interior from the outside.

"A woman comes in twice a week to clean up and sweep," Jenks explained, trailing Cochrane. "She'll also tend to the laundry, take care of any dirty dishes, and replenish the cupboards with fresh groceries," Jenks said.

Replenish: so Hoover was still hiring English majors as his errand boys, Cochrane thought to himself. It figured.

"Any special grocery requests or maintenance

items," Jenks continued, "can be arranged by leaving a note on the kitchen table. She'll take care of it."

"Who will?"

"The woman, sir."

"Ever seen her?"

"Never, sir."

"Do you think she might be one of the Bureau's stable of nymphomaniacs?"

"A *what,* sir?" Then, realizing, Jenks exclaimed. "Oh, *no,* sir. Not a chance, sir! Why, to my knowledge, sir, there's no stable of—"

"Just show me the upstairs and all the escapes," Cochrane requested.

God! Humorless *English majors from small, bad midwestern colleges,* Cochrane thought, refining his earlier appraisal.

There was an exit through the kitchen and an exit through the basement. Both led to an alleyway that connected with the street on both ends of the block. And all the downstairs windows opened wide.

Upstairs, a chain fire ladder was poised by a window in each bedroom and there was also one in the hallway. Each of the two bedrooms was furnished as sparsely as the downstairs room: a bed, a night table, one lamp, a dresser, and a chair. Each bed was a single. The Bureau brain trust—Morality Division—had anticipated everything, and did their best to discourage it. Bureau safe houses were not to turn into hotels for non-Bureau female guests. The rule wasn't stated, surprisingly, it was just there. Cochrane opened a night-table drawer and uncovered the final Hooverism: a Holy Bible for light bedside reading.

"And that's it?" Cochrane finally asked, downstairs

again and shadowed diligently by Jenks.

"Not entirely, sir."

"What else could there be?"

"Mr. Wheeler wishes you to come straight to Bureau headquarters as soon as your bags are unpacked. I'm to wait."

"Of course," said Cochrane. "It's a workday, isn't it? Saturdays always are, aren't they, Jenks?"

"Usually we get Saturdays off, sir. Today is the exception."

Jenks drove him an hour later to the Justice Department. At the guard's desk in the lobby was a balding man who flicked through a list of special passes when Cochrane announced his name. Cochrane watched the gnarled, unsteady fingers twice pass his name before finding it.

"Cochrane. Cochrane, *William*. There!" the man looked up and smiled. "Of course." He handed Cochrane his pass.

Cochrane proceeded to one of three new elevators, swift, smartly polished and chrome, and a Negro elevator man in a verdant uniform deposited him at Wheeler's sixth floor where yet another assistant was waiting for him.

Hoover was doing a fine job on the Senate Appropriations Committee, Cochrane concluded. Hoover had the FBI wing all polished, modernized, and shining, a veritable temple to America's only federal policy agency. Hoover always knew where bodies were buried, Cochrane reminded himself.

Cochrane was announced and stood for a moment in a reception area, studying a collection of framed photographs on the wall, each depicting J. Edgar

Hoover's personal role in the apprehension of various American bandits. Then Cochrane heard something midway between a bellow and a roar.

"Bill! Fine to see you! Thanks for being so prompt, though I knew you wouldn't be anything but."

Cochrane turned away from a portrait of J. Edgar Hoover with a granite-faced President Coolidge to see Big Dick Wheeler hulking massively into the reception area, his hand extended in greeting, a huge smile across his face.

Wheeler, all five foot fifteen inches of him, clad in a gray suit, white shirt, and tie, lumbered to Cochrane's side. He took Cochrane's hand into his paw, crushed it with a welcoming pump, and wrapped his other arm around Cochrane's shoulders.

"Damned good of you to come by on a Saturday morning," Wheeler said. "You saw your house? Your new residence for the duration?"

"Your driver took me there. Yes. Thanks."

"I know it's not a home, but it will have to do," Wheeler said. "Tell you what. One of these nights the missus and I will have you over for a roast chicken. How's that? God Almighty! A man's got to live, doesn't he?"

Predictably, Dick Wheeler was louder, more garrulous, and more of a dominant force on the sixth floor, his own, than on the second, Hoover's.

"Why am I here today?" Cochrane asked eventually.

"I want to show you through Section Seven," Wheeler said. "Much easier on a Saturday. Fewer interruptions."

"What *is* Section Seven?"

"Espionage and Counterespionage," Wheeler said,

plucking a Missouri meerschaum pipe from a breast pocket. "Call it 'Spying' if you want to use the current profanity."

"I didn't know we actually had such a division."

"Officially, we don't. Fact is, we've been turned down six times since 1935 for congressional funding for it. The money comes out of General Appropriations." Wheeler stuffed tobacco into his pipe with his thumb and struggled to get a fire started. They walked down a hall, closing doors behind them.

"You'll feel at home here. I read your reports from Germany last night. Damned fine work. I'm surprised you're alive."

"So am I."

"My office first," said Wheeler, leading Cochrane into the largest quarters on the floor. A picture window looked toward the Capitol.

"Have a seat," Wheeler said. "We need to chat first."

Cochrane chose an armchair, and Wheeler did likewise, staying away from his desk.

"Just out of curiosity," Cochrane asked, "what are Sections One through Six?"

"They don't exist."

"Then what's this seven?"

"Seven is everyone's lucky number. And that's what you're going to need, you know. Luck. Just like J.E.H. to toss a good capable man into an impossible situation. But, come on. It beats banking fraud in Baltimore, doesn't it? I'll give you the grand tour anyway. You're going to need all the help you can get. Someone's here all the time, of course. That's another reason for the name. 'Section Seven' seven days a week." Wheeler mustered a groan. "One of *those*

254

assignments. Like Racketeering in the Kansas City office. You remember?"

Cochrane nodded.

Wheeler foraged through a drawer of his desk and produced a bottle of twelve-year-old bourbon. "Want a drink before we start?"

"No, thanks."

Wheeler poured himself a taste of Tennessee's best in a small glass. "You're sure? God Almighty, we've worked together three times now and I'm in charge here, you know."

"It's all right," Cochrane reaffirmed.

"Okay then," said Wheeler, sipping and positioning himself massively in his chair. "Just remember this is top-secret stuff. You don't even discuss this with any other agent. Only the people you see here."

Cochrane nodded.

"Let me explain," said Wheeler.

SEVENTEEN

As background in Section Seven, there wasn't much. Some counterespionage and intelligence gathering had been done in Europe, Wheeler said, but Cochrane himself had done the best of it and had a working knowledge of the rest. Bill Cochrane nodded and a flood of images came back to him, from Theresia dead on her bed to Engle carefully taking the order for a set of Swiss passports.

As for German espionage within the forty-eight United States, Wheeler continued academically, as his pipe smoldered in the ashtray, it had all been haphazard at best—at least as far as they knew. Cochrane nodded again.

"We've dropped down hard on a ring of sympathizers here and there, gotten the local police to hassle a few others. But there's no war, so there's no law being broken. A saboteur with some bombs is something else. He gets priority. Roosevelt's pissed as hell." Wheeler sipped. "If we were just out to run down pro-Hitler groups, we'd be arresting half the Republicans in the Senate, William Randolph Hearst, Charles Lindbergh, and probably eighty percent of the Daughters of the American Revolution."

Cochrane mustered an uneasy grin.

"So you see, we're in a swampy area. Very few real rules. The laws we have to enforce are the usual civil and criminal laws. And many of them are state laws, so we don't have jurisdiction. Added to that, we have a peacetime espionage situation. Confusing?"

"No."

"Good." Wheeler drew a breath. "Because that leads us to the radio emissions. And the 'Bluebirds.'"

"The who?"

Wheeler finished his bourbon and poured himself a refill. He tossed Cochrane a sly smile. "So glad you asked," he said.

The Bluebirds' official name was Monitoring Division and they had been formed in the queasy days of 1937 upon a suggestion by William Donovan. On an evening in Washington, Roosevelt had casually mentioned a marked increase in mysterious radio emissions from the northeastern United States. Triangulation detectors had traced many of them to Newark and Manhattan, particularly Yorkville, in the East Eighties, and Little Hungary, in the East Seventies.

"I can't see that there's too much question what these emissions are," Roosevelt said.

"Why not listen to them?" Donovan asked. "Monitor them. Record them. Then decipher them."

Donovan explained how a skeletal monitoring station could be set up by the FBI on the sixth floor of the Justice Department. FDR signaled to an aide to take notes. Then the notes were typed and organized.

"Have Mr. Hoover do something about this," he said to the aide.

Hoover assembled a division called Monitoring under the shadowy umbrella of Section Seven. Those who worked in Monitoring quickly self-administered the nickname of the Bluebirds. They were a number of men and women, usually somewhere between twenty-five and thirty in number who spent their time in the hastily constructed plywood stalls of the largest room in the east wing of the sixth floor. These were the foot soldiers of Section Seven. Day after day, but mostly night after night, they turned dials on an endless succession of shortwave radios. Each man or woman, fluent in the international Morse code, monitored no fewer than three frequencies each, or read a book if nothing was coming across. Anything mysterious was recorded, particularly in the evening when emissions to Europe could be at optimum strength.

Each Bluebird worked a four-hour shift, and most, particularly those who finished between four and eight in the morning, acquired the sunken, narcoleptic look of the truly deranged. But each also emerged with a sheaf of papers, a scramble of notes, and notations of precise time, along with too many spools of wire recordings.

"Everything gets passed along to Deciphering and Cryptology," Wheeler said. "That's one unit, next door to the Bluebirds, on this floor also. I'll give you a look."

Wheeler set aside his bourbon. They rose and went a few paces down the hall. Cochrane was admitted to a large chamber where seven Bluebirds were at work, Saturday morning being a slow time to bounce signals around the clouds. Everyone in the room looked sleepy. No one had much to say, even to Wheeler, and Cochrane and Wheeler were gone from the room in ten minutes.

The next door down was another large room, this one cramped with wall-to-wall files and several large tables at its center. There was no activity whatsoever, because this was the CAR Division, as Wheeler described it. He pronounced it as if it had something to do with automobiles, and explained that the letters stood for Central Alien Registry.

"Everyone still has weekends off," Wheeler said. "But not for much longer."

Central Alien Registry was a nightmare. Stuffed into the files in varying degrees of order were alien registration forms dating back through the waves of immigration that flooded Boston, New York, and Philadelphia in the 1920s.

"If someone came into this country legally, he's in these files," said Wheeler, motioning. "If he came in *il*legally," he added with a grimace, "he might be here, also."

Two hundred and sixty thousand names were crammed into the files of the CAR Division, along with any criminal reports or FBI dossiers which might be pertinent. The files were divided into Asian and European—European being vastly larger—and there were cross-references of points of origin, many designated FRIENDLY, such as Britain or Canada or Australia, and others designated as UNFRIENDLY, such as Germany or Hungary.

"Where's Spain?" Cochrane inquired. "Or the Soviet Union?"

"Somewhere in the murky middle," answered

Wheeler. "Maybe by the end of 1940 we'll have it all straight."

Cochrane opened a file drawer and fingered a few cards to familiarize himself with the format. Then they were out into the hall again, nearing a right-angle turn in the endless corridor, strolling deeper into the belly of Section Seven, when Wheeler sniffed the air and stopped in his tracks. His feet shuffled, almost in the manner of an Ozark brown bear pawing the ground.

"Who the *hell* is smoking a *cigarette* on this floor?" he bellowed. "Standing orders. No cigarette smoking in any section I have anything to do with!" He continued down the corridor and around the corner. "Who the hell *is* the malefactor?"

The culprit was no less a personage than tiny Mr. Hay himself, who was discovered stuffing a smoldering butt into a potted hallway plant.

"Mr. Hay, you little gnome!" Wheeler roared, not half as angrily or aggressively as he might have. "Are you trying to asphyxiate us?"

"No, sir."

"Then why don't you scramble back upstairs before the cat catches you!"

"Yes, sir," said Mr. Hay, who drew a nasty bead on Cochrane, then returned a terrified defensive gaze to Wheeler. "Right away, sir. Just delivering some files for the CAR Division, sir."

"Go!" ordered Wheeler. "Vanish!"

And the dwarf went, scurrying back to the elevators.

"But *you're* smoking," Cochrane said softly to Wheeler.

"I'm smoking a pipe. Pipes, yes. Cigarettes and cigars, no, on my floors. Power is wielded arbitrarily and unfairly in this Bureau."

They arrived at another door and Wheeler pushed it open without knocking. "This is Deciphering and Cryptology," said Wheeler, leading Cochrane into a large room that was a messy warren of desks and small plywood partitions. "Also known as our history and Romance-language department."

Present today were perhaps a dozen loyal workers, most of whom glanced up when Wheeler passed. All were obsessed with various forms of code evaluation, mostly from sequential series of intercepted dots and dashes passed on to them by the pilfering Bluebirds. Many worked with wire recorders, playing back the unidentified blips, and others worked with pens, pencils, papers, notebooks, or improbable-looking little black and gray calculators.

Among the drones of the D&C Chamber were one civil engineer, two math instructors, one high school history teacher, two housewives who were said to be good at solving mathematical puzzles, and a bespectacled, adenoidal eighteen-year-old chess grand master from Brooklyn, New York, named Lanny Slotkin. The latter was currently pursuing his doctoral studies in chemistry at George Washington University. "I'm a genius," Lanny said to Cochrane upon introduction, simultaneously munching a cream cheese sandwich. Then he went back to his work.

"I love little Lanny," Wheeler said evenly, moving away from him, "almost as much as I love going to the dentist. But he *is* smart, the little bugger."

Then they came to a Chinese woman named Hope See Ming, who smiled very politely, offered Cochrane a dead fish of a handshake, and interrupted her work on an abacus to answer a question in perfectly textured English. Out of her earshot, Wheeler said she was the most able person in the room.

"Hope See Ming is our own little China doll," mused Wheeler, holding the door open for Cochrane as they departed. "Lanny is our pet Jew. Adam Hay is our pet squirrel." He closed the door and they were back in the corridor. "But you know what?" Wheeler continued. "They're smart as whips, all of them. Wouldn't be here if they weren't. Imagine what we could do if we could trade information with other intelligence services. British and Canadian are formidable, but we can't even admit we're in the same line of work."

"Don't you think they might soon figure it out?"

"So what if they do?" Wheeler shrugged. "We still have to lie. Neither Hoover nor Roosevelt are ready to go to the great unwashed American public and admit that we're running a spy service. That's just politics, William."

Wheeler led Cochrane onward, introducing him first to Roddy Schwarzkopf and Elizabeth Pfeifer, known as Hansel and Gretel in Section Seven, and who abruptly stopped talking when they saw Wheeler. Hansel and Gretel were an infiltration team that Hoover and Wheeler were getting ready for something. God knew what. Wheeler motioned down the corridor to a private office.

Therein was Bobby Charles Martin, a fingerprint expert formerly of the Ohio State Police, whose hobby was cartography, and who now merrily spent his days assessing recent European maps and navigational

263

charts. "Just in case we have to send a few lucky souls abroad again," Wheeler said as he handled the introduction.

Dora McNeil, the secretary of the D&C Division, looked up as they approached and gave Wheeler a sweet complacent smile. Then she stared at Cochrane, and fixed her posture.

Dora, Wheeler explained much later, was the house floozy whom no one had the heart to fire. This month she was a strawberry blonde. She was a more than competent secretary, blessed with an ample bosom, good legs, and a pair of buttocks which, when snugly nestled into a form-fitting skirt, had just the proper air of provocation. Dora, in Bureau parlance, was that good time who'd been had by all. Her blouse never seemed to be buttoned quite properly and at least once a week her eyeliner would be slightly off or a speck of lipstick would spend several hours on a front tooth.

But no one complained.

So Dora McNeil flounced around Section Seven at will, occasionally typing a letter or reheating coffee. J. Edgar Hoover did not know about her, and Lanny Slotkin was in deep, unrequited love with her. To him, at age twenty-five, she was a classy older woman.

"Hi," Bill Cochrane said to her as they passed.

"Hi," Dora returned with an eager smile and a twinkle in her green eyes.

"Introductions later, Dora," Wheeler grumbled with sudden curtness. Dora answered Wheeler with a downward turn of her smile.

"That's something else," Wheeler brooded. "The Bureau rule book, again. This city is filled with young secretaries who can't keep their knees together after six

264

in the evening. But do your prowling somewhere else. No dirtying sheets with another employee, hear?"

"I understand."

Then a smile emerged and Wheeler became the back-slapping, beer-guzzling good ole boy again. "God Almighty, I wouldn't mind if little Dora back there gave me a few tumbles. But we all got a directive two months ago over J.E.H.'s signature. One of the field agents from Chicago-Racketeering was in town for a month, just long enough to impregnate one of the file clerks from Central Recordkeeping."

"These things happen," said Cochrane generously.

"She happened to be the daughter of a bigshot over at Senate Budget and Appropriations," Wheeler said. "Frank Lerrick got a call asking us what kind of orgy we were running over here. J.E.H. went through the roof and made us all monks and nuns. Well, anyway. That's the entire show. I guess you can see how this all works."

Cochrane said he did, but Wheeler recapitulated anyway.

Bluebirds were the thieves who plucked the signals out of the airwaves. Then they sent them to Deciphering and Cryptology where people like Lanny Slotkin and Hope See Ming tried to find a pattern. "Letters, numbers, hieroglyphics, cuneiform, anything," Wheeler said. "There's only one principle involved. If a man can think up a code, another man can pull it apart."

They were toward the end of the corridor and Wheeler held out his fist and knuckles just above a door as a prelude to knocking. He turned and dropped his voice to a whisper.

"I'm going to introduce you to the 'Virgin Mary,'" he

said. Then he rapped. An agreeable female voice from within a final chamber gave them entry.

The Virgin Mary was Mary Ryan, a eighty-one years old, a graduate of Vassar, 1882, and the only current employee of the Bureau who had spent half of her life in the previous century. Mary came and went as she pleased, Wheeler explained, and did astonishing things with numbers, sequential series, probability, factorials, logarithms, and the other numerical complexities of cryptology. She had earned an office of her own.

Mary was an elfin white-haired woman with a small impish face, dazzling deep-green Irish eyes, and ruddy red cheeks. She wore her hair pinned back into a loose bun, and despite Cochrane's protestations, she stood when they entered the room and remained standing as they spoke.

Mary's desk was an outrageous scramble of papers, clippings, pencils, erasers, and simple additions and subtractions. As they entered she turned facedown onto the table whatever it was she had been working on.

All the great mysterious things that the Virgin Mary did with numbers she did in her head—conceived them immaculately, someone from the Bluebirds had once said—and could beat Deciphering's primitive computers. Only Mary's simple arithmetic was on paper.

Mary offered Cochrane a delicate hand, lined with thin bluish veins, but surprised him with a secure, sound grip. As part of her introduction, Wheeler mentioned that Mary was an alumna of the State Department's "Black Chamber" from the Great War of 1914–18. The Black Chamber was that dubious wing of the State Department in which the government spied upon anything and anyone for whom they were in the mood. Secretary of State Henry Stimson had disbanded the chamber in 1929 stating, "Gentlemen do *not* read other people's mail."

"Maybe gentlemen don't," Mary Ryan had snarled back when furloughed, "but Mary Ryan sure as hell enjoys it. Oh, well . . ."

And she went quietly out to pasture, only to be called back in 1937 when the FBI started picking up strange blips and dots bouncing through the stars.

"Bill Cochrane's going to be working on special assignment for us," Wheeler informed her. "I've assured him that he'll have the support of everyone in Section Seven."

"Oh, how wonderful," Mary Ryan answered. "It's not so often that we get some handsome young men up here. What sort of assignment?"

"I'm trying to catch a spy."

"On *our* floor? Figures!"

"No, no. Out in the United States somewhere."

"I wish you luck." She winked at him. "Section Seven isn't always too good about keeping its own secrets," she said. "What a bunch of detectives! If the power failed in this building half the male population couldn't find its way to the street. Oh, well, a woman pays a price to have herself surrounded by younger men. What did you say your name was?"

"Cochrane. Bill Cochrane."

"If you have a numerical sequence or code type, let me have the first look at it. Mary will save you a lot of time. Despite what this Mr. Wheeler tells you, you can skip Deciphering altogether. Them with their machines. Claptrap! Haven't the foggiest idea what they're about.

267

Bring it to Mary first and Mary will help you in every way she can."

"Thank you, Mary."

"You *are* a handsome young man," she said to Cochrane as they left. "I *do* so hope that wasn't why you were hired."

"Thank you, Mary," Wheeler said this time, and he and Bill Cochrane continued to the end of the corridor.

Then Wheeler spoke again, relighting his pipe, sucking furiously to pick up the flame and then exuding a long cloud of smoke. "Mary's got the sharpest intellect in this whole damned section, including yours and mine combined," he said. He stopped, produced a key from his pocket and unlocked a final door. "If Mary Ryan were a man she'd probably be running the Bureau. But she's not. So J.E.H. has the job, for the time being, anyway." Wheeler lowered his voice. "I hear Roosevelt wants to replace him."

"That rumor's been around for seven years," Cochrane said. "Hoover always lands on his feet. Other people come and go, including Presidents."

"True enough," Wheeler mused. "What do you think?" He opened the door. "This is your office."

Cochrane stepped in and found a plain desk and chair in a carpeted room. There was ample filing space, sufficient lighting, and two telephones. There were extra chairs and a sofa. No glamour, just creeping Bureau utilitarianism.

"It's fine," Cochrane said. The window behind the desk overlooked the inner quadrangle, which was currently a parking lot.

"It's nothing fancy, of course," Wheeler said with a

268

tinge of apology, cupping the bowl of his pipe in his hand. "But I figured you'd be better off near your back-up people in Section Seven."

"Of course. No complaints," Cochrane said again.

"Oh! I knew there was something else," Wheeler said suddenly. "This is just a sample of what's floating around our atmosphere at night."

Wheeler handed Cochrane a memo. "Bluebirds picked up a transmission in German coming from somewhere between New York and Philadelphia, or so they think. Whoever was sending it was pretty cool. Beat the listeners by hustling his message along. Bluebirds got the end of it," Wheeler explained, motioning to the sheet of paper. "Make of it what you will."

Cochrane scanned the words scrawled before him:

> . . . *Blumen von Berlin.*
> Siegfried

"And that's it?" Cochrane asked. "That's all of the message they picked up? 'Flowers from Berlin'? 'Siegfried'?"

"The hand on the key was too quick," Wheeler answered. "Like I said, clever emission. Shrewd to the point of arrogance. Quick and even-toned, yet nervy enough to spout off in German. Didn't even bother to code it, the prick."

Cochrane stared at the words before him, not knowing what significance to draw, if any. A rank amateur? A practical joker? A seasoned professional?

Wheeler was speaking again. "You might file it

269

somewhere, Bill. God knows, we're going to have to take anything on the East Coast seriously from here on."

Cochrane nodded. "Did the Bluebirds get the transmission pattern?" he asked.

"Damned straight." Wheeler grinned, appreciating Cochrane's insight. "They've got the frequency pegged twenty-four hours a day now. If our Kraut pal goes back on the air, the Bluebirds will be perched on his shoulder. We'll try some triangulation right away, too. God Almighty, can't run any risks."

"Let's hope he doesn't change frequencies," Cochrane said absently. "Of course, it might be nothing at all, also."

"What are you doing? Reading my mind?"

Cochrane folded away the paper. Then Wheeler slung his arm around Cochrane's shoulders, leading Cochrane back down the corridor in the direction in which they had come. Somewhere in the distance, Lanny Slotkin and Hope See Ming were having a noisy argument and someone had passed through Section Seven again with another cigarette.

"Hey," Wheeler said. "There's a new chili parlor in Georgetown that'll set fire to your esophagus. My treat. You got to be hungry after all this, Bill. By the way, there's been one slight change from the other evening. You'll be reporting directly to J.E.H. yourself. Doesn't change anything, does it?"

"Not much, it doesn't," Cochrane answered. He then changed the subject, leaving Wheeler to wonder exactly what he'd meant.

EIGHTEEN

The next day at 8 A.M., Bill Cochrane sat in his office and reviewed the material placed at his disposal. His sense of mission heightened, as did his bewilderment. Cochrane drew a long breath and exhaled slowly. For a moment he tried to recall how he had been maneuvered into this assignment. Then he remembered Banking Fraud in Baltimore. He looked back to the files before him, trying to conjure up an image of the man he might be looking for. No image appeared.

Cochrane was not beset with the self-doubts that had tormented him during his sabbatical with Mr. Hay. He knew he had it within him to be an outstanding detective. But he also knew that 95 percent of good detective work is routine, unspectacular inquiry, posing the right questions, ferreting out the proper responses. There are hours, no, *weeks,* of checking and double-checking. And there is the laborious placing together of disparate parts, never knowing exactly which parts are missing, which parts are incomplete, or how many make the whole.

Further, any successful federal investigation relied heavily at its inception on information received from local American police departments. Just as the cop on the beat had a better idea what was happening in his neighborhood than his commanding officer did, local police departments had a better insight than FBI offices into their respective cities. The departments knew who was in town to cause trouble or what unusual crimes had occurred. They knew what was perplexing and what was unsolved. They quickly noticed things out of the ordinary.

Over the years, Cochrane had always dealt respectfully with local police, from the department chiefs down to the rookies on patrol. Unlike most other special agents of the Bureau, Cochrane saw local cops as plodders perhaps, but men of a special sort of dedication. They were overworked and besieged. But they did their work to the best of their ability.

Equally, Cochrane reasoned that the man he was looking for had to break the law from time to time. By the very nature of the spy's profession, he had to have an assumed identity, at least part of the time. That meant the forgery of papers. Similarly, this particular spy had to have entered restricted areas to plant his devices. Had anyone gotten in his way? Somewhere along the line, the spy had probably stolen certain items. Who was a suspect in that theft? And where had the saboteur obtained the explosives to sink the *Wolfe?* Was *that* stolen? Purchased? From whom?

Somewhere, Cochrane knew, there were witnesses to this man. No one floated around like Peter Pan. No one failed to leave fingerprints. No one had no other human contact. Where did the spy live? To whom did he pay the rent? With whom did he sleep? Where did he buy his food? His clothes?

Cochrane began making notes.

In the early afternoon Cochrane reached for his telephone. He dialed numbers in Boston, Providence, Hartford, New York, Trenton, Philadelphia, Baltimore, and Washington. Since the Great War, every major American city had had a bomb disposal unit. Cochrane spoke to the head of that unit in each city. In many cases, such as New York, where the head of the Bomb Squad was Lieutenant Francis Xavier Sullivan, Cochrane spoke to men whom he knew personally.

Cochrane guided the conversations carefully. Each took on an identical drift.

"Yes," Cochrane would answer to the first query, "I am acting in an official capacity . . . Conducting an investigation given the FBI's highest priority . . . We are looking for a man about whom we know very little . . . No, no name, yet. Not even a description . . . We know he is an expert on incendiary devices . . . Yes, there is loss of life involved. A considerable amount, in fact . . ."

In each case, the man on the other end of the line quickly asked why an inquiry was being lodged in his area. Further, what federal laws had been violated? Why was the FBI pawing the ground for criminal activity in his city?

Cochrane was ready with a response which invariably brought a rising silence from the other end of the line.

"Unfortunately, it's not a simple matter of criminal

activity," Cochrane explained. "It's a matter of military security. *National* security would actually not be stretching the point. Our conjecture is that the man is either a well-trained mercenary or has extremely strong pro-Nazi sentiments . . . We assume he is a German, probably an infiltrator . . . No, we cannot confirm that. It's at the stage of theory, only . . . We'd like to know if you have anybody in this category in your files. Or if anyone springs to mind."

Inevitably, the men who received these calls promised that their files would be scoured immediately and that their top lieutenants would also be questioned. Cochrane thanked the men generously, asked that they each get back to him within twenty-four hours, and at length apologized for disturbing them at their homes on a Sunday afternoon.

Then, with the eastern calls complete, Cochrane placed a series of identical calls to the cities of the American Midwest with large German-American populations: Milwaukee, Cincinnati, Minneapolis-St. Paul, Chicago, and St. Louis. It was not until past seven in the evening that all Cochrane's telephone contacts had been established.

Cochrane then completed a printed form known within the Bureau as an LKW. The form, headed with the words LAST KNOWN WHEREABOUTS beneath the Bureau's imprimatur, was an official investigative request within the Bureau. Once filled in, and sent through proper channels, the paperwork would pass through one or another of the Bureau's clerical divisions and yield the current (or last known) place of residence for whoever was named on the form.

Carefully, Cochrane filled in a name. Otto Mauer,

late of the Abwehr. Minutes later, he left his own office, locked the door behind him, and dropped the inquiry at Central Alien Registry, where they would trace it in the morning. Cochrane had not seen Otto Mauer since Germany. He knew only—this from Frank Lerrick— that Mauer had fully defected late in 1938.

As Cochrane left the Bureau's sixth floor, the day in Washington was dying. He saw through one of the venetian blinds the redness of the evening sky. Almost simultaneously, he noticed that several of the Blue-birds, like owls, were reporting to work. All other offices on the floor were quiet, with the exception of one poor soul slumped over a table in Cryptology. And like Dick Wheeler, the Virgin Mary had not been seen all day.

Quite unusually, Laura was given cause to smile. At Barrett's, the antiquarian bookseller in Salisbury, she had invested one shilling in a thirty-year-old biography of Eleanore of Aquitaine. She spent the afternoon reading it on a bench on the cathedral clos.

Eleanore had been the Queen consort first of Louis VII of France, then of Henry II of England. The peasants of each country contended that Eleanore had the devil's tail beneath her skirts and that, as the jargon happily put it, was how she hopped around from throne to throne.

The devil's tail, for heaven's sake! Laura nearly laughed out loud, wondering how many women in the world had slept with and married two kings.

Such thoughts amused her, as it was a poor August for finding amusement elsewhere. Earlier in the month

Chamberlain had spoken over the BBC on the recurrent Polish question. Anglo-French guarantees over Polish sovereignty would be fulfilled by force, if necessary, should Germany seize the Polish corridor and annex Danzig.

Hitler, as usual, was not to be outmaneuvered. On the previous day Germany had concluded a ten-year nonaggression pact with the Soviet Union. With one stroke of the pen, Hitler had rid himself of the specter of a two-front war with France and Britain in the West and the Soviet Union in the East. War in Europe appeared more certain than ever. And if war began, sea travel would be precarious. It might be years before Laura could return to America. A decision pressed upon her.

She returned to Salisbury Plain on a rare, partly sunny day late in the month. Out there, in God's open green fields, she felt at ease enough to think. She walked the plain by herself for the better part of an hour. The sun was confused as to seasons: it seemed more April than August. She wore a tweed skirt and cardigan, which sufficed for the day.

Laura examined her own life. She considered what a return to America offered her; she weighed her future in England.

Toward three in the afternoon, she saw a single figure strolling purposefully toward her from across the plain. Watching him as he approached, she saw that he was lean and tall, clad in a black raincoat and a hat. He had smooth easy movements and carried a walking stick, which he did not use.

She recognized his gait when he was a hundred yards from her. Peter Whiteside. Laura waited. Then a few minutes later, he was close enough so that she could see his face. Then his smile. Then his eyes. He wore the regimental tie that she recognized from her own father.

"Laura . . . my dear Laura," he said. He embraced her as they met.

"I knew you would find me, Peter," she said.

"Find you? *Find* you? Course I'd find you. My top female dispatched to America. Gets married without my blessing. Mad at me still, I'd wager." His eyes shone.

"Peter, I—"

"Don't deny it. I can tell," he said, making light of it. "When a girl doesn't write back to me, I can take a hint as well as the next man."

"The flowers were lovely," she said. He looked blank for a moment and she added, "At the wedding. The roses."

"Oh, yes. Yes. The *wedding*. I'm so glad." He held out an arm, shifting a folded *Telegraph* to his other side. "Walk with me," he offered.

She took his arm and they proceeded. Laura noticed that Peter, like her father, had aged since she had last seen him. And she noticed too that the grass was still damp, despite the day's sun. A typical Londoner out for a hike: Peter had worn the wrong shoes.

They covered several hundred meters, moving in no particular direction at all, when Laura took the initiative. "I want you to tell me about my husband," she said.

A shrewd smile crept across Peter Whiteside's face. It merged with the lines near his mouth, nose, and eyes and for a split second gave him the appearance of an aging harlequin.

277

"You have it backward, Laura, dear," he said indulgently. "It's *I* who should be asking *you* about your husband."

"You had something against him," she said. "I could tell by your reaction. You kept asking for details. Every letter you wrote you wanted to know about him. I asked my father, too. When he returned to England after the wedding, you were all over him with questions."

"My, my," Peter continued. "I have raised a clever little girl as my spy."

Laura stopped walking, stopping Peter Whiteside with her.

"Peter, don't withhold information from me."

"Laura, it's *you* who have the information. I've never met your husband."

"I want to know why his family was on your list," she said.

Whiteside held her gaze with his.

"The Fowlers are a prominent family," Whiteside said. "That's all. Influential. That's what all the names on your list are. Influential American families. That's all you were reporting to me. Very simple, very white intelligence."

"Peter, you're lying to me." She felt his uneasiness.

"There's really nothing I can tell you, Laura."

"You didn't deny that you're lying to me," she said. "Is that because you don't wish to lie a second time?"

"Laura, there's nothing for me to say. Listen to me carefully. There's nothing I *can* say. I'm certain that you're a much better judge of Stephen Fowler than I. He's your husband."

"I want to know why his family was on your list," she

278

said again.

"I'm sorry, Laura. I have nothing to tell you."

"You're such a damned bore, Peter," she snapped. "All right, then. I'm going back to America in a week. When I arrive I intend to tell my husband that British Secret Service was investigating his family."

She turned and felt his hand on her arm. It was very firm and very insistent, much stronger than she had imagined it could be.

"Laura, you'll do no such thing!" he said.

"And why not, Peter? You tell me! Why *not?*"

"You insist you don't know?" His anger rose to equal hers.

"I know nothing!"

"Very well, then," he snapped back, accepting her challenge. "The man you married happens to be an agent of the Soviet Union. Hence, the leftwing editorials. Hence, the so-called humanist Christian ruminations which we've all been treated to in print. And hence, if you'll forgive my liberties, his secretive nature and his day-to-day ramblings from one American city to another."

For a moment entire new panoramas of deceit opened to Laura: her husband was a wealthy rebel who did nurture a suspiciously Marxist heart; he had traveled the world a bit in the years before she knew him and somewhere in that time must have turned his eyes eastward to the "Russian experiment"; he had women, or worse, *one* woman, somewhere else, and them, or *her,* he truly loved; and there was no wonder that he didn't sleep with her anymore—the passion had never really been there in the first place. His marriage, like everything else, was a deceit.

Then she rejected all of it. "That's the most monstrous lie I've ever heard in my life," she said.

"Think so?"

"Yes."

"Then prove me wrong." He bit off the words. A cloud covered the sun and Peter Whiteside stolidly held forth on Salisbury Plain, quoting from memory his file on the Fowler family.

Stephen Fowler had been pink, Whiteside insisted, as long ago as his undergraduate days at Princeton. "It was during the Depression, don't forget," Whiteside said, "and that brought a lot of bright young men to some rather radical conclusions."

Capitalism had failed both the nation and the Fowler family, Whiteside clipped along, and young Stephen sought an explanation. A student of history and political science, he wished symmetry in his solution. Marxism offered it in generous doses. There was further the romanticism of the era as well as the intellectualism. Stephen obviously thrived upon both as an undergraduate of Princeton and a divinity student at Yale.

"He traveled abroad and would have you believe he was in England and France," Whiteside concluded. "Which he was, for a while. But the fact is, he made the pilgrimage. *The* pilgrimage," Whiteside repeated for emphasis. "All the way to the Kremlin wall and mother Russia itself. At that time he offered his services to Stalin's government and the offer was accepted. What he's doing in America now, I don't know, Laura. Whether he's an active agent or simply a pulpit propagandizer is another question, too. I don't know. *We* don't know. I'd wager even money that the

American authorities themselves haven't the faintest clue as to what Rev. Stephen Fowler is up to. And to some degree it might not even matter. It doesn't even mean the man is evil or even any more dishonest than the rest of us. God knows, if Hitler steps another inch in any direction, we'll all be praying for the damned Bolshevik army to step in and pin down fifty panzer divisions along the Vistula. Stephen's your husband and I hope you're happy. But you wanted to know, Laura. So I've told you."

Peter Whiteside gently released her arm. He wore an expression that almost begged her forgiveness. Her own thoughts conflicted in more ways than they came together. And there was something very awkward and very terrible about the whole moment. For several seconds she lived and breathed in limbo. She was terribly shaken and knew it.

Yet, beneath this all, there was Stephen. *Her* Stephen. What right did these men like Peter, with the agencies of government behind them, have prying into the beliefs of a New Jersey minister?

It took Laura several seconds to rally. "Damn you and all those like you, Peter," she said in remarkably civil tones. "Whatever my husband believes, it is his right to believe it. He's done nothing to you or anyone else, has he?"

Whiteside answered softly. "Not that we know."

"Then stay away from him. Let him live his life. For all I know, people like you are the reason he has to behave as he does."

She turned to walk away from him, but his hand was on her arm again. "Just one condition, Laura," Peter Whiteside said.

281

She looked at him and waited.

"We spoke in confidence," he said. "You must respect that much. We spoke in strict confidence."

"I'll give you that much, Peter," she answered. "But no more. I cherish you as a family friend. But don't come to me with any of your bloody cloak-and-dagger stuff ever again. It's a dishonorable, dirty activity. I don't like it. I refuse to take part in it."

She turned away.

"Laura . . . ?" he called as she left. "Good luck to you, Laura. I mean it. Good luck to you."

But she never looked back. She felt Peter Whiteside's eyes boring into her for several hundred yards as she hiked. Only once did she look over her shoulder and that was from a considerable distance. Peter was just a distant figure in black by then. Very small, he was, and very undistinguished and unimportant from that perspective. She was angry with herself for ever allowing him to get her so upset. What kind of world was it, after all, where grown men played such games?

She took the bus from High Street, and when she arrived home there were raindrops again. She pushed through the iron gate before her father's home and, once indoors, saw the day's post waiting for her.

The letter from Stephen was on top. She set down her book and opened it. She began to read as she walked upstairs, thinking her father might be napping.

At the top of the stairs she stopped. She reread, as if Stephen's handwriting made no sense. But it did make sense. And her old Stephen had emerged from his year-and-a-half rumination.

. . . Nothing in the world more precious than you . . . my own fault that you left me . . . more than anything else I pray for your safe and early return . . . darling, Laura . . .

The phrases leaped out at her. It was as if a prayer had been answered.

Laura yelled with joy. She ran from room to room looking for her father.

He was not in his bedroom, nor the sitting room. Her concern grew as she rushed downstairs, the letter still in her hand, and moved to his study where he often fell asleep on the couch. She still didn't see him. She ran to the music room, the conservatory, and the library.

"Papa? . . . Papa!" No answer. She returned to the front door, where he often left a note if he'd been called away suddenly. No note. And his raincoat was still on its hanger in the closet.

Frantic, she turned and looked in the kitchen in the rear of the main floor.

Then she saw her father. She stared in horror through the kitchen window and saw her father on the lawn behind the house. He was slumped in a frightful angle against one of his prized pear trees. From the distance, his face seemed ashen and lifeless, his arms at his side like those of a marionette with severed strings.

Then she was moving faster than she had ever moved in her life. She was down the back stairs to the pantry, out the back door, and across twenty yards of garden.

"No! No!" she shrieked, tears flowing down her cheeks now, mingling with the raindrops that failed to rouse her father.

Nigel Worthington did not move.

She slid to her knees beside him, embraced him, and

283

yelled again, shaking him as if to raise him from the dead, and for half of a tormented moment, she thought that was exactly what she had done.

Dr. Worthington's eyes flickered dumbly, failed to focus, wandered, then zeroed in on his daughter.

"Papa!" she cried, half a gasp, half a plea.

"What the . . . ?" he asked. He raised his arm and put it around Laura's shoulder. "Can't a man take a nap without scaring his daughter half to death?"

She was crying so hard she was laughing now, or maybe it was the other way. "No!" she said. "Not under a tree in the rain!"

He looked around. He heard the rustle of raindrops on his fruit trees.

"It doesn't rain under trees," he protested mildly. "It only rains *on* trees." He paused, rallied, wakened some more, and added, "What's Stephen got to say?" he asked. "The good-for-nothing parson wrote to you, did he?"

"He loves me, Papa!" she said. "He still loves me! I'm booking passage. I'm going home!"

Nigel Worthington hugged his daughter as hard as he could. He laughed with her in a way in which he had once laughed with her mother. Then he reminded her of something that he'd always believed; that sometimes things work out on their own.

Laura laughed with him, grinned, and nodded, now comfortable in the fact that, like Eleanore of Aquitaine, two men loved her and there were no silly rumors about the devil's tale beneath her skirts.

Or none, at least, that she had heard.

NINETEEN

I

On Monday, August 28, the German ambassadors to Belgium, Holland, and Luxembourg announced that the Third Reich would respect the sovereignty and neutrality of those countries. On Wednesday, Hitler received from Britain a warning not to attack Poland, and on Thursday, Hitler published the terms of a peace plan which he claimed Poland had rejected. In reality, the terms had never been presented.

On the same evening, Siegfried transmitted triumphantly at eleven o'clock. He no longer used the German language. Instead, he finally switched to the German naval code, a complex five-digit cipher system drawing upon a code book given him that morning by Duquaine. The book contained several thousand numerical five-digit code groups, each one representing a different word, letter, or phrase. The complete code book would have been of extreme interest to either the FBI or M.I. 6—they had been able to capture only a partial one. The entire code book might have revealed, for example, that the five-digit group for *ship* was 54734. But the book would not reveal the key to the German High Command's system of supercipherment. This was the *additive,* a second five-digit group known only to the particular spy and his spymaster. The additive might be 12121. With the additive, in such an enciphered message the word *ship* would appear as 54734 plus 12121, or 66855. Since each spy might use a different additive, the result was a virtual infinity of codes.

Siegfried prepared his message in advance. His hand was diligent upon the telegraph key. He reminded Hamburg that some handsome flowers had been planted aboard the *Adriana.* Then he added that the *Adriana* had pulled out of port the preceding evening. She was unescorted and would develop severe engine problems as soon as she reached the continental shelf. The German Navy could then pursue the matter.

Hamburg asked Siegfried if he wanted a new assignment. The spy answered that he already had given himself a grand one and added—to a long silence from the other end—that this would be his final assignment.

Hamburg replied with a clarification request. Siegfried shot back:

CLARIFICATION IN DUE COURSE. YOUR SIGNAL HOPELESS. END.

CQDXVW-2

Then Siegfried shut down, his total transmission time being ninety-seven seconds. He congratulated himself. Short and to the point. The way it should be. Siegfried loathed unnecessary risks.

"Damn!" an irate Bluebird said to another. "He's gone."

The blips had disappeared so quickly that the Bluebirds had fumbled the opportunity. The first sixty-two seconds of Siegfried's transmission had been lost while a Bluebird groped for the wire recorder. The rest had been recorded. Wheeler and Cochrane were telephoned at their homes. "We picked up the man who discusses flowers in German," a Bluebird told Cochrane over the telephone. "Or, what I mean is, sir, that we picked up his signal. Just his signal, sir."

Cochrane started to Bureau headquarters, as did Wheeler. They met on the marble steps and charged into Deciphering and Cryptology to find Hope See Ming and Lanny Slotkin furiously working cipher combinations.

"Fuckin' A!" said Lanny, a stall away from Mrs. Ming. Lanny was used to having his way with formulas. "Numbers!" he raged. "He's gone on a friggin' numerical code. This is going to be tougher than a bull's ass!"

Hope See Ming worked calmly but with equal futility. Her command of English, Cochrane noted with a certain refreshment, was highly selective, particularly when Lanny spoke.

"You're the genius, God Almighty, Lanny," Wheeler said with a sudden tension that Cochrane had not seen before. "Why can't you figure it?"

"Weren't you listening? It's a *code!*"

287

"Well, crack it anyway."

"Give me time. Give me time," Lanny Slotkin fumed. "I've never seen a scramble like this before."

"No one else has, either," Cochrane said.

Which included the Virgin Mary the next morning. "Doesn't even follow the *format* of the previous transmissions, does it?" she said. "Are you sure Monitoring transcribed it right before you brought it in here to Mary?"

Cochrane referred her directly to a wire recording. She sat, listened, nodded her white head, and tapped along with her fingers.

"Are you sure our Bluebirds had the right frequency?" she asked next.

"Too sure," Cochrane answered. Monitoring Division, he explained, knew how to monitor, after all.

"God Almighty," Wheeler added. "He was off the air so fast that they didn't even have time to *say* 'triangulation detection,' much less attempt it." Wheeler shrouded himself in white smoke from his pipe. "Think he's our bomber?" he asked.

"It's worth a try, isn't it?" Cochrane answered. "Same precision and secrecy on the air as with bombs. How many pros could be working this area, anyway?"

"Maybe a lot," Wheeler said.

"Maybe only one," Cochrane answered.

The two men stood by a sixth-floor window which overlooked the Washington Mall. City lights were long since out, but the slender Washington Monument rose like a gray finger in the reflection of the quarter moon.

"Our Siegfried's been busy lately, Bill," mused Wheeler in a low, brooding rumination. "Lots of dots and dashes. Lots of numbers that mean nothing to us and everything to him. All of Europe's going to hell and our Siegfried-boy is busy as a rooster in a barnyard." A long cone of white smoke, then: "What's he doing next?"

Bill Cochrane answered with a frustrated shrug. "I don't know," he admitted.

Friday, September 1. The German armies invaded Poland from the west. Chamberlain's government demanded that they withdraw. Luftwaffe bombers attacked Warsaw day and night while the British and French armies mobilized.

Six hundred seventy nautical miles southeast of Nantucket an enormous explosion ripped through the engine room of the HMS *Adriana*. Seven crew members, all boiler and furnace men, died in the blast. Another five were critically injured. Part of the ship was aflame for four hours, but the blaze was eventually quelled. But there was a greater problem now. There was a fissure in the center of the hull and the *Adriana* was taking on water. There was a red alert on board, and help from the nearest American port remained two days away in choppy seas.

On Saturday, September 2, a civilian evacuation of London began. And on Sunday, September 3, England and France declared war on Nazi Germany. So when dawn broke in the northwest Atlantic Ocean that same morning, the *Adriana* was officially a ship of a combatant nation.

A German U-boat lined her up from a distance of two miles. The *Adriana*'s sonar had occasionally picked up the submarine since ten hours out of Red

Bank. But now the hobbled frigate was helpless and the U-boat advanced for the kill. Audaciously, the German submarine commander pulled to within a half mile of his prey, knowing the British vessel had no defense.

Then six torpedoes were launched.

The first hit the *Adriana* in the stern, almost squarely in the rudder. It blew out the entire screw propeller and rocked the ship mercilessly with the subsequent explosion. The *Adriana* convulsed first with fire, then with water. The panic among the crew would have spread in all directions, except it didn't have time.

A second of the six torpedoes found its mark, blasting the *Adriana* at the midpoint on the port side, thirty feet below the waterline. The explosion blew the ship sideways in the water and left a wound as wide as ten trucks in the frigate's side. The damage would have been enough to sink the *Adriana* by itself, but the weakened hull was in no condition to withstand the vibrations of the hit, either. Thus the second torpedo had the effect of breaking the ship in two, as the entire hull began to go. Fuel leaked into the fires left by the dual explosions and then there were further smaller explosions. Then there was black smoke everywhere, and suddenly the bow of the ship was raising itself toward the lightening morning sky, and then there was one final shattering explosion brought on by another torpedo. The ship blew into more pieces than anyone aboard would ever be able to comprehend.

There was no time for lifeboats. The *Adriana* capsized within five minutes and went under, like a child's toy in a boat pond, within nine. The entire crew of 186 English seamen, plus seven British and two American civilians, went down with her.

In Washington on Monday evening, Bill Cochrane was in the living room of his new quarters. He sat in shirt sleeves and his suit pants in a faded armchair, a brandy by his side and his arms folded behind his aching, sorrowful head. He thought of the three sailors he had seen in Union Station. They would have done better, he thought, to have gotten so drunk that they never could have found their ship again.

He turned on the Philco console at one minute after nine. The President of the United States came on the air with what had been announced previously as "an extraordinary message to the American people."

In truth, it was. France and Great Britain were finally at war with the little Austrian corporal and his Thousand Year Reich. Roosevelt, speaking from the White House, asked for "an adjournment of all partisanship and selfishness," and asked that Americans join together to work toward "a true neutrality" which would "keep this newest world war from the western hemisphere."

The President added that he could not, however, expect every American to be neutral in thoughts. "A neutral," Franklin Roosevelt concluded, "cannot be asked to close his mind or his conscience."

"I know what that means," Bill Cochrane spoke aloud to the console. And he saw the old alliances from the First Great War drifting slowly back into place. And then for another moment he was a boy again, skipping stones into the Rivanna River when his own father went off to war.

Each new generation, he thought, fails to learn from

the one before.

J. Edgar Hoover was also very good at grasping Roosevelt's meanings, particularly when beckoned anew to the White House the next day. Roosevelt had allotted ten minutes for Hoover, less if possible.

The President was livid. The *Adriana* had been in touch by shortwave with the British Naval Chancellery at Foggy Bottom in the hours between her crippling and her annihilation.

There was little question that the *Adriana* had been sabotaged on American shores and German naval intelligence had known. A submarine had been sent specifically to stalk and kill her after she left port.

"And you know, of course, J. Edgar," said Roosevelt, his face already drawn with tension, "the only way the German Navy could have known that quickly would have been by wireless."

"That's correct, Mr. President," Hoover answered.

Roosevelt looked up from his desk. He wore a gray cardigan sweater belonging to his son; his eyes were drawn and haggard. "J. Edgar," he said. "If you think this is beyond the scope of your Bureau, other arrangements could be made."

Hoover's response was chilly. "I assure you, Mr. President, that our field agents should be very close to a resolution by now."

"See that it's resolved quickly," Roosevelt concluded. "Or I'll expect your resignation. That's all."

It was the moment to shake Hamburg to its foundations. Siegfried leaned into his transmission key a few moments past eleven on Wednesday. He gave Hamburg a coded lesson in American civics:

MY ASSESSMENT OF U.S. POLITICS AS FOLLOWS: THERE IS ONLY ONE ROOSEVELT. AMERICANS HAVE NO OTHER LEFTIST PRO-JEWISH PRO-BRITISH LEADER OF SIGNIFICANCE. PREDICT CONFIDENTLY THAT REMOVAL OF ROOSEVELT WOULD RESULT IN NEW ADMINISTRATION EITHER NOW OR AFTER 1940 ELECTION MORE AMICABLE TO NEW ORDER OF GERMAN NATIONAL SOCIALISM, OR AT LEAST TO HISTORIC AMERICAN ISOLATIONISM. IN THIS MANNER, AMERICANS CAN BE EFFECTIVELY KEPT FROM JOINING EUROPEAN WAR.

Siegfried grinned. He pictured the reactions of those thick-browed Gestapo dolts at AOR-3. Then he fired off his conclusion.

CAN EASILY PLANT FLOWERS FROM BERLIN FOR PRESIDENT F.D. ROOSEVELT. SEEK PERMISSION FROM NO ONE LOWER THAN THE FUEHRER HIMSELF BEFORE I PROCEED. END.

CQDXVW-2

Siegfried relaxed and treated himself to a Pall Mall. Almost forty-five seconds expired before his receiver was alive with a response from Hamburg. Siegfried grinned at the jittery dots and dashes.

"The frightened little Gestapo assholes," he cursed to himself, blowing out a long stream of smoke.

Hamburg began,

DO NOT HAVE AUTHORITY TO ASSIGN—

Siegfried angrily whirled from his receiver to his transmission key. God, how these underlings could waste precious time! He slashed into their message:

I AM NOT SEEKING YOUR PERMISSION, YOU INCOMPETENT MORONS! WILL PROCEED ONLY ON DIRECT PERSONAL ORDERS OF ADOLPH HITLER. OBTAIN SAID PERMISSION THROUGH APPROPRIATE GESTAPO CHANNELS! AWAITING RESPONSE SUNDAY NIGHT. END.

CQDXVW-2

Siegfried boldly leaned back from his key, his shoulders square and erect. He stared at the receiver. Not a whimper from Hamburg. It was about time they learned who was in control. About time, indeed.

Siegfried's entire transmission had come in clear as a bell and the Bluebirds had a complete recording. Cochrane, who had come up corpse-cold in his responses from twelve chiefs of urban bomb units, oversaw the Bluebirds' progress, then oversaw everyone in Cryptology as they tried to distill Siegfried's anguishing blips.

"Mary Ryan has been in this repulsive business for a long time," Mary Ryan said with pride late on Thursday, "and she has never seen a cipher like this one. Alphabet soup, that's what it is. Heavy on the boiled pork and roast potatoes."

Cochrane nodded. The Virgin Mary remained at her desk. Cochrane went by Bobby Charles Martin's cell in Section Seven. Together, Cochrane and the cartographer from Ohio spread out a huge map of the states of New Jersey, New York, and Pennsylvania. Martin, creeping forward with the minimal new results obtained from triangulation, motioned with his finger and drew a circle with a fifty-mile radius around the area of New Jersey just south of New York City.

"He's somewhere in here," the former Ohio state trooper announced solemnly. "But that's all I can say."

A few minutes later, Wheeler passed Cochrane in the hallway. "Hoover's still screaming bloody murder," Wheeler said routinely as he passed. "I can keep him at bay for another couple of days."

Mr. Hay chose that moment to pass both of them in the hallway, concealing a lit cigarette in his palm. He knew better than to even look up.

It was Hermann Goering, himself, founder of the Gestapo and currently Minister of the Air Force, who had the pleasure of passing along the report from the nervous Hamburg station to Hitler.

War meetings at 9 A.M. were common in early September. Each day the Wehrmacht made extraordinary progress in every direction, pulverizing anything that stood in its way. The Luftwaffe, meanwhile, softened any potential resistance through its merciless aerial bombardment. Already, Warsaw was in ruins, Danzig had been taken, and Hitler had received ebullient reports on a potentially swift victory in

France and a tougher but eventual victory over the Royal Air Force.

Goering found Hitler in the map room of the Berlin Chancellery. Hitler wore a gray shirt, black tie, black trousers, and the mandatory armband. Goering noticed for the first time since he had ever known Hitler that the Fuehrer's eyes looked drawn and tired.

There were a dozen men there, cabinet members and generals, to discuss war preparations. The mood of the men in the room, considering Nazi successes in the field and in the air, was suitably cheerful.

Goering waited until noon when the meeting was adjourned and when all others had departed. Then he spoke privately to Hitler. He showed him the record of transmissions from AOR-3 in Hamburg. He recounted the successes of Siegfried in the United States.

Hitler's eyes narrowed and sparkled at the same time. "Ah, yes," he said in his soft Austrian whine, "you have spoken of this man before." Hitler scanned the previous successes of the agent in America. Hitler's eyebrows were raised. "He has sunk two English ships? Once by himself, once with the help of our Navy."

"He has always succeeded in whatever he has tried. I'm sure the Fuehrer recalls the bombing in Birmingham, England, a few years ago."

"Ah, yes. Of course." Hitler's eyes were merry.

"And now," Goering continued, nodding to the report before them, "he proposes—"

"I see what he proposes," Hitler said softly. He pursed his rosy lips. "Do you think this is possible?"

Goering quoted. "'Americans have no other . . . leader of significance,'" he said slowly in German. "Can easily plant flowers from Berlin for President F.D.

296

Roosevelt.' The man has never yet been wrong," Goering said.

Hitler still considered it. "Where did we find this man?" he asked.

"We didn't, Mein Fuehrer," Goering said. "He came to us. He is completely outside all of our services. If we authorize him to proceed, then even we cannot stop—"

"Completely outside?" Hitler asked abruptly, looking Goering in the eye. "Then he could never be conclusively traced to us?"

"No, Mein Fuehrer."

"Then let us wish him luck," Hitler concluded. He reached for a fountain pen with a brisk single movement of his ivory-hued wrist.

Hitler had entertained a savage hatred of Roosevelt since 1937 when the American President had made a speech in Chicago urging a world "quarantine of dictators and aggressors." Hitler had taken that speech to have been aimed directly at him—which it only partially had been—and had since borne Roosevelt nothing but venom. Hitler insisted that Roosevelt was partially Jewish and attributed all of Roosevelt's actions to "this basic fact." Now he initialed with great fervor a document which would dispatch a homicidal Siegfried toward Roosevelt.

"Let us hope this will be the end of that cripple in the White House," Hitler muttered, withdrawing his pen. "You know, of course, Goering, that Roosevelt suffers from syphilitic paralysis, not infantile paralysis."

"Of course, Mein Fuehrer," Goering answered.

He clapped the file shut and raised his hand in a salute. Hitler returned to his battle maps. Goering was halfway out the door when Hitler, almost as an afterthought, jerked his head up.

"Goering!" he shrieked suddenly.

The Air Minister turned.

"It is more urgent than ever that we obtain a victory in England before the Americans become involved." Hitler motioned toward the folder in Goering's hand. "This 'Siegfried' is more crucial than ever. See that he succeeds."

"We will do everything to assist him," Goering said. Then he saluted again, turned, and departed. That evening in his radio chamber, four thousand miles to the west, Siegfried rejoiced in the unqualified authorization from Berlin that he had dreamed of for years:

PROCEED!
ADOLF HITLER

PART FIVE

September-
October
1939

TWENTY

"Not very pretty to look at, Mr. Cochrane, sir," said Chief Martin Kugler of the Red Bank, New Jersey, Police Department. The two men stepped from a rusting green and white police car on the side of the road. Nearby there already stood an entire delegation of police vehicles. Men in various uniforms—local police, county sheriff's office, state police—stood with folded arms and waited. Police Chief Martin Kugler led Cochrane through a trail in the woods. The ground steamed with unexpected September heat, and a cloud of gnats pursued them.

Kugler's tones were apologetic. "We knew a boy was missing from the navy yard, but they get AWOL's all the time. Generally they turn up a thousand miles away at their parents' home. Wish it had been the same with this one, right?"

"Right," Cochrane mumbled, looking ahead. Kugler's waddling, measured steps set the pace. The police chief was a squat, sincere, balding little man with thick arms, an imposing paunch, and a .45 that hung like a cannon at his left side. This was Chief Kugler's second homicide in nine years, and the first that didn't fit into a neat pattern of victim-knowing-killer. He and Cochrane neared a group of men standing around a body in the center of the woods. Kugler continued. "We read all the FBI circulars, you know. Read them carefully. Think they had your name on them."

"They did," Cochrane answered.

"Well, you know. Since the *Adriana* we been looking for anything funny around here. Then this morning two kids are playing in the woods and they find this."

Billy Pritchard's corpse was in a middle stage of decomposition. The skin was dark and ulcerated, the teeth horribly accentuated by the rotting flesh of the lips, and the hair matted badly from dirt and rain. The entire corpse crawled with insects.

Cochrane stared. The body of an American boy in his underclothes was more real than a thousand ships exploding at sea.

Kugler stared also. The last few hours had been unpleasantly unique in his experience.

First the body had been discovered in the woods. He'd immediately filed the homicide report with the state police in Trenton. The state police—noting the proximity of the body to the navy yard, that an American sailor was still AWOL, and the events surrounding the *Adriana*—called it in to Washington.

Moments later, Chief Kugler had found himself talking long distance to someone named Special Agent Cochrane who wanted more of the specifics.

"See, I don't want to make something out of nothing, Mr. Cochrane, sir," Kugler had offered, "but the boy's uniform is gone. Now, you know that British boat that

302

blew up? I was thinking . . ."

"Don't touch anything," answered Cochrane. "I'll be there in three hours."

Cochrane telephoned the Newark Bureau office and asked for two special agents, Mike Cianfrani and Jim Hearn—whom Cochrane knew from New York—to be placed on local special assignment. As Cochrane took a taxi to Washington's Union Station, Cianfrani and Hearn took their own car to Red Bank to safeguard the crime scene.

Kugler broke the deep silence that enshrouded the dead sailor. "God awful hot out here, ain't it?" the police chief said. "Goddamn. Poor kid. Body stinks to high hell."

"How do you know it's the sailor?" Cochrane asked, still looking down. The eye sockets were dark and discolored.

"Dog tags." Kugler motioned toward what used to be the boy's neck.

"Yes," said Cochrane softly, seeing the flat gray shape of something metal. "Of course."

"That's all that was touched here, sir," Kugler rushed to reassure. "Absolutely all. Rest of the area's as virgin as a Girl Scout tea party."

"I'm sure," Cochrane muttered.

Cianfrani and Hearn supervised the search of the area.

Meanwhile, Cochrane excused himself to wander the area on his own. He had seen enough of the victim. The local police placed a sheet across the corpse. Moments later, Cochrane heard a body bag unzipping.

Cochrane walked farther into the woods, looking for the odd item—a scrap of cloth, a bottle, a button, *anything*—which might yield a fingerprint or a clue. He found nothing.

The gnats pursued him but his thoughts focused upon Billy Pritchard. It was doubtful that the young man had been taken to the woods and strangled. So where had the crime been committed? And why? Had Siegfried simply wanted a uniform to gain access to the *Adriana?* Or was this homicide one of those maddening coincidences that send a detective in the wrong direction for months? Cochrane pondered as he continued to walk. He saw a clearing ahead and, when he reached it, was surprised to come upon an old gravel and dirt parking lot. He stood perfectly still for a full minute and stared at the abandoned diner and the lonesome telephone booth.

He took a few more steps forward and noted that a road wound down the other side of the hill toward Red Bank. "Accessible by car," he said to himself. Then he walked back to where Billy Pritchard's remains were now in a yellow canvas body bag on a stretcher.

Chief Kugler, looking more and more shaken, glanced up to Cochrane. "Don't get much of this around here," said the police chief. "This is a family region. Worst thing that'll normally happen is a man'll take a deer out of season."

"This incident didn't happen, Chief," Cochrane said. "The boys who made this discovery actually found a wino sleeping in the woods. That's all."

Several heads turned.

"Oh, well, that's just dandy," Chief Kugler snapped. "As soon as the county medical examiner gets the body—"

"The corpse is going to Newark for a postmortem.

FBI forensics lab." Cochrane nodded to Cianfrani and Hearn. "Twelve hours should be sufficient for a thorough autopsy. If there are any doubts or delays, this is upon the authority of J. Edgar Hoover's office. Any questions?"

There weren't.

Two state troopers accompanied the Newark agents down the hill with the yellow canvas bag. Cochrane turned back to Kugler.

"Did this Pritchard boy have friends?" Cochrane asked.

"A boatload. Down at the yard." Kugler paused. "Parents, too."

"I'll start with the friends," Cochrane answered.

What emerged that afternoon was a portrait of a homesick, clean-cut, dutiful young naval officer, half-man and half-boy, and totally naïve to the malevolence of the world beyond Kansas.

"Is he dead?" asked one shipmate. Cochrane was at home with the lie. "This is a standard investigation. Ensign Pritchard is AWOL from a sensitive installation. Now, perhaps," Cochrane nudged firmly, "you could recall your friend's daily routine . . . ?"

At Reilly's, Pritchard's friend recalled, the young man liked to hobnob with the local females, and even shoot a round of darts with some of the English sailors, to whom he always lost.

"A terrible dart player!" another of Pritchard's friends remarked. "The worst in the house."

"Second worst," Buck Reilly, the bartender and owner, recalled that evening as he removed the padlock from his front doors and opened for business. "The worst was Pritchard's pal. The old man."

"What old man?" Cochrane asked.

"Elmer," said Buck Reilly, his ham-hock arms swinging at his sides as Cochrane followed. "And come to think of it, he's disappeared, too."

Cochrane took up a place at the end of the bar. "Elmer who?" he asked.

"I don't know Elmer who," said Reilly. "I don't learn last names unless a customer is behind on his tab. Elmer used to hang around here at nights."

"Continue," Cochrane asked.

Reilly blew his breath into a glass and polished the glass with his apron. "Well, he was an old guy. I don't know how old, but he said he fought in the last war. Tall, but up a bit. Sallow complexion. Gray hair. Looked like a thousand other old men."

"Nothing strange about him?"

"Not that I recall."

"How did he get here?"

"What? To the bar?"

"Yes."

"Damned if I know."

"You never saw a car? Or a bicycle?"

"No, but I wouldn't have. Hey, I'm busy serving when this place is open. Stay around. You'll see."

"If he didn't live around here, he couldn't have walked," Cochrane said. "Particularly if he was old."

Reilly shrugged. "Now you tell me something," he said.

"If I can."

"Is Rosenfeld going to get us into the war? He *is,* isn't he? Franklin D. Rosenfeld?"

"I only work for the FBI," Cochrane answered, a sudden fatigue overtaking him. "I've never been to the White House."

"Seems to me there's still eleven thousand Americans buried in France from the last war," Reilly said. "And for what? Know what I think? I think Mussolini is just what the dagos deserve. I can't buy a drop of liquor in New Jersey without paying something to the Don Macaronis. I hear Mussolini put them all out of business in Italy. That's why they all come here. And as for Hitler . . . *as for Hitler,*" he repeated for emphasis, "well if there's anything worse than the Jews it's those filthy fucking English. So I say, let Adolph eat them both alive."

Cochrane felt anger swelling inside him and didn't understand how he suppressed it. Maybe it was professionalism, because his overwhelming instinct was to knock the flinty-eyed Reilly squarely in the jaw.

Instead, he flipped shut the palm-sized notebook in which he'd been writing and recognized that it was time to leave. To his abiding shame, he answered Reilly. "Who knows, Buck? Maybe you're right."

A pair of brutal thunderclaps toward five in the afternoon shook the very foundations of everything that was standing. There followed a few heartbeats later a deluge and all Cochrane could think about was, *There goes any clue that we missed in the woods this morning.* Cochrane had taken refuge in a Red Bank guest house.

He sighed and a depression was upon him. Billy Pritchard was dead needlessly as were scores of other people. Cochrane bought an afternoon Newark *Star,* and lost himself in the sports. Not surprisingly, the Senators had been thrashed a second day in a row by the formidable Yankees: home runs by DiMaggio, Keller, and Henrich. Then he found himself laughing out loud.

DiMaggio, Keller, and Henrich. Wait till he told Hoover, he fantasized. An Axis connection on the New York Yankees!

The rain continued. Mike Cianfrani telephoned from Newark in the evening.

"The killer used a hard, flexible tool. There were scars on the neck," said Cianfrani. "Strangled the Pritchard kid."

Cochrane lay restlessly in bed much of the night. A sense of Siegfried was beginning to emerge:

A six-foot German. Young. Strong. A talent with makeup, explosives, and probably dialects, too. The man had a car. He could work ably with a wireless and was privy to a complex code. Cochrane was certain that young Pritchard had been lured from Reilly's, murdered, conveyed to the parking lot, and dumped in the woods.

On his way back to Washington, a vision of Bobby Charles Martin, the cartographer, was before Cochrane. He thought back to the circles Martin had drawn on the maps of New Jersey, courtesy of the Bluebirds' triangulation.

Red Bank was within the circle. The saboteur had spied on the United States Navy by day and transmitted to Germany at night. Cozy, Cochrane concluded. FDR would be apoplectic.

Cochrane returned to his office and telephoned

Newark again, ordering reports of the Pritchard slaying to be sent to all town police chiefs in northern New Jersey, as well as the chief homicide investigators of all principal cities between Washington and Boston. Somewhere, Cochrane prayed, the Pritchard killing might strike a parallel with something else. Moments later, Dick Wheeler lumbered into Cochrane's office.

"Hoover's called a meeting for Monday morning," Wheeler said. "The Chief wants all the Indians present. All three of us tribe members. You, me, Lerrick." Wheeler curled an upper lip. So did Cochrane.

"Now, more bad news," Wheeler added. "For you, that is."

"Let's have it."

"The LKW you requested. Last Known Whereabouts of one Otto Mauer."

"Yes?"

"No can do," Wheeler answered. "The Bureau slapped a red tag on them just forty-eight hours ago. From your own happy days working with that smelly little gnome up in the seventh-floor archives, you know what that means."

"Removed to Hoover's own personal files," said Bill Cochrane.

"Where they will probably sit until icicles hang in hell," surmised Wheeler. A pensive silence shrouded them both, then Wheeler concluded. "Monday morning early," he reminded Cochrane. "Second floor conference room."

Wheeler left and Cochrane suddenly felt himself very alone. The sensation made him think of Heather.

He stared out the window for a moment. That odd question was upon him again. If she came back for five minutes, what would he say?

I've missed you . . .

I love you . . .

I've been given the goddamnedest problem, and I cannot solve it . . .

"Then you had better keep working on it," he could almost hear her answer in her proper, magnolia-scented way. "Work comes first. Fun comes later."

But, Cochrane recalled, there would be no fun. Not today. Mourning ends, he reminded himself. Pain sometimes doesn't. He sympathized with the family of Billy Pritchard, who that day was attending the twenty-two-year-old's funeral. The burial was in Kansas, where Berlin was something very distant. All the Pritchard family knew was that their son was dead. On the death certificate the circumstances had been "redefined," as Bureau parlance tactfully put it. Mike Cianfrani, from the Newark office, had taken care of everything.

Billy Pritchard had died, the report said, when a stockpiled harbor mine had accidentally been detonated. The military was dangerous even in peacetime, the family was begged to understand. And these things did occur on the odd occasion.

TWENTY-ONE

I

The powwow was scheduled for 8 A.M., Monday. In actuality, it was a war party.

Cochrane arrived at twenty to eight. The building was quiet. The door to Hoover's office was closed. But Cochrane had seen both Hoover's and Clyde Tolson's cars outside in the lot. The Director was lurking somewhere.

Cochrane entered the conference room and found Dick Wheeler already seated. "J.E.H. is furious this morning," Wheeler said. "Keep your wits about you."

Wheeler removed his pipe from his breast pocket, skewered the stem with a green pipe cleaner, and set it down on the table near an ashtray. "Just give me enough room to talk when I need to," Wheeler warned. "J.E.H. listens to me, don't forget."

Cochrane settled into a chair. "What's going on?" he asked.

"We have company. From the executive branch."

Wheeler grimaced and they both heard the door from Hoover's office open across the corridor. There were voices, including Hoover's.

A pulsebeat later the door opened fully. Wheeler and Cochrane were on their feet as Hoover entered in a brisk, energetic shuffle. The Director wore a fiercer scowl than usual, and his cheeks and brow were florid. He looked angry, particularly when he spotted Cochrane. But then again, he always looked angry from a distance of fifty feet or less.

Frank Lerrick was with him and handled the introduction of a third man: tall and thin, with a squat, pug nose and big ears that almost seemed to flop. His name was Russell Middlebrook and he was an undersecretary of state. Cordell Hull's office was to be kept informed of progress in the case, Lerrick announced. Middlebrook took a place between Lerrick and Wheeler. At the table he gave no more than a nod in Cochrane's direction and settled in with a pad of paper and a pencil.

"He's a creep," Wheeler would announce with a contemptuous grin to Cochrane in a later, lighter moment. "Over at State they refer to him as 'Rabbit.' Went to Penn State University and took the right exams. What can you expect? He's second-string. If there's such a thing as simultaneously honest and untrustworthy, he's it. Big ears, get it? Mouth to match."

"Okay, okay," said Hoover waspishly after the introductions. "Let's get started." It was ten of eight. Hoover nodded toward Cochrane, who was expected to summarize activity since the previous meeting.

"A great deal of positive progress," Cochrane began.

"Have we made an arrest yet?" Hoover demanded.

A pause, then Cochrane answered, "We have a portrait emerging of a key suspect." For several minutes, he provided details.

There followed a long glacial silence with which no one seemed inclined to tamper. "We cannot arrest a *profile,* young Agent Cochrane," Hoover scolded. "How many more targets do we allow this man? How many ships do we lose?" Without stopping, the director shifted his own gears. "How long have you been on this case?"

"Six weeks, sir."

"Six weeks," Hoover repeated flatly. "And in six weeks you've managed to draw a profile." Cochrane held his own indignation in check as Hoover bore ahead. "You were taken off a relatively easy assignment in Baltimore. You should have been well rested. Do you know that I have a meeting with the President early this very afternoon. Mr. Roosevelt is going to ask me for a progress report. Apparently there isn't one." Hoover glared, set down a pencil across the table with a loud clack, and let go with his characteristic low, whining curses.

"Jesus Christ," he wheezed. "Jesus, Jesus, Jesus," he said. His eyes bulged, his cheeks rouged and his lips tightened. Ruddy-faced and angry, he looked like a deranged Mr. Toad of Toad Hall. His puffy eyes then darted to each of the other men at the table for help or sympathy.

Dick Wheeler, who knew better than ever to interrupt, had been waiting for just such a silence to rescue Cochrane.

"I think, Mr. Director," Wheeler suggested mildly,

"that the President will be very impressed with the Bureau's progress over the last few days. I've reviewed it myself," emphasized Wheeler, who hadn't reviewed it at all. "I think a written summation of Bureau progress should be represented to the President. I think we can also safely state that we're extremely close to the key arrest."

Cochrane shot Wheeler a beseeching glance but Wheeler's eyes were upon Hoover.

"Are we? *Are we?*" asked Hoover in his rushed, clipped voice. He looked at Cochrane without allowing him to answer. "Well, all right. Much better." He looked back to Wheeler.

"I think we have enough to please the President," Wheeler said.

"Who'll make the report?" Hoover asked. "I want this agent"—he indicated Cochrane with a sharp nod of the skull—"still out in the field. No point to take a fieldman to the White House."

"I'd be happy to make the presentation," Wheeler offered. Frank Lerrick looked at Wheeler with vexation.

"All right," Hoover agreed. "A report. Something in writing that we can both present verbally and submit." Lerrick's small intense eyes still glowed like simmering charcoal in Wheeler's direction as Hoover spoke. Hoover turned to Lerrick and the red glow vanished. "That sounds good to you, Frank? One o'clock."

"Very good, Mr. Director," Lerrick said with enthusiasm.

"I think this field agent, Mr. Cochrane, has done excellent work," Wheeler continued, soothingly. "I'd stake the reputation of my own office upon Mr.

Cochrane's work."

Hoover seemed pleased by, or at least content with, the endorsement. His mood now mellowed considerably.

Undersecretary Middlebrook was taking short, precise notes—much to Cochrane's unease—and Frank Lerrick just watched and listened with his arms folded. J. Edgar Hoover looked absently to Frank Lerrick and then across to Wheeler. Everyone in the room knew the director had something on his mind. J. Edgar Hoover had, as Dick Wheeler had once termed it privately, "his own cute ways of doing things."

"I think some arrests should be made," Hoover announced portentously.

A silence held the room. Hoover spoke from the throne:

"Yes. I think maybe a dozen or so arrests should be made. German-Americans. Hit the Bunds in New York and Chicago. Let them know we're still alive." He turned back to Lerrick. "Can CAR Division come up with a dozen to twenty names by noon?" he asked. "I want the President to know that we're making a sweep."

"It can be done," Frank Lerrick answered, making note of it.

"Sir?" Cochrane interrupted. Hoover looked his way. "With all due respect, I think any arrests at this time would be a particularly bad idea."

"You think that, do you?" Hoover retorted, his eyes tightening.

"I've been through Central Alien Registry myself," Cochrane explained. "No names stand out. I'd even guess that the man we want is not in CAR Division's

315

files. Random arrests will only alert the other side."

Hoover's fingers were drumming the table. Persistent tapping in the same spot.

Hoover's little eyes darted around the room. "Other opinions?" Hoover challenged.

"The arrests can be made by, uh, this evening," Frank Lerrick chimed in solidly.

Hoover looked to Dick Wheeler, whose eyes narrowed dreamily as he worked his pipe between clenched teeth. A slight sucking noise emanated from the briar. "I think some arrests might be in order," Wheeler agreed. "Flex a little muscle. Show Old Glory to the swastika set. Read them the riot act."

Cochrane felt the conversation exclude him. "Wasn't there a Portuguese or Spanish operation out of Yorkville?" Hoover asked. "Didn't I see a report on that recently?"

"That's correct, sir," Wheeler answered.

"Well, that's one that we can roll up for starters," Hoover commanded. "Then see what else is around."

"Done, Chief," Lerrick said.

"Now," the Director concluded, "if there isn't anything else . . . I have another meeting this morning."

The seat of Hoover's suit had just taken leave from his chair when Cochrane again interrupted.

"Yes, there is one thing," Cochrane said.

Half-up, Hoover eased back down. "What?" Hoover inquired tartly.

"I need permission from the Director to use a source currently unavailable to me."

Hoover frowned. Cochrane forged on.

"This Bureau apparently repatriated a German defector. A man named Otto Mauer, whom I used as a

316

source in Germany."

"A German?" Hoover asked with an odd blend of xenophobia and surprise. "A *German?*" he repeated. There was a stark, telling silence after Hoover's second exclamation.

"We have Mauer in the relocation program, Mr. Director," Wheeler said flatly. "There's a red tag on his file, meaning it's inaccessible to field agents."

"Without specific permission of the director of the FBI," Cochrane added. "Which is what I'm requesting."

"You're requesting permission to break the rules?" Hoover asked with the intonation of a statement. "Permission denied."

"Sir," Cochrane tried again, "the infor—"

Hoover's eyes shot upward from the desk. "Permission *denied!*" Hoover blurted again. "Did you fail to hear me the first time? Rules are rules!"

"It is absolutely vital," Cochrane answered, "that I find out everything possible on Abwehr or Gestapo structure within the United States. We have no other trustworthy defectors. Mauer will talk. He's been a solid, unimpeachable source since the first day I—"

Hoover looked like a hammer in search of an anvil. "Agent Cochrane," Hoover interrupted. "I run the cleanest, most honest police agency in the world. I'll not have it rely on a . . . a"—Hoover sputtered slightly and searched for just the right word—"a German," he concluded. Then, nodding toward Cochrane, he issued his instructions to Dick Wheeler. "He may leave now," J. Edgar Hoover said.

Cochrane left first and Wheeler hulked after him.

The latter caught Cochrane on the marble steps outside on Constitution Avenue.

"Well, I warned you," Wheeler said, falling into stride beside Cochrane. "I tried to take the heat off you."

Cochrane cast him a sidelong glance and continued to walk. "You put the heat *on* me, Dick," he said.

"On? How?"

Cochrane stopped and turned to face Wheeler. Wheeler, an inch or two taller, looked downward and peered through his pipe smoke. "This fiction of being near an arrest. How can you put me on the spot like that?"

"Had to, old man."

"Had to, how?"

"I've been in Bureau headquarters more than a few years now, Bill," Wheeler answered. "I know how to deal with the Chief. Look, Hoover always has to think a resolution is close. Otherwise he brings in a new team. That means you go back to Baltimore."

"Not a chance. That means I'd retire. Become a banker again."

To Cochrane's surprise, Wheeler only shrugged. "That would be your own choice. The only indispensable man in Washington these days is Roosevelt."

"I'll be sure to tell Hoover you said so," Cochrane retorted.

"Bill, don't be an ass."

"Further, I need Mauer. Where is he? Do you know?"

"You don't need him," Wheeler insisted. "Are you forgetting? The man is a Nazi. Worse, he's a defector. Last time you dealt with him you were lucky to get away alive. Take some free advice, Bill. On something as vital as this, how can you believe a man who already betrayed his own country?"

"He's never betrayed me," Cochrane countered.

"Rules are rules."

"That never bothered you in Kansas City."

"That was Kansas City and that's all over with. I now know better."

"Then I'll find Mauer on my own."

Cochrane drew away from Wheeler on the sidewalk but Wheeler reached to him and held his arm, not in confrontation, but as a friend might. "Bill, look," he offered. "Please understand." Cochrane stopped and turning back, albeit with mounting irritation. "You have to understand about J. Edgar Hoover. When he came into this agency in 1924, it was a corrupt little federal cop outfit operating out of a converted warehouse—the type of thing you'd get in some small hot banana republic in Central America. Say anything you want about the man, but he built this Bureau. He wants it spic and span. His greatest fear is that his FBI will have a moral relapse. If it did, a lifetime of his work would go down the tubes."

Cochrane tried to find the rationale. But he wanted Mauer. "Those are great excuses and a masterful apology for the man. Dick, you must be fabulous raising funds over on Capitol Hill."

"I'll take that as a compliment, Bill, because I'm not givng you Otto Mauer's new name or location. Hoover is intelligent and honest. He has reasons for his rules. You have to work around them."

"So we have a spy out there, a killer. He can do anything he wishes. But I have to deal with rules."

Wheeler shrugged his shoulders. "Fascist methods versus democratic methods, Bill," Wheeler reminded him. "In the long run, which do you really prefer? Honestly now?"

Wheeler kept a hand on Cochrane's elbow until he felt it safe to release it. He looked at the younger man half as a chiding uncle, half as an older brother.

Cochrane seethed quietly. "Do you think Hoover is pro-Fascist?" Cochrane asked at length, cooling slightly.

"What the devil makes you ask *that?*"

"Answer me."

"No, I don't think he's pro-Fascist. He's just a goddamned born-and-bred Washington Republican."

"What about Lerrick?"

Wheeler laughed. "A card-carrying New Dealer from Illinois. Same as me, except I'm from Missouri. You want pro-Fascists, I'll find you some in the Senate, lurking like a nest of copperheads. Or in the House, where there's about a hundred. Or do you want the more visible ones—Colonel Lindbergh. Ambassador Kennedy. Huey Long. The Silver Shirts. What the hell are you getting at, Bill?"

Several thoughts came together at once: thoughts about Hoover, security, fascism and socialism, communism and democracies, loyalties and betrayals. But Bill Cochrane gave voice to none of them. Instead he sighed disgustedly.

"Know what I think?" Wheeler confided. "I think you should take a day off. Collect your thoughts. Get your mind back on the right course. God knows, Bill, no man can eat and sleep this stuff with no respite. Do

320

us all a favor. Take the day. Please. I'll cover for you."

Prompted by such enticements from an immediate superior, Cochrane took up Wheeler's offer. It was as good a way as any of disappearing for a few hours, then circling back to Bureau headquarters while Wheeler was in the Oval Office on Pennsylvania Avenue.

Cochrane wandered the sixth floor in an ostensibly jovial mood and buttonholed one Bluebird after another, taking them into his confidence. Those he could trust, at least. There was Lanny Slotkin first and then the two house-brand Germans, Roddy Schwarzkopf and Elizabeth Pfeiffer. Then of course there was the Virgin Mary and even Bobby Charles Martin, whom Cochrane found reading an ominous report on Gestapo interrogation techniques.

To each, when drawn aside, he made a grinning offer. "I'd like you to help me in a little intrigue," he said. "Consider it a game. Office politics, really. So don't speak to anyone who's not in on it."

Each accepted the challenge. And each was equally nonplused to learn that the victim of the intrigue was known to all and stood a full, towering forty-six inches tall.

II

Laura lay in bed beside her husband in the bedroom of their home. Stephen's eyes were closed; Laura's were open. He breathed evenly. She could not sleep. Her mind was teeming with the events of the day.

Laura quietly pulled the sheet off and stepped from the bed. The room was cool and she had no clothes on. She reached to the cotton robe and pulled it on. Sometimes when she couldn't sleep, it helped to walk around.

She went to the dormer window of the bedroom and sat on the plum-colored cushions on the bench within the window. Laura loved that view of sleepy Liberty Circle. She could see the stars, the moon, and the trees. The church across the street left a light on all night and a dim streetlight lit the road and walkway.

She looked out and heaved a long sigh. There was no way around it: it was good to be home. Good to be back with Stephen.

He had met her that morning when the French liner *La Normandie* had docked. He had embraced her passionately, handed her a two-pound box of Louis Sherry chocolates, and instantly made her glad that she'd avoided the shipboard fling with the Swedish businessman who had been arduously chasing her.

Then Stephen had driven her home. The house had been clean and fresh (Stephen had hired a maid) and the little town was resplendent in the burnt orange of September. Stephen's mood was much more loving than when she had left. He behaved as if some burden had been lifted. He said that his parish had taken to him well and that the neighbors had asked about her. Above all, he said that he had missed her horribly.

He apologized in advance on one matter: the Lutheran Council on the East Coast had taken a shine to him and he would have to take the occasional trip to other parishes or other cities. But he would hurry back.

He would not ignore her again. Things, Stephen promised, would be different.

Then it was evening. Time for an early bed. She undressed with all the excitement of a young woman taking a new lover. And he was just as impassioned.

"I've been starving for you!" he had said to Laura at the moment when he climbed on top of her. And she had been starving for him. He led her and himself to a hurried but robust climax, made all the better by the fact that, to Laura's way of thinking, her husband behaved like a man who hadn't touched another woman since her departure.

Yes, she decided as she lay beside him afterward. Some things were still important. Politics were not. Fidelity was.

Laura was deeply within this line of thought when she realized what she was watching through the dormer windows. Across the street was a man. She couldn't recognize him, and would never have noticed him at all because he was moving carefully within the shadows of trees. But she had happened to be staring at his precise location and she had picked up the movement.

He walked toward the church. Laura looked across the room at the clock. It was past 2 A.M. Every tenet of surveillance that Peter Whiteside had impressed upon her came thundering back.

Details. Details. The man was tall and lean and wore a dark coat. She could not tell age and she could not see the color of his hair. She squinted. She watched the man walk and a hunch was upon her.

For some reason—and she couldn't place the genesis of the reason—the man struck her as foreign. He was neither English nor American. Something about his movement told her that. Or was that part of a 2 A.M. fantasy?

For that matter, was the *man* a fantasy? She stared again. No, he was real. He entered the church.

Laura held her position for ten minutes, barely blinking. Her heart beat so loudly that she thought Stephen could hear it clear across the room. But he didn't budge. No lights changed in the church. Nothing went on or off.

She thought back. A light remained on in the vestry and a very dim light in the pews. The altar was dim and visible at night; so was the cross.

The man emerged. He went quickly on his way. Nothing indicated that he was anyone she knew.

Several unhappy visions were upon her all at once: the man was from the American government. They were after Stephen—he *was* a Communist spy. Or, the man she had seen was part of Stephen's network. A fellow traveler along the red road. Or, she shuddered, had she seen one of her own countrymen? Had Peter Whiteside dispatched someone to watch *her?*

Or was it none of these? Was she lost in a wilderness of deceptions that, like the smile of the Cheshire cat, receded as she approached them? Was it all too grand for her to even conceptualize?

She felt the wetness of her palms. She drew a long breath. Then a final thought was upon her.

The man who had entered the church was a member of the church. He sought solace with God in the lonely, early dark hours of the morning. Somewhere there was illness. Somewhere there was despair. Somewhere there was a need for spiritual strength and a prayer and that need did not observe the conventional rules of time.

A man had simply felt the need for a prayer at an unorthodox hour. Was that not, in fact, why her husband left the church open?

Now the memory of Peter Whiteside was before her, burning with the intensity of a flare. Peter's account of her husband rang shrilly in her ears.

Turned his eyes eastward . . . offered his services to the Soviet Union and his offer was accepted . . . Made the pilgrimage to the Kremlin, itself. . . .

Suddenly she had to know. She tiptoed from the bedroom and to the stairs. Then she went down to the library, where she turned on the light on her husband's desk. She began to open drawers, riffling through his papers and belongings and shuffling purposefully through his official licenses and documents.

"So this is spying, Peter," she mumbled to herself. She felt disgraced. "I hope you're proud of yourself."

Then she found what she wanted: his United States passport. Her hands trembled slightly as she opened it. She studied his picture and the date and stamp of issue at New York. Then she flipped to the pages that bore travel stamps.

Entry into the United Kingdom via Southampton: April 20, 1935. Departure to France via Calais ("Probably the ferry," she thought) on May 3 of the same year. Arrival in New York on board the SS *America* on the thirtieth of May.

Some Communist agent, she thought. *Some pilgrimage to Moscow!* She flicked through each page of the passport. No other stamps save their Canadian stamps from their honeymoon in 1937. *Where, oh where, Peter Whiteside,* Laura asked within her soul, *is the vaunted pilgrimage to Red Square?*

Stephen's own words returned to her: "I was sick

from the water in England and the cheese in France, so I came home early." What emerged from his passport was the documentation of a Princeton graduate student seeing the cathedral cities of England and France. Nothing more. His passport was the physical refutation of all that Peter Whiteside had claimed. Where had Peter come upon such a tale? Who had fabricated it for him?

Laura returned the passport to its drawer. She piled the other papers and documents upon it so it looked undisturbed.

She turned off the light in his study. She climbed the stairs to the bedroom.

In her mind, Peter Whiteside was still talking to her: *"Facts, Laura, facts! My office deals in facts!"*

In her mind, she answered him.

Facts: the man who had entered and left St. Paul's Lutheran Church in Liberty Circle several minutes earlier was tall, angular, had a hint of a foreigner about him, and moved in and out of shadows with considerable ease. Like Marley's ghost, she reckoned, he was not an undigested clot of mustard. He had been there.

More facts, as she entered her bedroom: she loved her husband. She had personally inspected his passport. He had never been to the Soviet Union and it was preposterous that he was a Communist agent.

Laura walked quietly to the bay window. It was 2:35 A.M. She sat down for a moment and loosened the cotton robe. She looked out the window and all was still.

Sleepily, Stephen spoke. "What are you watching?" he asked.

She looked back to him. "I thought you were

326

asleep," she answered.

"Half asleep. I heard you coming up the stairs. Are you all right?"

She rose and returned to the bed. She untied her sash and slipped out of the robe. She stood near the light from the window intentionally so that he could see and admire her. She took care of her body and kept her figure. She wanted Stephen to know it was for him.

She saw his eyes open appreciatively. "What were you watching?" he asked again.

"Someone went into your church," she said. "To say a prayer, I imagine."

There was a slight pause, then he answered, "Happens all the time," he said. "Funny little town. People can't sleep. Get up, take a walk. Church is the only thing open." Sleep hung heavily in his voice. "They say a prayer, go home, go to bed. St. Paul's is a public service." Another slight pause and: "I love to look at you without your clothes."

He reached to her and slipped his hand between her legs, cupping it behind one trim thigh. He gently pulled her back to him, caressing her from the top of her leg to the buttock.

"As long as we're both awake," he said, "and as long as we're together again . . ."

She sat on his side of the bed and then was beside him, her flesh to his, as he kissed her.

"You don't have to talk me into anything," she giggled. "I'm your wife, remember? Saying 'no' isn't allowed."

TWENTY-TWO

Cochrane turned predatory upon tiny Mr. Adam Hay, the archivist in the Bureau's musty attic.

It began on Wednesday, shortly after nine when Mr. Hay found Cochrane lounging in the small chair near the east file cabinets. Mr. Hay froze when he saw Cochrane, then turned a sour expression upon him and closed the door.

"Morning, Adam." Cochrane had a knee up, folded into his hands, and was rocking slightly in the only chair in the room.

"What do you want?" Mr. Hay answered.

Cochrane motioned to two cups of hot coffee and a tray of fresh doughnuts. "I thought we'd review old times."

The dwarf looked at the food as if it were poison. "What do you want?" he asked again.

Cochrane got to his feet and ambled through the room, glancing at a file here, a file there, picking up a document, looking at it and discarding it. Mr. Hay eyed the doughnuts. "I grew nostalgic for the time I spent up here, Adam," Cochrane said. "You know they reassigned me to Baltimore. Banking fraud. Then they brought me back. I have an office downstairs."

"Bully for you."

Cochrane took a doughnut and held the tray out to Mr. Hay. The dwarf selected a doughnut, then exchanged it for the one Cochrane held. The dwarf munched.

"I remember certain things from when I worked up here," Cochrane said. "The lively conversation, the way the days passed so quickly, the sheer, unbridled inspiration of dealing with . . . all this." Cochrane motioned toward the files.

"Cochrane, get to the point."

"I remember in particular," Cochrane recalled carefully, "a funny little—you'll excuse the terminology—mannerism of yours. Two, in fact. You used to study the racing form at noon. Hoover goes to the races, too, you know. Were you aware of that?"

"I've seen him at Pimlico. On weekends."

"Then there was that second mannerism of yours," Cochrane said, moving closer. The dwarf slipped into the chair. Cochrane stalked him like a panther. "And this one was the truly endearing one, Adam. When requests came up here for specific files, even those to be red-tagged and sealed, you used to open them up, sit there at your desk," Cochrane motioned with his head, "and read them. Start to finish."

Mr. Hay was getting the point. "I don't know what you're talking about," he countered.

"I think you do," Cochrane said. "Further, you have a photographic memory."

"You're wacko, Cochrane. You got your balls

slammed in the bank vault once too often."

Cochrane leaned forward onto the arm of Mr. Hay's chair. He patently menaced the little man. "Otto Mauer," said Cochrane. "The file was requested from this office last week. It got red-tagged. I'm betting you looked at it."

"Maybe," fretted the dwarf. "Maybe not."

"Now, you need recall only two things. I want Mauer's new name. And I want his location.

The dwarf looked petulantly at Cochrane.

"Get the file from Lerrick. Or Wheeler. Or ask Hoover, himself," he retorted.

"I want the answers from you. You may whisper them in my ear. Or inscribe them on a piece of paper."

Cochrane leaned over the smaller man. Mr. Hay's eyes raged. "Go piss up a rope, Cochrane," Mr. Hay snapped. Then he stamped with all his eighty pounds on Cochrane's left foot, catching the instep cleanly with the heel of his shoe.

A searing pain shot through Cochrane, exploding upward from the foot. The archivist burst from the chair and took up a defensive position on the other side of a table, a letter opener clenched in his paw.

"Don't come near me, Cochrane," Mr. Hay instructed. "Pull my whiskers again and there'll be bloodshed, I swear it to you."

Cochrane held his temper and looked at his small adversary. "Obviously," Cochrane concluded, "you need more time to think."

At lunch that same day Mr. Hay fled to a park bench across the street from the White House. The archivist sat undisturbed, opening a liverwurst sandwich and a thermos of iced tea, for a full and glorious minute and a half before Cochrane appeared from nowhere and sat down next to him.

"Mauer's new name, Adam. Plus town and state," Cochrane said simply. "That's all. Then we'll be friends again."

Mr. Hay choked down his sandwich and could barely concentrate on his racing form. He gulped his tea and fled into the noontime crowds on Connecticut Avenue, then was horrified to see, upon his return to his seventh-floor archives, Cochrane lounging again in the small chair.

"The name. The town. The state," Cochrane repeated as if it were a catechism.

The dwarf was rattled, but compensated. "Blow it out your ass, Cochrane!" he yelped.

Cochrane sighed. "If the Chief could hear your language, Adam . . ." Cochrane shook his head in disappointment.

Cochrane brought an hour's worth of work with him, reports from urban police chiefs in the East. He tried, as he ferreted through several dozen homicide cases, to link something with the Billy Pritchard slaying. And when he finished that task, unsuccessfully, he prowled uneasily through the Bluebirds' reports from previous evenings. Nothing there again. Nothing from Siegfried. Deciphering drew a similar blank and so did Cryptology. As Cochrane worked, spreading out his tasks before him on Mr. Hay's table, he raised his eyes and stared at the dwarf every few minutes. "The name. The town. The state," he repeated. "The name. The town. The state."

Toward three in the afternoon, Cochrane got to his feet, winked one eye at his nemesis, and strode from the room. Adam Hay's spirits soared. Alone at last! Then his spirits were quickly crushed with the arrival of Lanny Slotkin, resident cur of the Bluebirds. Mr. Hay had never in his life encountered Lanny Slotkin or anything like him.

"The name. The town. The state," Lanny said, not even certain of what he had been dispatched to inquire. "Cochrane sent me. I'm supposed to stay here until eight o'clock tonight or until I get answers."

Mr. Hay made himself scarce behind a file, working on the lower shelf. But Slotkin was a bulldog, as well as a high priest of rudeness.

"Come on, you little shit," Slotkin screamed after only ten minutes. "I don't want to stay up here all fucking day! What is it he wants to know?" Slotkin entertained the urge to pick up Mr. Hay and shake him. But he resisted.

Mr. Hay was unofficially married to an Indian woman from Bombay. She was of normal dimensions and they lived together in a rear apartment on a grim side street in Georgetown. When he returned home that night, he found Cochrane sitting on the front steps.

"Name. Town. State." The words shot into Mr. Hay's mind faster than Cochrane could mouth them. Mr. Hay bolted up the shabby staircase and scampered in the direction of an apartment door, from behind which emanated pungent smells of Manipur curry and incense.

Adam Hay jammed his key in the lock, turned it, and slammed the door behind him, thinking himself safe within the sanctuary of his own home.

His wife appeared in a saffron and purple robe, kissed him, and spoke. "We have a guest," she said. "A lovely gentlewoman." The dwarf shuddered.

Mr. Hay crept warily into his own living room where he encountered Mary Ryan, the Virgin Mary herself, all eighty-two years of her. She offered him a lined hand.

"This is Mrs. Ryan. From your Bureau," said Mrs. Hay.

"I *do* think," said Mary Ryan, who would go along with any intrigue if it was either work or fun, "that you *really* ought to tell us the name, the town, and the state."

The dwarf turned crimson. Unfortunately, Mrs. Hay had already invited Mary to stay for dinner. Mary Ryan loved curry.

Friday was no better. Every time Mr. Hay looked up, there was Cochrane or one of his deputies. Among those Bluebirds whom Cochrane could trust, it became a passing parlor game. Go talk to the archivist. Pick the dwarf for information. It could save us months of work, and don't tell Wheeler. "I'll take the responsibility," Cochrane had told them all. The name, they demanded. The name. The name. The name. The town. The state. Three quick answers would liberate Mr. Hay from all of this, Cochrane reminded him by telephone a few minutes before Friday midnight.

Totally unnerved, Mr. Hay went to the window and stared downward. And there were the Bureau's two Germans, Roddy Schwarzkopf and Elizabeth Pfeiffer from Section Seven. They stared upward from an alleyway, then waved. Mr. Hay jerked the curtains shut and moaned.

Cochrane spent Saturday morning in Cartography and Central Alien Registry. With the help of Bobby

Charles Martin, late of the Ohio State Police, he marshaled a list of every township within the fifty-mile map radius that the Bluebirds had charted in northern New Jersey. Then CAR Division went through their own files and came up with a list of 256 names of German emigrees living within that area. The towns ran from Passaic and Hoboken to little map dots like Bernardsville and Liberty Circle.

"Monday," promised Cochrane, "we get some staff in here from another division. We check out every name." Then a second list was drawn, one comprising immigrants from the other unfriendly nations: Italy and Japan, just in case.

"That's three hundred wops and seventeen Japs," Bobby Charles Martin surmised with his usual egalitarian candor. "Guess those get checked out, too."

"You guess right," said Cochrane, reaching for a jacket and hat. "Let's go watch some horse races."

Mr. Hay was at Arlington Park for all nine races that afternoon. He seemed to wear his own saddle, with Bobby Martin and Bill Cochrane in it.

Ditto, Sunday. And late afternoon, the archivist began to crack. But as the ninth race was finished, Adam Hay looked up and they were all gone. Every one of them. No one was breathing down his eleven-inch collar.

It was Mr. Hay's custom on Sunday afternoons to relax in the grandstand after the final race. He would peruse the next week's racing card, enjoy the solitude of six thousand empty seats, then amble to his car—a senile old Ford that rattled in every gear including neutral—which he always parked in the far end of the parking lot.

He thought of many things as he handicapped his ponies that afternoon. Name, town, and state were among them. He studied furlongs, sires, and first quarters, late brushes, jockey changes, and trainers. Name. Town. And state. It was a litany.

He folded the racing form into his pocket a few minutes before six. He walked to his car and, his eyes barely to the height of the window, he unlocked it in the vast, deserted parking lot.

The car door flew open. It burst toward Mr. Hay with a commotion that made the small man scream and recoil. A human body, strong and powerful, burst upward from low behind the front seat, pushed the seats apart, and rushed from concealment to confront the archivist.

The tiny archivist yelped and his eyes went wide as demitasse saucers with two brown marbles at their center. It was an emissary from the devil, Mr. Hay thought, risen from purgatory!

Then he saw the truth. It was the devil himself! Cochrane! Glaring, menacing, scowling, looking downward with his twenty-four inches of superior height. Cochrane's eyes gleamed. He said nothing. By now the week's catechism spoke for him.

"Name . . . town . . . state . . ." Mr. Hay's heart fluttered somewhere ten feet above his head.

"Otto Mauer is now Henry Naismith," Mr. Hay confessed sullenly. "The town is Ringtown. The state is Pennsylvania. Now leave me alone."

TWENTY-THREE

It was raining in Manhattan the day Marjorie next saw her mysterious clock manufacturer. Her face still smarted when she thought of the way he had struck her last time. But that was in the past. Perhaps she *had* been too forward with him. He did seem like a very proper man. If only she knew more about him. . . .

She saw him as she stepped out of a taxi on West Thirty-second Street, near Macy's. The man who so fascinated her was disappearing into a sporting-goods store. Marjorie was wearing a wide-brimmed rain hat and a heavy trench coat, so she arranged the hat slightly more over her eyes. Then she moved to the window of the store and peered in. What type of sports did her man like? she wondered. She watched him carefully. He was examining some diving equipment. Rubber wet suits. Snorkels. Marjorie was surprised. Equally, she was surprised when he kept looking up and surveying the people around him. It was as if he thought someone might be spying on him.

Perhaps he was embarrassed, she concluded. Perhaps he was just learning about deep-sea diving. But no. He bought an elaborate combination of equipment. A complete wet suit. A diver's knife. A mask. Then he paid with cash and turned toward the door.

Marjorie crossed the street. The intrigue now excited her. She would follow him and find out what she could. But she would have to behave cleverly, she told herself. Otherwise he would see her.

He was an easy mark, a man wearing a tan trench coat and carrying a large shopping bag. He crossed Seventh Avenue at Thirty-fourth Street, then oddly reversed himself and walked south. If he was going to Pennsylvania Station, she wondered, why hadn't he walked there directly?

She followed from a distance of half a block. Sure enough, he went into the train station.

She lost him. She darted through the gates and looked in every direction. ("Really, girl," she giggled to herself, "there's a war beginning and you make such a lousy spy!") But her spirits were high now. The game was on. For a change, Marjorie could stalk a man, rather than lie passively beneath one.

But her Mr. Bolton was gone. She scanned the huge lobby. Then she spotted him walking toward the Lackawanna Railroad Line. She pursued and saw him glance at his watch. The gate for his train was already open. He hurried through it, then stopped short. He turned and Marjorie stopped also. Much too obviously, she thought. Then she made a point of examining a billboard for the new movie, *Gone With the Wind*.

She looked back a moment later. Maybe he had noticed her, maybe not. He would have to have excellent vision to recognize her from that distance beneath her hat, she told herself. She saw him getting onto a train. Less than thirty seconds later, the conductor standing at the rear signaled up the track to the flagman. The train gave a slight lurch.

Marjorie made a split-second decision. She bolted for the rear of the train. "Hey, lady!" the conductor barked. "Make up your mind!" He almost had the doors closed when she hopped on.

"Oh, I . . ." She admitted breathlessly, "I wasn't sure whether this was my train."

"Where you going?" he asked.

She had no idea. "Um . . . end of the line," she decided.

"That's Liberty Circle."

"Can you sell me a ticket?"

The conductor was a white-haired man named Jeffrey, who looked at Marjorie very strangely. She was heavily perfumed and very overdone. Perhaps, he sensed what she was.

He sold her a ticket, breaking a five-dollar bill.

"You're very kind," she said.

Marjorie found a seat in the rear car. She knew Mr. Bolton was three cars up. The train was only five cars. She wondered what to do.

Mr. Bolton solved her problem for her. He did something strange again. Ten minutes into the trip she saw him slowly walking down the aisle of the next car. Then he entered her car. Marjorie borrowed a Newark *Star* from the man sitting next to her. She buried her face in it as Mr. Bolton walked to the rear and stared out over the tracks. Then he returned up the aisle. What was he doing? Looking to see if he knew anyone?

339

Or just getting a walk?

He left the car. Then a few minutes later, he returned carrying his shopping bag. He sat a few rows in front of her on the opposite side of the aisle. Was he trying to tell her something? There would be no mystery at all where he got off.

The train stopped in Newark and East Orange. Then Madison, New Providence, and Far Hills. Only one stop left. There were only a handful of passengers left. Mr. Bolton was one of them. Marjorie was another.

At Liberty Circle, Mr. Bolton rose. He went to the exit and descended the steps onto the railroad platform. Marjorie followed. Mr. Bolton pulled his coat close to him against the rain, then quickly paced down a flight of steps that led to an underpass. Marjorie pulled her own hat and coat tightly to her body. It was teeming. She followed him.

And suddenly the idiocy of it all struck her. What in hell had propelled her so blindly onward? He had been right when he'd slapped her. She *was* a whore! And he was, like most of her customers, a family man. How dare she follow him to his home! What on earth did she think she was doing?

Marjorie slowed her pace and a wave of desolation was upon her. The underpass was starting to flood and her shoes were being ruined. She knew, because she was looking downward and crying.

Mr. Bolton, any man like Mr. Bolton, was the unattainable for Marjorie. She could only be his whore. She could never be a wife or the mother of such a man's children.

She ascended the steps on the other side of the tracks. She walked very slowly, the chase finished. All she wanted now was the next train back to the city.

She stood in the rain. At the far end of the platform was a small building where the tickets had to be sold. She walked in that direction, hoping to find a timetable.

She opened the door and there he was. Standing behind the door, holding his shopping bag, gazing into her eyes from six feet away. "Marjorie . . ." he said softly. She was speechless. She stammered for words.

"I can't believe this," Mr. Bolton said. He seemed genuinely glad to see her. "I thought it was you on the train. So I came back." He reached to her. "I'm sorry I hit you," he said. "I never should have."

She could hardly believe it. Away from the tensions of the city, he was a different man. So friendly. So relaxed. He took her in his arms.

"My wife is away for a week," he whispered. "Come to my house. Come right now. We can make dinner and make love all night."

It sounded so wonderful. It was almost dark outside now and the rain was torrential.

"Do you have a car?" she asked.

"No need," he said. "I live just near here. I always walk to the station. There's a short cut."

"You must get soaked," she said.

"We'll get toweled off together," he said. He took her arm. "Of course," he added suggestively, "it will take some time for your clothes to dry out. You won't be getting dressed again right away."

Marjorie was thrilled. And his wife was away. Maybe the Boltons were separating. Maybe the world wasn't so cruel after all.

He led her down a quiet country lane where there

were no houses. Then he motioned to a pathway just off from the road.

"I'm sorry about this part," he said. "The path cuts through a few feet of woods. We're behind an old churchyard. But this saves us about a quarter mile of hiking."

Like a gentleman, he offered her his hand. There was just enough daylight left to see.

"Watch your step, Marjorie," he said, leading her. "Don't twist an ankle."

It hardly seemed like a path at all. The footing was treacherous, filled with twigs and stones. Suddenly her man was very quiet. Seconds earlier it had all been a thrill. But now she felt herself turning against this. This was no path at all. And now he was stopping. *Why?*

He turned. They were far from a road and she saw no church and no churchyard. There was just a man standing before her, his hands on her shoulders. And suddenly she was very cold and very wet. She was very aware of the rain and very frightened. There was something horrible in his eyes . . .

"Fred . . . ?" she asked. She was aware of his size. His strength. His hands. He was touching her differently now. There was a scream brewing if only she could summon up the courage to—

"You should never have come here, Marjorie," he said in perfect English. "I don't know what possessed you to follow me. All the way from Thirty-fourth Street. Foolish fucking bitch!"

The scream was in her throat now but hardly any of it rose beyond her lips. His hands were beneath her jaw, and it felt as if someone were wrapping a steel pipe around her neck.

She scratched at his face but he pulled back a hand, formed a fist, and punched her directly in the face. The pain was excruciating. She felt something warm and wet dripping to her mouth. Her whole head throbbed. And the nose seemed crushed.

But all that was secondary. *No air! He is killing me!* The horror of it wrenched her soul and for a moment she saw her girlhood again. She imagined the family that she would never have, and then a vile vision was upon her of Brooklyn, alcohol, and a thousand ugly, dirty men defiling her.

And this man, she thought as she died, was the ugliest and dirtiest of them all.

The orders for arrests were issued above J. Edgar Hoover's signature, though drawn by Frank Lerrick. They were confined to the East: Philadelphia, Boston, New York, and the occasional freight stop in between.

Agents of the Federal Bureau of Investigation struck in the early morning while their targets slept. In Boston, the owner of a small bakery was taken into custody, as was his wife and younger brother. They protested that they knew nothing about Bund activities. Their warrant said otherwise.

Similary, a mechanic in Philadelphia, a film importer and distributor in New York, and the owner of a small foreign-language bookstore in Bridgeport were all arrested for espionage-related activities.

There were others, too. But the only one of significance was arrested two days later when the SS

Panama docked at Pier Thirty-four on the Hudson River. He was the chief butcher on the ship and had long been suspected of being a Gestapo courier. His name was Wilhelm Hunsicker.

He was on the deck at the time of his arrest, speaking to a South African who had been born with the name of Fritz Duquaine but who had been through various aliases since.

Duquaine stepped away when he saw the federal agents approach. And when Hunsicker put up a vicious fistfight, Duquaine valiantly offered to call the city police. The city police never received the call, and Duquaine, unrecognized by the agents to whom he'd spoken, drifted into the pedestrians on Twelfth Avenue and disappeared.

A team of four special agents drove Hunsicker by armored van from New York to Washington. Cochrane was at the Bureau at 10 P.M. when it arrived. Frank Lerrick supervised.

"What's going on?" Cochrane asked. "Is he my suspect?"

"Not until he makes a statement."

"I'm the case officer, aren't I?"

"Cochrane, for once in your fucking life, would you control yourself?" Lerrick snapped. "We turn him over to you when he's ready. Not before. You get a transcript of everything."

"I'm so glad," Cochrane answered.

Hunsicker's arrival coincided with the arrival of two men whom Cochrane had never seen before: Jack Burns and Allen Wilson. "Burns and Allen," Dick Wheeler liked to call them. They were from Ohio, knew Bobby Charles Martin from previous intrigues, and

344

were nowhere nearly as funny as the real Burns and Allen.

"Professional interrogators," Wheeler mumbled to Cochrane toward midnight. They had already guided Hunsicker to a room in the basement. Cochrane shuddered, called it a day, went home, and slept fitfully.

TWENTY-FOUR

Cochrane left Washington in the morning and was driving through Pennsylvania farmland by early afternoon. The sky was clear as vapor, though a few cumulus clouds rolled in toward 3 P.M.

The needle of the gas gauge was perched insistently toward the big white E of empty, so Cochrane pulled his 1937 Hudson into a town called Mahanoy City. It was a town like the others of the area, several churches, factories at each end, an enormous anthracite breaker at the outskirts of town, and mountains of black silt bracketing the highway which led in and out. Farmland had given way to coal country.

Cochrane stepped out of the car at an Esso station. The day was cool. The heat of the summer had finally broken and brown leaves in coiled whirlpools hissed and swirled near the two red and white gas pumps.

"How much farther to Ringtown?" Cochrane asked the attendant, a young man in overalls and a green flannel shirt.

The attendant motioned down the road. "'Bout

fifteen miles," he said. For three dollars, he filled the car's tank and washed the windshield.

Mahanoy City. Frackville. Shenandoah. Shamokin. The towns got smaller as Cochrane drove through them: row houses built by the Reading Coal Company, churches, shops and trees. Ringtown was the smallest, with one main street.

Cochrane stopped at the police station, entered, and found Police Chief Stan Zawadski, a tall thin man with dark hair, with his feet up on the desk. Chief Zawadski glanced to the stranger from the sports pages of the local paper. "Yeah?" he asked.

Cochrane offered his FBI shield by way of greeting. The chief's shoes hit the floor as he sat up.

"Don't see many of those around here," the police chief said. Cochrane smiled amiably, folded the shield case away, and inquired of a man named Henry Naismith.

Zawadski gave directions to a farmhouse on a road diverging from the main highway. Cochrane thanked him.

"Now, you do one thing for me," Zawadski asked. Cochrane listened.

"You tell Mr. Hoover that he should run against Roosevelt next time," the police chief said. "Three terms. That's a lot for one man. This ain't a kingdom, after all. You tell your boss he should run for President."

"I'll tell him," Cochrane said. He returned to his car. He noted in passing that Chief Zawadski's car was parked at the town's only fire hydrant. No one seemed to care.

*　　　*　　　*

The farmhouse was five minutes out from town and Cochrane saw it on the dirt and gravel road for a mile before he arrived. The building was big and white, wooden and rambling, with a dark shingled roof that sagged. As he drew closer, he saw that an occasional window was broken and every shade was drawn. More critically, Cochrane observed as he pulled into a semicircular driveway before the house, there were no approaches to the house that were not visible from a distance. He noted, too, that there were two strings of outside lights. He guessed they were illuminated on most nights.

Cochrane parked and had barely stepped from his car when he heard the front door of the house open. Cochrane walked a pace or two and almost did not recognize the man who stood before him.

It was Mauer.

But it was an older, more sober, less-dignified man than Cochrane remembered, with more lines and a more hardened, hard-bitten cast to his face. The German stood on the front steps to the house staring at his arrival. He wore a neat white shirt, gray flannel pants, and a cloth tie, as if he had been interrupted while dressing for an afternoon hike in the mountains south of Munich.

But more important was the look of sheer hatred on the man's face. That, and the shotgun cradled like a baby in his arms.

"Hello, Otto," Cochrane said.

"You . . . !" said Mauer, breathing low and with evident animosity. "What the devil are you doing here?" He spoke in English.

"I came to talk to you."

Mauer's arms unfolded like a soldier's. He held the

shotgun across his chest and Cochrane stopped in his tracks.

"I ought to shoot you right here. Right now. No questions, just shoot!"

"Otto . . . ?"

Then the German pointed the weapon at his visitor, the butt end of the stock poised near the right shoulder in anticipation of firing. Cochrane dared not step in either direction.

"You leave me behind to be butchered! You leave my family to Gestapo and you make your own escape! Damn you! *Damn* you!" The weapon was still trained.

"Otto, I had passports sent to you from Zurich. By courier."

"No passports. Never any passports. Thanks to you. You were turncoat. Traded us for your own freedom at Freiburg. Why do you come here? To be shot? I bury you out back. No one know. No one care. Tell me, turncoat, you ready to die?"

Cochrane felt his own anger rising to his defense.

"Otto, who's been telling you these things?"

"*They* tell me," Mauer insisted, very loud.

"Who in hell is 'they'?"

"No matter to you!"

Cochrane groped for some other angle and tried the most obvious. "Otto, where's your family?" he asked. "Have they separated you from your family?"

Cochrane saw the German stiffen. He saw, too, from the crooked curtains in the window and the untrimmed shrubs near the door that no woman was on the premises. Further, Mauer had the air of a desperate, lonely man.

Cochrane switched into German, seeking any common bond. "Otto, I trusted you with my life in Germany. I wouldn't come here if I'd betrayed you. We must talk. It's crucial for both of us."

"Turncoat!" Mauer said again. The German jabbed the air with the two barrels of the shotgun. Cochrane flirted with the idea of turning and running, but quickly rejected it. One step and Mauer would fire. From twenty feet, the shotgun would tear a hole in Cochrane the size of a watermelon.

"Herr Mauer," Cochrane tried again, "I'm here on official business. *Bureau* business. I can prove it."

Cochrane made a motion toward a jacket pocket, but Mauer stopped him with another jerk of the weapon.

"Not a move!" Mauer continued in German.

Cochrane kept talking. "I'm trying to catch a spy. Gestapo, we think. A man who's in America, Otto. Here. Where we are!"

"There is no Gestapo in America," Mauer retorted.

To which, Cochrane's anger rose again to the occasion. "Are you crazy," he demanded, "or just uninformed? They sit in New York and Newark all night with radios. They blow up ships, they sabotage plants. They derail trains and they kill people."

"Saboteurs," the German answered. "A few insane people. Malcontents."

"I'm looking for a very dangerous man," Cochrane said. "I can prove it. But you and I have to talk."

Mauer peered at him for the longest fifteen seconds of Cochrane's life, straight over the double barrels of the shotgun. Cochrane half-expected to see the flash and the eruption from the nozzle of the gun. He would feel the agonizing pain for only a second or two, then

351

there would be darkness. For some reason, as all these black thoughts coalesced at once, Cochrane thought of the country graveyard in Virginia where his family was buried. He wondered if he would be returned there. He fought off the thought. It had never occurred to him before.

And worse, he was out of words. Long ago at the National Police Academy they had taught him: always keep a gunman talking. They don't shoot when they're talking.

But Cochrane's mouth had gone desert-dry. He'd said everything. There was no further appeal. All he could do was glare at Mauer. If the German was to kill him, he would have to look him in the eye.

Mauer still spoke in German. "You have a gun?"

Cochrane nodded.

"Loaded?"

"It's not much use unloaded, Otto."

"Very slowly. You drop it." Very slowly, Cochrane reached with his right hand.

"Left hand! Left hand! Thumb and forefinger!" the German shouted.

Cochrane's right hand drew back and he reached his service weapon. He pulled the gun from the holster and he tossed it gently away.

"Now," said Mauer, his own weapon never budging, "if you're with the FBI, let's see identification. Again, left hand. Very *very* slowly."

Again Cochrane obeyed. He removed his shield case from a pocket and tossed it toward the German. Mercifully, it landed open, the bronze shield facing upward. Mauer crouched down and picked it up. He stared at it so hard that Cochrane thought he was trying to memorize it.

Then Mauer looked back to his visitor. He spoke in tones that were not in the least apologetic.

"You come inside," he said.

Cochrane felt the moment slowly defuse. He moved forward. Mauer stepped back a little and kept his distance, just in case. In Cochrane's experience, however, shotguns were rarely used indoors. Too messy. Frightfully noisy. Mauer appreciated that, too.

If he were going to kill me, Cochrane later recalled thinking, *he would have done it there. Right there. While I was holding the gun.*

He entered the farmhouse at shotgun point and later recalled a second thought: *I've been wrong before,* he reminded himself.

But Cochrane was not wrong.

As the men entered the house, Mauer retreated to a stuffed, fading armchair on one side of the room. Beside it was a bottle of bourbon, already open and half consumed, a carving knife, and a pair of shot glasses. The German motioned to a sofa across the room. He indicated that he'd be happiest if Cochrane sat there. Cochrane did. Then Mauer eased into his own chair, cradling his shotgun across his lap, like a dog or a small blanket, and he stared at his visitor.

No one spoke. It was a time of observation. Cochrane noted first the shabby state of the house's interior, the walls crying out for paint, the furniture that had outlived its brighter days. An odd number of coffee cups and plates presided upon nearby tables and a general pallor of imprisonment hung ponderously upon everything within the room, particularly Mauer.

Mauer had lost weight since Cochrane had seen him last. And patches of his hair were now a drab gray, like a small animal's. He scrutinized his visitor, trying to read what lurked behind Cochrane's eyes. He was unable, and his own eyes lost their menace and retreated into anxiety.

Cochrane rushed to a new conclusion about Mauer. Here before him was a lonely, broken man. A former officer of the Abwehr, Mauer now dwelt in the professional purgatory of the exiled defector, untrusted where he was, reviled where he came from. With the final days of his middle years slipping away, Mauer spent his weeks in isolation, fearing the advance of a lonely old age. He had the look of a man under siege.

"I want you to know at the outset," Cochrane began, "that I'll help you in any way I can. But I need to know certain things. You must be honest with me, as I believe you always have been."

Mauer's glare was unyielding. Then it broke into a rueful smile and a scoff laced with cynicism. *"Me* help *you?"* Mauer answered, switching into English. "Almost as funny as you helping me."

Cochrane saw no humor and was about to open his mouth when Mauer reached for a week-old Philadelphia *Bulletin*. "See this?" he asked. "War already." He shook his head sadly. "I do not know if Germany can win. Not with its current leadership." He glanced at the headlines and a newspaper map on the front page, a map bedecked with firm black arrows showing paths of German invasion.

"Poland," Mauer said with contempt. "Imagine

England going to war over a corrupt, backward, ill-educated dictatorship of idiot colonels. Imagine Chamberlain complaining that Hitler has taken another part of Czechoslovakia when it was Chamberlain who agreed to its partition one year ago." Mauer poured himself bourbon and sipped. "Imagine England taking a stand on the so-called Polish city of Danzig when Danzig was part of Prussia from 1793 until the Treaty of Versailles in 1919. Are you a student of history, Herr Cochrane?"

"I try to be."

"Would you not agree that the Allies themselves created Hitler when they partitioned Germany and wrote such an odious settlement to the Great War? It was such a settlement that built up the resentment in Germany that gave credibility to Hitler."

"I wouldn't disagree. Not completely."

"An insane document, the Versailles treaty. We are, in a sense, fighting the same war. A sad, oppressive settlement."

Forgetting the weapon across Mauer's lap, Cochrane took issue. "Similar to the settlement the Kaiser inflicted upon the Czar two years earlier. Wouldn't you say?"

Mauer, savoring a sip, set down his shot glass. His reaction surprised Cochrane. "Point," he said philosophically. "Now, tell me why you are here so I might decide whether or not to shoot you."

For the first time, in sunlight reflecting through the door, Cochrane caught a glimpse of the stock of the shotgun. Upon the stock was a beautifully carved scene of two men cornering a bear, the penultimate act of a presumed hunt. Then Cochrane's gaze slipped to the knife near the bourbon bottle. There were wood chips and slivers on the floor. Mauer was marking time by engraving the stock of his own weapon.

"I want to talk about Abwehr operations within the United States. Anything covert. Anything at all."

"It won't take time too much. I know nothing."

"But you were in the Abwehr. You know the procedures if not the specifics." When Mauer said nothing, Cochrane forged ahead. "I'm after a single man. I think he's working alone."

Mauer relied loftily. "Absolutely impossible," he said.

"The man exists."

"In your mind perhaps, mein Herr."

Cochrane thought of Billy Pritchard's corpse rotting in the New Jersey woods. "No. The man is real," he answered.

"You've seen him?" Mauer asked quickly, switching back into German.

"I've seen his work."

"But you haven't seen *him?*"

"Otto, I wouldn't be here if I'd been that close."

Mauer laughed mirthlessly. "You were a banker once. Probably not even a bad one. But, if you'll excuse me, you have no aptitude for intelligence work whatsoever." Cochrane felt the rebuke like a school-boy, but kept quiet. "You are like most other Americans. This is what I tried to tell you a year ago in Berlin. You fail to understand Germany. And when you fail to understand Germany, you fail to understand Hitler or German methods of doing things."

But Cochrane did not fail to understand the German language. So he allowed Mauer to continue.

"There is no such thing as one man working alone. Nowhere, I repeat, *nowhere* in German society today. Particularly in the military. Or in the Abwehr. Or anywhere in the intelligence systems. The entire concept is totally antithetical to the Reich. Look," he said. The German's eyes came alive with intrigue for the first time. "A private in the Wehrmacht, the lowliest private, has a sergeant. The sergeant has a lieutenant. The lieutenant has a major, the major has a colonel, and so on up until you reach the field marshal. But the field marshal has commanders in Berlin, the strategists who plan the war. And they have their commander— Hitler himself."

Mauer replenished his shot glass. "Similarly with a spy," said Mauer. "A spy in America will have a command in his region. A spy based here in Pennsylvania, for example, may have a master in Washington. The master may be Portuguese or Spanish or Hungarian. But he is the master, nonetheless. The master would report by courier or by radio to Hamburg. Hamburg reports to the Intelligence Chancellery in Berlin and that agency reports to Admiral Canaris. Canaris reports to Goering. Goering reports to Hitler. Orders go down the chain of command. Reports go up. See? Very simple, very orderly. Very German. No man works alone."

"But someone *is!*" Cochrane insisted.

"Then he is not German," said Mauer sharply.

Cochrane rejected the notion. He was struck instead by the absurdity of being unarmed and interrogating a man who had a shotgun across his lap.

"So," Mauer said. "Now. I've told you what you wanted to know?"

"Only partially."

"What else?"

"I'd like to know how you arrived here from Germany. Particularly," said Cochrane, trying to maintain an easy, discursive tone, "if you didn't use the Swiss passports intended for you."

Mauer fingered the weapon again. "Look in your own damned files," he said.

"I want to hear it in your own words," Cochrane said.

"You, too? Everyone wants to hear my own words. They sat here with a wire recorder and transcribed me."

"*Who* did?"

"Your superior. This Herr Lerrick."

Cochrane was thunderstruck and did his best to conceal it. *Lerrick?*

"He sat where you're sitting now," Mauer said. Then he motioned across the room to a worn straw chair with a ladder back. "And the other man. He sat over there." Mauer indicated with his gaze.

"Yes. Of course," Cochrane said, recovering. "And when was this again? Shortly after your arrival, right?" he guessed.

"About two weeks. I go to Washington first of course," the German said, switching back to English for no apparent reason other than that the events recalled themselves that way. "Then they put me here. Lerrick and the other man, both of FBI, badges like yours, come to talk to me here."

"The second man . . . ?"

"I do not recall a name."

"What did he look like? Large? Small?"

"Big and tall. Broad like a bear. Looked German but

wasn't. Smokes a pipe. Looked clumsy but wasn't."

Richard Wheeler, Cochrane realized. "What was discussed?"

"Everything I previously tell you."

"Nothing else?"

A long, hesitant pause, then: "How I escape." Mauer's indignation toward Cochrane returned. "How I lose my family." A vacant, uneasy glare came over the German, thinking back to his escape and its ultimate circumstances.

"Please, Otto," Cochrane begged. "Run through it once more. It's vital. And I may be able to help. Please believe me."

"I want my son and my wife back," he said. "Nothing else. Not this damned house, this damned gun, not your damned passports or money."

"I understand that," said Cochrane with legitimate sympathy. "And as God is my witness, I will do everything to get your family back to you. But you must tell me everything that happened. We're on the same side, you and I. I swear we are."

For the first time since he'd entered the farmhouse, Cochrane felt the relationship rekindling between the two men. Or was it wishful thinking?

"Please, Otto," Cochrane said.

"All right," Mauer said at length, looking away resolutely. "All right."

TWENTY-FIVE

The Swiss passports from Zurich never arrived, Mauer recalled. Either Swiss authorities intercepted them at customs or German authorities picked them off. Either was possible. In 1938, like people, things had a way of disappearing.

"Or, of course," Mauer couldn't help but add, scrutinizing Cochrane closely, "the passports never left Zurich at all. They never existed."

Failing to receive the help as promised, Mauer continued, he took matters into his own hands. He was under twenty-four-hour watch now, but the number of thugs had increased to four. Mauer could read the message. It was time to tour Europe.

He practiced a bit of private capitalism on his own, Mauer admitted, working a deal with a pair of Dresden-born clerks in the Nazi documentation office in Berlin. He'd come out of it with a pair of impeccable passports, one for a woman and one for a child and both on thirty-six hours' notice. The passports were Swedish and bore diplomatic numbers. Better than forgeries, they were the real thing, having disappeared from the Stockholm registry and reappeared blank in Berlin. No one admitted exactly how.

Mauer's wife and son were to leave Germany immediately for Spain. They would arrive in Madrid by air, then travel southward by train. They would cross the tenuous border to Gibraltar where they would contact an M.I. 5 agent, a self-styled nobleman called Major Aseña, who ran a cafe in the afternoon and a network of anti-Franco infiltrators for the English at night. In exactly what force Aseña was a major was open to dispute, and the conventional wisdom in Gibraltar had it that his rank was as self-proclaimed as his nobility. But no one pressed such questions; Major Aseña solved problems.

From Gibraltar, Frau Mauer and her son were to take an Irish liner—named with the uncanny half-poet, half-warrior sense of Gaelic irony, *The Empress of Belfast*—to New York. There Otto Mauer and his family would rendezvous, at least according to prearrangements.

Mauer saw his wife and son to the airport in Munich. He watched them safely onto the aircraft, then stood on the observation deck as the airplane disappeared into the sky. He went to work for three more days. Then on a Friday morning, he threw his own ace.

I.G. Gehringer, the sprawling German electrical supply company, had a plant in Helsinki. It was constantly under surveillance by both Russian and English operatives. Using his own passport and Abwehr identification, Mauer flew to Helsinki on a Luftwaffe civilian transport, ostensibly to run a spot security check on the plant.

362

He arrived, conducted his check, disappeared into a cafe, and convinced himself he was alone.

He ordered a single Polish vodka, drank it, and waltzed out the side door and down two short, busy blocks. He reported to the American Consulate, which was busy, overworked, and functioned with a staff of six. There Mauer demanded to see the chief diplomatic officer, who happened that day to be the consul himself.

The consul was a trim, laconic Vermonter named Fred Godfrey. Mauer introduced himself as Count Choulakoff, just in from Munich, and demanded passage at least as far as London. Godfrey damned near threw him out, having, in his experience in White River Junction, never encountered Russians making demands for free travel.

Godfrey would in fact have thrown the bogus count off the premises after two minutes discussion, but Mauer drew a Luger from his overcoat. He suggested in concise English that Mr. Godfrey rethink his position.

Godfrey went sheet white and followed instructions. He cabled the FBI in Washington, citing an emergency of the highest order and asking guidance. He cited that a gentleman of the Russian aristocracy, name of Choulakoff, recently of Munich, was sitting in his office. What should be done?

As they awaited a response, Godfrey drew up an American passport. The count just happened to have a recent photograph handy and Godfrey had no deeply rooted instincts toward martyrdom.

The cable came back after ten very sweaty hours, all of which Mauer spent sitting in Godfrey's office, his loaded Luger in his coat pocket, making small talk with the consular staff. Washington's instructions were to "assist the count in travel westward." Godfrey heaved a huge sigh and handed Mauer a passport with five hundred dollars. Mauer apologized profusely for the mailfist techniques, politely accepted the passport and cash, and was on his way. Within a minute he was gone.

"I was in Oslo by steamer within thirty-six hours," Mauer recalled to Cochrane as the shadows elongated across the floor of the Pennsylvania farmhouse. "I was in England via a second steamer within two more days."

M.I. 6 pounced upon Mauer as his feet touched the dock in Southampton. Their agents at the harbor were expecting him, knew from the very outset that he was German, not Russian, and arranged to escort him onward to London, but very politely.

"Two of them brought me to London," Mauer said, "two very neat young men in Chesterfields. They both spoke perfectly fluent German and posed everything as a civil request." He paused. "They put me up at Claridge's," Mauer recalled, not without a certain appreciation. "A suite overlooking Brook Street."

Mauer's eyes danced for a moment. Cochrane nodded and then a shadow came across the German again. "But you see," Mauer continued, "my family was nowhere to be seen. And within a few hours I had been turned over to yet another Englishman. A Major Richards, a man in his thirties with very short dark hair and tortoise-shell glasses. He wore no uniform, of course. He told me that he was in a branch of M.I. 5 called B.A. 1. I don't know what the letters stood for. But I knew what the branch did. Double-crossing enemy intelligence, both German and Italian. They would trap enemy agents and turn them back against the German or Italian spy masters who'd dispatched them. That, or execute them, I suppose, so the poor agents had little choice."

Cochrane interrupted. "Had you ever heard of B.A. 1 before?"

Mauer's whitish eyebrows shot skyward. "Good God, young man! Of course. Abwehr has a thorough file on them. I even had heard of Major Richards. That's why Major Richards' offer was so laughable."

"What offer?"

"He wanted to feed me back into Germany to work for England. I told him that I had already worked for the Americans and felt I was compromised. He laughed and said that the Americans had no intelligence service abroad yet. He told me that if I had worked for an American, I had actually probably been working for an American Communist in the employ of Stalin."

"How did you answer that one?" Cochrane asked, choosing his words very carefully.

"I ripped into him. I said, 'Major, sir, you and the Americans share a common language. If you don't know what they're doing, why don't you go ask them for yourself?' He didn't like that and suggested that perhaps I was not really Abwehr, but rather some sort of criminal. Maybe I should be returned. He said this, I know, just to get me hot. So I said very calmly, 'No, Major. I am in truth Abwehr. That is how I know you studied at Oxford and Heidelberg, were born in Taunton, married, and used to work in war office before being recruited into intelligence.' Major Richards withdrew very slightly, then nodded. 'Very good,'

365

he answered me. Then I told him ten of his B.A. 1 agents who'd been discovered by the Gestapo. He didn't like that, either. He tried to make another offer to me, but I was getting very mad now. So I said to him, 'Major, you talk to your Major Aseña in Gibraltar. You get my wife and son here and I'll see what else I can do for you. Until then, nothing!' I folded my arms and did not answer him for another half hour. Finally he grew tired and left. Good riddance."

"You didn't care for him?" Cochrane asked as Mauer reached again for the bourbon.

"Pest," retorted Mauer. "But, ah," he added with a brisk, contemptuous wave of his hand, "he's paying my Claridge's bill. So naturally in two days he's back. But now he visits with five other men. Muscle. Looked like Englishmen off the docks, all standing around my suite in Basil Rathbone-type coats, getting my walls dirty. He shows me a handwritten note from Major Aseña in Gibraltar saying that my family never arrived there. Then they quickly team up on me. They tell me that I cannot stay in England. They're squeezing me, you see. They tell me that I entered the country on a no-good American passport and I will be put in jail. I tell them to go directly to hell. They make me another offer. They want to give me new identification, money, and let me run networks of German doubles in Morocco or Egypt, I take my pick. I ask them if they are completely crazy. I mention my wife and family and suddenly I realize—they never believed my story about a wife and son in Spain. Maybe they did not even believe my identity within the Abwehr. But this they must have believed. My information had to check with theirs."

There was a long silence and Mauer needed to be

prodded again. "So what did you do, Otto?" Cochrane nudged.

"What the hell do you think I did?" he snapped. "I say to this man, hey, I have an American passport. That makes me citizen of United States. I want to notify my embassy that I am here being recruited by foreign agents. Well, there was a pained expression around the room. They all filed out. But two of them stayed at my door for two days. I'm under house arrest now, can you believe? Then Richards came back yet again. Very *very* reverential this time. Full of apologies. And an American diplomat comes in a minute later. We go through the Count Choulakoff charade again and the American turns to the major. 'Yeah, this is our man, buddy,' the American says. He tells me that my family is in Washington waiting for me. They put me on a disguised American military cargo ship that next night. I'm in Philadelphia in eight days, Washington in ten. I'm greeted by the FBI. I demand proof that they have my family safe. They say, proof takes time. Just some questions first. I'm going crazy but I have no choice. I try to cooperate. We go through the whole damned story again, everything I tell you in Germany, everything I tell the English in London. I know what they're doing. They're testing my story against yours. Then they discredit you to see if I change my story. I stick to the truth. It's all I have. Then I demand, absolutely demand, to see my family."

"Who was doing the interrogation?"

"Several. The little idiot who stutters a lot was the leader. Moustache. Little thin Don Ameche-type moustache."

"Lerrick," muttered Cochrane, almost unwillingly.

"That's the one." Mauer grew angry again. "He stands, walks to me with a smile, and slaps me across the face! He's fifteen years younger, but I jump out of my seat to strangle him. But other Bureau toughs grab me, put me back in chair. He says I'm in America now and in American they don't like Nazis. I tell him I'm not a Nazi, never was, but he doesn't want to listen. He hits me again and I'm held down. He says his Bureau gives the instructions, not me. He says I will cooperate or he will make sure I never see family again ever. Then they keep me awake. They change me from room to room. They take off my watch and change my clothing. I have nothing familiar anymore. I lose track of days. I tell them everything I know. Everything. At the end, this man simply says to his assistants. 'All right. That's enough. No more.' 'My family?' I said to him"— Mauer's voice was deeply plaintive here, almost brittle with emotion—"'What about my family, you liar!' But he left the room."

More bourbon, then Mauer moved toward a conclusion.

"Later that same day the other man arrives. The big hulking one who looks like a bear and who visits me sometimes here. He says there is a terrible difficulty, but he can help. My family is still in Spain, he says. I explode. I scream at him that I'm betrayed three times now by his same rotten Bureau. I go for him, but he grabs my hands. He is very calm. Then he shows me. He has a picture. He shows me a photograph of Natalie and Rudy in Madrid. 'They are being cared for,' he promises me. 'They will be brought to America when it is safe to travel.' He gives me his word."

Mauer exuded a long sigh. "Here," he said. The

German reached to a drawer and handed Cochrane a black and white photo. Cochrane looked down at it as Mauer rubbed his own eyes. In the photo Natalie Mauer stood with her son, Rudy, an image in black and white at Plaza Mayor in Madrid. Natalie looked happy. The young boy looked sorrowful, as did the city in the background, which still bore scars from the civil war.

Cochrane returned the photograph to Mauer, who tucked it into his pocket.

"They tell me I must wait," Mauer said. "I ask for asylum and they give me this house. I ask for a bodyguard and they give me this gun." He shook it with controlled venom and Cochrane leaned backward slightly. "I ask them to move my family immediately; Madrid crawls with Gestapo and SS and Franco's national police. But they give me excuses. I ask them to use Major Aseña in Gibraltar and the Americans say they know of no such agent. So I sit here. I know nothing. Helpless. I've told everything I know." He took his longest pause yet. "God in heaven," he said as a benediction.

An absolute silence enshrouded the two men, the isolated farmhouse, and Mauer's whole black story. Slowly, as if it made no difference anymore, the German set aside his weapon and stood. He got to his feet slowly, as if battling a stiffness in the legs, and walked fretfully across the room. Cochrane watched him go. Mauer was in the kitchen and drew himself a glass of water. Cochrane glanced back to the shotgun. He was closer to it than the German. But now it barely mattered.

In the fading light from the outdoors, Cochrane

watched Otto Mauer. A wave of commiseration swept over him. Despite the risks, Cochrane knew that he had enjoyed their first meeting much more. Back then, just a short year ago, Mauer was a dashing senior Abwehr officer of substantial influence. Now he was an aging defector, broken in spirit, separated from the things that he loved, and drifting into an uncertain murky future. Worse, he knew it. Stripped of his nationality and his influence, he remained a husband and a father. But even his family had been taken from him.

Cochrane broke the depressing spell of the room by reaching to a lamp and lighting it. Mauer returned, carrying a glass, obviously lost in thought. The German sat down.

"Anything else?" Cochrane asked.

Mauer looked up. "I told you, you know everything."

"Well, it simply occurs to me," the American said. "You've been driven from your country by a bunch of cutthroats, separated from your family, placed here by people you don't know and can't trust . . ." Cochrane probed the German's narrowing eyes for some resonance. He thought he found some. "You must have done some time thinking, Otto. You must have theorized on what went wrong. And where."

Mauer looked at him glumly and his own voice was defensive again. "No theories," the German said. "I know."

"Then tell me."

"From the very start, young William Cochrane," Mauer said, "Gestapo had your number in Germany. And I should have known. But Abwehr didn't know at all. Only Gestapo. Trouble is, how do they have you before you even set foot in the Reich? How are they watching you every step of the way?"

"Exactly," Bill Cochrane answered.

"Better still, how did you escape when few others do?"

"I don't know."

"Then I tell you."

"Go ahead."

"You got very lucky, boy," Mauer said. "That's all. Like I said, Americans are bumbling amateurs in matters of intelligence and security. No match for Germans at all. When you get into the war—and make no mistake, England and France will drag you in again—you're all in great trouble. No doubt."

"We'll see."

"Ah." Mauer waved his hand contemptuously and dismissively again. "I show you!" he snapped, very angrily.

Impulsively he grabbed the shotgun again and whirled it upward as he remained in his chair. The moment seemed frozen in both time and horror to Cochrane because when the gun came up it was trained directly at Cochrane's upper chest, where it would blow a hole where his heart was. "I show you for sure!" the German said.

The German snapped the weapon open to check the ammunition and then clacked it shut again. "Ready?" he asked, and Cochrane didn't have a half second to move before both triggers of the double-gauge were squeezed.

There were two clicks. Two of the loudest clicks Cochrane had ever heard in his life. He stared at Mauer.

"When your Bureau gave me a weapon, they gave me no ammunition," he said. "Fools!" He reached to his jacket pocket and pulled out a pair of shells. He opened the weapon and slid them in. "Now, you go. You help me if you think you can. But you remember. When I am ready to shoot someone, I will be prepared, also." A long final silence and then: "Remember, too—I could have shot you. You owe me your life. Bring me my family in return. Your own words once, 'One gentleman to another.' Now, go. We still have our agreement."

Silence, darkness, and loneliness were the three great interrogators. Before them, a man's soul was bare and vulnerable.

All three worked upon Cochrane as he drove the winding, black highway through the hills of northeastern Pennsylvania. It was night now and he had left Mauer standing on the farmhouse doorstep, cradling the shotgun, seeing his visitor off. The image stayed with Cochrane. But now the entire sky was the color of Mauer's eyes and mood. And the darkness accused.

The headlights of the Hudson shone a frail yellow beam on the road ahead, but Cochrane saw the road only absently. Other visions descended. Distant voices asked questions.

Why had his own Bureau endeavored so carefully to keep him away from Mauer? Similarly, why had he been discredited in Mauer's eyes?

Why was Hoover personally guarding Mauer's file?

Was Mauer telling the truth? If so, how much? If not, how much? Why had neither Lerrick nor Wheeler ever

*admitted that Mauer was in the United States in
Bureau custody?*

Cochrane worked the stories forward and backward,
and turned everyone's account inside out. He searched
for the detail that didn't fit, the subtle imperfection or
the gross inconsistency. He found none. He found
instead only other images and other voices.

And other questions.

Along the dark two-lane interstate, a vision came to
him from somewhere deep in his own childhood. He
was a boy again on a muggy summer day and he was
skipping flat rocks across the river outside Charlottesville. Every once in a while he would throw wrong. The
rock would plunge and not skip.

A smooth circle would emerge on the water,
followed by another and another, round and concentric from the point where the rock had disappeared.

The perplexities now before him reminded him of
the rocks that didn't skip—disappearing into a
fathomless surface, with other, deeper concentric
questions rippling out from the epicenter.

*At what point in 1937 had Cochrane actually been
compromised in Berlin? And by whom? And how? Or
was Mauer's "defection" a clever design to suggest just
such unnerving questions? The purpose? To provoke
America's embryonic intelligence service into jumping
at its own shadow.*

Cochrane turned on the car radio, trying to cleanse
his mind of Otto Mauer, Germany, Siegfried, and how
they linked together, if they did at all. He lowered the
window to draw some fresh air into the car, and, as the
radio warmed, first there was a rush of static and then a
high pure swath of bigband music from some ersatz

ballroom in New York or Philadelphia. Glenn Miller filled the car and Cochrane felt a momentary joy, almost a euphoria, disconnected from all the thoughts of this and previous days. It lasted for several minutes as, seemingly in a dark void, propelled by the evenness of the car's engine, and drawn forward apparently by the two yellow beams of light, he sailed smoothly through a universe separate from any other.

But then the purity of Glenn Miller's sound receded, just as Mauer's story had, and it was replaced by a screaming all-night preacher on KDKA in Pittsburgh who wanted to tell Bill Cochrane about salvation.

It occurred to Cochrane that he should be tired and he considered stopping. But then he realized that he wasn't tired at all, so instead of looking for lodgings, he drove like a banshee past the sleeping coal towns, figuring he could see the Washington Monument by dawn.

The static began to suffocate the preacher, too, and Cochrane took his eyes off the road long enough to look to the knob of the radio. And when he looked up again, like a mirage, there was a massive stag leaping into Cochrane's lane from the grassy divider in the highway's center.

He swerved wildly and his tires screeched. Somehow he missed the animal and then it was gone. Cochrane's heart was leaping like the stag, then—his heart still pounding—he wondered if he'd been nodding off and it had all been a dream, sent from somewhere, to keep him awake.

He didn't know. There were a lot of things, he reminded himself, that he didn't know.

What was Siegfried's final, ultrasecret mission? Why

did Mauer insist that a Gestapo agent would not be working alone? Why, when Cochrane himself had seen the proof: the dead body of Ensign Pritchard?

What, in fact, did any of this have to do with Siegfried? After weeks of investigation, Cochrane hadn't a clue.

He arrived in Washington just past dawn. He parked in front of his own house and, bordering on spiritual and physical collapse, climbed the stairs and slept.

Like Police Chief Zawadski in Ringtown, Cochrane parked in front of a hydrant. But unlike Chief Zawadski, Cochrane drew a summons when he slept past 8 A.M.

TWENTY-SIX

"You're a bachelor, Mr. Glover?" Mr. Fields, the rental agent, asked as they moved through the hallway.

"That's correct, sir," Siegfried answered. "Single." He managed a boyish smile. "Came close once or twice, but never married."

"Lucky you," said the rumpled little man in shirt sleeves and suspenders. "You've saved yourself one enormous pain in the ass, if you don't mind my saying."

Mr. Fields owned the apartment house in Alexandria, Virginia, and lived downstairs with his suety bride of thirty-eight years. Mr. Fields was tart-tongued, smelled of sweat, and had a small apartment for rent at forty dollars a month.

Fields turned the key in the door and flicked the light switch as they entered the apartment. Nothing lit.

"I'll get you a new bulb if you take the place," Fields said. "Look around. See what you think." He glanced at his watch. Fields had fringes of hair on the side of his skull, somewhat like a monk, and nibbled from a bag of salted peanuts.

The apartment was small and furnished, one long "L" with kitchen facilities and three windows. One of the windows overlooked the Potomac, four blocks away, if the tenant craned his neck.

"Like it?" Mr. Fields asked. "That's a new mattress over there, too." He motioned toward the bed.

Siegfried surprised Mr. Fields. "I'll take it," the spy said.

"You will?" Mr. Fields came to attention. Then from somewhere a smile danced across his lips for all of five seconds. "You *will?*"

"I travel a lot. I only have occasional business in Washington," Siegfried said. "I won't even be here that often."

Siegfried took out his wallet and paid a month's security and two months in advance. Mr. Fields felt rich.

"What sort of business are you in, Mr. Glover?" Fields asked as they walked down two flights to the main floor.

"Government. I'm a consultant."

"Oh. I see." Mr. Fields was impressed.

Using his forged driver's license, Siegfried applied for a passport via the Alexandria address. It would be delivered, the clerk told him, within a week. Later that same day, he visited the used-car lots along Rhode Island Avenue in the District of Columbia. He came away an hour later with a beige 1934 Ford with twenty-five thousand miles on the odometer. He was two hundred dollars poorer.

Then he drove to Union Station and turned in a claim check for two suitcases he had placed in storage. These contained his diving gear and his explosives. The

378

man who handed him the suitcase containing six sticks of dynamite was smoking.

He returned to Alexandria and "moved into" his new, occasional quarters. He went to the window and craned his neck. Yes, he could see the river. And he could see the capital beyond. Then he looked at the sky and smiled. Everything was coming together. He would have a very light dinner, perhaps just a sandwich, he told himself, then come back and unpack his diving gear. It promised to be a fine night for a swim.

In actuality, it was a *perfect* night for a plunge. Siegfried prayed it would be as perfect the next time. President and Mrs. Roosevelt always began their Thanksgiving sojourn to Warm Springs by boat from Washington. This year, Siegfried had noted in the newspapers, the President's schedule would be the same. But Siegfried would be sending a special bouquet this coming November, one that would shake the world.

The moon was at the first quarter, just as the almanac said it would be. Siegfried walked from his car on the Arlington side of the Potomac. It was almost 11 P.M. He wore a tweed suit and carried a walking stick. He could see Washington very clearly from a promenade across the Potomac.

Siegfried cut through a brambly area by the side of the road and the land led him to the shore of the river. There was not a human being anywhere in sight, which was the way he wanted it. Human beings only caused trouble. Like that damned woman. That Marjorie.

Women had their purposes, Siegfried thought, but it was not to inhibit important work. Marjorie had gotten what she had deserved. Siegfried barely gave it a second thought. Yet . . . it would trouble him until he got her into a permanent grave. Then the matter could rest.

By the water, he began to undress. He deftly pulled off his jacket, his shoes, and his pants. His shirt followed. He wore his wet suit beneath the tweed. He was ready for the river. He looked across and saw the object of his rehearsal: the *Sequoia,* moored at the basin just south of the Francis Scott Key Bridge. It was a two-mile swim across the river and two miles back. Siegfried enjoyed exercise.

Marjorie. His mind kept coming back to her. Siegfried hated unfinished business, and now that's exactly what she was. Lying in a makeshift area in the woods like that. It was an invitation to disaster. He would have to return to Liberty Circle as soon as possible and . . . and what? *Deal* with the situation.

Siegfried consoled himself with the fact that the sailor he had murdered in another set of woods had never been discovered. He would have heard of it if the corpse of that foolish midwestern kid had surfaced. The news would have been all over, in fact. Nazis would have been blamed and there would have been a localized hysteria.

Americans! What fools!

Siegfried methodically rolled his clothing into the shape of a thin bed blanket. He tied them with string. Then he checked his equipment.

A diver's knife was lashed to one leg. He fitted a loaded Luger, wrapped tightly in waterproof canvas and sealed, into a specially designed rubber holster at his waist. Beneath his left arm was a small, tightly bound package containing a pair of red clay bricks.

The bricks exceeded the size and shape of the bomb that Siegfried would plant against the President's yacht. But this was the rehearsal. If it was feasible to cross the Potomac twice by moonlight, bring the bricks to rest against the slumbering ship and return, then Siegfried would have proven his method of murdering the socialist thirty-second President of the United States.

He checked his watch. It was 11:22. He entered the water.

The bricks were heavy, but Siegfried was a strong swimmer. He would take his time and conserve his energy. Speed was not an element. Not tonight, and not the next time when he would use a much shorter route. Accuracy and practicality were the elements Siegfried tested. He moved his arms in slow, patient overhand strokes. It was almost fun. Out for a midnight swim.

By his own estimate, he had done a half mile. Then a mile. He felt his muscles loosen and he found an even, steady pace. It was inordinately peaceful and quiet in the middle of the river. He could see very clearly. The moonlight was just enough to guide him along, but not enough to give him away.

He covered the first mile in twenty minutes. The second mile seemed a little quicker. His watch told him he was correct. The *Sequoia,* which had seemed like a toy on the horizon when he began, now was in front of him with the majesty of a small ocean liner. He was a hundred yards from it and could clearly see through portholes and windows on the main deck. An occasional crew member wandered the main deck's promenade. Siegfried studied the port side of the ship, the side facing him, to check for any sailors who might be leaning against the railing. He saw none. He was fifty yards away.

Then he was within forty. And he could practically drift the rest of the way. He cut his strokes and paddled quietly to his left, moving into a giant shadow cast by the ship's hull against the lights from the shore. The stern of the ship was before him. The rudder and the screw were like appendages to a moderately sized building.

He looked up and saw nothing human. A few more strokes and he was within reach of the ship. Then he threw his hand forward and touched it.

A sense of victory coursed through him, a foreshadowing of the victory that would eventually be his. It *was* possible! He had reached the presidential yacht unobserved. He placed his hands against the cold steel of the Bathbuilt hull and an exhilaration was upon him that was almost religious. He felt himself grin. He almost wanted to scream with joy.

He looked up. Again he was thrilled by the discovery. The area of the stern that housed the rudder and propeller was recessed from the main deck of the ship. This would be the ideal place to work, to bolt his bomb—the *flowers*—for the leftist President. In this space he could tread water unobserved from either ship or shore. Like the night, it was perfect.

He examined the hull again and marked its seaworthiness and sturdiness. He made one mental note. The bomb would have to be even more powerful than he'd previously estimated. He had to be sure it would blast through the steel. Siegfried would make certain that it would.

Carefully now, he rehearsed every move that he would make when he returned. He dived beneath the waterline and felt for a place where a waterproof plastic cement could solidify the bomb in place in a matter of minutes. He also looked for, and found, areas of iron in the hull in case he opted for a magnetized attachment on his return. Then, using the package of bricks as his dummy, he rehearsed the placement of the bomb. Once satisfied, he pushed off from the ship and let the bricks sink into the Potomac. No use carrying the extra weight back to Virginia.

Siegfried took a final look and pushed off. The next time he saw the ship from such a distance he would be playing a game in dead earnest. The bomb would be live and triggered. It would be, in fact, ticking.

Someone would die. Probably many people. They would deserve it, he told himself, for being on board with Roosevelt. Imagine! An aristocrat leading America toward communism. Siegfried felt a wave of contempt overtake him. He spat at Roosevelt's boat. Then he saw sailors moving on the deck.

Very quietly, with hushed strokes, he turned in the water and pointed himself toward Virginia. He retraced his route, swimming easily with the current, and arrived on the opposite shore completely unobserved.

A chair scraped on the basement floor. The screech of wood upon the cement was momentarily the only sound in the room. Then there were the sounds of murmurs and heavy, panting breathing.

Hunsicker, his brow thick, puffed, and bruised, sat unrestrained in a wooden chair at the center. There was a single lamp at a small wooden desk. Behind the lamp sat Frank Lerrick, watching studiously as the light cast shadows like a Halloween mask across his moustache and cheeks. Bobby Charles Martin, who was an expert on things beyond basic map reading, sat to one side facing Hunsicker. He raised his eyebrows, puffed on a cigarette, and dropped it onto the floor. He extinguished it with the toc of one shoe.

He raised his gaze from Hunsicker to the two men who circled Hunsicker like hungry wolves, Allen Wilson and Jack Burns. Burns passed in front of Hunsicker and the German flinched. Then Wilson rushed to him from the side and delivered a heavy, punishing, open-handed half-punch half-slap to the side of the German's skull.

The German reeled and the chair tipped. Burns grabbed the silent German by the lapels, picked up his enormous body, and slammed it down again on the hard-backed chair. Then Burns took his own turn and delivered a similarly punishing blow from the other side. But this time his partner held the chair and the German did not fall.

Lerrick spoke almost from boredom. This had been going on for the better part of a day and a half. Hunsicker, with blood now trickling from the corner of an eye, looked at the man behind the desk with heavy, painful, dark tired eyes.

"Herr Hunsicker," Lerrick began with an air that suggested an impending end to the kindness and the patience. "You're a very noble man, Herr Hunsicker. You have held out for what you believe in. You have not told us anything for a very long time. Your own officers in the Gestapo would be proud of you. Truly proud. But how long can this continue? How long *must* it continue?"

Lerrick stared at the subject. Hunsicker's face was sweating profusely and his head sagged slightly to one side. The eyes, which had looked mean, now looked hollow and unfocused.

Burns rushed Hunsicker again, began to wind up with a tremendous punch, and Bobby Charles Martin raised a hand to halt him. The blow stopped in midair as the German flinched.

"Not just yet, Jack," Martin said to his interrogator in kindly tones. "Mr. Hunsicker is conversing with Mr. Lerrick."

"Wilhelm," Lerrick said with sincerity, leaning forward, "I am being very candid with you. This will go on for weeks. We will not stop until you tell us what we wish to learn." A tangible pause and: "You have worked for the Gestapo yourself. You know that no man can hold out forever. You know that in the end the unfortunate man in your position always must talk. That is human nature." A lesser pause, and Lerrick concluded, "There are limits to pain, Wilhelm. There are things that you have heard about from your own people, but have barely dreamed about here. Injections. Electricity. Wires."

There was a response from Hunsicker's listless eyes.

"Yes, Wilhelm," Lerrick continued. "The worst is yet to come. And that will be followed by a long imprisonment. Unless you choose to speak."

The German's mouth moved and Lerrick smiled appreciatively.

"And after you speak with us, we will make you comfortable. We will let you sleep. A doctor will ease your physical pain. Would you like a woman, Wilhelm? We could even bring you a nice young fraulein who will take care of your other needs. Wouldn't that be much better than this, Wilhelm?"

Words formed on the German's lips. He mumbled. It was only an obscenity, but it was a start.

Then there was more silence. Lerrick glanced amiably to Burns and Allen.

"Hurt him," he said evenly.

As Burns steadied Hunsicker, Allen Wilson stepped behind him, brought the German's wrists together, and began to pull them sharply upward. It was too much even for Frank Lerrick.

Lerrick rose from his desk and went to the door. Bobby Charles Martin followed. The men went outside into a quiet, guarded corridor in a Washington basement.

"Jesus," Lerrick said, shaking his head in disgust. "I, uh, can't stand this stuff." He glanced at his watch. It was three in the afternoon. He lit a cigarette.

"A few more hours," said Martin. "He's ready to break." He glanced at his own watch. "He'll be talking by midnight."

"And what if he doesn't?"

"He will," Martin said, taking out his own pack of cigarettes. "What are you feeling so bad about? They do it to their own people, you know."

"Of course, but . . ." Lerrick's words were punctuated by a loud piercing scream from the room behind him. "But, Jesus . . ." he concluded, shaking his head. "I, uh, understand national interest and all, but we never did anything like *that* back in Illinois."

"Really?" answered Martin, genuinely surprised, his furry eyebrows shooting toward the ceiling. "Back in Ohio we do it all the time."

TWENTY-SEVEN

Questions. Answers.

Siegfried had more of the former than the latter. So did Laura. So did everyone.

Exactly which type of explosive would be best? Siegfried wondered as he drove his car northward. And how much of it? Should the *Sequoia* blow up at night when the President was sleeping? If so, the explosive could be placed just above the rudder and screw of the yacht, enough to blow the whole ship apart. But attaching that much explosive to the *Sequoia* could be cumbersome. And if the President boarded the ship in the morning, the charge would have to sit in place for a full twenty-four hours before detonation.

Or, Siegfried wondered, would a smaller charge be a better idea? A small charge fixed to a point below the President and Mrs. Roosevelt's chamber. Siegfried had studied the layout of the ship. Surely a 2 A.M. detonation below the waterline—about ten yards beneath the sleeping First Couple—would annihilate them. A relatively simple timing device could be used.

Much easier, Siegfried realized, than the elaborate work that sank the *Wolfe*.

What about boarding the ship? he wondered. Not necessary, he quickly concluded. The point was to kill one man in particular. Siegfried grinned. The President's yacht would no doubt have a naval escort. And right in their midst . . . a few hours after departure . . .

The spy laughed. How Goering and Hitler would welcome him to the Reich! What a hero he would be!

Questions. Answers.

Laura wondered about her husband. He was being so wonderful to her. Since her return, the marriage had been spectacular. It was like the old days in New Haven. He came to her every night minutes after the lights went out. He would reach to her—a strong, lustful primitive—and pull her to his side of the bed. Then their love games would start. Maybe the banter was silly. Maybe it was childish. She blushed to think of it. But it thrilled her.

"You are my prisoner now, little girl," he would say. "You must do as I say."

"And what do you say?"

He would answer with his hands. He would take her nightclothes from her with just the right amount of roughness. She would be naked. His hands, his lips, and his tongue would be all over her until she would ache with her own desires and pray that he would hurry and satisfy her.

Then she would realize that he, too, was completely naked. She would reach to his legs and feel the strong hard muscles. She would guide her hand in the proper direction. And her fingers would flirt with his hardness.

Then he would be upon her, strong and rigid and powerful, kissing her passionately as he pressed himself far inside her.

Bed was delicious again. It was like having a new lover. The honeymoon all over again.

What was Peter Whiteside ever talking about? Laura wondered. There wasn't a Soviet spy anywhere within miles. Laura would be happy to help England, but being a wife came first. After a few days back with her husband, England and the rest of Europe seemed very distant again, very small and very marginal to one's daily existence. Laura began to understand the Americans. From their point of view, why should they get involved?

Of course, Stephen Fowler disagreed. Moral obligation, and all. Thy brother's keeper. She stayed out of political discussions with him, left him to his sermons, his writings, his occasional guest sermon at another parish, and his frequent visits to Protestant convocations in the surrounding cities.

Peter Whiteside, Laura had finally convinced herself, didn't know what he was talking about. "A typically stuffy English windbag," as an American might say.

Laura smiled. It was a beautiful clear late autumn afternoon. Her husband was away that day but it was much too nice to be indoors. So she would go for a walk. That would be perfect. Through the woods, back behind the churchyard.

She felt a certain elation. Her life had come together at last. And this time, she felt, no one could take it away from her.

Hunsicker had not been listening to Bobby Charles

Martin's predictions. Burns and Allens worked him relentlessly. By dawn the confession started trickling out.

To those who listened, the words of the German contained little of substance and much of times and places that no longer mattered. It was an hour before Siegfried's name passed Hunsicker's lips. By that time the German's jaw was about touching his belt.

Roddy Schwarzkopf, who was on duty, was called down to the basement. Schwarzkopf was stunned to find a bleeding, battered prisoner sitting in the center of the room. Four members of his own Bureau stood in soaked shirts with rolled-up sleeves. There wasn't an eye in the room that didn't have a pupil like a pinpoint.

"Don't ask what we've been doing, Roddy," Lerrick snapped. "We're going to feed you some questions. You will pose them in German. That will be easier for the King of Prussia here."

Bobby Charles Martin operated the wire recorder and kept the microphone close. As if by osmosis, Schwarzkopf broke out in a sweat also.

"National interest, Roddy," Lerrick purred. "Now, uh, please . . . if you will . . ."

Hunsicker poured out as much as he knew. His drop point for contact with Fritz Duquaine ("Probably no good anymore," Lerrick said) and the address of the apartment in Yorkville ("Long since empty, I'm sure," Lerrick added). Then there were other names, key pieces of several networks, and then they were back to Siegfried.

"What does the man look like? Tell us what he looks like, Wilhelm."

Schwarzkopf translated and Hunsicker rambled. As

Schwarzkopf translated back to English, a portrait emerged that matched the one Cochrane had evolved from the Pritchard case in New Jersey.

"So we are talking about the same man," Lerrick breathed. "Keep sweating him, Roddy."

There were the meetings with Duquaine, Hunsicker babbled, and the saboteur known as Siegfried had been at several of them. Dapper. Guarded. Tall. Strong. Speaking aristocratic German to Hunsicker's working-class ears.

"A gentleman," Hunsicker stressed with fading strength. "A true gentleman."

"Where does he come from?" the interrogators pressed. Hunsicker didn't know.

"Where does he go to?" they asked. Hunsicker didn't know that, either.

"Slap him around a little more," Bobby Charles Martin instructed. "If he still doesn't tell us, it means he doesn't know. Careful not to kill him, by the way."

The German still didn't know. And before he lost consciousness the rest was a garble. He recalled his most recent conversation with Duquaine: how the spy master had arrogantly instructed him on American politics and how they would not be seeing Siegfried again.

Ein . . . letzter . . . Angriffszeil . . . One final target.

Then the German had collapsed. Stiff and weary, the interrogation team rose from their own seats and stretched. Horrified, Roddy Schwarzkopf was the only one in the room to check if Hunsicker was still breathing.

He was.

Hunsicker's confession was transcribed onto paper

by three different typists that same morning. There was a copy sitting on Wheeler's lap when Cochrane, punchy from only five hours' sleep, entered his own office at eleven and found Wheeler sitting there reading.

"Our German friend has been mildly helpful," Wheeler concluded as a cloud of pipe smoke rolled from his direction. "He's confirmed some of what we already knew. But he's added little. It's rambling. Damn Lerrick and his filthy methods." He tossed the report onto Cochrane's desk. Cochrane picked it up. "So this is what they beat out of him, huh?"

"If you want to call it that," Wheeler said.

"What would you call it?"

"Doing what had to be done."

Cochrane glanced down to the transcript but didn't read it. Not yet. Wheeler wouldn't let the subject drop.

"Sounds like you don't approve," Wheeler suggested.

"Whether or not I approve doesn't matter, does it?"

"No."

"So why ask me?" Cochrane countered. Wheeler was testing his patience these days, same as he had tested it in Kansas City and Chicago. But Dick Wheeler was always like that. Testing, testing, testing, then drawing the best performance from the men in his command.

"Does Hoover know?" Cochrane asked. "About Bobby Martin's interrogation techniques?"

Wheeler's pipe was in his mouth and he puffed out a prodigious cloud. "Bill, how long have you been with this Bureau? Since 1934, right? The Chief doesn't want to know about techniques. Results count, not methods. If you can't appreciate that, you're dreadfully naïve for a man your age."

There was a pause, then Wheeler continued. "You know what, Bill?" Wheeler asked, his mood shifting tangibly as he cupped the bowl of his pipe in his right palm. "I don't like shit like that, either. Frank Lerrick authorized it and I know for a fact that it turns his stomach, too. But what the hell do you do? Give the other side a chance to kill us first? You can be damned well sure that the other side doesn't behave any better."

"So what separates them from us?"

"We're right," Wheeler answered quickly. He motioned to the transcript again. "Well, enough philosophy. Maybe you'll see something that I didn't in those papers. What are you doing for lunch?"

Cochrane wasn't doing anything, including eating. He had the transcript for lunch. He read it once, twice, three times, closed into his office before the skein of it began to make sense. He tried to purge the delirium from the German's voice. He picked up his pencil and wrote isolated sentences on a yellow pad. He felt himself go very cold, though the room was warm.

Hunsicker's final meeting with Duquaine. That was the key. Cochrane isolated the sentences because the account of the meeting was scattered across thirty-eight pages.

" . . . Siegfried . . . All alone . . . Approved by Berlin . . . Special mission . . . to change American politics . . . One final target . . . Keep America out of the war . . . *One final target* . . ."

Then Cochrane was on his feet and hurrying down the hall, bumping into buxom Dora McNeil and continuing around the corner to Wheeler's office, where he entered without knocking.

Wheeler's head shot upward, then relaxed when he

recognized Cochrane. "Decipher it, did you?" Wheeler asked. Then he read Cochrane's expression and turned very serious. "Well, God Almighty," he grumbled, removing the pipe and setting it aside. "Don't be shy about it. What have you got?"

"We've got this invisible German floating around the country. No one sees him, no one recognizes him. We only know where he's been, never where he is." Cochrane looked down to what he'd written on a yellow legal pad as if to check that it was still there. Then he handed it to Wheeler. "And this is what he's up to. The final mission."

Wheeler read Cochrane's sprawling but semi-inspired handwriting.

"Now," said Cochrane. "You tell me. What does this mean to you? There's only one target that changes American politics. Am I right or am I crazy? And note carefully the wording. 'Approved by *Berlin*.' Normally the fifth column works out of Hamburg. But this went up and down the chain of command, into and out of Hitler's own office on the Prinz Albrechtstrasse, if my guess is anywhere accurate."

Wheeler scanned and Cochrane saw his superior's face go white. Roosevelt. Of course, Roosevelt. What else could it possibly be?

"Holy Mother of Christ," Wheeler breathed. He tossed the pad back onto his desk. He reached to his telephone and dialed Hoover. "Who the hell *is* this Siegfried?" Wheeler ranted as he listened to an unanswered ringing on Hoover's end. "*Who* is he? *Where* is he? And why in Christ's name can't we catch him?"

"He can't stay out there forever," Cochrane said

stubbornly to the skeptical gaze of Wheeler. "He has to show himself somewhere."

Then Hoover came on the line, and Wheeler, with unusual deference, began to speak.

Siegfried was in Liberty Circle.

He stepped out of his car and gazed at the clean white spire of St. Paul's Lutheran Church. It was a crisp day today, the kind Siegfried liked, and he felt invigorated. He looked to the tower of the church where his radio room was concealed within the walls.

He began to think. And absently, he reached to the pocket of his jacket and pulled out a pack of Pall Malls.

He drew one with his lips, lit it, and began to smoke. He lowered his eyes away from the spire and his radio room. No use calling extra attention. There were people on the sidewalk. People who didn't even know there was a Siegfried.

He puffed on the cigarette. Then he heard a woman's voice, which jarred him.

"Why, Reverend Fowler!" the woman said, glaring at the spy. "Smoking! I never knew!"

It was Mrs. Dobson, a plain little woman whose husband owned the hardware store, and her friend Mrs. Jarvis, who worked for Bell Telephone of New Jersey.

"I'm surprised at you, Reverend!" Mrs. Jarvis chimed in. "I didn't know you had any vices. Such an otherwise decent young man! But, *smoking!*"

The two ladies, both parishioners, laughed good-naturedly.

Reverend Fowler extinguished the cigarette against

the side of the car.

"I apologize, ladies," he said, grinning and shaking his head. "I quite forgot myself! See you both on Sunday, now, hear?" He laughed, too, making light of his small sin.

Then they were gone and Siegfried shuddered. The cigarettes. He'd neglected to throw them away. They were part of Siegfried, not part of Reverend Fowler. A little mistake like that again could cost him everything!

He shivered. Marjorie. The swim across the Potomac to the presidential yacht. The necessity of now assembling the biggest, most lethal bomb he had ever made. The pressure was mounting on him. Why else would he have forgotten a detail like the cigarettes?

He calmed himself. Perhaps it was a good thing. He would be more careful now. More careful than ever. Nothing short of perfection would do, not until Roosevelt was dead and he was safely in Germany, an American-born hero of the Third Reich.

Cigarettes! A man like Siegfried didn't need them anyway. Siegfried was an Aryan! Made of steel! Better than the rabble that surrounded him!

Stephen Fowler turned toward the parish house, which was quiet. Where, he wondered, was Laura?

PART SIX

November
1939

TWENTY-EIGHT

"A Mrs. Laura Fowler found the body," said Chief of Police Bob Higgins of Liberty Circle. "Horrible thing. Just horrible. The poor woman went out for a walk behind her husband's church. About an hour before the Reverend returned from a trip. There's a cemetery behind St. Paul's, then a couple of acres of woods. Well, sir, she's walking and her foot hits something."

Bill Cochrane followed Chief Higgins closely, listening to each word. They walked from the police station only about two blocks to the church. Higgins was not used to having FBI visitors. It was still a nice afternoon.

"She sees what hit her foot and she looks down. Well, sir," said the red-haired, lean Higgins, "sure enough. It's the arm of a dead woman reaching up from a makeshift grave."

Cochrane nodded. They walked quickly. "Thank you for telephoning," he said. He hadn't been off the train from Washington for ten minutes.

"Well, sir," answered Higgins. "I got that FBI

circular about that sailor who was murdered. Wasn't that a horrible thing? Well, it stuck with me. Couldn't get the case out of my mind. The boy's body lying out there in the woods. Well, sir. Then we get this one right here in Liberty Circle. Almost the exact same thing. So, well, sir, I made up my mind to call."

The local police officer was correct. It was like Billy Pritchard all over again. Higgins led Cochrane fifty yards through the woods and they came to a black blanket that covered a corpse. The rest of the Liberty Circle Police Department, two deputies, sprung to attention when they saw that Chief Higgins had a visitor.

"This killer you're looking for . . ." Higgins said. "Must be important."

"Why's that?"

"Murder don't bring the FBI in unless it's real important. Well, sir, I'm just a country cop, but I know that much."

"Fact is, Chief," Cochrane said, "there's both kidnapping and bank robbery involved. That's what brings us in."

"Holy shit," he said. "Is that a fact?"

The deputies uncovered the corpse. Cochrane grimaced and looked down. The odor of the corpse was building.

"Strangled," said Higgins helpfully. "Just like the boy in New Jersey."

Cochrane stooped down and looked at the neck. "Looks like a pair of hands did this," he said. He didn't volunteer that a chain had been used in Red Bank.

"She's been dead for two days at the most," said Higgins. "I went to a forensics science course in

Trenton last year. And I'll tell you something else, Mr. Cochrane, sir, she was here on Wednesday."

Cochrane had already noted the clothing. The undergarments were still wet. "Why's that?" Cochrane asked.

"It hasn't rained since Wednesday," he said, looking to his deputies, who were suitably impressed. "But she was here in the rain. That means she was killed Wednesday afternoon."

Cochrane was looking carefully at the neck now. A pair of very strong hands, he noted. The throat was crushed.

"Very observant," he said, glancing up. "But I thought you didn't touch the body."

"Didn't *move* anything," the chief said with sudden defensiveness. "But we checked the body."

"No one recognizes her?"

"It's a town of four thousand," Higgins said. "I know everyone. I don't know her."

"What about the neighboring towns?"

Higgins suppressed a chuckle. "Well, sir, I had the other police chiefs over here this morning. Wanted to give you as much as I could. None of them could identify her, either, Mr. Cochrane. She's from out of the area."

"No identification?" Cochrane asked.

"No, sir."

"No purse? No wallet?"

"Well, sir, no."

Cochrane wondered if the chief had checked the dead woman for sexual contact, too. But he didn't ask.

"Out of the area," the chief repeated. "I'm sure."

"So am I."

403

"You are?"

Cochrane stood. He nodded to the deputies, who placed the blanket back over the corpse.

"Yes."

"How so sure?" Higgins asked.

"Expensive high heels. Black lamé dress. Three gold bracelets, a ruby ring, and silk stockings. How many women dress like that around here on a rainy afternoon, Chief?"

"Well, sir. Not very many, I got to admit."

Cochrane noted that the woman also wore a raincoat. Clear days since Wednesday gave further credence to that day as the time of the murder. Cochrane glanced over his shoulder. If the body had been dragged to this spot and dumped, the trail had been beaten away by eager footsteps. But more likely, the woman had been lured here by someone she knew, someone she liked, or someone who coerced her. But there had been no robbery or, apparently, sexual assault. Her clothes were neat, which argued against coercion.

Cochrane looked back to the police chief and pondered: murder was the crime least frequently committed by professional criminals. Rather, it was the province of jittery amateurs seeking to cover their mistakes. Why was Siegfried jittery? What mistake had he sought to cover?

Then again, in the twilight world of espionage, such statistics could be tossed to the wind. But such questions couldn't be.

"Okay. So what else?" Chief Higgins asked.

"She came from the city," Cochrane said. "She came out here to visit, perhaps. Must have known someone.

Maybe the killer."

"You think the killer lives here?"

"I didn't say that. But it happened on Wednesday, Chief, give or take a day. Now maybe you can get a couple of volunteers and go door to door. Find out who saw any strangers on Wednesday of this past week. J. Edgar Hoover would be thankful if you'd help."

"Well, sir, gosh. I'd be happy to help a great policeman like J. Edgar Hoover."

"I'll tell him we can count on you."

Chief Higgins was beaming.

"Now, the state police will be by for photographs," Cochrane said. "They'll also handle the removal of the body. Where do I find this Mrs. . . . Mrs. . . . ?"

"Fowler? The one who discovered the body?"

"Right," Cochrane said.

"Well, sir, just follow me. It'll just take a minute."

Chief Higgins led Bill Cochrane to the home of Reverend and Mrs. Fowler. Cochrane and Chief Higgins waited in the Fowlers' living room as Reverend Fowler appeared first. "She's extremely upset," Reverend Fowler explained in low tones before his wife entered the room. "I hope you won't dwell on too many of the details."

"I'll proceed gently," said Cochrane.

"What are you, by the way?" Fowler asked. "New Jersey State Police?"

"Federal Bureau of Investigation."

Cochrane saw an unwitting flinch in the minister's eyes. He chalked it up to surprise.

405

"Investigating a *homicide?*" Reverend Fowler asked, his tone of voice strange.

Cochrane repeated the lie about banking and kidnapping. The minister appeared content with the explanation.

The woman who entered the room a minute late was as beautiful as she was shaken. Laura wore a navy-blue sweater and a gray skirt. Bill Cochrane looked at her and wondered why he always met the truly extraordinary women in the line of duty or after they had married someone else. Then he reminded himself that a woman in city clothing was dead beyond the churchyard. He exchanged a few pleasantries with the Fowlers, sat down, and turned to business. Chief Higgins remained in the room.

Laura recounted what she had found and how she had found it. She had little more to say. She had, after all, turned and run from the area in horror upon her discovery. And she had not been back to the location since.

Reverend Fowler tried to take some of the attention away from his wife.

"Really, Officer," Fowler said, "I don't know what else my wife can tell you. She only made the discovery."

"Had either of you been up in that area of the woods on previous days?" Cochrane asked.

The Fowlers shook their heads.

"What about suspicious individuals?" Cochrane asked. "Or people you haven't recognized in town recently?"

"I saw the woman's face," Laura said with a shudder. "I can still see her face." She stifled a tremor, and her husband, sitting on a sofa next to her, took her hand.

She raised her eyes back to Bill Cochrane. "I had never seen her before. Ever."

Fowler looked at his wife carefully and shifted his eyes back to Cochrane. It was at that moment that Fowler was unnerved to notice that Cochrane had been watching him as his wife spoke.

"Reverend," Cochrane asked, "do you know anyone in the habit of using that area for any purpose?"

Fowler said he didn't.

"But the only access is through the churchyard, isn't it?" Cochrane asked.

Chief Higgins interjected. "Well, sir, no. Not exactly. The woods come out near the train station."

"They do, do they?" asked Cochrane, intrigued.

"They also border upon more than three dozen private homes," Fowler seemed anxious to add. "Really, Officer, there're probably a hundred ways to get to that location. None of them are particularly well watched."

"Of course," said Cochrane. He looked at Laura again. Another man's woman. His attention lagged again and he wondered what such a woman had seen in her husband. Then, of course, he sensed it. Fowler was well-spoken, and handsome. Chief Higgins had already confided that their parish minister was from a moneyed Main Line family. "I suspect that's all for today," Cochrane said. "Thank you."

What was it, Cochrane wondered, that he didn't like about the minister? Then he realized: Fowler had the type of woman that Cochrane had once upon a time wanted. Reactions like this, he warned himself, often made people see others not so clearly.

"Officer?" Fowler asked, as they all stood and as

Cochrane moved toward the door.

"Yes?"

"Tomorrow's Sunday," he said. "If you're here in the morning, St. Paul's would welcome you. We have services at eight and nine-thirty."

Cochrane's response surprised the minister. "That's very kind of you," he answered. "I'll try to be there."

Once again, Bill Cochrane thought he saw something strange in the man's eyes.

"Wonderful," Laura said. "My husband gives an excellent sermon."

"People like it because it's short," laughed Fowler. "They can get home to breakfast at a reasonable hour."

Then Bill Cochrane and Chief Higgins were outside the Fowlers' home again and Chief Higgins was talking as they walked down the lane that passed the church.

Higgins was saying how popular the new minister was, how he'd just come from seminary at Yale, and how he'd eased the transition from the older Reverend Dryer, who was now quite ill.

Cochrane listened with one ear as they walked past the white wooden church. Cochrane looked skyward toward the spire.

Then several thoughts came together. The steeple of St. Paul's was the highest man-made point anywhere in the area. And then he suddenly recalled why the name Liberty Circle had leaped out at him. The town was almost dead center on the radius map drawn by the Bluebirds of radio transmissions.

His mind played Satanic games as he thought back to Wilhelm Hunsicker's description of an elusive spy.

Except for one detail: Siegfried was German.

Wasn't he?

"What the hell's wrong with you?" Chief Higgins' voice was urgent. Then his hand was on Cochrane's shoulder, shaking him, jarring him. ". . . wrong with you?" Cochrane heard him say.

Cochrane snapped back to where he was. "Sorry," he said.

"We're strolling along here, sir, and you plain stopped walking. You all right?"

"Yes," Cochrane said, realizing that he had in fact stopped walking when a certain realization was upon him. "I was thinking. That's all."

"Must have been some thought."

"Yes. Frankly, it was. Something personal though. Sorry, I can't share it."

Fact: *no one had ever established that Siegfried was a native German. That had been supposition. Dick Wheeler's, seconded by Hoover.*

And, fact: *there was no such thing as coincidence in this line of work.*

Bill Cochrane checked into an inn situated in nearby Moorestown. From there he telephoned Dick Wheeler in Washington. He was staying here for a few days, Cochrane explained. Siegfried had been there four or five days earlier and no one had seen a stranger. So perhaps the spy wasn't a stranger.

"Don't get carried away, Bill," Wheeler warned. "Why would Brother Siegfried kill in his own backyard?" Cochrane could almost smell the white pipe smoke seeping through the line. Dick Wheeler cast his own spells.

"I don't know," Cochrane answered. "But it's as warm a lead as we've seen. So I'm staying."

TWENTY-NINE

The turnout for both church services that Sunday morning was larger than usual. The news of a murder within friendly Liberty Circle had spread through town. By Saturday evening everyone knew. By Sunday morning townspeople wanted to see each other and know that the world would safely go on. So they went to church.

St. Paul's had pews of deep burgundy, two side aisles, light oak panels on the floor and the walls, and a pulpit to the center left. An ethereal, benevolent fair-haired Christ appeared on the stained glass behind the altar. Bill Cochrane was only an occasional church-goer, but even he was moved by the old church (1797, said the historical marker outside), the congregation that filled it, the service, and the pastor.

Stephen Fowler was a man of great seriousness that Sunday morning. The congregation joined the choir in "Holy, Holy, Holy!"—the processional hymn—and after an opening prayer and psalm, those assembled sang "A Mighty Fortress." ("At least one Lutheran hymn a week," Reverend Fowler liked to tell parishioners with a wink.)

411

Then came the sermon. Stephen Fowler met head-on the subject that troubled his parish most. He avoided words "murder" and "homicide," but he talked of the "tragedy" in their midst. He spoke eloquently of death as part of life, touched upon guilt and original sin, and then moved to both forgiveness and trust: trust in God, trust in Christ; trust in the teachings of Christ. Follow me.

"Some follow and some stray," Reverend Fowler concluded. "It is up to each of us to decide which we are. But I promise you this." He held his congregation in rapt attention. "Those who follow are not those who need have fear now. Fear," he said, "is for those who have strayed. Let us pray. . . ."

The recessional hymn, appropriately, was "Faith of Our Fathers," which keyed something within Cochrane and summoned up memories of a Methodist childhood in Virginia. After the service he felt good, as if the service itself had routed the specter of war and murder.

But, of course, it hadn't. Afterward, outside on a sunny cool November morning, he found himself glancing upward at the spire again. Then he saw Reverend Fowler and Laura exchanging greetings with the faithful in the vestibule, so he joined them.

"It was good of you to come," Fowler said to Cochrane, shaking his hand. "I like to see new faces each Sunday."

"It was a lovely service," Cochrane said. "Thanks for skipping 'Onward, Christian Soldiers.'"

Reverend Fowler chuckled. "I'll tell you," he said, lowering his voice, "we get *requests* for that mawkish piece. Once a year will do us fine on that."

"Anything new?" Laura asked, changing the subject.

412

"On the . . ." She wasn't sure what to call it.

"The investigation? No. I suspect I'll be turning it over to the state police this evening."

"Then you're not staying?" she asked.

Cochrane shook his head. "I'm on my way back to Washington," he said. "Federal employees can only get away for so long before it starts to look like a vacation."

"I'm on my way to New York, myself," Fowler said. "Later today. Sorry we're not going in the same direction. We could have had a fine talk."

"Maybe some other time."

"Maybe." Bill Cochrane turned to Laura and looked into the loveliest pair of brown eyes he could ever have imagined. "Thank you for your time, Mrs. Fowler," he said.

"I wish I could have helped more."

For some reason, he was short of words. "I'm sure you did your best," he said lamely. Then he left, feeling their eyes on his back as he walked away.

From a slatted window in the church spire, just above the antique clock, and just a few feet from Siegfried's cramped transmission chamber, a man could see the railroad station.

Reverend Fowler found it convenient to be in the spire that afternoon when the train to Philadelphia and Washington departed. He focused a pair of binoculars on the depot, scanned the voyagers assembled, and eventually found the snooping FBI agent.

Fowler kept the glasses carefully on Bill Cochrane. There was nothing about the man that he liked.

His presence there. His sharp, penetrating mind. His

observance of detail. The way he looked at Laura. The way she looked back at him.

The train pulled into the station and Fowler kept the glasses on the troublemaker. Fowler thought of his wife. His wife was his *possession,* after all. She might have to be taught a lesson sometime soon. After all, he mused further, with Marjorie gone, Laura would have to fulfill other functions. A man needed a wife *and* a whore sometimes, Fowler mused wistfully. Laura would have to be both.

The train pulled to a halt at Liberty Circle. The first three cars would be transferred at Trenton to an engine and train of the Pennsylvania Railroad. Fowler watched Bill Cochrane carefully and was relieved when the FBI agent boarded the second car. Fowler scanned all the exits until the train pulled out of the station.

Cochrane had not disembarked. He was gone. Fowler placed his binoculars back in their case, content with Cochrane's departure. He was further satisfied that he could travel to New York, himself, later that evening.

Fowler paid no attention at all to three other travelers who disembarked at Liberty Circle. One was a tall dark-haired Englishman in a coat and a bowler. The other two men were younger and more heavyset. They were bareheaded and followed their senior partner.

But Siegfried, thinking ahead to his own departure that day, had no way of recognizing Peter Whiteside. Nor did he have any way of guessing his business in Liberty Circle. Nor, in his wildest fantasies, would he have imagined that Whiteside would have brought some M.I. 6 muscle along with him, just for good measure.

THIRTY

Fritz Duquaine, the Boer and Siegfried's onetime spy master, felt like a damned fool. Twice he'd been to St. Paul's by night to leave messages for Fowler. Twice he had urged the stubborn minister to contact him. Protocol forbade a direct meeting anywhere outside of New York. And they had made rendezvous arrangements in the summer. But Fowler, Duquaine cursed, has this fixation: his independence and his self-professed anonymity. Siegfried hadn't made contact for three weeks, since the last signal left in the church.

Duquaine stood before the Sailors' Monument in New York's Battery Park. Beneath his left arm he held an umbrella and an attaché case. In his right hand he held a New York *Mirror*. The weather had turned sharply colder and wind swept in from the harbor. Duquaine was reminded of the docks in Bremen or Cape Town in the winter. Yet another exercise in futility, Duquaine thought. In a raincoat, he was freezing. It was a Tuesday a few minutes after noon. Few other people were in the park. Apparently few

New Yorkers enjoyed having their ears turned to ice.

Duquaine walked to a bench near a park exit toward Wall Street. He hunched his shoulders. Even here the wind found him. He cursed Siegfried again and muttered a special oath for all self-styled spies. Someday one of them would get him killed.

What in hell, he wondered, was Siegfried doing that would get direct approval from Hitler? How far could Siegfried have managed to get, seeing how the Gestapo's contact within the FBI had sent out an alarm?

Duquaine lit a cigarette, using three matches within his cupped hands. He glanced at his watch. Twelve minutes past noon. Well, he decided, he wasn't going to freeze more than three more minutes. That was certain. He turned to his left, squinted slightly against the brightness, and eyed the ferry and a British frigate leaving the harbor.

The damnable British, he thought again, thinking back to his own boyhood. Filthiest colonialists in the world. Now at least England was in the war against Hitler. Over the pretext of Polish territorial integrity, of all things! Duquaine wondered whether he would soon be assigned to infiltrate England in advance of the German invasion. It was not without reason. He had relatives up north, toward Sunderland and Edinburgh, and under a colonial guise he could probably get a good look at submarine activity.

Duquaine was in the midst of this thought when he turned quickly and was startled to see Reverend Fowler standing beside him, looking down in the ominous squinting glare that Duquaine had always disliked.

416

"Daydreaming?" Fowler asked in English.

"Waiting for you and freezing," said Duquaine. "And not for the first time."

"But possibly for the last," said Fowler. "Shall we walk?"

"Of course." Anything, Duquaine thought, to get moving and get business accomplished. They walked toward Wall Street.

"I am instructed to warn you," Duquaine began, "the Federal Bureau of Investigation has picked up your trail. Apparently, they do not know who you are yet, but—"

"I'm aware of it," said Fowler flatly.

"There is a particular agent. His name is William Cochrane. He—"

"I'm at least a week ahead of you, Duquaine," Fowler said. They paused. A policeman walked by and gave them a nod, which they returned. "I know about the FBI and I know about the agent. I want from you two things. One is the agent's home location. Do you have that for me?"

"I do," Duquaine said. He gave it and Fowler memorized it.

Then Fowler continued. "Now, I need an escape route and it must be ready immediately. I assume Berlin has arranged such?"

"Berlin has. You are to travel under a pseudonym or do you need identity papers, too?"

"Duquaine," Siegfried responded curtly, "if I needed papers I would have told you so. I need a route," he said. "That is all."

Duqaine hesitated and held his own temper. "You are to travel to Mexico City," he said. "There is a

417

German Embassy there, as you know. The undersecretary of consular affairs is a Herr Jaccard. You will go to a restaurant called Renato's, which is down the boulevard from the embassy. Do you speak Spanish?"

"Adequately," Fowler answered.

"Inquire at the bar for Señor López-García between six and seven on your first evening. The bartender will say that he does not know your name. You will move to the end of the bar and drink. Señor López-García is Herr Jaccard. He is available each evening for such emergencies. He will find you. Remain ready to travel; have no more than one small suitcase. You will be sent to either Tampico or Veracruz the next day and will leave on whatever German ship is first scheduled out of port. Probably a freighter."

"A freighter?"

"What did you prefer? The *Bismarck?* Or perhaps the Fuehrer's personal vessel?"

"Something more than a freighter," Fowler said acidly. "What am I? A deckhand? I'm going to keep America out of the war, all by myself."

"If you are unhappy," Duquaine replied with evident relish, "arrange your own passage."

"What I shall arrange," said Fowler, stopping and breaking off the conversation, "is that you will be placed on latrine duty in Gestapo headquarters in Berlin. Good day to you Duquaine. You've been of some small help."

Duqaine held his silence but looked furiously at Fowler. The American, however, turned his back on the South African and walked away.

"Bloody Nazis," Duquaine mumbled when Fowler was far out of earshot. If he never saw any of them again, it would be too soon. The Nazi true believers were almost as repellent as the English. Then, as Duquaine disappeared toward Worth Street, in search of a Longchamps for lunch, a few of Siegfried's words came back to him.

What in hell had Siegfried meant, "Keep America out of the war"? Fowler, Duquaine was now convinced, had delusions of grandeur. What a shame that Berlin was actually dealing with him.

"Where *is* your husband?" Peter Whiteside inquired on Wednesday.

Laura, seated on the sofa in her own living room, cocked her head. "So this *is* a business call, isn't it, Peter?" she snapped. Whiteside lowered his eyes and set aside the cup of tea she had brewed for him. She folded her arms and glared indignantly at him.

The two tall, sturdy men who had accompanied Whiteside found subjects to amuse them outside of the room. One sat on the front doorstep and Laura assumed he was a guard. The other was in the kitchen, and she knew he was covering the rear access to the house. Whiteside had introduced them as his associates, Andrew McPherson and Mick Fussel. It had not taken inspiration to peg them as M.I. 6, like Peter.

"You ought to be ashamed of yourself, Peter Whiteside," she said sternly. "Coming into my home, pretending you're glad to see me, asking your idiotic, insinuating questions . . ."

"I am ashamed, Laura," he attempted, "but not for coming here today. I lied to you last time we spoke. And I let you remain in considerable danger."

419

"You're trying to change your story now? Is that it?"

"After a fashion, yes."

"Well, I damned well don't believe you!"

Whiteside groaned imperceptibly.

"I don't want to hear your new account of things, Peter. Can you understand that?"

"I can understand how you feel, but you must listen to me."

"I should *never* have listened to you!" she snapped, getting hotter.

Fussel appeared in the doorway from the kitchen, and disappeared again.

Now Whiteside was angering. "No, Laura, perhaps you shouldn't have. But you did. So you made an error, too, didn't you? So now you have to listen to the truth. For your sake, for your father's sake, for England's sake—"

"And for the sake of yourself and all those who sail with you." She glanced at her watch, a black-faced oval Tiffany timepiece with Roman numerals, a wedding gift from Stephen's parents. "You have five minutes to set the accounts straight, Peter Whiteside," she said sternly. "After that, I will thank you to leave my home."

"I shall need more than five minutes, Laura," he warned.

She looked back to the watch. "I'm counting already," she said.

Siegfried was counting, also. Or, taking inventory, actually, in the apartment in Alexandria. His wet suit was in perfect order and packed within a locked

420

suitcase. He had U.S. currency, Mexican currency, a small amount of gold, and some Third Reich currency.

He turned his attention to the explosives. He still had enough TNT to sink a ship, but now there would be a change of plans. He hated changes, but sometimes last-minute quirks could not be avoided.

He drew all the window shades in the small apartment, then carefully threw the extra bolt on his door. He loaded his Luger, just in case he was disturbed. He liked the feel of the weapon in his hand. For the Third Reich, he would not hesitate to fire it.

He laid the Luger at the right side of a desk that he had converted to a work space. He then went to his mattress, undid part of the seam, and withdrew one stick of dynamite.

Intent on his work now, he conjured up plans for a second bomb. Four sticks of dynamite should pierce the hull of the *Sequoia* and do away with Roosevelt. But first there was this meddlesome FBI agent. . . .

Siegfried sat down at his desk and worked meticulously. He opened one stick of dynamite and poured out an ounce of TNT. He removed from a paper bag one of two inexpensive watches he had purchased at Grand Central Station in New York. With the help of a knife, he removed the crystal from the watch, then used a pair of tweezers to snap off the minute hand. Next Siegfried laid out a large section of iron pipe, three inches in diameter and seven inches in length. He unfolded a thick black woolen sock, acquired in New Hamsphire, the type used by lumberjacks on winter work details, and cut two six-inch lengths of copper wire. Then he withdrew from his pocket a nine-volt radio battery.

Damned fool FBI agent, Siegfried thought. *Who did he think he was going to stop? The early word on the FBI had been correct,* he mused to himself: *a bunch of amateurs, led by that incompetent vainglorious Hoover.*

Siegfried used surgical rubber gloves. He held to his ear the watch with only the hour hand. It was not ticking. Perfect. Not yet time to wind it. He set it aside.

The thought came back: Cochrane. The FBI agent deserved what he was going to get. Fowler didn't like the way Cochrane looked at Laura. Laura was *his,* to do with, to use, and to dispose of at times suiting his benefit and convenience.

Siegfried was angry. He set to work with unusual vengeance.

Whiteside held Laura's attention for a full twenty-two minutes. He watched her face as he spoke and he laid before her every bit of evidence. The Birmingham May Day bombing. The circumstantial notion that Fowler *could* have acquired knowledge of explosives from German agents in America and further *could* have been the saboteur who sunk the *Wolfe* and the *Adriana.*

Whiteside felt he was winning, but toward the conclusion, he saw skepticism growing again. She refolded her arms. And by the end, she was studying the floor, not looking at Peter Whiteside.

Fussel and McPherson were still at their sentry posts. It was five in the afternoon. There was a long silence as Whiteside finished.

"Well . . . ?" he asked.

"Every bit as fatuous and disreputable as your previous tale, Peter," she said. Her tone wasn't hostile now. It was simply disappointed. Before her eyes, Peter Whiteside had shrunk to something small, mean, and mendacious, and petulant.

"Laura, please—"

"I'm sorry, Peter," she said. "You'd better go." Her eyes flashed. "Now!" She was furious. "I mean it. I don't want you in my home and I don't want to hear any more of these stories. Please leave before I call the police!"

Whiteside puckered his lips, then let slip a long sigh of resolution. He nodded to Fussel, who was watching, arms folded, leaning against the doorframe to the kitchen.

"If you should change your mind, Laura," Whiteside tried, "I—"

"I shall not."

"I can be reached," he spoke through her, "through the British Consulate in Washington. It's on Connecticut Avenue. Ask for me by name."

She was raging and he knew it.

"I'm ready to arrange for your protection at any time. Please remember that."

"Go," she demanded, not looking at him.

Whiteside gave Fussel a slight nod of the head. And he went, no further word spoken, taking McPherson from the front door with him.

THIRTY-ONE

Bill Cochrane lay on the bed in the house on Twenty-sixth Street. He stared at the ceiling. It was a Sunday night, Fibber McGee was on the radio, but Cochrane wasn't listening.

There was something tangibly *wrong* at Liberty Circle. The Lutheran minister and his English wife. There was something within Stephen Fowler that Cochrane couldn't place, something hard and secretive. And how had an Englishwoman of Laura Fowler's rank landed in a quiet American whistlestop?

Then Cochrane piled on the coincidences that he had been trained to believe did not exist. St. Paul's was in the center of the Bluebirds' triangulation pattern. Siegfried unmistakably had passed through the town. But had he ever left?

Then there was his own attraction to Laura Fowler. Combined with his long pursuit of Siegfried and his worn-down nerves, was he now seeing shadows where there was no sun to cast them?

What *was* wrong with Stephen Fowler? Why were

Cochrane's internal alarms sounding? Instinct? Nerves?

Or attraction to Laura?

For the hell of it, he ran both their names through the United States Passport Bureau on Monday morning. Then he caught the one o'clock train north. Liberty Circle was worth a second look.

Laura found Bill Cochrane meandering along the side of St. Paul's. He had been waiting to be spotted, and sight him she did as she walked back to the rectory from town. She walked to him and smiled.

"Back again?" she asked.

"Hello, Mrs. Fowler," he said, having seen her the second she appeared at the roadside. "Hope your husband won't mind. I thought I'd take a second look at things. Paths to the woods through the churchyard."

"Must be an important case," she said.

"A murder's important," he answered swiftly, wondering how lame he sounded. "How's your husband?"

"Away again," she said. "Visiting a parish in Connecticut, I think."

"You think?"

The vagueness of her response surprised her when he called attention to it. "I *know,*" she said with an effacing smile. She walked with him until they came to the front door of St. Paul's. It was late afternoon now and the sky was darkening. "Wait here," she said.

She walked inside the church as Bill Cochrane stood outside. Then two small outside lights went on and another set illuminated the steeple. Laura reappeared. "The duties of the parson's wife," she said. "Lighting the steeple when he's out of town."

He smiled. "Short hours, no heavy lifting. Not bad duties, wouldn't you say?"

"Find anything?" she asked, suddenly quite serious. She motioned to the woods. The murder continued to disturb her.

"No," he said.

"Would you tell me if you had?"

"Maybe."

She smiled again. "Is it considered a bribe to brew a cup of tea for an FBI agent?" she inquired. "It's chilly out here. Interested?"

He was. He followed her to the rectory, wondering what kind of fool or madman Stephen Fowler was to so often leave alone a woman like Laura. He wondered if they were happily married. A small wave of depression touched him: he concluded that he had no reason to believe they were not.

She made Earl Gray in a blue and white ceramic pot that she had brought from England. They sat in the warm living room of the rectory and the tea was delicious, even though Bill Cochrane wasn't a tea drinker. She also served a plate of cookies, setting them on a table between them.

Laura sat on a sofa, her feet curled under her. Bill Cochrane sat in an armchair on the other side of the table. He tried to draw a sense of the Fowlers. Somehow he failed. See a woman in too bright a light and everything else is obscured, he reminded himself. He recalled that he was there, after all, on business.

But Laura was talking and he was listening. Somehow he had nudged the conversation to her past, and she told him about Wiltshire, her father, and Edward Shawcross. Then she told about Lake Contontic, the ballroom, and the young Princeton graduate, Stephen Fowler.

"And you've lived happily ever after?" he inquired.

She held his gaze for several long seconds. "Why do you guess that?" she answered.

"Nice home. Attractive husband. Comfortable, secure life-style," he said, probing.

She found herself telling the truth. "It hasn't always been easy," she said. "Stephen is away too much. There are times when I've thought of . . ." Her voice trailed off into silence.

"Not divorce, surely," he said.

"No," she answered quickly. "Returning home indefinitely," she said. "Until Stephen could decide whether he wants to be married to me."

"Home to England?"

"Yes."

And according to immigration records, you did, he thought, not saying it. *For two and a half months this past summer. Just when some of the worst bombs were planted.*

"And did you?" he asked, testing.

"June of this year," she said. "Until mid-August. I went to see my father in Salisbury."

"A pretty cathedral city if my fifth-grade geography still serves me," he said.

"It serves you quite well."

"Did Stephen travel with you?"

"No, he didn't."

Cochrane sipped his tea. Laura refilled his cup when he set it down. He waited for her to speak.

"Stephen was here in America," she said. "We weren't getting along. I thought some time away from each other might help."

"Did it?"

She found herself answering defensively. "Yes," she said firmly. "I think it did." Then she turned the questions back on him.

"And what about you?" she asked. "You should be ashamed of yourself," she said with mock severity, "turning your federal interrogation techniques upon an innocent Englishwoman. What about you, Mr. Cochrane? Happily married, I suppose, with a beautiful wife from a patrician American family. You have two little ones, a boy and a girl at a manageable interval, and a lovely home outside Washington, D.C."

He shook his head. "I have a three-room apartment in Baltimore when I'm not on an assignment. Right now I'm lodged in a crumbling old wooden structure in Georgetown. No children. I'm widowed," he said.

There was a heavy pause.

"Oh, I *am* sorry," said Laura, feeling inordinately clumsy. "I didn't meant to—"

"It's all right," he said. "It was several years ago. But you were almost right. She was a very pretty woman from an old Virginia family. We had grown up together."

"What was her name?"

"Heather."

"A pretty name," she said. "I can remember when my mother died," she said after a pause. "Death creates such a horrible void. It's so difficult to fill it."

"One *can't* fill it," he answered. "One can only get on with the rest of one's life. Sometimes you have to go in new directions. I would never have joined the FBI, for example, if my wife hadn't been killed in a car accident. I needed new challenges. New scenery. New faces. Does that make sense?"

She nodded. "There's only one thing that doesn't make sense about you so far, Mr. Cochrane."

"Which is that?"

"Why you're lying to me."

"Lying? About what?"

"You're investigating Stephen," she said. "You came here ostensibly to investigate a murder. But a murder is a state crime, as you yourself said. And you've even come back for a second look. Or, should I say, a second snoop. What are you looking for, Mr. Cochrane? Be as honest as you can with me. Maybe I could even help you."

He studied her and was struck by the manner in which he had foolishly both underestimated her and talked too much. He reached for a cookie as she silently held him in view. Every bit of his training dictated that he stay with his cover story. But then there was instinct. That, and the most enticing brown eyes that had ever drawn a bead on him.

"I'm waiting," she said.

"Everything I've told you is true."

"Of course it is," she answered. She folded her arms and waited.

It was a decision based on instinct and hunch, just as trusting Otto Mauer had been:

"I'm looking for a spy," he said. "A murderer and a spy. Same man. And I'm drawing close."

Then he told a story which fit astonishingly with the account given by Peter Whiteside. By the end of it, half an hour later, all the bombing dates coincided with Stephen's absences. As for Birmingham a few years ago, Laura thought, one could only draw certain conclusions. When he finished, she was greatly shaken. She spent a long time in the midst of several dark thoughts.

"I can't believe that my husband is the man you're looking for, Mr. Cochrane," she said at length. "He has his faults like any other man. But he's not the monster you described."

"I never said that he was," Bill Cochrane answered. "You came to that conclusion yourself. Same as I did."

There was a silence. Then the monstrosity of the whole thing was upon her, and it was too big, too horrible, and too terrifying to even comprehend. So she rejected it completely, and Bill Cochrane with it.

"How *dare* you!" she said, suddenly turning on him. "You come in here, accept our hospitality, and then make these accusations about my husband. I'll thank you, sir, to be on your way. And unless you have something concrete, don't ever come here with such stories again. Now, out!"

THIRTY-TWO

The vision was filled with its usual irrationality. It was familiar; Cochrane had suffered it before.

President Roosevelt was sitting on the east portico of the White House, sunning himself, making pencil notes in the margin of a typewritten report. Cochrane stood to the right, arms folded behind his back, as a man who was no more than an unidentifiable specter approached Roosevelt.

"Oh. Hello, my friend," Roosevelt said, looking up and grinning. The cigarette holder was in place.

The visitor handed Roosevelt a package as Cochrane tried to protest. But words would not escape his lips.

"Das ist für Sie," the man said as Roosevelt accepted it.

Cochrane twisted and turned. His feet were cemented in place; his throat empty.

"Für mich?" Roosevelt asked.

"Jawohl." The man nodded courteously.

"Danke schoen," said the grateful President. "I hope you'll consider voting next November. Are you a Democrat?"

"Nein," said the visitor, "I'm a National Socialist. *Heil Hitler!"*

Roosevelt looked quizzically at the man, then grinned at Cochrane, who was waving his arms to protest. Next there was a tremendous explosion in red and gray and black; and upon the explosion, Cochrane saw the largest swastika he had ever envisioned.

Then everything settled and Cochrane was far away, as if in an airplane. The White House was tranquil down below him, except it flew the red, white, and black banner of the Third Reich from its flagpole and Hitler stood at the east portico, his arm raised in the Nazi salute as one million cheering people stretched from the lawn of the White House across the city to the Washington Monument.

Cochrane tossed himself upright in his bed and came awake. His neck and face were wet and warm. The bedside clock, when he turned the light on, said 1:30 A.M. His mouth was parched. Cochrane wished his mind would behave itself when he was trying to sleep. Wasn't Siegfried furtive enough without creeping into his dreams?

Cochrane stalked down the creaky staircase. He was midway between a fitful sleep and a fatigued wakefulness. Some ice water, which he found in the Frigidaire, might help.

He stood by the kitchen counter and sipped. He thought of Laura and wondered where her husband really was. What was it about Reverend Fowler and his church, in the midst of the Bluebirds' triangulated zone of suspicion, that rankled him?

He wondered if Reverend Fowler was making love to Laura right then, as he stood in the kitchen finishing his ice water. He tossed the cubes into the sink, then thought of his own late wife. He had put Heather's photograph away recently, but now missed seeing her. Maybe he would get the picture out, try to cull more warmth than sadness from the memory, then go back to bed.

Then sleep, maybe.

He set down the glass in the sink. He turned, then noticed something. He looked again.

The window over the sink was closed but crooked. Cochrane eyed it closely, leaned forward, and inspected it. Then he reached for the lock above the lower panel of the window and felt it.

Something inside him flashed. Someone had tampered with the lock. He opened the window itself and saw the telltale marks left by a flat blade—either a knife or a screwdriver—that had been used to pry the window. He climbed onto the porcelain sink and looked at the lock at the midpoint of the window. It had been forced, then bent back into shape. An intruder had worked well, but not perfectly.

Cochrane placed himself within the mind of Siegfried. Where was he, Cochrane, most vulnerable?

He tore up the stairs and threw on every light in the house. He grabbed pants, a sweater, and a pair of shoes. He did not open any drawer or door that hadn't already been touched. No use springing a booby trap that he'd so far been lucky enough to escape.

He stood in the bedroom, his heart pounding. Then he stared at the bed. Logic told him where anyone is most vulnerable.

Gingerly he went to his hands and knees. He crept to the edge of the bed and took a flashlight from the night table. He pushed aside the bed spread. The fear was in his throat as he shined the light.

He saw the device, planted in a long black woolen sock. He had little doubt as to who had planted it, when, why, or what the device was.

He also knew that he was not dreaming. Less than a minute later, he was down the stairs and out the door, standing on Twenty-sixth Street, flagging down a police car like a maniac.

Cochrane stood outside, huddled against the November night, when the District of Columbia bomb squad arrived. One man arrived by a police car. The other two came with a truck that looked to be a cross between a tank and a covered wagon. It was covered by six-inch-thick steel cable, and Cochrane, from his days as an ordnance officer in the Army, knew just how much of a wallop the truck could contain if anything inside it exploded.

The three men from the bomb squad donned greenish-brown suits of armor plating. They pulled on squarish helmets that shielded their heads. There was a shatter-resistant visor that allowed them to see right in front of them, but barely to the side at all.

One man, a graying, angular District police lieutenant, who said his name was McConnell, remained outside. The other two men dragged their equipment inside and crept cautiously up the stairs to where Cochrane had located the thing in the black sock.

Fifteen minutes passed. The two men emerged from the house, holding between them two ten-foot poles. An iron basket dangled from the middle of the poles, about three feet off the ground. McConnell opened the rear of the bomb truck and the men eased the poles onto hangers within the truck. McConnell quickly closed the door.

"Now where?" Cochrane asked.

"Fort Meade, Maryland," he said. "Detonation range. Coming? Nice night for it," he added sourly.

Cochrane heaved a long sigh. "Yeah. Coming."

The truck made its way slowly through the quiet avenues of Washington, then onto the new highway that led to Maryland and the Northeast. The trip took an hour. Cochrane followed a quarter of a mile behind the bomb truck, in Lieutenant McConnell's car. All other traffic was diverted from the highway as the truck passed.

At Fort Meade, Cochrane looked at his watch. It was now 3 A.M. and McConnell was the ranking officer on the scene. He told the driver of the bomb truck to take the device to Detonation Range B.

"You're going to blow it up, huh?" Cochrane asked.

"Got a better idea?" McConnell was a twenty-year veteran of the District police. He behaved accordingly.

"I want it defused."

"You want what?"

"There are components in there that might lead to the bomber. There are fingerprints possibly."

"Yeah, and let me tell you, Mr. FBI, judging by the weight of that little birthday cake in there, there could be enough sauce to take out a building and everything living inside it."

"Your squad defuses bombs all the time."

"When we're on an assigned case. Otherwise, we dispose of them." McConnell's irritation was evident.

"Well, *I'm* on a case."

"Then *you* defuse it, chief."

Cochrane looked at the truck and the driver waiting disgustedly. The vehicle's enormous diesel engine idled noisily in the cold night. "You have a good lab?" Cochrane asked.

"Best within two hundred miles."

"You got an extra suit and helmet?"

"If you're crazy enough."

"Then I'll take it apart."

"One hitch," demanded McConnell. "I need authorization to let you blow yourself up. Who's your superior?"

Cochrane reached to his pocket, pulled out a paper, and wrote out a telephone number. "Richard Wheeler. Assistant Director, Special Operations. Call him at home."

McConnell took the number and looked at Cochrane with something less than affection. "Fuckin' FBI!" he said. "Always a hassle." Then he instructed his driver to rush the thing in the sock over to the laboratory.

The bomb lab was a converted airplane hanger on the south end of the army base. The actual work area was a room within a room within a room, with extra steel plating against each wall. Cochrane dressed in the outer area, struggling into the unbearably warm antiexplosives suit and pulling on the helmet. He donned the iron-plated gloves, which weighed five pounds each, and passed through the final door to the work area.

The "birthday cake," as Lieutenant McConnell called it, was still in the iron basket, sitting on a long steel table.

The two men who had taken the bomb onto the truck were assigned to work with Cochrane. They, however, would be backups and would not handle the actual device.

"All right," he told them, at 3:32. "I'm ready."

They entered the room as a team. There was a large tub of number ten lubricating oil beside the device. Gingerly, feeling the sweat roll beneath his uniform, Cochrane nodded as the other two men held the ends of the poles. Then Cochrane removed the steel lid of the basket and reached in with a five-foot pair of tongs. He lifted the device out and gently submerged it in the tub of oil. Immediately, one of the two assistants immersed the end of a stethoscope into the oil. All three men stepped back to a range of twenty feet and knelt.

The stethoscope had fifty feet of tubing and led behind a partition of four-inch-thick glass. There sat Lieutenant McConnell, who listened. The stethoscope also contained a miniaturized microphone. The oil acted as a sound conductor. If there were any noise from within the bomb, such as ticking and whirring—which could denote a live device—McConnell would hear it.

Cochrane squinted through the glass visor of his helmet. McConnell listened for an unbearably long time—at least ten seconds. Then he shook his head.

No noise. Either the device was dead or set to blow. There was a difference.

Cochrane crept slowly forward again, signaling for one of the men to follow him.

The lubricating oil served a second purpose. If the bomb casing was not airtight, the oil would seep into it, clog whatever mechanism was involved, and possibly prevent a blast.

Cochrane signaled for the tongs. His assistant picked them up, then reached for the bomb. The device came up out of the oil. Now Cochrane steadied his hands and drew his breath. This was the part that could kill.

He moved in close and touched Siegfried's device, fully aware that no one could survive a blast at that range. With large rubberized shears, he cut away the sock. The wool fell back into the oil. Cochrane saw a hefty section of pipe—potential shrapnel that would tear him and his assistant apart—sealed at each end by iron industrial plugs.

"Put it in the vise," he said to his assistant.

The third man left the lab.

Several yards from the worktable was a vise attached to an immovable iron base. The bomb was carried in the tongs to the vise. Cochrane moved quickly to the device, secured it in an upright position, and tightened a wrench horizontally to the upper plug on the bomb. He then threaded a heavy industrial wire through the end of the wrench. Both men retreated. Cochrane unraveled the wire to a distance of twenty feet.

"I got it now," he said to his remaining assistant. The man withdrew from the lab.

Cochrane stood across the room from Siegfried's concoction. Beneath his iron-plated gloves, his hands were soaked. The wire that linked him to the bomb was taut in his palms. He pulled until it was tight as piano wire.

His eyes were glued on the bomb. He half expected . . . at any moment . . .

He wondered if he were crazy. Why was he here? What did he hope to gain? It was the middle of the night and he had forgotten. Adrenaline was giving way to exhaustion.

Slowly, Cochrane began to move. He took the first steps of a grand circle around the bomb. The wrench tremored slightly, then, pulled by the wire, followed. Cochrane moved cautiously but resolutely. He circled the device one full time. Then a second. Then a third.

Lieutenant McConnell and his two squad members watched from behind the plate glass. Cochrane continued to move. Each step was an eternity. The route around the bomb seemed larger than the Bluebirds' fifty-mile radius on the map of New Jersey.

Midway through the seventh revolution, the plug came loose from the pipe. It fell with a horrible clatter onto the copper sheeting on the laboratory floor. Cochrane dropped the wire, turned toward the device, and crept.

He crept cautiously but quickly. No properly constructed bomb remained dormant forever. Cochrane moved to within ten feet of the open pipe. Then five feet. Then two. Now speed was paramount, as long as he didn't jar the thing into detonating.

He reached to the bomb and unscrewed the vise. He turned quickly and eased the bomb onto the copper sheeting of the floor. He lay flush to the ground and lifted the closed end of the bomb upward so that the mechanism slid out.

Behind his visor, his eyes widened. Before him was the craft of his madman: a charge of black TNT in a large capsule, a tiny wristwatch with one hand broken off, a flash bulb, a battery, and copper wire to form an electrical circuit.

Without looking, Cochrane knew what Siegfried had done: a small hole had been bored in the face of the watch and one end of the wire protruded through it. The other end of the wire was linked to the hour hand, with the TNT, the flash bulb, and the battery in between. Had the hour hand come around to the 2 on the watch, the circuit would have completed and the bomb would have detonated. Currently, the hour hand was seven-eighths of the way from 1 to 2.

Cochrane felt his heart in his mouth. He threw the lead pipe across the room and he reached for the rubberized shears. He poked the tip of them to the battery and he clipped the wires from both battery terminals. He took the battery in his hand and moved it five feet from the TNT and copper wire. *The circuit was broken.*

Then he leaned back. He reached to his helmet and pulled it off. It had to have been one hundred degrees within the suit. He looked to the plate-glass window and the four men—Dick Wheeler had arrived—who watched him through it.

"Done!" he said breathlessly. "Get someone in here for fingerprints."

As the four men came around from the window and entered the work lab, Cochrane looked down at what he had gained. A few ounces of powder. Some common bits of hardware. Some routine copper wire. Elements that added up to death, surely, but ordinary ingredients.

The bulb, the battery, the wire, and the watch could have come from anywhere. The TNT was untraceable. It could have been mixed in any of a thousand places in North America.

He glanced across the room to where he had tossed the pipe. Siegfried was no fool. Most assuredly the metal had been wiped clean of fingerprints. What in hell had even possessed him to risk his life like that? he wondered.

He didn't move. Wheeler and the bomb squad officers approached him. Sitting on the copper sheeting, his helmet beside him, he felt like some beached hard-hat diver from the 1920s.

He looked up.

"Fella," said McConnell, "you got balls the size of watermelons, you know that?"

"A lot of good it did," Cochrane answered.

Dick Wheeler seemed very pale, with dark crescents under his eyes. He gazed down at Cochrane, then at the components of the bomb. He pulled on a pair of rubber gloves.

"What are you doing?" Cochrane asked.

"May I?" Wheeler motioned toward the bomb.

"You're asking *my* permission? I work for you, remember?"

Wheeler rested a hand on Cochrane's shoulder, then reached down to the watch. He picked up the bomb's timing mechanism, held it to his ear, then set it back down.

"I'll tell you one thing, Billy Boy," he said portentously and with tired, raised eyebrows. "I think you're getting on Brother Bomber's nerves."

"Is that a fact?" Cochrane looked upward at Wheeler and suddenly felt all of his patience depart him. "What the hell does that mean?" he snapped. "Would you stop talking in riddles? It's four A.M. What's going on?"

"Siegfried," Wheeler explained silkily, "forgot to wind that watch. It stopped at one fifty-two. I reckon that's why you're alive."

With wide, confused eyes, Cochrane turned and assessed again the components that he had just separated. "I defused it," he said.

"It was already dead. Lucky for everyone, of course." Wheeler spoke calmly and gracefully. Cochrane was suddenly aware that the bomb squad members were now forming a small audience.

"I *defused* it!" he insisted again.

"Yes, Bill. I know."

Cochrane's head shot upward and he glared furiously at Wheeler. "Well, goddamn it, he's starting to make mistakes! That proves it! I'm closing in on him! I'll have him in another week. You'll see!"

"Bill . . ."

"You tell Hoover that! One more week and I'll give him goddamned Siegfried's head on a plate."

Wheeler eased to a crouching position, then sat down next to Cochrane. "Bill, a decision has been made at headquarters. There's going to be a change."

For several long seconds, Cochrane stared at Wheeler. "What are you talking about?"

"I want you to go home and get some rest. Be in J. Edgar's conference room not this morning, but tomorrow morning. We'll run through everything then. Don't do anything further on the case."

"No, I will *not* go home and get some rest! Would you tell me what's going on?"

Wheeler looked away, then looked back. "You're being dismissed," Wheeler said.

It was too absurd to comprehend. It had to be another of those wretched dreams. He began to laugh. "That's nonsense! Dismissed from Siegfried just when I'm lining him up? Idiotic! Hoover wouldn't dare!"

Wheeler appeared truly uneasy with what followed. But he managed the words, anyway. "You're being dismissed, Bill. And it's not just the case. It's dismissed from the Bureau. Do you understand that? You've been fired."

THIRTY-THREE

Hoover sat at the head of the table and glared when Cochrane entered. They were in the second-floor conference room again, arranged at proper intervals around the oval table, and if the last meeting had been a war party, this was to be the burning at the stake.

Lerrick was two seats away from Hoover to the right and Wheeler was three empty spaces to the left, almost suggesting that Cochrane take a seat directly across from the Chief.

"Come in! Sit down, damn it!" Hoover growled, drumming his fingers on the table, his round swollen face getting redder by the second. "Let's get on with it!"

Cochrane noted that he was ten minutes early and the other three men were already there. Usually Hoover was the last to enter. The door was still open.

Hoover glanced over his shoulder. "Where's Adam?" he asked. And suddenly an entire vista of disbelief overtook Cochrane.

Adam Hay padded softly into the room and closed the door behind him. He looked at Cochrane, then approached a seat directly next to Hoover, with Lerrick on his other side. Cochrane had the notion of watching a small boy called into a meeting of adults, taking up a position between his parents.

The chair squeaked as Adam Hay pulled it out and tucked himself into the table. Dick Wheeler made a comical sour face, and even Frank Lerrick turned his head away to mask a grin. Cochrane, confronted with the absurd, was not smiling. Seated, the small archivist was the same height as when he'd been standing.

Hoover was all business.

"Listen to me very carefully, Agent Cochrane. This is an unpleasant meeting, but you deserve your own say before any departmental action is taken."

Meaning, it's already decided, Cochrane thought bitterly.

"Mr. Hay," Hoover began, "has been a very valuable member of this Bureau since 1931. I daresay, Agent Cochrane, that our archives would not function without him. Yet, Mr. Hay has reported to Personnel"—Cochrane's eyes shifted to Lerrick, who seemed to be memorizing something invisible on the table— "that you've been engaged in bullying, abusive behavior toward him. What have you to say?"

"Behavior of what sort?" Cochrane asked.

Hoover stared at him, then, with evident displeasure, opened a file in front of him. He read a thorough account of Cochrane's efforts to pry Otto Mauer's name, town, and state from him. The account mentioned Arlington Park, the hours up in the archives, and visits from various unnamed other members of the Bureau, i.e., the Bluebirds.

"What have you to say?" Hoover asked.

"Substantially accurate," Cochrane answered.

Hoover flipped the file shut. "Any explanation?"

"Yes, indeed," said Cochrane, his anger rising. "I'm trying to catch a man who's intent on killing President Roosevelt. The info—"

"Goddamn it, Cochrane!" Hoover raged, hitting a fist on the desk and turning violet. "There are rules in this Bureau! Do you understand that? Rules have to be followed! This was explained to you once before!"

"There is no way," Cochrane began defenselessly, "that I could humanly complete the job I've been assigned without talking to the one defector who—"

"The German," agreed Hoover in a flash. "That's what makes your behavior all the less pardonable. You were distinctly forbidden to contact Mr. . . . . Mr. . . . ."

"Mauer," Lerrick interjected, helping the Chief.

"Mauer. But you attempted anyway. Did you find him?"

"With Mr. Hay's help, yes. Yes, I did."

"What was the nature of your discussions with Otto Mauer?" Hoover asked as Mr. Hay belched softly.

Cochrane paused before answering. An entire kaleidoscope of distrust was before him now. He began to edit his own answers.

"I wanted to know how he had reached America."

"He reached safely. That was all you needed to know."

Cochrane felt Lerrick's eyes and Wheeler's eyes boring in on him.

"I needed to know about Abwehr structure."

Wheeler summoned the nerve to interrupt. "Bill," he said sorrowfully, "your German simply isn't a reliable source. Don't you think we would have let you use him if we considered him reliable?"

"He *is* reliable!" Cochrane shot back. "And why you don't want me to use him raises more questions than I can count."

Wheeler's bushy eyebrows lowered severely. "Now, what in hell is that supposed to mean?" he asked.

"It doesn't—"

"And, uh, one other thing"—Frank Lerrick speaking suddenly—"these other 'Bluebirds' who helped you torment our friend here. Would you care to give us the names?"

"No," Cochrane answered, "I wouldn't care to. Does Roosevelt know there's a man stalking him?"

Silence all around. Cochrane turned squarely back toward Hoover. "You haven't even alerted the Secret Service, have you?"

"Gentlemen," Hoover cut in sharply, "we're getting far afield. There are certain facts before us." Briefly, Hoover's tongue emerged from his mouth, moistened his pink lips, then withdrew like the head of a turtle. "Special Agent Cochrane does not deny the abusive and bullying behavior imparted toward another employee of this Bureau. Similarly, Special Agent Cochrane admits to having disobeyed the orders of this particular office by contacting a proscribed source."

Cochrane leaned back in his chair and waited for the hammer to fall. Lerrick and Wheeler fixed their gazes elsewhere. Cochrane looked Hoover in the eye, but his peripheral vision caught a gloating toupeed dwarf. Suddenly the preposterousness of it all weighed heavily.

And meanwhile, Siegfried is out there, Cochrane cursed to himself. *While we're discussing table man-*

ners, Siegfried is stalking Roosevelt.

Hoover held Cochrane in a long stare, and finally Cochrane, as he returned the gaze, reached the end of his patience.

"Should I stand for sentencing?" he asked.

Hoover let the remark pass. "Agent Cochrane," he finally said, "your letter of resignation from this Bureau would be greatly appreciated. It should be dated the end of this month: effective November 30, 1939."

Resentment, anger, perplexity: Cochrane clung to them all in ample amounts. But there was, of course, no court of appeal. Not here. And in a strange way, exhilaration finally swept over him. It *was* done. His job *was* finished here. Hoover had fired his final shot and Cochrane still lived and breathed and saw a future in front of him—peacefully in a bank somewhere in another city.

"That's just splendid," Cochrane answered, surprising everyone in the room with the calmness of his reply. "Fact is, Mr. Hoover, sir, I've an excellent letter already written. All I need to do is change the date."

"I'm placing Frank Lerrick in charge of this investigation," Hoover concluded softly. Then he turned to his dismissed employee: "Special Agent Cochrane," he said. "I'm deeply disappointed in you."

THIRTY-FOUR

Laura was noticing the little things.

Her husband had been home for two days and had again become the moody, uncommunicative Stephen that she did not like. He had hardly spoken to her. The least he could have done was tell her about his trip. To her, New York was an exciting, bustling exotic city. She wished he would at least excite her with stories of what he had seen, people he had met.

But nothing. No talk. And heaven knew, he hadn't much been interested in touching her, either. What was she to think? She was a woman of twenty-five with the physical desires of a woman of twenty-five. Why couldn't they make love when he came home? Why wasn't he interested?

Little things, she repeated. She sat in the living room of their home and stared out the window, through the rain, across the lawn to St. Paul's. Her husband had disappeared into the church two hours ago, citing the need to work on Sunday's sermon. Little things, like ignoring her as if she wasn't there.

She caught herself thinking the unthinkable: maybe, long-range, this marriage simply wasn't destined to work. If Stephen was going to neglect her, well, she could see her reflection in the mirror. She was an attractive woman. She took care of her body and groomed herself well. If this man couldn't love her and appreciate her, maybe another man would.

She dismissed the idea, but with effort.

Then there were the big things. There were the tales told by Peter Whiteside, suggestions and accusations that grew upon Laura like a series of cancers. Combined with Stephen's behavior, Peter's damnable insinuations nurtured suspicion within her. She sought to acquit him. But when she compared his time of return by train two days earlier from New York, she found that no New York train had stopped at Liberty Circle at that hour. There had only been the train that connected with Philadelphia, Baltimore, and Washington.

Wrong cities, wrong timetable, Stephen, she thought. *Wrong husband, wrong wife?* she wondered.

There were too many questions now. Too much unexplained behavior. Laura rose from the window and went to the closet. She pulled on her raincoat. It had been raining hard that day, a cold wet downpour which did nothing to elevate her mood and much to trigger a residual dissatisfaction and homesickness. A wife could be expected to tolerate only so much. It was time to discuss things. Now. Damn his sermon.

Laura took an umbrella from the rack in the foyer and she crossed the street to the church. Outside the red front door she shook out her umbrella and slipped out of her coat as she entered.

452

The minister's chambers were in the rear, past the pews and the altar. When Laura looked for him there, he was gone. The light was off and his small desk looked untouched. She stared at it for several seconds trying to grasp the meaning.

"Stephen?" she called out. "Stephen?"

There was only the sound of empty rooms in return. It occurred to Laura that Stephen may have left the church through the rear exit, and, as variations of deceit swirled and unraveled before her, she contemplated why. She passed quietly to the doorway adjacent to his chambers. It was locked from the inside.

Facts, Peter Whiteside: Stephen came into this building two hours ago. I have been staring at the front door from across the street. Either I have failed Basic Surveillance or he has not left. He is in this building.

Where? What is he doing?

There remained only the balcony, which was empty, and the front stairway to the belfry and steeple. When she looked at the latter, she found the doorway ajar. She ascended the narrow staircase that wound up to the spire.

As she climbed she listened. She heard her own footsteps on the stairs and the creaks of the aged wood. She came to a first landing, where there was a small window. She stopped, listened, and looked out.

She was higher than the nearest trees. She looked down at the rectory house where she lived and watched the rain sweep over it. She lifted her gaze and could see the road stretching into Liberty Circle. She could see part of the town.

It was a fine view, probably even finer and more dramatic on a clear day or at the next level. Why, she

453

wondered, had Stephen never called her attention to it?

The staircase led to another landing just below the bells. She could smell the mustiness of the seldom-used stairs and could hear the rain driving against the wooden walls. It almost distracted her from the entire point of the search. *Where was Steven?*

She took the final turn in the staircase and arrived in the bell-tower landing. It was a narrow, squarish chamber about eight by eight, ringed by panels and several storage closets. The door of one closet was slightly open and she stepped toward it. But as she made her first movement, she saw that several of the panels on the opposite wall had been hastily replaced. She stepped toward them instead.

"Stephen?" she said aloud.

Behind her a closet door exploded open. Laura screamed. She wasn't fast enough to turn to confront the figure that lunged toward her.

It was a man, she was sure, and he hooked one arm around her with his hand covering her mouth. The other hand came up to her throat with a knife and she felt the side of the blade pressed hard—it was hurting her!—to the flesh by the jugular.

And he was rough. He forced her all the way forward to the small window in the tower. Her face was pressed roughly to the cold glass.

There he held her and hurt her, until she recognized the hand, the wrists, and the feel of the strong body.

Slowly his hand moved away. Slowly he relaxed the knife.

"Stephen . . . !"

He allowed her to turn slowly to face him. His gray eyes were blazing with a furious cruelty that she had never seen in the man with whom she had shared part of her life.

"You damned fool!" he said. "What are you doing here?"

"I was looking for you!"

"Why? Why do you have to prowl? Why can't you leave me alone!"

Laura could feel the tears welling up in her eyes. And she was fully aware that he had not for an instant relaxed the grip on the knife.

"You're my husband!" she cried. "I wanted to see you! I wanted to talk to you!"

"You should have stayed home and waited for me!"

She felt her courage rallying. "And wait for what?" she demanded. "Wait until you bloody well felt like coming home and talking to me? What *are* you doing up here?"

"Nothing that you would understand."

"No? And *that?*" She stared angrily at the knife, then back at her silent husband. And next there was a horrible moment as she looked into Stephen Fowler's eyes and no longer saw her husband. She saw something cold, mean, and evil that had always before been beneath the surface. But now, when she saw it, the look explained everything.

She saw the man before her for what he was. For a moment, as his eyes riveted upon her, there was only sheer, paralyzing terror, knowing that the hands that had been intimate hundreds of times with her had manufactured bombs and strangled a strange woman. She knew that Peter Whiteside had been right in everything he had last said about him. And she knew that somehow she had come very close to her husband's secret. Something about this place . . .

Then she realized. Bill Cochrane had told her. Radio transmissions. A spy. The steeple was the highest point for miles around. That's what had attracted the FBI agent and that was its significance to her husband.

It all came together to her in the space of three seconds, along with the fact that Stephen was intent on killing her. Now! She could tell from his eyes. She could tell by the way his fingers played nervously on the hilt of the knife.

She could think of only one way to save her life.

As his eyes remained locked with hers, she pressed her hand between his thighs. Gently, as she suppressed a shudder, she rubbed him.

The savagery in his face softened with the surprise. Good, she thought, she had done the unexpected.

"Don't you understand?" she asked with a conciliatory voice. "I don't know what you're doing and I don't care. I just want my husband to make love to me. I've missed you. Can't you comprehend that?"

She massaged his genitals and within a few seconds felt the firmness rising beneath the wool of his trousers. She did her best to smile receptively. All the while she feared that he would stab her with one sudden upward thrust of the knife.

"I love you, Stephen," she said. "I'd never do anything to betray you. Don't you know that?" The words were barely out of her mouth when she realized it was the first lie she had told him in more than two years of marriage.

Before he could stop her, she unzipped his fly. She reached in and held his firm penis in her palm and continued to caress him. From the corner of her eye, she could see his fingers still flexing nervously on the knife.

"Let's undress," she said. "Now. Right here. Please, Stephen?" She unbuttoned her blouse as she spoke.

"I'm going to teach you who the master is," he said. "I'm going to punish you for following me."

"Stephen . . . ?"

He raised the knife, then threw it onto the floor, where, point-first, it stuck. Then he looked at his wife, drew back his hand, and slapped her hard across the face, just as he'd once struck Marjorie.

Laura's face was on fire where he had hit her. She raised both her hands to where she'd been struck and looked at her husband with wide horrified eyes. He grinned. He struck her again. She bolted to flee him, but he held her by the wrist.

"You'll finish undressing," he told her, biting off the words. "You'll do exactly what I tell you, Laura. Nothing less! You belong to me, Laura. You said so yourself. Now don't you forget it."

She undressed as he watched her in silence. As her undergarments came off, Stephen seemed to be devouring her with his eyes, assessing her as a rapist might a naked schoolgirl. She was completely nude. She covered a small area on the floor with her clothing. When she turned and looked at Stephen again she realized that there had always been within him a need to brutalize a woman. He had never done it to her before, but obviously he had been doing it somewhere else. She wondered what connection it had with the dead woman behind the church.

Then as he pulled his own clothes off, he made her kneel. He held her by the hair and forced her to take him into her mouth. She had never done that to him before, much less been forced to. As an act of love, had he ever asked, she would have. Today, with a deceitful man whom she knew to be a spy and a killer, it filled her with revulsion.

But then he made her lie back, and he was on top of her. She managed to keep her face away from his as he pushed inside her. He could not see her tears. He was rough and fast, like she imagined a man might be in a whorehouse. And when she felt him finish, she was relieved. Horrible as it was, at least it was over.

He moved off her, breathing heavily. He lay near her and she sensed him to be more of a stranger than any man she had ever made love with. She was afraid to speak. She looked at the knife, which still stuck in the floor nearby. She realized that he could still kill her. She would have to see this terrifying hour through to the end.

She moved her hand to his flaccid penis and touched it gently.

"I like you as a sexual animal," she lied, wondering all the time how she was managing to maintain her facade.

"Get dressed and get out of here," he said. Apparently, she realized, he had decided to keep her alive. She stood and reached for her clothing. Stephen grabbed her by the wrist. "And Laura," he snapped, holding her so tight that it hurt, "you never come up here again. I have things to do that a woman couldn't begin to understand. Do you hear me?"

"Yes, Stephen," she said.

"Now, go."

She did.

Laura returned to their bedroom in the rectory. She looked in the mirror at her ashen, tear-streaked face, felt something welling inside her, and threw up.

Then she went downstairs. She found a bottle of scotch, took a drink, and after several minutes it seemed to calm her. She would have to maintain the act until the right opportunity came along, she told herself. No, she could barely tolerate thinking about or looking at this man again, much less have him violate her. But she did know where she could find friends. She only needed the right moment.

Stephen forced his new, brutal form of sex upon her again that night and the next. Then, mercifully, he announced on Wednesday morning that he was traveling again. He departed on the noon train to Trenton and Philadelphia.

Within another hour, she too was gone. She traveled first by bus, using some dollars she had put aside in her kitchen. In Newark she walked from the bus depot to the train station and found a southbound express for Washington. There, at Union Station, she deciphered a confusing city map and started her way to the British Consulate, praying that Peter Whiteside would still be there.

THIRTY-FIVE

The drive to Pennsylvania from Washington wasn't as smooth as Cochrane's previous trip. There had been traffic around Philadelphia, then a closed two-lane highway around Stroudsburg. Cochrane had to drive along the slower route that went through the mountains. Then, as was Mauer's quaint habit, there had been the meeting at the farmhouse door with the German holding a shotgun across his chest. Mauer lowered the weapon as soon as he saw Cochrane was alone.

Mauer shuffled back into the house, leading Cochrane, and went to the armchair from which he ruled his domain in exile. He stood his shotgun against a table, no more than an arm's length away. He sat down.

"You'll excuse the gun again, I hope," Mauer began in German. "Only a precaution."

The two men gazed at each other for a moment and a slow, ironic smile crept across Mauer's lips. "So, you were saying," Mauer said. "Fired? From your Bureau?"

"Fired," Cochrane confirmed.

"Why?"

Cochrane paused. "The reason given was rudeness to a subordinate." He explained about Adam Hay. Otto Mauer clearly enjoyed the story. Otto Mauer, for that matter, clearly enjoyed having a visitor. He poured a brandy for each of them as Cochrane spoke. He walked the drink to Cochrane and stepped past two large crates of books.

Cochrane finished speaking.

"So you were impertinent to this gremlin, who is a file clerk, and for this J. Edgar Hoover dismisses you from his FBI?"

"That's correct."

Mauer sipped his brandy as visions of his own bureaucratic nightmares flashed through his mind. "In Germany," he finally said, "it is the burden of inferiors to be polite to their superiors. Not the other way around. Prosit."

Mauer sipped and replenished his own glass.

"Prosit," Cochrane answered.

Mauer set down his brandy. "Do you think this was the only reason you were dismissed from the FBI?" the German asked.

"I have my doubts."

Several thoughts went through both men's minds and all were unspoken and contained by a long silence. "I see," Mauer said at length. Then he cocked his head in a peculiar manner, as if to examine Cochrane in a new light.

"So," Mauer finally asked, "why then have you come to see me again? You are no longer looking for your spy. You no longer have any authority. You cannot help me and I cannot help you. We are both in exile, my friend, and exiles are eunuchs."

"Well," Cochrane started slowly, "my plans will move me to New York to take a private job. I wanted to reassure you that there are other good men in the FBI. I'm asking two friends from the Newark office to remain apprised of your case. Concerning your family, that is. If it's possible to move your wife and son here, they will expedite things for you."

"You're very kind," said Mauer flatly. Cochrane wasn't sure how much cynicism laced the remark. But he continued. "Second, there's one thing I cannot comprehend."

"And what's that?"

"The code system," said Cochrane. "If the FBI knew Siegfried's five-digit additive, they could break the German naval code. You must know how such systems work."

"And so?"

"Why didn't the FBI ever ask you about the additive?"

"They *did* ask me."

"And?"

"And until my family is returned I cannot help."

"Then you know more than you told them?"

"I only know that they lied to me. I do not have my family."

There was cautious ambiguity in Mauer's reply. It was the same sort of charade that had transpired between the two men in Germany.

"Is that what you told them?" Cochrane asked.

"That's what I told them," he said, sipping again, "and that is what I now tell you." Mauer watched Cochrane. "You look puzzled," he suggested airily.

"I am."

"Why?"

Thinking of Hunsicker, Cochrane answered, "They have new methods. The Bureau badly wants the code broken. I'm surprised you were not subjected to—"

"'Coercion'?"

"Yes."

"I'm surprised, also," said Mauer. "Perhaps they are not as anxious to break the code as they maintain."

"I can't believe that," Cochrane said instinctively. It dawned on him also that he couldn't believe he had been dismissed merely for the contretemps with Adam Hay.

"My friend," Mauer said, finishing his second shot of brandy, "we are entering an age in which much happens that we cannot believe. Look at Germany again," he said with a sigh. "Who can believe that Hitler is the chosen leader? But he didn't seize power. His party was elected to a majority. Hindenburg asked him to form a government. May I pour you another drink? Cognac makes reality less harsh."

"Thank you, I'm fine," demurred Cochrane, who wasn't fine at all.

Mauer poured himself another drink. "We live in an age of unreality," the German expanded philosophically. "Why was Germany allowed to rearm? Who financed Hitler? Why does the capitalistic West align itself with the Soviets? Will America allow Germany to conquer all of Western Europe? Who else will stop the Wehrmacht? Yet will America risk joining a much greater war than the one a generation ago? I ask you, young man, does *any* of this flirt with reality? Yet it happens."

Mauer rambled on for half an hour, then tossed

down his third cognac with one enthusiastic gulp. Cochrane knew it was time to think about departure.

"I'll pass along the details about your family," he said again. "That's all I can do. Good luck."

Mauer answered with a complacent, resolute shrug and raised an eyebrow as if to wish Cochrane good fortune, also.

"Need anything to read?" Mauer asked as he switched into English. He motioned to two cartons of books and explained that this seemed to be part of an FBI program to keep him amused and, presumably, out of trouble. "Duplicate copies from the library of the U.S. Congress," said Mauer, picking through the top copies of two corrugated cartons of books. "Foreign copies, originals, and in translation. I once complained to your Bureau that I couldn't find anything to read. Now they send me five dozen books every four weeks."

Cochrane could see the grim humor of some bureaucrat somewhere in the headquarters building.

"Honest. Take anything you like," said Mauer. Mauer stood and weaved slightly from the cognac.

Graciously, Cochrane stood and leaned over to see what Mauer offered. Most were translations of technical manuals. Others dealt with butterfly collecting in Bohemia or beekeeping in Austria.

One large volume caught Cochrane's eyes immediately, *The Fighting Liners of the Great War*. Published in London five years earlier, it recounted in text and pictures the reoutfitting of the luxury cruise ships of the mid-teens as troop transports. Cochrane flicked it open.

"Take it," insisted Mauer. It was a fresh copy.

465

"You're serious?" Cochrane asked.

"Just bring me my family in return," Mauer said, switching back to German. "Before I turn the shotgun on myself."

Cochrane reiterated: no promises, but he'd see what he could do.

The parking spaces were filled in front of the ramshackle house on Twenty-sixth Street, so Cochrane parked down the block.

He was halfway to his house when he saw two visitors on his front porch, and at first he thought someone had to be mistaken. Who would visit him? He was a professional leper this afternoon, received only by brooding expatriates. He was several steps closer when he recognized Reverend Fowler's wife. Laura saw him at the same time.

She stood, and so did the tall man with black hair who was with her. Cochrane stopped on the sidewalk before them. As he looked up, she gazed down at him. Bill Cochrane sensed trouble.

"I didn't think I'd see you again so quickly," he said.

"Nor I, you," she answered. Then after an awkward moment: "Oh, sorry," she said. "This is Peter Whiteside. He's been a friend of my family all my life."

Cochrane offered a hand, reaching upward. Whiteside took it and shook.

Then Cochrane turned back to Laura. "Look," he said, "I should tell you . . ."

"I know," she said. "The FBI dismissed you."

A pause for a second. "Oh. I get it. You tried me there first?"

She nodded. "I made a pest of myself," Laura said. "Pretended that my interest was romantic. Finally a young man gave me your home address. On the sly, of course."

"I'm leaving Washington," Cochrane said.

"What a shame."

"Not really. I look forward to living quietly."

"But if you'll excuse the suggestion," Peter Whiteside interrupted, "you're leaving with business unfinished."

There was accusation in Cochrane's voice. "Now how would you know that, sir?" Cochrane asked.

To which Laura lowered her voice, though there was not another human being in sight. "Peter is with Britain's SIS," Laura said calmly. "Secret Intelligence Service. I work for them also. I think if we go inside and put our heads together," she suggested, "we'll all be able to help each other."

Cochrane looked at them quizzically, from beautiful Laura to the lean, dapper Whiteside, then back again. And suddenly the whole kaleidoscope—Hoover, Siegfried, Roosevelt; Fowler, Laura, and Mauer—took on new shapes, shades, and hues.

"Unless I'm mistaken," Whiteside added as a teaser, "you're looking for a man named Siegfried. Well, we are too."

Cochrane pulled his house keys from his pocket. "Let's go," he said, motioning to the door.

THIRTY-SIX

"You wouldn't have any tea, would you?" Whiteside asked. "Bloody cold out there all day. Last time I was in Washington was a July, I think. Nearly broiled."

"We've hit a cold streak for the last week," Cochrane said. He led Laura and Peter Whiteside into the kitchen and prowled through jars and cans that had been there since young Jenks had first assigned a housekeeper to the premises. He found a small square carton of Twinings. It was unopened.

"How's this?" Cochrane asked.

"Perfect."

Laura took over. She found a teapot, and soon had water boiling as Whiteside and Bill Cochrane sat down in the dining room. Laura kept an ear to the conversation.

Whiteside marked time at first, rambling pleasantly along about inconsequential topics, and Cochrane studied him carefully. Top of the line British intelligence officer; Cochrane could tell by the alertness and the eyes, as well as the accent and way he carried himself. As if on cue, when Laura appeared with three teacups, Whiteside began talking about the city of Birmingham in 1935. Not until Whiteside honed in on the topic of labor unrest and Communist marchers did Cochrane fully understand where the conversation was leading. By that time he was watching Laura more and more, wondering why he was thinking the thoughts he was about another man's wife, and fondly appreciating the way she crossed her slender legs beneath her skirt.

". . . and it was when the marchers reached St. Chad's Circus," Whiteside continued, "that the first of two devastating antipersonnel explosives was detonated." The sentence jolted Cochrane's attention back to where it belonged.

Explosives. Of course. That was what it was all about. Bombs. Sabotaged ships. A threat to the life of President Roosevelt.

Now Cochrane hung on every word that passed Whiteside's lips, and gradually the missing pieces of Siegfried came into view. The story took an hour, with several refills of tea, and if there were any details lost, Cochrane didn't miss them.

The grand design was before him. The footnotes, such as why a man like Stephen Fowler would embark on a career as Hitler's disciple in America, could wait.

Which leaves me with Otto Mauer, Bill Cochrane thought. *There has to be a way to tie it all together. How, for example, did a pipe bomb in a sock arrive under my bed?*

Cochrane recalled from Mauer's story in the Pennsylvania farmhouse: "Tell me about B.A. 1,"

Cochrane said out of the blue.

Whiteside looked considerably surprised. "Pardon me?"

"B.A. 1," Cochrane said confidently. "And a Major Richards, if I remember correctly. Based in London, charged with double-crossing of German and Italian agents."

Whiteside was silent.

"It's not enough just to talk," Cochrane insisted. "You have to answer questions, too."

"What about B.A. 1? It's part of M.I. 5, as I'm certain you know."

"I have a defector named Otto Mauer," Cochrane said. "He passed through the hands of Major Richards in London. Surely you know all about it."

Another pause. "Surely, I do," Whiteside said at length.

"If my guess is any good," Cochrane said, "you can tell me about Mauer's wife and child, also."

"Your guess is good," Whiteside answered. "Why is it so good?"

"Because I know Bureau tactics," Cochrane said. "They flashed the man a photograph of his wife and son in Spain. But they couldn't deliver the goods. If they could have, they would have at least brought them here and shown them around. So someone else is holding them. If the Nazis grabbed them in Spain, then Mauer's been feeding us bad information from the time he arrived here. But I don't think he is. So the only other possibility is M.I. 5."

"That's correct."

"Then *you* have them?"

Another pause and Laura eyed Peter Whiteside with

considerable suspicion.

"That's correct," Whiteside said again.

"Where?"

"Is it relevant to Siegfried?"

"It's relevant if you want any cooperation out of me."

"The precise location is classified," Whiteside said. "But we moved them from Spain. They're nearby."

"How far away? In days?"

"Two. Maybe three, depending on transport."

"So your people took their picture in Madrid and turned it over to the Americans, right?"

Whiteside nodded.

"Why?"

'Well, we didn't know what to do with them, obviously," Whiteside said, as if it were self-evident. "We had them in inventory, so to speak, but there was no way to cash them in. So we offered them to the Americans. Free. Had to move them from Spain, anyway. Franco's national police run the country and are like this"—briefly Whiteside's hands clasped each other—"with the Gestapo." Whiteside sipped some tea, which was cool in his cup by now. Cochrane noticed through the window that the afternoon had faded and already the darkness of evening was upon Washington. He heard a car go by. Whiteside continued. "We wanted to give them to the Americans. A favor for the future when we needed a favor in return. It was as simple as that. So we notified State Department. Got a man who used to sell cars in Colorado, but is now a career diplomat. Said he'd pass the picture on to FBI, but that was all he could do. We never heard anything more."

472

Cochrane now sat leaning back, his arms folded across his stomach, his head forward and his clear eyes upon the Englishman. He had a sense of constantly being shown a moving picture—Mauer's story—with frames missing or out of order.

"Wait a minute," he finally interjected. "You've forgotten an entire step."

"Have I?"

"How did you know to intercept Natalie and Rudy to begin with?"

"We *knew*," Whiteside said cryptically. "We knew a major defection was under way. Double guards of Gestapo, SS, and SD at all the rail and air terminals. We knew something was afoot. So we kept our eyes also on Major Aseña in Gibraltar."

Cochrane nodded.

"Major Aseña is very capable and very able. Both sides play ball with him, we all know that. Not a major in anybody's army except his own. A mercenary, follow? Our sources in Gibraltar told us he was waiting for a woman and a boy. Germans, the sources said. At the same time, Norwegian intelligence shared with us the fact that one Otto Mauer, traveling alone, had passed through. So we watched the obvious route for the family of a German aristocrat and that meant Madrid."

Whiteside's eyes clouded and Cochrane saw a cunning that had previously escaped his notice. "Now," Whiteside said, reckoning with the past, "figure, one— Major Aseña is a total mercenary. Sells to the highest bidder. Figure, two—if Mauer of the Abwehr knows him, other Abwehr officers know him, also. Conclusion?"

"Natalie and Rudy could have been up for grabs. The Abwehr could have bought them back and forced Mauer to 're-defect.' He would have been in a position to serve massive disinformation to the FBI just in the hope of seeing his family alive again."

Now Whiteside leaned back. "You understand quite well," he said.

"I'm learning," Cochrane answered.

"Well, that's exactly what was going to happen. As soon as Mauer hit Helsinki and defected, he was safe. He was in British and American hands every step of the way. But the Abwehr had already contacted Major Aseña. They had reached an agreement to pay the major ten thousand American dollars to hold Mauer's wife and children if they crossed to Gibraltar."

Seeing Cochrane's intrigue, Whiteside purred soothingly. "Our source on that is excellent," Whiteside said. "That's all I can tell you, of course."

Your own infiltrator in the Abwehr, mused Cochrane, thinking but not speaking. *Good for the damned Brits.* "Congratulations," Cochrane said.

Whiteside went ahead. "So we picked up the missus and the boy in Madrid. I'd dare guess that we had every street man in town looking for them. It wasn't difficult," Whiteside smirked. "The bell captain at the Ritz was ours for several years. He's in London now so I can tell you that."

From there it was simple. Whiteside's people in Spain assigned a photographer within hours, took some nice touristy photographs of the mother and child in the Plaza Mayor to prove they had arrived there and were all right, then went back up to the hotel room and took some photographs for passports. The Mauers were moved to a British safe house the next morning and British passports were drawn by noon.

"And if I'm guessing right you had them out of the country within two days," Cochrane said.

"Within one day," said Whiteside. "Not that it was easy. The airports were being covered, Otto Mauer by now being considered a significant defector. There was Gestapo manpower and hardware everywhere. So we used a soft route by car into France. Then we moved them to Ireland from Bordeaux. It was the only route open at the time."

"But if they're close by, they're not in Ireland," said Cochrane. "You said you could have them here within three days. That's not Ireland."

"No it's not."

"That means Canada or one of the islands in this hemisphere."

"You're getting warm."

"Canada's not warm this time of year."

Even Whiteside laughed. Laura sat nearby, quietly taking it in, working on the cup of tea, holding it in her hand to preserve its warmth. For several minutes, Cochrane had all but forgotten about her.

"Let's say they're on a very safe island about three hundred miles off the coast of South Carolina. Very coral, very sunny, and very secure."

"Lucky them in Bermuda," Cochrane said.

"They're miserable. They want to be reunited. This is where you come in, Mr. Cochrane, you see. Your FBI is holding Mauer and we haven't a damned notion where he is. Further . . ." he began shrewdly.

"Further, you've invested a lot in the operation. You're holding a woman and a child to use as a lever.

475

You want something in return."

"A vulgar but accurate way of putting it."

"What do you want?" Cochrane asked, ignoring the distasteful expression that Laura had made.

Whiteside drew a fatigued breath and turned unexpectedly to Laura. "Are you certain you wish to hear this?" he asked.

"Yes, I'm certain," she said.

Whiteside turned back to Cochrane. "We want Siegfried out of the operational picture," he said. "And we want whatever network goes with him."

"He's said to work alone," Cochrane tried.

"Poppycock. Somewhere there's a control. Or at least a guardian angel. He can do a lot of things on his own, but not everything. Look. You can arrest him here. I cannot. And so far SIS has no authority to take, shall we say, more physically forceful means of action on U.S. soil. We need the goodwill for the future, you understand."

"I understand," said Cochrane. And he did. Whiteside preferred that Siegfried be arrested or shot, perhaps preferably the latter, by his own countrymen. No use having an international flap among friends. The logic was sound, the situation a classic trade-off. Everyone in the room, even Laura, recognized that.

"Then there's the matter of your own Bureau," said Whiteside. "Seems they're handling the intelligence end of things on this side of the ocean. It would help us in the future if we knew how clean Mr. Hoover's Bureau is. Contacts we could trust, and all."

"We'll take care of Siegfried," Cochrane said. "As for the Bureau's bill of health and Siegfried's control, I need Natalie Mauer and her son for that. What can you arrange?"

"Where do you want them?"

"Philadelphia would be fine."

"When?"

Cochrane shrugged. "As quickly as possible."

"Two days," Whiteside promised. "Consider it done."

Whiteside offered his hand and the two men shook. "A gentlemen's agreement," Whiteside said gleefully. The words sent spasms of anxiety through Cochrane, as he remembered so well where he had heard a similar phrase before.

THIRTY-SEVEN

As Thanksgiving 1939 approached, the mood at the White House was grim. Liberals pleaded that Roosevelt must run again to preserve eight years of the New Deal. Added now, however, was the powerful and irrefutable argument that no true leader could walk away from the nation's most serious crisis since the Civil War.

Yet Roosevelt was, in many ways, a conservative and a traditionalist. A third term flew in the face of established American political custom. So, the pressures mounted.

The German and Russian armies had met at the confluence of the Bug and Muchavec rivers; Poland had been successfully partitioned within four weeks. With peace on his western front, Stalin looked toward Finland. And with the Soviet Union neutralized—temporarily at least—Hitler turned his attention toward Western Europe.

A desperate French Premier, Albert Lebrun, begged Roosevelt daily to issue a declaration of war against

Hitler. An equally impassioned but more restrained Prime Minister Chamberlain asked for more aircraft and more heavy artillery for Great Britain. Winston Churchill, who returned to Chamberlain's coalition cabinet at the outbreak of war as First Lord of the Admiralty, exchanged a private series of letters with the American President. The two men had met only once, in London in 1920, but each had long been impressed with the other: they had occupied parallel positions during the World War and had each opposed Hitler since the early 1930s. Now they exchanged confidential correspondences through the office of Ambassador Joseph Kennedy. Each letter from Churchill underscored the urgency of Chamberlain's requests.

But to Churchill and all others, Roosevelt agonized in his reply. Direct American involvement in the European war was politically impossible, even though he personally understood how severely the safety of the United States would be imperiled by the collapse of France and Great Britain.

"Eleanor, I am a tired and weary man," he told the First Lady one evening in mid-November, following the delivery to the White House of yet another pessimistic dispatch from Churchill: six Soviet armored divisions had been redeployed to the Finnish border, and an ongoing buildup of German naval strength in the North Sea and North Atlantic now threatened to cut off British supply lines from Canada and the United States. "There is only so much I can do," Roosevelt grumbled darkly.

Politically, he meant. Socially, he meant. With the physical strength that remained in him, he meant.

He was the most powerful man in the world in November of 1939, yet uncertainties were everywhere. He was pinned in by everything from his physical condition to his relations with a recalcitrant Congress. The little ailments plagued him again: his sinuses; his arthritis; his sleeplessness. Franklin Roosevelt was fifty-seven years old, his health was declining, and he deeply feared dying in office. To make matters complete, his third son, Elliott, was in Texas campaigning for John Nance Garner for President.

Roosevelt became bad-tempered and uncommunicative, particularly to those whom he loved or trusted. He took no one into his confidence. The American Communists belittled him and the isolationists sniped at him. Big city bosses withheld their support on major issues until they could be assured what would be in the pork barrel for them in 1940. Southern senators, upon whose support Roosevelt's shaky Capitol Hill coalition rested, were incensed by Eleanor Roosevelt's embrace of "civil rights" for Negro Americans, and now balked at the President's every word. The Negro civil rights groups themselves, who had nowhere to go outside the Democratic Party, overtly criticized Roosevelt's pared-down social budget for 1940. And John L. Lewis, the pugnacious labor leader, savagely assailed FDR for allegedly patronizing him, ignoring his movement, and "treating the leadership of organized labor as if it has no brains."

"It clearly doesn't," FDR snapped in response, but not in public.

The President's insomnia worsened. He took what solace he could find from the bookshelves of the White House. He would frequently rise from bed in the hours

481

after midnight and ask the Secret Service to open the library. Then the President of the United States would don his silk bathrobe, take the elevator to the second floor, and bury himself in histories, biographies, and his collection on the navies of the world.

One evening Eleanor followed him down at 2 A.M. She found him in his favorite reading chair, a single light on beside him. But Franklin wasn't reading. The book was open and folded across his lap. The President of the United States was staring gloomily at a paned window that overlooked a sleeping, unsettled Washington.

"You need desperately to get away, Franklin," she said, seating herself on the edge of his chair. "Only so much can be expected from one man."

The *Sequoia* was already docked at the Potomac boat basin, she reminded him. As soon as Congress adjourned on the Friday before Thanksgiving, the presidential yacht could take them part of the way to Warm Springs, Georgia, as it had done in every previous year of his presidency.

She saw a flicker of approval in her husband's eyes. She further reminded him that he could then be away from Washington for a full week, surrounded by friends and relatives. If he could keep his spirits up until then, he could draw strength and renewal from the holiday.

Roosevelt nodded very slightly. Eleanor's hand gently rested on the back of his neck. She leaned down to Franklin and kissed him on the side of his forehead.

He looked up to her and she saw what she had not otherwise seen for days: a very slight, and very wan, smile.

"I'm so damned tired," he said. "How can I accomplish anything anymore?"

Eleanor, who always had an answer for the press, had none for her husband.

Cochrane found a pair of hotel rooms while Peter Whiteside found a ship.

The ship in question was *The Fundy Rover,* a Canadian freighter out of Halifax that plied a textile trade between Nova Scotia and Bermuda, with the odd stopover in between. Whiteside flew to Bermuda himself both to be a baby-sitter and to arrange for one of the ports of call.

Whiteside brought Natalie and Rudy Mauer aboard *The Fundy Rover* himself, abetted by two members of the Royal Bermudian Police, who stayed for the transit and shared the three eight-hour watches with Whiteside. Passage to Philadelphia, and the unscheduled stop there, would take three days.

Cochrane, meanwhile, had driven like a wild man into the hills of northeastern Pennsylvania. He took no chances on anyone beating him to Mauer, who met him *de rigueur* at the farmhouse door with a shotgun.

"Is it loaded today?" Cochrane asked in German as he stepped out of the car.

"It's loaded every day now," Mauer answered. He was unshaven and looked surprisingly older. He weaved slightly, the result Cochrane supposed of his growing predilection for schnapps and brandy for breakfast.

"What other company do you get these days?" Cochrane asked.

"The idiots from Washington called again," Mauer said, this time in English. "Told me there would be more questions. A man would come to see me."

Cochrane felt a chilly tingling through his chest. Dead leaves swirled across the flagstone walkway between him and Mauer. He stopped, looking down the shotgun barrel.

"What man?" Cochrane asked.

"I don't know."

"Who did you talk to?"

"The sneaky one with the moustache. Herr Lerrick."

"Otto," Cochrane said, "I came here to take you to Philadelphia. British intelligence is bringing Natalie and Rudy into the country by steamer."

"More lies," said Mauer. He made a disturbing cocking sound with the shotgun.

Cochrane's anger rose. "Jesus Christ," he snorted furiously. "If you don't believe me, blow my head off with that infernal weapon! Then you can stay here and rot until someone comes along to put a bullet in your skull. But if you do believe me, pack one bag and don't plan to come back here. You're moving again, Otto. I've got your family and you know a five-digit additive. Even trade, damn it. Now go pack your bag and be in my car in fifteen minutes. That's all I'm waiting!"

Cochrane stared for a final second at the nose of the weapon. Then he turned on his heels and walked back toward the car.

"Cochrane! *Bill Cochrane!*" The German cried out now, his voice fevered, intense, and tortured.

Cochrane stopped and slowly turned, keeping his hands visible. His eyes met Mauer's from a distance of a dozen yards.

The German glared down the site of the firearm, then withdrew slowly.

"I'm *already* packed," Mauer proclaimed.

They were gone in six minutes, not fifteen. Cochrane pushed the speedometer as far as he could without risking the Hudson's becoming airborne, but such was his desire to escape the highways of the area before any "official" escort from the Bureau might arrive. He pressed the car around sharp turns on narrow two-lane highways until the road flattened out south of Wilkes-Barre just as the sun set. From there it was a clear sail. Their destination was a place famous for cream cheese, W.C. Fields jokes, hoagies, and incompetent athletic teams. It was only slightly less famous as the location of the Bellevue-Stratford Hotel, where Cochrane had already reserved a pair of adjoining rooms. There in Philadelphia he and his German would uneasily spend the night.

And the next night. And the one after that. Mauer's fury mounted, and Cochrane himself began to entertain terrifying doubts about Peter Whiteside, the Bureau, and exactly which direction what sort of operation was leading.

"Now is not the time to panic," Cochrane explained over the course of their wait. "If you trusted me ever," he said as if to read Mauer's darkest thoughts, "you must trust me now."

"*Must* I?" Mauer was asking ominously by three o'clock on the second afternoon.

"Yes. You must." Cochrane spoke with utter calm, no mean accomplishment for a man himself on the verge of panic. But he had shored some of his own defenses, also. A third room had been rented close by.

485

Therein resided special agents Cianfrani and Hearn, on leave from the Newark office and willing to act as witness, muscle, and, if need be, firepower for Cochrane.

For her part, Laura Worthington Fowler sat and waited, also. In the empty white house in Liberty Circle, the minister's wife bolted awake at night with every creak in the floorboards or at every tree branch that scratched its November fingers against a windowpane. Her husband was gone, absent, vanished. He was somewhere but he was everywhere. And though the M.I. 6 agents Fussel and McPherson maintained twenty-four-hour sentry duty from the church, how did she know that Stephen wouldn't materialize suddenly and unobserved on the dangerous inner side of the bolted doors?

Laura slept fitfully when she slept at all. Twice she sprang upright from a half-sleep in her bed, convinced that her husband was standing above her with a knife. Twice there was a scream in her throat. Both times when she threw on the bedside light, the room was still, quiet, and safe. One time she cried, feeling herself alone and betrayed. But she rallied her spirits, telling herself, as Bill Cochrane had told her, that in the days ahead there would not be time for fear.

Laura saw herself at the center of a triangle at whose corners stood three men: Stephen, Peter Whiteside, and Bill Cochrane. They threatened to pull her apart if she did not maintain a tenacious grip on her sanity. She settled in to sleep, her hands beneath her pillow, a small steel paring knife from the kitchen beneath her mattress.

On both fronts it ended as if with a single jolt.

The Fundy Rover churned without fanfare into the port of Philadelphia late in the afternoon on its third day out of Hamilton. The Mauers were traveling now on two of the crispest, finest, freshest Canadian passports that Ottawa had never issued. The ship docked on a Cunard pier a few slips away from the United States Navy Yard in South Philadelphia. Whiteside guided mother and child off the freighter, through customs, and into a red and white taxi for the ride up Broad Street.

They arrived at the Bellevue-Stratford at a few minutes past five. Whiteside rang Cochrane's suite from the lobby.

"I've got your visitors," he said. "We've had a wonderful voyage. Little chilly for a cruise this time of year, don't you think? Do you have our Hun?"

Cochrane, on his feet with the telephone to his ear, turned and looked at Mauer, who stood and stared expectantly at him. "Got him," said Cochrane, who gave Mauer the thumbs-up signal at the same time. "Bring them up."

Cochrane set down the telephone.

"No tricks? Natalie and Rudy? They're here?" Otto Mauer asked in deteriorating English.

"No tricks. They're here."

"I can't believe."

"See for yourself, Otto. An agreement between gentlemen, remember. I haven't lied to you."

The doorbell rang a few seconds later. Mauer's instinct was to rush to the door and throw it open, but Cochrane took the final precautions. Holding his service pistol in his hand, he went to the door and peered through. It was Whiteside, as expected. And

Cochrane recognized Natalie and Rudy from several months earlier in Berlin.

He opened the door.

There was one moment made up of too much emotion for anyone to bear, then the woman and the child rushed into the room. The boy was noisy, his mother was tearful. Somewhere, Otto Mauer magically shed ten years. His face was alive and joyful. He managed in one movement to sweep up his son in his arms and embrace his wife.

Cochrane watched from the doorway. Whiteside sauntered into the room a few steps behind his guests. Cochrane gave a nod to the peephole across the hall, through which either Cianfrani or Hearn was watching. Then he closed the door. He and Whiteside sat and exchanged idle chatter over the merits of steamer travel from Bermuda as they allowed the Mauer family to reacquaint themselves with one another.

Then Whiteside looked up at the Germans. "You know of course that we'll have to move them again," he said.

"Can you keep them?" Cochrane asked.

Whiteside nodded thoughtfully.

"I have a safe house ready on Spruce Street here in this city," he said. "Two blocks from the British Consulate. It should serve well for a few days. I want to move them to Canada as soon as I'm able."

"I don't even want to know about it," Cochrane said. "I just need one number from Herr Mauer."

Whiteside watched the Germans, who spoke so briskly in their own language that both he and Cochrane had difficulty. "I think you've earned it," Whiteside said.

Mauer thought so, too. Before dinner he stepped into the adjoining room with Cochrane. A five-digit additive to the naval code should be all Cochrane needed, Mauer agreed. And there had been a standing Abwehr order in effect since 1937, known only to those of his own rank or higher:

All operatives in North America were to maintain the same additive. Changes over such a distance would be too difficult to effect. Any serious agent in America was working the code books with the same combination.

"So what is it?" Cochrane pressed.

"April 20, 1889," Mauer said. "It's so frightfully evident that I'm surprised no one tried it."

Cochrane blanched for a moment, then the realization was upon him.

"Four, two zero, eight nine," he said. "The date. Naturally."

Mauer was grinning with the ugly irony of it.

"A significant date to all Germans," Cochrane said.

"To all Nazis," Mauer corrected. Cochrane did not argue the point.

"The date of birth of Adolph Hitler," Cochrane said. And Whiteside grimaced with him.

In Liberty Circle, Reverend Fowler appeared on foot leaving the railroad depot. He was halfway to his home when a DeSoto with New York plates pulled to the curb next to him. Fowler was more than mildly surprised to be confronted by two Englishmen, one with a northern brogue and the other who'd evidently been born within sight of another St. Paul's. Fowler was even more perplexed to find that both had weapons aimed in his direction.

Both Englishmen leaped from the DeSoto while Fowler froze. He held his hands aloft, as if accosted by highwaymen, and protested that if they wanted his wallet, they were welcome to it.

"Fuck your bloody wallet," said McPherson, who grabbed the minister by the top rear of his coat and slammed him hard against the car. A frisk revealed nothing. Then they handcuffed him, shoved him into the rear of the DeSoto, and were off, reporting to Peter Whiteside by telephone much later that evening.

Stephen Fowler offered no resistance, even when given no explanation for his abduction. For his captors, he had only forgiveness and advice:

"I don't know who you are or what you think you're doing," Stephen Fowler said. "But you've made the most dreadful of mistakes."

THIRTY-EIGHT

When Lanny Slotkin entered Foley's on Washington's Twenty-fifth Street, Cochrane was at the bar, seemingly planted in one place, concerned with the magical contents of a beer mug.

Lanny couldn't resist. He ambled to the bar and overtook an unsuspecting Cochrane from behind.

"Bill Cochrane. Imagine. Never seen you here before." Cochrane looked up, made a show of staring first at the mirror behind the bar, then turned.

"Hello, Lanny," he said. "Long time no . . . no what?" Cochrane grimaced. Slotkin glanced at the beer, and several dollar bills and some coins at Cochrane's solitary place at the bar. Cochrane breathed heavily.

"No see," said Lanny, suddenly quite chummy. "Long time no see."

"I'll buy you a beer," Cochrane offered.

He wrapped an arm around Slotkin and held him to the brass rim of the bar. "Hey! Bartender!" he boomed, his Virginia accent more evident than Slotkin, of Utica

Avenue in Brooklyn, had ever noticed. "My friend here is an FBI man. Set him up!"

"Not so loud," Slotkin urged. "I don't want people to know—"

"Ah, who the hell cares, anyway?" Cochrane scoffed.

The bartender drew a stein of beer for Slotkin, gave the younger man an indulgent grin, and departed.

"You bust your ass for the damned FBI and they put you on the street," Cochrane said in more subdued, sorrowful tones. "Well, I'm through busting mine. You just look out for yours, Lanny. That's tonight's advice from this old war horse." Cochrane lifted his mug. "Cheers." He drained it.

"Cheers," answered Slotkin, not knowing what else to say. He sipped generously.

"I hear that fuck-all Frank Lerrick has taken over my game," said Cochrane in a low, confiding grumble. "Well, we'll see what he can accomplish that Bill Cochrane couldn't, right, Lanny?"

"I suppose so."

Cochrane received a refill on the beer.

"The trouble with Frank Lerrick is the same as the trouble with Hoover," Cochrane rambled unsteadily. "They never get laid, 'cept maybe with each other with Clyde Tolson sandwiched in between."

"Cochrane, would you cut it out?"

"A man's got a right to bitch about his former employers, Lanny."

"Yeah, but I come here every night," Slotkin snapped back, trying to hush Cochrane. "Now, knock it off."

Cochrane was silent for a moment. "Every night? How come I've never seen you?"

"Because you never came here. Until now."

"That must be it!" Cochrane slapped his side. Slotkin tried to move away but Cochrane planted an arm around his shoulders.

"Not so fast, Lanny. I want you to tell me your secrets."

"What secrets?"

"Hope See Ming. That's the lady's name, isn't it?"

"What about it?"

"'What about it?'" rejoined Cochrane, repeating. "You sit there looking at her the whole time. Do you mean you can't tell *me* about it now? What do you do in the evenings, anyway? Play with Sally Fivefingers?"

"Cochrane, you're really smashed!"

"I can't believe you, Lanny," Cochrane said in astonished tones. "Hope's Chinese, right?"

"So?"

"So her you-know-what is sideways, Lanny. You mean you didn't know that? You mean you—"

"Oh, for . . . !" Slotkin turned crimson. Cochrane held him with an arm like a tentacle.

"The sideways ones are the best, Lanny. You're a genius and you didn't know that? Haven't you even *tried* to get into her?"

"Cochrane . . ."

"What about little Dora McNeil, Lanny? You work with her all day. You got anything going there?"

Slotkin was searching for an escape. There wasn't one.

"Do you know what little Dora puts behind her ears to make herself attractive to men, Lanny?"

"What?" Slotkin asked unwillingly.

"Her ankles," Cochrane replied drunkenly. "She

puts her ankles behind her ears."

Slotkin started to physically struggle against Cochrane's arm. It was hopeless. "What's the matter with you, Lanny?" Cochrane asked. "Two lovely ladies and you haven't serviced either of them. Are you a pansy, Lanny?"

"I'm not a pansy!" Slotkin snapped. Three heads turned in his direction from the far end of the bar. "I don't want to drink with you, Cochrane," Lanny howled. Cochrane let Slotkin push his arm away. "I don't want to talk, either. You're shit-faced drunk and—"

"Some thanks I get."

"I don't owe you thanks for anything."

"No?"

"No."

"How about the time you leaned on poor little Mr. Hay? Hoover was looking for names. I could have mentioned you, Lanny."

"That was your idea."

"You didn't have to go along with it."

"Cochrane, what do you want from me? What are you doing here, aside from making a spectacle of yourself?"

Cochrane recoiled with sudden earnestness and sobriety. Then his expression was one of mournfulness. "Lanny, I want nothing from you except sympathy," Cochrane said. "I lost the best job I'd ever had. Hell. It hurts. I'm sorry if I'm sounding off. I've been overserved here by a sadistic barkeep."

Slotkin was off stride from Cochrane's mercurial shift in mood. "Hey, no offense," he said. "I understand."

"The fucking thing is," said Cochrane in confidence, "we had those numbers lined up. The naval code? I think I had it," he said drunkenly. "I was going to go through some of the old intercepts and try out my numbers. Now Wheeler or Lerrick's going to try it and grab all the gravy."

Slotkin's ears twitched and stood up straight. "What numbers?" he asked.

Cochrane took a long appraising look at Lanny Slotkin. "What the hell. You did a favor for me once, pushing around Hoover's pet dwarf." His voice went very low and he withdrew a fresh yellow pencil from his jacket pocket. He took a cardboard coaster from the bar.

"I think this was it, Lanny," Cochrane said. "But play around with it. Don't jump to conclusions. And for Christ's sake, don't say where you got this. You'll get yourself fired."

"I won't say anything."

"And you promise you'll wait two or three days?"

"Promise."

Cochrane blinked, as if to clear his brain. Then he wrote on the coaster in a labored, stumbling scrawl:

Four. Two zero. Eight nine.

"I think that's the additive, Lanny boy," Cochrane said.

"Where'd *you* get it?" Slotkin asked, accepting it, staring at it, and placing it within his coat pocket.

"I got lucky. Trial and error. What else works in life?" Cochrane reached for his beer. "Cheers, Lanny." He raised his mug. "Wear your glory in good health."

Slotkin raised his own mug and couldn't believe his good fortune. "Cheers," he answered. "Yes, cheers."

So this was it, Laura thought the next evening. The irrefutable evidence. The smoking gun. Her husband was what they said he was. That, and more.

Laura stood in the cramped hollow behind the wall within the spire of St. Paul's. Downstairs, Cianfrania and Hearn had secured the doors of the church, front and back respectively, while Whiteside and Bill Cochrane had led her upstairs. They had pried loose the outer panels of the chamber with a pair of butcher's knives—they broke one steel blade in the process—and had then, once the panels were loose, simply removed the nails.

And there, behind a second set of board, were the instruments of Siegfried's transmissions. The streamlined, gray metal transmitter that could fit into a small suitcase, the electrical wire, the receiver in a wooden crate, the copper antenna leads, and a German naval code book, fresh and complete, unlike the one at Bureau headquarters.

Whiteside and Cochrane hooked a sixty-watt bulb into an overhead light and reassembled the transmitter.

"We should send at seven in the evening," Cochrane said. "That's when Siegfried used to send."

"Who has the steadier hand?" Whiteside asked toward six-thirty. "You or I?"

They dummied the transmission key and took turns trying.

"It has to feel like Siegfried on the receiving end, too," Cochrane said. "Or no one's going to buy the act."

Cochrane's hand was steadier. Laura watched and said nothing, taking it all in, alternating her thoughts between her husband, Bill Cochrane, and Whiteside.

Cochrane wrote out a brief exchange for transmission. He and Whiteside buttoned into five digits per word for sending, then Laura double-checked their work.

Cochrane sat down at the telegraph key at precisely seven. He began launching numbers into the stratosphere. When they came down in Hamburg, the unscrambled text read:

FDR OPERATION COMPROMISED BY DISLOYAL AGENT OF REICH WITHIN FBI. ABORTING MISSION. WILL ALSO IMMEDIATELY REVEAL TO FBI IDENTITY OF AGENT AND DEPTH OF DUPLICITY.
CQDXVW-2

Unscrambled in Bureau headquarters by the officious Lanny Slotkin, the message unraveled the same way. Slotkin burst from his seat as if it were on fire. He waved his hand in the air triumphantly, screamed, "I got it!" and hit his hip on Hope See Ming's desk as he dashed from the Bluebirds' chamber. He scurried through the hall, passing Bobby Charles Martin, who instinctively always wanted to trip him, and was virtually airborne past Dora McNeil, who had herself all gussied up for someone's benefit that evening.

Slotkin burst unannounced into Frank Lerrick's office. Lerrick, whose desk was piled high with classified documents, bolted to his feet, his face turning red, and was set to explode with the ferocity of one of Siegfried's most potent creations.

But Slotkin silenced him.

"I got it. I cracked it. It makes perfect since in English. Here," he said, handing the white pad with the interpretation to Lerrick.

Lerrick took it and read.

Slotkin gushed excitedly. "It works, fuck it, it works!"

At which time, Dick Wheeler loomed like a Kodiak bear in the doorway, glared in, and puffed his pipe furiously.

"What in *hell* is all this racket about?" he snarled. "Lanny?"

Frank Lerrick looked up. "Our little resident genius from Brooklyn has done us proud," he said, not without an edge. "Take a look for yourself, Dick. This just came in. Our Lanny has grabbed the brass ring. Cracked the naval code for us."

Wheeler came forward and looked as Lerrick handed him Slotkin's notation pad.

"My, but we're in business," said Lerrick. "But what's this all mean—'compromised,' 'duplicity' within the Bureau?" His thin moustache twitched. "Not our Bureau. Can't be. *Can't* be!"

Fussel and McPherson had never guarded such an amiable, complacent prisoner.

"What exactly did your commander say about me?" Stephen Fowler asked when locked into a British safe house off Clifton Park in Baltimore.

"He said you were a dangerous lad," said McPherson in his rumbling Caledonian brogue. "Said we were to shoot you, sir, if you tried anything naughty, sir."

"You won't have to shoot me," said Reverend Fowler in conciliatory tones.

"Certainly hope not, sir," added Mick Fussel. "Have

to fill out a whole bloody report if I fire a weapon. Bugger up the whole day, it would."

"Somewhere someone has made a terrible mistake," Fowler said. "I intend to be the perfect guest, sit here until the mistake has been realized, and then wait for your commander to issue me his apology."

"That being the case, lad," Andrew McPherson said, "you'll be making life much easier for everyone."

"Mr. Whiteside never apologizes to anyone for anything," Fussel noted as if it were relevant. "Doesn't make mistakes."

"He made one this time," Fowler said calmly.

McPherson was a huge, burly man with a wide thick face, powerful shoulders, and a neck to properly connect the two. The son of a miner, he had been born in Dunfermline, worked in the mines a bit himself, done a stint in the Army in Africa, then moved permanently south from Scotland to Liverpool, where he'd become a constable. In the mid-thirties, the talent scouts from M.I. 5 were looking for some muscle with brains attached. They recruited him.

Mick Fussel came to his post as an M.I. 5 baby-sitter in much the same manner. A humorless Cockney who was a lanky but strong six feet two inches tall, Fussel had taken a job after the Depression in an automotive parts warehouse in north London. When the day-to-day drudgery of shipping bumpers and fenders to railway stations proved too much for him, he noticed a recruiting poster at a bus depot for the Metropolitan Police. The poster showed a beaming young man in a crisp, smart uniform and the text beneath the photograph promised a job with a future and an interesting life.

Fussel applied, became a police officer, and was destined for quick promotion when the same recruiting drive that tapped McPherson tapped Fussel also. A man of thirty-five, his arms were long and he often had five to six inches of shirt cuff showing. His hair was streaked with gray, as if from some tour of duty he never spoke of, and, unlike McPherson, who wore his handgun beneath his armpit, Fussel kept his on his left hip.

Through the first evening of his capture, Reverend Fowler exchanged a calm banter with both men. Fussel and McPherson were under specific instructions to keep Fowler handcuffed and ankle-shackled at all times.

This they did. The only exceptions were when the minister asked if he could shower. His hands were free, and Fussel, pistol drawn, stood ten feet from the shower stall watching the minister. Afterward, when Fowler toweled off and was dry and dressed, he held out his hands obediently for the cuffs to be put back in place.

"That was very kind of you," said Fowler. "My wrists were killing me."

"I'm not here to be kind to you," answered the tall Cockney.

"No. Of course you're not. You're simply following your orders."

"Too bloody right," Fussel said. "Now let's get on with you."

He motioned to a doorway that led to a flight of steps that led downstairs. When the minister reached the first floor, he saw that McPherson was waiting, also with gun drawn.

"Your Mr. Whiteside must have given me some kind

of advance billing." The American grinned.

"He just said you were extremely dangerous," McPherson growled. "Keep moving and shut up."

"Have you heard from him?" Fowler asked, hopefully, ushered toward a downstairs room.

"What would it be to you if we did?" Fussel asked.

The minister sounded apologetic. "I'm waiting for him to realize his error."

"From what Mr. Whiteside says, lad, you've got one bloody long wait," Fussel said. "Now get in there and sit." The Englishman indicated a sofa in a small bare room.

"Yes. Of course," Stephen Fowler said, sadness in his voice.

He obeyed his captors with a docility that surprised even them. They exchanged a look or two of confusion, themselves, but remained vigilant. About an hour later, Fowler asked for a Bible and they found one for him. He spent his evening reading and his captors played cards. There was not a peep or complaint from the prisoner.

"What do you make of all this?" McPherson asked Fussel toward midnight.

"Our guest is trying to lure us into a sense of complacency," Fussel said. "Don't trust him for a minute."

"He's a parson, you know," McPherson said in a low whisper. "Imagine that!"

"Mr. Whiteside says he's more than a country church mouse," Fussel snapped back. "Keep your wits about you, you Caledonian fish merchant, or you'll end up going home in a box."

*   *   *

501

At half-past eight in the evening, a figure walked from the back steps of Bureau headquarters. He hit the sidewalk with a purposeful cadence to his walk, continued two blocks, and turned into Connecticut Avenue. It was a man, a coat pulled unevenly to him against a freezing Washington wind, striding with short but intent paces. He found his car and looked in each direction as he unlocked it, behaving for all the world as if he *expected* some sort of trap.

But it wouldn't be sprung there, anyway, the man reasoned. It would be sprung in goddamned New Jersey. Damn clever Lanny Slotkin and his numbers, the man thought. Curse Hoover, curse Roosevelt, curse Stephen Fowler, and for that matter curse Bill Cochrane, too. One way or another the game was over, his cover blown.

The man unlocked his car, entered it, and gunned his engine. He checked his supply of gas. He had already checked the revolver on his hip.

He pulled out onto Connecticut Avenue, allowed a bus to pass him, then proceeded due north. It would be a long drive.

THIRTY-NINE

Laura was the first to see the man across the street in the shadows. She was upstairs with her bedroom light off. There were few leaves left on the trees this late in November and she had an improved view of the church entrance. It was 2 A.M.

She was sure this was a different man than the ones she had seen before. He walked differently and wore different clothing. She felt her heart race. This was the man they expected downstairs.

She stepped back from the window and kept the man in view. He disappeared into the church. For the first time she felt truly like a spy; but she was too frightened to savor the moment. She only gave the signal that Bill Cochrane had asked of her.

One sharp rap to the floor: the man had appeared. He was in the church.

Downstairs, four men had spoken from one station to the next in whispers. Now pulses raced. Nerves tightened like taut rubber bands and each man fell to a death of silence.

Hearn and Cianfrani took cover in the dining room and living room respectively, feeling like bloody fools or, worse, schoolboys at play. Hearn was under the tablecloth of the dining table, his Colt drawn, listening to his own pulsebeat in the darkness. Cianfrani had found a suitable place between a couch and a wall in the Fowler living room. He too had his weapon drawn and ready in a darkened silent room.

He felt his own hands sweating against the weapon. The whole catechism came back from the National Police Academy.

Rounds, chambered, *sir!* . . .

Safety catch up, *sir!* . . .

Set to fire, *sir!* . . .

Between them they had covered the only access to Fowler's study. Back door chained. Windows locked. Cellar door bolted.

Front door open.

In the study burned the only light in the house. The light was from Reverend Fowler's desk lamp, the one with the green glass shade. At the sound of Laura's heel on the wooden floor, Peter Whiteside sprang to his feet and took his position within the stationery closet of the arrested minister's study. Whiteside had fallen silent over the last hour, wondering just what to expect, wondering just how to phrase his report to Whitehall, and inevitably—as does any spy when he has too much time to think in a foreign place—sorting out the loves, accomplishments, and failures of his own life. But then Laura's rap had come, and his weapon was ready and he was on his feet. He drew the closet door three quarters closed and if he could have held his breath for an hour he would have.

He held his pistol upraised. Easier to lower and aim than raise and aim. He saw his watch: 2:04 A.M. It seemed like 5 A.M. His eyes were aching and his stomach was in open revolt with his nerves.

Bill Cochrane had found a black shirt, black jacket, and white collar belonging to Siegfried. He had donned all three. Better to set the final stage, all four men agreed. Then he had settled in at Fowler's desk and waited, his pistol across his lap, never more than a few beads of sweat away from his hand.

Over the course of the evening he had stared for several hours—interrupted only by occasional conversation with the moody Whiteside—at the curios on Reverend Fowler's desk: a silver framed color photograph of Fowler and Laura, presumably from their honeymoon, a handsome couple arm in arm before the Château Frontenac and the St. Lawrence in Quebec; a worn leather Bible, probably family, which made Cochrane reflect for hours if the Bible's value was that of an heirloom or a prop; an oval crystal paperweight and a brass scissor and letter-opener set.

Over the course of the evening Cochrane had studied these artifacts intensively, as if they were clues to some great puzzle. They yielded nothing. He tried, as he sat at Fowler's desk and coveted Fowler's wife, to move into the psyche of the man. What mad flywheel made Siegfried run? What furies besieged him? What demons possessed him?

He thought of the minister, calm and conciliatory even at the moment of his arrest. He thought of the helpless anonymous woman murdered in the woods behind the church and he pondered a sailor from landlocked Kansas slaughtered two miles from Red

Bank. Nothing had connected by the time Cochrane heard Laura's foot on the ceiling above him.

The traitor—Fowler's guardian angel within the FBI—was in the church.

Then, upstairs, Laura saw the man emerge, clinging to the shadows cast by the streetlamp and the trees. He crossed the lane and Laura practically felt her heart explode.

The man opened the gate before her home and briskly approached the house via the flagstone path. As bold and as blatant as that! She almost forgot the second signal. Then her foot—or was it her fear?—took over for her.

She rapped a second time. The man was on his way.

All at once, and unfolding in all its complexities within the breadth of a second, an appalling notion was upon Bill Cochrane. It was so neat and clear that Cochrane could not understand why it had never come to him before:

Tiny Mr. Hay was the demon within the FBI! Toupeed, scheming, malevolent Mr. Hay:

I know everything, Cochrane. . . .

Pull my whiskers again and there'll be bloodshed, I swear it to you. . . .

If there's a fire, I figure I can be assistant director. . . .

The little imp was probably assembling matches and kerosene already!

In Bill Cochrane's tired mind, allegiances blew apart, swirled into a vortex of confusion, then reassembled in queer, bright ominous new formations. Before Bill Cochrane was a panoply of deceit.

Mr. Hay sat astride a network that involved both

Dick Wheeler and Frank Lerrick, at least as subalterns. Hoover was kept in the dark, which wasn't difficult, and the entire floor of Bluebirds in Section Seven were legmen for the cabal on the second floor.

Hope See Ming, Lanny Slotkin, and, yes, even Mary Ryan had deciphered Siegfried's code long ago. But they weren't telling. The Germans—Roddy Schwarzkopf and Liz Pfeiffer—were doubles, quite obviously now, and Bobby Charles Martin was a crypto-Nazi from the Rhineland of Ohio. At 2 A.M. it all made perfect sense. Cochrane had been the fall guy for the entire operation, the one to whom Hoover had turned for an answer and who had not been able to supply one. Hoover was thus destroyed at the White House and Cochrane was ruined as a public servant. And, most important in this scenario, America's fledgling intelligence networks would be washed away. A reorganization would be forced going into an election year, 1940, and then everything would again be wiped clean by a new President.

Then the whole conspiracy flew apart, spiraled, and reformed. Peter Whiteside and Laura Fowler were Gestapo. So was Otto Mauer. So was Stephen Fowler, who had been hauled away not by M.I. 6 agents but by coconspirators. The transmitter at the top of the church tower was dead and the man now lured to Liberty Circle was not an FBI traitor but an executioner who would in a few moments treat Cochrane to a bullet between the eyes. The only betrayal within the FBI, Cochrane reasoned, was Cochrane himself, who, against all entreaties of rational, professional men like Dick Wheeler, had thrown in his lot with the opposition.

"I'm going crazy," Bill Cochrane said softly. His hand was on his pistol, which was across his lap.

Then there was a sound. It was the front door of the house opening and then softly shutting. Peter Whiteside stood in the doorway of the stationery closet with a .38 drawn and upraised. Even in the dim light cast from Fowler's green desk lamp, Cochrane could find his eyes.

"No shooting unless absolutely necessary," Cochrane said again, his voice no stronger than a whisper. But no one could hear and that had been decided a day ago, anyway.

The footsteps moved closer.

No shooting, Cochrane reasoned. Why then was his own hand soaking wet upon the pistol? Why was there a cramp in his wrist and a pulsebeat in his neck? Why was the sweat on his face unbearable?

Why was he taking a final glance at the sturdiness of the wooden desk to see what parts of it might stop a bullet?

The footsteps had found the sliver of light cast by the partly open door to the minister's study. They drew closer now, careful footfalls on a carpet, then upon a bare floor.

Cochrane swiveled in his chair to place his back to the door and he prayed—perhaps as Stephen Fowler had ultimately failed to pray—that the intruder would speak before shooting.

A large man or a small man? Cochrane wondered. Then, to his abiding horror as he heard the door push open, he realized that if the man started shooting, size made little final difference at all.

The door was open. One footfall, then a second into

Fowler's study. And Cochrane was thinking, *Dear God, let me see who it is before I'm shot! Dear God, this one last wish!*

"Reverend Fowler?"

Cochrane knew the voice from a thousand other times that he'd heard it. But it was only when he swiveled quickly in his chair to face the intruder that the reality was upon him.

Cochrane stared as Peter Whiteside pushed his closet door open and faced Dick Wheeler with a drawn pistol. Wheeler jumped in astonishment when he saw the movement, then gave an involuntary quake a second time when Hearn and Cianfrani appeared quietly behind him, weapons drawn.

There was little said, considering the moment. Cochrane spoke first, and his own voice sounded very distant in what was otherwise total silence.

"Please remain calm, Dick," he said, still stunned, "and keep your hands in full view. You're being placed under arrest."

A bewildered Wheeler looked at the Englishman. Simultaneously, Cianfrani held a cocked pistol to Wheeler's ribs while his hand darted very professionally under Wheeler's coat to remove the service revolver.

From the desk, Cochrane saw Laura appear. Then his attention went back to all the guns that were drawn and he prayed that nothing would happen accidentally. The evening had already been blackened enough.

Then another mood swept Cochrane and his overwhelming emotion was that of disappointment. He could barely bring himself to look Wheeler in the eye. "Give him a thorough frisk," Cochrane said in a subdued, sullen voice. "He's probably carrying more than one." He was: a two-shot derringer was at the elbow in the left coat sleeve.

To which Dick Wheeler feigned confusion. "Bill, what the devil is all this about? Some sort of joke? Not funny, brother, if it is."

For several seconds Cochrane could not answer. He merely held Wheeler—who was moved to the wall and frisked by Cianfrani as Hearn stood guard—in a chilly assessing eye while several images flashed before him: Kurkevics, the dead FBI contact in Berlin, Theresia bloody and dead in her home, Mauer worried to the point of homicide and hysteria over the plight of his family, and then Cochrane's own long days of exile with the flatulent dwarf in the archives.

Then disappointment gave way to anger and anger to confusion. Dick Wheeler, the ascendant star of the Bureau; the FBI emissary and diplomatic courier to the House and Senate; Dick Wheeler, who stood to inherit the leadership of the whole damned department if any President ever had the temerity to send J. Edgar packing.

Wheeler had betrayed all this and betrayed every human being he knew within the Bureau. Why? For what in return? Bill Cochrane sat in the quiet room and watched Cianfrani and Hearn complete an all but routine arrest and search. But Bill Cochrane did not understand.

"No joke at all, Dick," was all Cochrane could say. "And you're right. It's not funny."

Whiteside withdrew slightly, lowered his pistol, but kept it drawn and pointed toward the floor. He knew better than to involve himself further in what was now a preponderantly American operation. Cochrane stood from the desk.

There was something about Fowler's clothing that now rested very uneasily upon Cochrane. The white celluloid collar was unbearably tight all of a sudden and he wanted to be rid of it. He unfastened it.

Laura stepped through the doorway. "There isn't anyone else," she said. "I kept watch."

She moved to Peter Whiteside, who took her under his arm. Cochrane later remembered thinking how tired she looked. And Agent Hearn, looking back and forth from Cochrane to the prisoner, finally spoke in confusion, addressing Cochrane.

"Hey, what's going on?" he asked. "You know this guy?"

"Somewhat," answered Cochrane. "But it's a long story."

Cochrane insisted that they leave for Washington immediately, drive through the night, and render their prisoner to a federal installation as soon as possible. Cianfrani suggested that a nice new cement and iron edifice in Newark was all ready, spiffy, and waiting, but Cochrane made the further point that this would only make another transfer inevitable.

"And we don't even know entirely what we're dealing with," Cochrane said, with an eye to security and a larger conspiracy.

It fell to Laura to make coffee for the drive, an irony which was not lost upon her. A strange parochial little scene transpired as the coffee brewed and they sat around waiting, all of them chitchatting except for

Wheeler, who had fallen silent, and Hearn, who sat with his pistol across his lap and stared at his shackled, manacled prisoner.

Then the whole crew was off to Washington in three cars. Hearn and Cianfrani drove the lead, transporting Wheeler in an enclosed rear seat designed for just such purposes: a leg chain linked him to the body of the car, an iron mesh divider separated him from the occupants of the front seat, and the rear doors locked from the outside.

Cochrane drove with Laura in the second car, his Hudson, and Whiteside drove the follow-up, staying a precautionary hundred yards behind the other two.

It was 7 A.M. when they reached Washington and the whole motley assemblage of three cars remained together all the way to the Federal House of Detention. Everyone's eyelids were heavy, even Wheeler's. The prisoner had little to say, but said all of it when Cochrane helped him out of the rear of the FBI car.

"You're making a hell of a goddamned mistake, Bill," he said, hulking out of the rear seat into an upright position. "I don't know what you think you're doing."

"Uh-huh," Cochrane answered.

"I'm just assuming that you've lost your mind completely and can't be legally held responsible for any of this."

"Cianfrani and Hearn will handle the booking," Cochrane answered.

Dick Wheeler looked at him sourly. Then Cianfrani and Hearn took Wheeler's arms and pulled him respectfully in the proper direction. Cochrane waited until the three figures disappeared into the federal jail.

Laura and Peter Whiteside moved to a spot a few feet behind Cochrane and were there when he turned.

"I'll take Laura over to the Shoreham," Whiteside said. "I'll check her in there, then I'll need some sleep myself. Been a bloody long stretch."

Cochrane nodded. "What about Fowler?"

"He'll be safe with my men in Baltimore for another day," Whiteside said. "Then I'll have him brought here. Acceptable?"

Cochrane didn't care for the delay. But he needed the sleep himself. He acquiesced to Whiteside's plan. His attention turned to Laura.

"I think you should stay away from your home until your husband is safely locked up," he said. And then for some reason, perhaps due to the fatigue that afflicted all of them, he added. "I'm sorry."

She nodded. Words were failing Laura at that hour, too. Something caught in both of their eyes and she reached to Cochrane and he embraced her. He gave her a comforting hug and slowly released her.

She pulled slowly from his arms. "Thank you," she said. "Come say hello tomorrow."

Cochrane promised that he would.

FORTY

"What you have to remember about the Germans," said Reverend Fowler, entrancing his two guards, "is that in the age of the Barbarians, we're talking about the 400s and 500s A.D. here, the first German converts to Christianity denied the divinity of Christ."

Fowler's eyes twinkled. He was at the card table with Fussel and McPherson. His feet were chained together and linked to a tall armoire. His wrists were cuffed. For the past hour, he had regaled his captors with historical and religious anecdotes ranging from the death of Catherine the Great to Cardinal Richelieu supporting Catholicism in France and Protestantism in the rest of Europe.

"That made the first German converts," Fowler concluded, "the first Christians to be both true believers and heretics at the same time."

McPherson was fascinated as Fussel listened warily. Reverend Fowler took aim on McPherson and began talking of what he called "Scotland's legitimate national feelings," to which Fussel moaned and turned a deaf ear.

There was some smoked meat on the table with a large serving fork. Both guards sat with their weapons on the opposite side from Fowler.

"Mind if I eat something?" Fowler asked in passing.

"Help yourself," McPherson said. Fussel dealt the cards and McPherson moved the serving knife from the plate.

Fowler picked up a salt shaker and shook it briskly over a slice of beef. He ate. He looked around.

"What's the matter?" McPherson asked.

"Overdid it with the salt," said Fowler. He eyed McPherson's beer.

"Nothing fucking doing!" Fussel interjected. "He doesn't get any alcohol. Whiteside's orders."

"Then get him some water," McPherson said. "You're closer than I am."

Fussel shot his partner a hostile stare. "Want to know something?" Fussel said. "I'll be happy when we can turn the bloody parson here back over to the Americans. If he's dangerous, we shouldn't have him. If he's not, we shouldn't have him, either."

"Just get him some water, huh?" McPherson said.

Fowler turned politely to Fussel. "Thank you," he said.

Fowler watched Fussel leave the room for the kitchen, one room away. With his cuffed wrists, he reached to Fussel's five-card poker hand. Fowler peeked. He looked back to McPherson.

"Two aces, a king, and two sevens," he whispered. "Is that good?"

McPherson's bushy brow furrowed and he looked studiously downward at his own hand.

Then everything was too fast for comprehension. the minister's shackled wrists flew toward the serving fork, grabbed it in both fists, and brought it upward into McPherson's throat.

McPherson howled, but at the same moment, Reverend Fowler was lunging across his body, pulling the pistol from the holster and withdrawing backward once he had it.

Fussel dropped what he was doing in the kitchen and raced back when he heard the commotion. He was fumbling for his own gun.

"God! No!" Fussel shouted, taking it all in at once—his partner anguished and clutching at the bloody fork stuck in his throat, and the parson whirling toward the doorway, a Smith & Wesson .38 in his two hands.

Then Fowler fired. Two bullets crashed into Fussel's chest. They slammed him backward and sent his own gun flying from his hand. Fussel felt the agony of the bullets ripping into his flesh and shattering his breastbone. He gasped several times, clutching his horrible wounds, and knew he was dying.

For several seconds, McPherson tried to struggle. But the fork seemed to have impaled his whole body. His eyes were thick with his own blood. Every inch of him convulsed with pain.

The last thing he understood was that the prisoner was placing the nose of the pistol to McPherson's head. There was a loud cracking sound, an indescribable pain, and then total blackness. . . .

With another bullet, Siegfried shot through the chain that linked his ankles to the armoire. Then he crawled to the body of Andrew Fussel, found no pulse, and emptied the Englishman's pockets.

He quickly found what he wanted: the keys to his handcuffs and leg chain. He unlocked himself, stood, flexed his wrist and leg muscles, and glanced at the bloody bodies of the two men he had killed. He exuded a long sigh, not of emotion, but of fatigue. The day in captivity had been excruciating. His whole schedule and method of operation had been sabotaged now. He would have to strike Roosevelt quickly and depart. The whole country would be looking for him within twenty-four hours.

Siegfried emptied the wallets of the men he had killed and took both of their pistols with him. He closed the door to the safe house behind him less than five minutes later. Then he taxied immediately to the bus terminal and was bound for Washington, then Alexandria, Virginia, within the hour while the two undiscovered bodies had an entire night to cool in the house off Clifton Park.

For the first time in recent days, Laura felt safe. Stephen was under arrest. Bill Cochrane told her that with the apprehension of the big strapping Missourian named Wheeler, his Bureau's internal troubles, as he called them, were apparently settled, too.

Then there was Bill, himself. She could feel the old warning signals. Her attraction to him had been no secret since the first time they sat and talked over tea. She felt, well, safe with him. He was a man she wanted to be with. Nothing sexual yet, she thought. Just being with him sufficed. Especially now, when she needed all the emotional support she could get.

Both of their minds were overladen with the events of the last few days. Now it was time to relax and to unwind.

Bill asked her to accompany him to dinner and she accepted. They spoke again of many things and Laura again found him to be a fine conversationalist and a good listener. He spoke about his boyhood in Virginia and his memories of two societies, one colored and one white, in his hometown in Virginia. In turn, she told him of the Georgian home with the high wall in Salisbury, her mother, and how she as a girl used to play with her father's ribbons from the 1914–18 campaign on the Continent.

The restaurant was informal and Italian, a quiet little family place called Mario's around the corner from the Library of Congress. After the meal, he offered her a port back at his place before returning her to the Shoreham.

Again, she accepted. She could almost feel—or was she imagining it?—a little tingle of the old girlish excitement: *a quiet glass of port at a man's place. Maybe things would get nicely out of hand. Tonight, who cared?*

It was only nine in the evening when they left the restaurant and they were in no hurry at all, enjoying each other's company. The night was chilly and even raw when the wind kicked up.

"Know what?" she asked, pulling her wool coat close to her, "it reminds me of Dorset in the winter. Mind if we walk a little?"

"You Brits never feel the cold, do you?" he asked with a smile.

"It's invigorating," she said, pulling her collar close. Her dark hair, pulled close to her by her collar, framed her beautiful face.

"May I?" he asked, offering her an arm.

"Why, yes. You may," she said. She took his arm.

Washington fascinated her. Unlike London, it was a city that seemed to be *only* government. There were uniforms everywhere, Army, Navy, Air Force, every third car that passed them as they strolled looked official, and the illuminated monuments and Capitol Hill, washed in yellow lights after dark, told her that this was the seat of American power. This was where decisions were made. If America entered the war, the entry would become official within view of where they walked.

A light cold rain began to fall and again it made her think of England. They hurried back to where the Hudson was parked on C Street and he was struck with an idea.

"It just occurred to me," he said. "You've barely seen Washington. I'll give you the grand tour before that nightcap."

"That would be wonderful," she said. They quickened their pace and almost trotted the last block back to the car. His arm was gently on her shoulders and then he unlocked the door on her side of the car. He helped her in, came around to his side, jumped in, and, almost on cue, the rain intensified. They both laughed. The car's engine whined, ground, then sprang to life. Then they were off across the shiny, rain-swept streets of the city: the White House, the Lincoln and Jefferson memorials, the Mall at the foot of the Capitol dome, and then, for the finale, he crossed into Virginia at Arlington, turned the car in the traffic circle, and took the same bridge back into the city.

She had come a long way, she was thinking, since Edward Shawcross and his plans for a country inn. Even the recent memory of her husband's attack on her seemed to recede. It was one of those magical evenings with a man who was so new to her life that by his very presence he conveyed novelty and excitement.

She began to think about the house on Twenty-sixth Street where he lived. "I'm ready for some port," she finally said.

He turned down Pennsylvania Avenue a final time. The flag was flying and lit above the White House. Roosevelt was in residence. There were three men in U.S. Navy uniforms standing in the rain before the iron gates, peering in. To Bill Cochrane, they keyed memories of the sailors from the *Adriana* in Union Station, singing on their way to their incendiary slaughter at sea. He had to work to suppress the unpleasant memory.

The sight of the sailors keyed a similar association to Laura, and Cochrane suspected as much, because she had been very talkative over the course of the evening—more about university, her husband, her girlhood, her father—and now she was very quiet, as suddenly, were the rain-slicked streets.

Envisioning her thoughts telepathically, or at least trying to, he sought to calm her.

"I know you're alarmed about Stephen," he said. "I know how traumatizing it is. But there's no way he'll harm you again. There's no way he'll harm anyone."

To which she had many reactions, but said nothing. Then they were parking near his house.

When they entered, he led Laura to the living room, eased her coat from her, and turned on only enough lights to maintain the pleasantness of the evening. She rubbed her hands together, still chilled from the outdoors, and he checked the radiator. The heat was low, so he used some newspaper to kindle some logs in

521

the fireplace.

Laura sat quietly as the fireplace slowly came alive. "Now," he finally said, "time for that nightcap. Port, still? I have brandy, also?"

"Port would be fine," she said.

He found some in a decanter on the dry sink in the dining room. He blessed the housekeepers for seeing to at least some eventualities.

He glanced at her and idly thought, *What in hell do I think I'm doing here with my suspect's wife?* Then he reminded himself that his resignation from the Bureau became effective within less than two weeks. He had no suspects any more because he had concluded his final case. So much for conflict of interest.

"Bill?" she asked at length. "What do you think will happen?"

He poured a tawny port into two cordial glasses, barely looking up as she spoke. "About what?" he asked.

"In Europe," she said. "Germany and England."

He drew a long breath and returned to the sofa. He handed her one glass and sat down near her.

"I suppose Hitler will topple what's already shaky," he answered. "France is totally unprepared for war. They'll fall the same way the Weimar Republic did."

"And England?" she asked.

"Chamberlain's been discredited because a war has started despite all his concessions. He'll be out of office within weeks, also."

"I'm not an expert," she said as she sipped very slowly, "but England doesn't have the ships and planes that Germany has. Do you think there will be an invasion?"

"I think there's a good chance."

She was looking straight ahead now, not at him, and Cochrane knew where her thoughts were: in Salisbury, at the Georgian home of her father, surrounded by memories and a peaceful garden from her girlhood. All the things she had told him about.

He placed an arm around her shoulder before he even realized what he was doing.

"I also think England will get some ships and airplanes," he said. "Very quickly, if she needs them."

She turned to him and smiled. Her eyes were soft, set like porcelain in her fair, unblemished complexion. She was, as he had noticed all along, very beautiful, in addition to being another man's wife.

"From Roosevelt?" she asked.

"That's the rumor on Capitol Hill," he said. "But who knows? There's an election coming, also. If Roosevelt leaves office, few of the other candidates have any international vision at all. Die-hard isolationists, they are. They'll travel to hell and back to keep America out of another European war."

"What will you do?" she asked. "Enlist if there's a war?"

"I don't know. Maybe."

"What would you like to do?"

"Go to New York, I suppose. Find some peaceful work. Make a few dollars. Want the full truth?" he asked.

She nodded and was half finished her port.

"Fall in love again," he said, finishing his. "And yourself?" he asked.

"Myself?"

"What would you like to do?"

She thought for a moment, looked away to the fire, then looked back to him. "You'll laugh," she insisted.

"No, I won't, Laura."

"I'd like to spend time with you," she said. "A lot of it."

He set down his glass of port and took her hand. It was surprisingly chilly, despite the fire. Then there was a long silence, as each attempted to rationalize the danger signals that flashed.

"That would be wonderful," he said in response. And his instinct was to add the conditions: wonderful, thank you, but you're married; wonderful, thank you, but I've buried the only other two women I've loved; wonderful, thank you, but I've totally given up on love, remember. I'd hoped to fall again, but figured I wouldn't.

Until I met you, that is, a voice within him said. *Until I saw this lovely, frightened, distraught English-woman standing in the woods behind a church.*

But there were no other words spoken. Instead, he kissed her. Then there was an urgent embrace and they sank back onto the sofa. Her eyes were closed and her arms were around his shoulders. When his hand moved gently to the buttons of her sweater, she did nothing to stop him. Rather, a delicious anticipatory warmth coursed through her. Much later in the evening she remembered thinking, *This isn't adultery at all, I'm simply going to bed with a man I love.*

When it was over, and when she lay next to him watching the final embers in the fire, words formed before she knew she was saying them.

"If America enters the war," she said softly, "don't you dare get killed."

FORTY-ONE

The sound of the persistent knocking, a fist on a wooden doorway, forced Laura to emerge from a deep, satisfying sleep.

There was the warmth of the strong male arm around her. His chest pressed to her back beneath a sheet and a blanket. There was, as she slowly woke, the excitement and strangeness of Bill Cochrane's bed. There was the sound of traffic outside and there was . . .

That damned knocking again. Who in bloody hell . . . ?

She felt Bill's arm leave her waist and she rolled over. She fluttered her eyes open and saw him hurriedly dressing. Slowly, her mind began to register. The previous evening. Dinner. Logs in the fireplace. A new lover.

He pulled on his clothes.

"Good morning," she said, sitting up.

Then came the knocking again.

"Morning," he said.

She sat up in bed, held the sheets to her, then figured, why bother? She liked her lovers to admire her. The sheet was across her lap.

"What is that?" she then asked, realizing that the persistent rapping would not go away. "Bill, what's going on?"

He sat down on the edge of the bed, wrapped an arm around her bare shoulders, and kissed her.

"You're very beautiful and you're a spectacular lover," he said to her. "And I have no idea who is downstairs at my door. So I thought I'd get dressed and find out."

"Oh," she said, feeling a trifle foolish.

He went to his dresser and withdrew his pistol from the second drawer. He checked it as he disappeared down the stairs. She listened.

Moments later, she heard the door unlock. Then there was an animated, tormented conversation. Bill's voice. Another man. She recognized it.

Peter Whiteside.

She found her own clothes, ran a comb through her hair, and paused at a mirror. She looked like a very sinful girl who had slept over at a strange man's house without even bringing her own things. Such was life, she reasoned. She was entitled to her own imperfections.

Then she stopped at the head of the stairs. Snatches of conversation rose up from the living room.

". . . shot to death by the filthy bastard. Two of my best bloody men . . ." Whiteside's impassioned voice: "My own damned fault, I should have assigned fifty men to guard him . . . and what the bloody *hell* do we do now? Fowler is loose again!"

"For starters, we don't panic," Bill Cochrane answered. Laura tiptoed down the stairs and saw a greatly shaken Peter Whiteside standing in the living room with Bill. Whiteside's face was ashen.

"Mind?" Whiteside asked, opening a decanter of scotch and pouring himself some.

"Suit yourself," Bill answered, his arms folded before him.

Whiteside gulped down three fingers of liquor as if it were water.

"And Laura's missing, too," Whiteside said urgently. "Tried to reach her since six this bloody morning. Called the hotel, finally had the bell captain check her room."

"And?" Cochrane asked.

"Never returned there last night." Whiteside threw down another gulp of whiskey.

"Is that a fact?"

Then she spoke. "Laura's perfectly safe," she said. Whiteside whirled as if addressed by a ghost. "But we're going to have to do something about her husband."

Whiteside stared at her, then his gaze shifted to Cochrane. "Oh. I see," he finally said. He looked as if he were about to deliver a lecture on morality.

Cochrane interceded and saved the moment. "After you've finished drinking your breakfast, Peter," he said, "we'll have to get moving. I suspect Fowler's right here in Washington."

"Here? *Why?*"

"He's stalking Roosevelt."

"Good Christ!" Whiteside, who was having a bad morning, exclaimed. He reached for the bottle again.

"Well," Cochrane said, "it's about time you both knew, isn't it? That's all we're doing. Preventing an assassination that could change the world."

There followed a day of quiet panic in the District of Columbia. Cochrane hit the pavements almost immediately—or, more accurately, the tires of the Hudson hit the city streets—and ferreted out anyone in the Bureau or Secret Service with whom he could still obtain an open ear.

To most field agents, he was still a leper. The Secret Service was not partial to obtaining their leads from the FBI and Frank Lerrick was either "out" or "unavailable" whenever Cochrane called.

All Bill Cochrane wished to convey was that Siegfried, or Rev. Stephen Fowler, had slipped the leash of British intelligence and was probably in Washington.

"So what's new about that?" asked one of the White House Secret Service detail.

"Just be extravigilant," Cochrane adviced.

"We'll keep our eyes extraopen," came the response, heavy with sarcasm.

In the early afternoon Cochrane found his way into Bureau headquarters and onto the sixth floor. Most of the Bluebirds were absent: more empty desks and listening posts than Cochrane had ever seen. The place had an air of summer vacation or lunch hour, this in late November and in the middle of the afternoon.

He looked again for Frank Lerrick and failed again to find him. Lerrick, just since that previous morning, had gained the title of Acting Operations Chief, whatever that meant. Bill Cochrane supposed it was some sort of move designed to fill the vacuum left by Dick Wheeler's "retirement due to illness," as insiders were asked to call it.

Cochrane drove by the White House and parked across on Pennsylvania Avenue by the curb. He sat and analyzed the street. He "made" as much of the plainclothes security as he could. His spirits were lifted slightly. Somewhere, perhaps, someone had been listening to him that afternoon. There was in fact extra security.

For Siegfried? Or simply because most of Washington knew the unofficial news anyway: Congress was an hour or two from Thanksgiving adjournment. The President would be leaving for Warm Springs as soon as the final gavel cracked.

Cochrane pondered: a man needing heavy security, he knew from his own experience, is most vulnerable en route. In public places—in transit—a ring of security is most difficult to set.

Lincoln, he recalled, was shot in a theater. Garfield was shot at a train station. McKinley took a bullet at a public meeting hall.

President Roosevelt, himself, escaped death in a Miami motorcade in 1933 when a bullet intended for him hit Mayor Cermack of Chicago instead.

Transit, thought Cochrane. Where in transit? He had been too close to Siegfried not to have some understanding of the man's moves. He knew a bomb was probably already made. Where was it?

Cochrane turned over the engine of the Hudson and drove to the Washington Naval Station.

Cochrane showed his FBI credentials at the main

529

gate. Already he could see that security was tighter than usual. The word *had* spread. Something *was* going on.

"Are you with the FBI contingent already here?" a Naval MP asked.

"That's right, sailor," Cochrane said.

The MP waved him past while another MP stood ten feet away with a carbine.

Cochrane parked in the first space available. He walked toward the presidential yacht. He pinned his FBI shield to his lapel and kept his hands visible.

The ship was ringed with sixteen MP's, eight different posts, two men at each post. Cochrane glanced to the deck and saw a stronger presence there than usual. He moved down the pier a hundred feet from where the *Sequoia* was berthed and stared at the water.

No movement at all along the waterline of the ship. He raised his eyes. There were two PT boats in the Potomac Harbor, visitors he had never seen before. One was a hundred yards upstream from the *Sequoia,* the other was a hundred yards downstream. Both dwarfed the presidential yacht. Cochrane studied them.

"Satisified, Cochrane?" a voice asked.

Cochrane's head turned to his left. There was Frank Lerrick, who had spotted him, then appeared quietly at his side.

"I'll be more satisfied when the President arrives safely wherever he's going," Cochrane answered.

Lerrick looked angry. "Same old Bill Cochrane," he said. "Not your case anymore, but you have to keep nosing into it. Don't you understand what 'dismissed' means?"

"Maybe not. But my resignation's not effective till the end of the month, anyway."

Lerrick drew a breath. The wind was kicking up and the banks of the river were chilly. "What can I do to get rid of you?" Lerrick asked. "Short of having you locked up?"

"Convince me that your security is more than ample. I think there'll be an attempt on the President before he leaves this harbor."

"Impossible."

"Convince me," Cochrane again challenged.

And Frank Lerrick went a long way toward convincing him. The yacht had been tossed inside out, Lerrick said. Even panels from walls had been taken off and riveted back on. Everything that could move had been picked up, shaken, and put back into place. Ten army demolitions experts had gone through the ship that very afternoon, and when they had finished, the District bomb squad had repeated the same procedure.

"You couldn't slip a wet cough drop on or off that fucking boat," Lerrick said.

"How about the harbor?" Cochrane asked.

Lerrick motioned to the PT boats. "Navy operation, uh, all the way."

"What about a mine at the mouth of the river?" Cochrane asked with sudden inspiration.

Lerrick grinned and appreciated the question. A chance to show off: "I was twenty-four hours ahead of you, Cochrane. Two mine sweepers from Annapolis covered the harbor this afternoon. They're also

531

proceeding along the coastal waterway as far as Georgia. An advance escort in addition to the PT boats."

"And the sides of the *Sequoia* itself?" Cochrane asked.

"Six marine frogmen spent the afternoon going over every inch of it," Lerrick said. "There's not a barnacle on that boat's belly. They finished at four-thirty. Half an hour ago. And nothing, *nothing,* has come within two hundred, uh, yards of the boat since. Satisfied?"

Cochrane had to admit it. Yes, he *was* satisfied. Lerrick had done all the right things. The facts were the facts. Why then, did his instincts still rebel?

He thanked Frank Lerrick and departed.

His mood and suspicions simmered. He considered going for dinner, but wasn't hungry. He wound his way slowly through Washington traffic and discovered that he was heading, for no real reason, back toward the White House and his previous post across the street from the presidential residence.

Where would the attack come? he kept demanding of himself. He couldn't see it. He couldn't sense it. His intuition had left town. He began to wonder whether his common sense had, too.

Maybe, he postulated, it's all a conceit at this point. Siegfried knew he had lost and fled the country: he saved himself, just as I should now save myself.

Cochrane tried to place himself within Siegfried's twisted psyche. And when he did so, a sense of impending disaster seized him.

He had the *damnedest* feeling. It was a sense he had developed involuntarily over the past five years. He knew when he was being tailed and he knew when he was close to his own quarry. His senses had never betrayed him. But tonight they were short-circuiting. He was getting messages, but didn't know what they were.

Was he close to Siegfried, or was Siegfried close to him? Had Fowler flown the coop completely—he had to have had an escape route or two lined up—or was he still lurking somewhere in the capital, waiting for his shot at Roosevelt?

Cochrane sat in his car on Pennsylvania Avenue, parked by a fire hydrant. The flag flew above the White House, a yellow spotlight upon it.

He ran through everything again. The White House itself was secure from within. It *had* to be. Similarly, the White House grounds were clean. Cochrane had seen the Secret Service and Bureau people spanning every inch that very afternoon. They had even used dogs.

The presidential limousine had been under guard for two weeks. Secure, Cochrane thought, checking off a mental list.

What about the route to the yacht? Unpublished, Cochrane recalled, and the first blocks away from the White House were under guard by Secret Service, plainclothes D.C. police, Army, and FBI. A cat couldn't slip in and out without being seen.

So that left the yacht, which had been searched and searched again from within. And the frogmen searched the outside at sunset.

So why did Cochrane sense disaster? Where, oh where, was the weak spot in security?

He started his car, just for the exercise, and pulled into traffic. He circled the White House in its entirety,

Pennsylvania Avenue, to Constitution, south, and back again. He had never seen such heavy security. He should have been reassured. But that damnable feeling was still upon him.

He parked again. The same spot. A brown sedan pulled from a parking area a hundred feet behind him, then cruised next to him and stopped.

They looked at him questioningly, a car full of hard-nosed Secret Service faces.

Cochrane kept his hands in full view on the top of the steering wheel. His window was already open.

"FBI," he said. He flicked one palm open in plain sight and showed a shield. They shined a searchlight in his face.

"What the fuck are you sitting here for?" the driver asked.

"Security's a joint operation, isn't it?" he asked. They looked at him resentfully, then rolled up their car window. They parked fifty feet down the block in front of him. They settled in to wait, and so did Cochrane.

Earlier that afternoon, Stephen Fowler had selected his key landmark on the Virginia side of the Potomac. It was—appropriately—the spire of St. Thomas's church, the tallest point near the riverside in Alexandria. The spire would be easily visible at all hours from the water, which was what counted.

Siegfried left his car one block from the Lutheran church. The trunk of the car contained the spy's escape material: fake passports, tickets, money, and dry clothing.

Then Fowler took a public bus into Washington. He

would start in the Washington Channel, upstream from the *Sequoia,* and swim downstream with the current to his target. Then the current of the Potomac would guide him back across the Potomac to Alexandria. For a strong swimmer, it was fiendishly simple.

He wore his black rubber wet suit beneath an overcoat and a pair of baggy workman's coveralls. He carried the bomb in a small suitcase.

He went to East Potomac Park at dusk, staked out a bench near the Washington Channel, and waited. A thousand thoughts were upon him: his proximity to killing the President . . . his escape through Mexico . . . his eventual reception in Germany.

His spirits rose. He was a commando, wasn't he? A bomb beneath his arm. A diving knife sheathed and strapped to his shin. A loaded pistol in a waterproofed canvas wrapping was taped to his chest within his wet suit.

He stared at the water. *Nothing* could stop him. Not the foolish English, not the amateurish Americans. Not even the muddle-headed women who occasionally got in his way.

At eight o'clock, his eyes accustomed to the dimness of the park, he stood up and began to stroll. He could almost feel the small watch ticking in its case.

Four sticks of dynamite, he pondered. Enough to depose Franklin and Eleanor from the White House, but probably not enough to sink the *Sequoia.* Well, he reasoned, some details didn't matter. He would be on the midnight flight to Mexico City by the time the blast detonated. And he would be on a German warship by 7 P.M. the next evening.

Siegfried stopped near a clump of trees. There was

not a soul within sight. Quickly, he undressed. He checked the waterproofing around the bomb and the plastic adhesives that would secure it to the ship. He tossed away the small suitcase.

He patted his knife and his pistol. He blackened his face with burnt cork. Then, at half-past eight, he entered the channel.

He carried his clothing and abandoned it a hundred feet into the river.

He took a few strokes and began his path downstream. The friendly current carried him. Even the weather cooperated. Dim moonlight masked by a November overcast. In the center of the river, or under the hull of the *Sequoia,* Siegfried would be invisible. His presence would be known only long after his flowers were planted, when explosion and death would shatter the night.

His strokes were firm now, long, smooth, and even. He felt like a sculler on the Charles or the Schuylkill. Genius propelled him, Siegfried decided. That and a sense of mission.

It would be a different America after Roosevelt died. A different world. The next American leadership would surely see the folly of war with the Third Reich.

How Hitler would welcome him! How he would be a hero in the week or two it would take to arrive in Berlin!

At five minutes past nine, Cochrane recognized a tall, lean man in a top coat and bowler walking past the White House. The man walked in Cochrane's direction. On his arm was a very beautiful woman.

Peter Whiteside and Laura Worthington Fowler approached Cochrane's car. "Anything happening?" Whiteside asked.

"Sure," Cochrane answered. "There are so many security people within two square blocks that we're falling over each other."

"I noticed," Whiteside answered.

"American overkill? Is that it?" Laura asked with mock reproach.

"It sure isn't classic English understatement," Cochrane allowed. "Why don't you both get in?"

They did, Laura in front with Bill Cochrane, Whiteside in the back. Out of the corner of his eye, Cochrane saw Whiteside remove his pistol from his overcoat pocket, check the six cylinders, and click it shut again. For one terrible second his instincts rebelled on him, a new horror seized him, and he was aware that he had his back to a man with a loaded weapon.

Then Whiteside tucked the pistol away. Cochrane became more aware of his own Colt revolver, sitting loaded where it always was, beneath his left armpit.

"I can't figure it out," Cochrane said idly. "I *know* Siegfried is going to try something. But everything is secure. The White House. The grounds. The Naval Station. The yacht. The Potomac itself has U.S. Navy ships perched practically on top of the *Sequoia*. Couldn't slip a dingy past a pair of PT boats."

"What about the mouth of the river?" Whiteside asked. "Could a small ship be waiting there?"

"The Navy cleared the area," Cochrane said. "You know about Roosevelt and his Navy. Well, maybe you don't. But the President looks out for the Navy and the Navy looks out for—"

"Excuse me," Laura interrupted. "But what about a single man in the water?"

"What do you mean?"

"Stephen," she said without emotion. She recalled, "Way back, when I first met him, he used to do lengths of the lake. He could swim for hours. Why—"

Cochrane turned the key in the Hudson's ignition. The auto roared to life. Cochrane cut a U-turn on Pennsylvania Avenue. He pointed the car toward the bridges that allowed vantage points over the Potomac and which led to Virginia.

At nine-fifteen, two minutes after Cochrane's car screeched its tires and headed toward Virginia, the yellow spotlight above the White House was extinguished. Two U.S. Marine lance corporals appeared on the White House roof and hauled down the Stars and Stripes. Congress had adjourned. Franklin Roosevelt was traveling.

On the ground-floor rear of the White House, the President's luggage was placed in the trunk of two customized Cadillac limousines. Two extra Secret Service agents were assigned to Roosevelt's car, an extra lead car was assigned, and six motorcycle escorts from the District police—instead of the usual two— were in place and ready to lead the motorcade to the Naval Station.

Roosevelt, in the snippish mood that he'd been in recently, noted the extra security immediately.

"What the damned hell *is* this?" he asked. "An official state visit to the *Sequoia?*"

"Just appropriate security, Mr. President," replied

dark-eyed, bushy-haired Mike Reilly, the ranking Secret Service agent assigned to the White House.

Roosevelt eyed the extra men as his chair was wheeled to the limousine. "I never knew there was so much Republican territory between the White House and the Potomac," he remarked, the smile returning for an instant.

His security people split with laughter. Then they helped him into the back seat of the customized presidential limousine. Two agents hopped along the running boards on each side of the automobile while Reilly strolled the short driveway that led from the White House garage to the exit gate.

He stared through, scanning to his left and right across the park behind the White House. He saw only Secret Service and FBI details. He walked back to the presidential entourage and spoke to the men under his command.

"Not a German in sight," Reilly said. "But what can you expect from FBI reports?"

His agents grinned.

"Let's move," he said.

Reilly hopped into the lead car. On command, the rear gate of the White House swung open and the motorcade was on its way.

FORTY-TWO

"A nation of sleepers and dreamers," thought Siegfried as he treaded water carefully past the first U.S. Navy PT boat. There were sailors on the deck and obviously their mission was to guard the harbor. But none spotted the agent of the Third Reich as he slipped through the dark water fifty yards off the PT boat's bow.

Siegfried reached the *Sequoia* after a swim of twenty-two minutes. The yacht was like a steel goliath when he reached it and touched the hull. The curve of the bow protected him from view from above. And the spy tingled with the same excitement as last time.

Then he set to work.

He unbound his bomb from where it was strapped to his suit. He pressed the adhesive cement to the aft starboard side of the vessel, then he pressed the metal-encased explosives firmly into the cement. He pressed hard for two minutes, treading water. The charge was just above the waterline, ten to fifteen feet below the precise spot where the President and Mrs. Roosevelt usually slept.

The bomb was secure. Siegfried pushed off from the ship. He reached to the metal case around the bomb and he rapped it gently with his arm.

It held. Waves and water would not remove it. Nothing would, until it detonated at 3 A.M.

He pushed off and slowly slipped away from the boat. Then he heard a commotion on the pier above him.

Siegfried treaded the water and slowly moved at an angle to the *Sequoia*. He could see the pier. His heart almost stopped.

There was the presidential motorcade. Two long black Cadillac limousines. Siegfried did not see the leftist Mrs. Roosevelt. But as he stared from the shadowy surface of the Potomac, he did see the President.

Secret Service agents were lifting the invalid from the back of his car. Siegfried, ever conscious of details, could even see the ugly steel braces jutting upward within the President's trousers. The most powerful man in the world, some people called him, and he couldn't even walk. A prisoner of his own degenerative affliction. Siegfried almost laughed. How could Adolph Hitler even be compared with a cripple?

The spy watched Roosevelt being wheeled up the gangplank and into the yacht. Then Siegfried turned in the water. The hardest work was done, he rejoiced. He treaded his way to a distance of a hundred yards from the yacht and continued smoothly through the water. He cut his speed as he successfully passed the second naval vessel.

He cut through the water purposefully now, with

542

long, even, far-reaching strokes. He was prideful and giddy with excitement. He had affected the course of the twentieth century!

The shoreline of Alexandria, Virginia beckoned to him and grew larger as he swam toward it. The current carried him. Ten minutes after leaving the *Sequoia,* he spotted the illuminated spire of St. Thomas's Church.

That was his landmark. His beacon. He knew his car was a hundred feet from the church.

He hurried his strokes. All that mattered now was his escape to Germany.

The shoreline on the capital side of the river, Cochrane reasoned, was impregnable. There was the United States Naval Station first, then Bolling Air Force Base due south. On the Virginia shore there was National Airport between Arlington and Alexandria. The most vulnerable coastline, Cochrane then reasoned, had to be Alexandria.

They stood on the Alexandria promenade on the west bank of the Potomac: Laura, Bill Cochrane, and Peter Whiteside. They looked at the dark river and they gazed upward to where the lights of Washington shone from a distance of two to four miles.

"Just tell me this, if you would," Whiteside said to Cochrane. "What exactly are we looking for?"

There was a lapse of several seconds before Cochrane could muster an answer. "Anything," he said. "Anything in that river that isn't motorized has to come downstream. That means here."

Cochrane took two heavy flashlights from the trunk of his car and handed one each to Laura and Peter

Whiteside. He kept a smaller flashlight for himself. "Why don't the two of you stay reasonably close," Cochrane suggested as they began to walk the promenade. He held in mind that of the two of them, only Whiteside was armed. "I'll go on ahead," he said, starting to move southward along the bank. "We'll do two or three hundred yards at a time, then I'll move the car to keep it with us. By the way," he warned, "keep your eyes on the water."

"Pound to a penny we're wasting our time," Whiteside said.

"Have a better idea?" Cochrane asked.

No one did and Cochrane moved on ahead. He scanned the surface of the water as he walked, squinting and trying to make the light from shore work for him. Why was the moon so damnably dark tonight? he agonized. Coincidence, or part of Siegfried's design?

A phrase came tumbling back to him out of the past. *No,* he thought, *there* were *no coincidences.* Fact: *the water was the least guarded area.* Conclusion: *Siegfried was out there somewhere!*

Cochrane cautiously walked twenty feet from the water. There was suddenly the sound of a male voice and Cochrane's hand was upon his pistol, drawing it, pointing it, and praying that Fowler didn't have the drop on him already.

He shone his own small light in the direction of the noise and yelled, "Freeze! FBI! Freeze or I'll shoot!" And the focal point of his body was his quaking finger on the trigger.

Then, stunned, he could barely react to what he saw. Two young men, one slighter than the other, their clothes askew, fresh from an embrace that Cochrane had interrupted, stood trembling and staring at him. One wore a woman's wig and an earring.

It took him a full five seconds to comprehend and relax. "Go on," he said, lowering the weapon. "Get out of here." He turned off his flashlight. Wordlessly, the two men fled, one whimpering in terror.

Can't be so nervous! Cochrane told himself, feeling his soaking palm against the black steel of his gun. *Can't react that fast. I'll kill the wrong person. Jesus!*

Cochrane replaced his pistol in its holster and continued to walk.

What were they doing with flashlights? Siegfried wondered. The man and the woman appeared to be looking for something. Siegfried was fifty feet off the shore and intently watched Peter Whiteside and Laura. With a pair of long quiet strokes, he moved closer to them. Then he heard their voices and recognized them.

Siegfried was incensed! How dare these benighted amateurs endanger him again! This time they would both pay dearly.

Laura turned and shone her light across the water. Siegfried was imperceptible amid the choppy surface of the Potomac. Then the beam was gone.

He watched them. Their lights were like beacons and they were not far from Siegfried's car. In the water, he watched their lights move farther down the promenade. Then the Englishman walked ahead of her by several paces.

Siegfried studied the situation. A few seconds earlier he had thought he had seen a third, smaller beam farther down the shore. But when he looked for it again, he did not detect it. Must have been an odd car light, he reckoned. He waited several seconds more.

First Laura . . . then the Englishman. A quick, essential military operation. He moved to a position behind them and slipped quietly through the water toward shore. He reached to his leg and unsheathed the knife.

Then Laura and Peter Whiteside made things easier. Laura stayed behind and Whiteside went on ahead. They split by about fifty feet.

Siegfried was out of the water. For good measure, he reached within his diving suit and unwrapped his pistol. He placed it back within the suit, ready to draw it if necessary.

There were benches and shade trees along the promenade. But Siegfried also would have to cross open spaces where he was exposed. He would have to kill Laura quickly, then catch the Englishman equally by surprise.

He started after her, holding the dagger in his fist. He would grab her from behind, he quickly calculated, cover her mouth, and put the knife between her ribs. She would never know what happened.

He was thirty feet behind her now. Laura stopped and again scanned the surface of the water with her flashlight. Siegfried moved to the side of a kiosk. He stood with his back flush to it on a side facing away from her.

Siegfried could hear his own heart pounding. He edged toward the corner of the kiosk and inclined his head to peer around the corner. She still had the flashlight beam illuminated. She looked back in his direction as if she might have heard something. She even took a step in his direction. But then she turned and followed Whiteside.

Siegfried studied his two victims. Now he understood what they were doing. Whiteside was covering the ground along the promenade. Laura was watching the water. By slipping behind them, Siegfried knew, he had them both at his mercy. He could blind-side both of them.

I will cut her throat, he consciously decided. *Messier, but there will be no scream.*

Same with the Englishman.

Laura was in the open and Siegfried started after her.

She held the lantern in her left hand and scanned the water, and he was within twenty feet of her. Then fifteen. He bolted forward in full flight, the knife aloft in his fist, ready to cut.

Laura swept a strand of hair from her face and turned her head slightly. Out of the corner of her eye, she thought she saw—!

She turned as he hit her. She ducked but he had her with one hand and her mouth opened in horror—*just like the poor woman who was murdered behind the church!* she thought—and she launched an unholy piercing scream unlike any other in her life.

As she clutched the lantern, she saw the glint of light off the blade of the knife. She cried out again as it moved toward her throat.

His hands were wet and cold. The rubber suit was wet and slick. His grip on her was not firm. She had one hand free and held off the knife. She managed to turn. Laura's other hand crashed into his face. The steel flashlight hit him in the eye with much more force than

547

he ever could have imagined.

Then she brought her knee upward and it was his turn to bellow. She hit him in the face again with the flashlight, across the bridge of the nose, and he slashed at her with the knife.

But he was off balance and missed. She broke away.

Siegfried cursed violently. The pain in his genitals rocketed through him, but he remained on his feet.

"Laura! Laura!" Whiteside called out, and Siegfried could see the Englishman running in their direction, marked by his own lantern beam.

Siegfried staggered for a step, then pulled his revolver. It was his only option now. He would shoot them both.

He raised the pistol. She was thirty, forty feet away and moving. The Englishman was maybe sixty. Easy pistol range, but Laura was directly in the line of fire. Thought to Siegfried was now all simultaneous: *Have to hit the Englishman first. No time. Just shoot!*

Whiteside dropped his lantern and raised his own weapon. But Siegfried fired first. Then bullets were everywhere, and Laura hit the ground.

Whiteside squeezed off two shots, then a third, but he was moving quickly to one side as he fired and his aim was off. Siegfried's first bullet hit him in the leg, and the next smacked into his flesh a few inches above the heart. His own weapon flew from his hand and he went down.

In his pain, as he held his hands to his wounds and felt the warmth of his own blood, Whiteside stared at Siegfried. Fowler was like a black specter, something evil and violent risen from hell itself, framed by the light from a distant streetlamp and standing erect, triumphant, and proud on the other side of Laura's fallen, prostrate body.

Whiteside gasped and went to find his pistol. But his left arm wouldn't work at all. He was helpless. Siegfried—the executioner—stepped closer. Then even closer.

Laura was moving again. She whirled and threw up her hands, turning back toward the man she had once loved.

"No! Stephen! No!" she cried out in terror. Fowler raised his gun again—*First Laura, then the Englishman, the proper order after all*—and the night was alive with the crackling of pistol fire. Laura closed her eyes.

She waited for the pain. She waited for the bullets to tear into her flesh, for the agony of death and the inevitability of the onrushing final blackness. . . . *three, four, five shots. Then a sixth!*

The first two shots from Cochrane's pistol sailed wide of Siegfried. Fowler was not the easiest target for Cochrane, shooting as he was from many yards behind Peter Whiteside. But the first shots had forced Siegfried to fire at the gunman, who must have been farther up the promenade, only to come racing back at the first sounds of violence.

Cochrane's third shot had found its mark. It hit Stephen Fowler in the center of the chest and drove him backward. On instinct and strength he fired again, but now for Siegfried all was pain and confusion. He fired again wildly and then his empty gun clicked harmlessly. From out of the darkness more bullets came at him.

Bill Cochrane emptied his gun at the Nazi. One bullet hit Stephen Fowler in the throat and, tumbling viciously from that range, tore open the flesh, ripping inward at the Adam's apple and bursting in a red explosion out of the back of the neck.

But in some ways it barely mattered. Siegfried was already falling. Half a second later he was sprawled on the cold grass in an unearthly configuration. Blood poured from him. Part of his body spasmed, then he was completely still.

Sounds: quiet, building sounds of pain. Laura was crying, but no bullet had touched her. When she had fallen she had dived forward and tumbled to avoid his gunfire.

More sounds, as Bill Cochrane rushed to Whiteside and Laura: Whiteside moaning and begging for a doctor. Then Laura was beside him, also, and she clutched Bill Cochrane, sobbing wretchedly and wanting to hold him very tightly and not look back at the dead man behind her.

"A doctor, please, a doctor . . ." Peter Whiteside begged.

Cochrane used Whiteside's necktie to tie a tourniquet around the Englishman's leg. He forced the lantern upon Laura and he pressed a handkerchief to the chest wound near the heart.

"Help him up, help him up!" Cochrane ordered. The Englishman's legs were unstable. But as quickly as they could they pointed him toward the car.

Alexandria County Hospital, Cochrane knew from his days at the National Police Academy, was ten blocks away.

Then all three of them froze. Their eyes were upon the Potomac. United States Navy PT 622 was moving down the river toward the ocean. It grew steadily larger as it approached. But the eyes of Laura, Bill, and even the wounded Whiteside were upon the vessel behind the naval patrol boat.

It was the *Sequoia,* smooth, white, and sleek compared with the gray naval gunboat. Like its escort, it moved resolutely through the black river.

"Fowler came out of the water," Cochrane said. "The bomb is already in place."

"A doctor," Whiteside moaned again, losing consciousness. "Please . . . I beg of you . . . a doctor."

FORTY-THREE

On their way to the hospital Cochrane practically took the corners on two wheels. They were at the emergency-room entrance within five minutes, and had Whiteside upstairs in an operating room within eight.

To the astonished nurses and physicians, Bill Cochrane brandished his FBI identification and asked the hospital staff to telephone the police.

"Tell the police they'll find another body on the promenade by the river," he told them as he assisted the wounded Englishman onto a stretcher. A more complete explanation would be forthcoming later, he promised, "But the body down by the river doesn't need an ambulance. Just the wagon from the morgue."

Then he and Laura drove at a dizzying speed back to Washington, picked up a pair of police cars, which chased him but for which he did not stop, and came to a screeching halt before the Naval Station basin, which, with the *Sequoia* departed, seemed all but asleep.

Cochrane and Laura were stopped at the iron gate by MP's who now had strict orders not to let anybody pass. The FBI shield did no service to him, and as he argued with one MP, another stood to the side, a mean glint in his eye, holding an M-1 carbine at port arms.

"What I'm telling you is that an explosive device may have been placed against the President's yacht. I want to see the officer currently on duty."

The MP's were both skeptical and impassive. "We'll make a note of it for the morning," one of them said.

"Morning's too late, goddamn it!" Cochrane raged. "Where's the duty officer?"

"I'm the duty officer," said one of the MP's, who bore on his sleeve the stripes of a warrant officer.

"The duty officer is never below the rank of a lieutenant at this station," Cochrane fumed. "Now would you call him?"

Laura stood by, her face tight with tension.

The MP gave Cochrane a look of extreme irritation, then disappeared into a booth and made a telephone call. He looked up twice at Cochrane as he spoke.

"Well?" Cochrane asked when the MP emerged.

"Wait here," he said.

The MP's withdrew into their regular posts behind a wire gate. Several minutes later appeared a naval lieutenant bearing the name tag of Symonds.

Symonds was a tall, sandy-haired officer in his late twenties with an honest, open face and a soft mid-South drawl which Cochrane placed as from the Tidewater region of Virginia.

"What can I do for you?" Lieutenant Symonds asked.

Cochrane showed his FBI identification again and mentioned a possible explosive device somewhere against the hull of the *Sequoia*.

"Begging your pardon, sir," Lieutenant Symonds answered. "But the ship was thoroughly searched, both inside and outside. And the harbor's been held secure for three days."

"Not secure enough," Laura said. "One man swam through."

The lieutenant looked at them with narrow eyes, trying to decide. *"Swam?"* he asked.

"A diver," Cochrane said. "He may have come from the other side of the Potomac. All I know is that the chances are excellent that the *Sequoia* will blow up at any minute."

"And who are you again?" the officer asked.

"FBI," Cochrane said, increasingly vexed.

"And who's your lady friend here?"

"British intelligence," Laura answered.

Lieutenant Symonds seemed to yield. "I'll radio to the two escort ships. Let me take all the information that you have. Both the PT's have frogmen aboard. They can do an extra check on the *Sequoia.*"

"That's fine," Cochrane said. He made a motion to step through the gate. Symonds placed a hand on his shoulder and the MP's stepped forward again.

"I have to take your statement here, sir," the officer said. "We're under strict orders. No one sets foot within the gate tonight without direct written permission of the Department of the Navy."

Cochrane eyed the young officer and the two MP's. "All right," he finally said.

Lieutenant Symonds took a pad and pencil from a booth and took Cochrane's statement. His pencil hesitated twice when Cochrane spoke of an assassin who had been shot on the opposite bank of the river. But Lieutenant Symonds politely recorded everything.

"I'll transmit this right away," he promised. "Thank you, sir."

He saluted smartly and returned within the naval yard, leaving Cochrane and Laura outside the gate.

"Now what?" she asked.

"Now," Cochrane said, "we hope the Navy divers get to that device before it detonates."

From within his office, Lieutenant Symonds watched the man and the woman step back into their car. He reached for a shore-to-ship telephone and the two MP's watched him.

The Hudson backed up from the gate, turned, and grew smaller as it moved toward the capital. Lieutenant Symonds put down the telephone without speaking a word.

The MP's laughed. Lieutenant Symonds shook his head.

"Jesus H. Christ," Symonds cursed. He tore up the statement he had taken from Cochrane. He sprinkled it into an ashtray.

"Don't think there was a chance he was for real, do you, sir?" one of the MP's asked.

"A snowball's chance in hell, gents," drawled Symonds. "I don't think a sea trout could have swum within a knot of that yacht tonight without being spotted. Do you?"

"No, sir," the MP's agreed in unison.

"See if you can get rid of the next crazy without breaking up my card game," Lieutenant Symonds said. The MP's grinned. "Carry on."

The lieutenant saluted smartly and the MP's returned it. There were no other "crazies" that evening.

This time Siegfried had wound the watch.

The *Sequoia* was one mile off the coast of Newport News on its journey to Augusta when the two copper wires met and the electrical charge from the dry cell detonated four sticks of black dynamite.

The *Sequoia* convulsed with the explosion. And while Siegfried had been correct in his estimate that he did not have enough dynamite to destroy the entire ship, he had also been correct that he had enough explosive material to do the intended job. Even the legendary steel and seaworthiness of the Bath shipworks of Maine were not enough for four sticks of TNT.

Everything in the President's bedchamber was destroyed. The dynamite blew the metal from the hull of the ship through the outer wall, then through the inner walls of the presidential cabins. A hole twenty feet wide from the waterline upward was gutted into the vessel, those near the explosion were practically deafened, and amid the smoke and shards of metal, the first seamen to make their way to President and Mrs. Roosevelt's suite found nothing but destruction, smoke, and ruin.

U.S. Navy PT 336, the escort vessel to the rear of the *Sequoia,* threw its throttle forward and was first to reach the scene of the catastrophe. What they saw when they shone their floodlights on the yacht was a pleasure craft that was remarkable in that it was still afloat. The hull was warped upward to a point above the waterline.

Several blackened crew members were picking through the rubble.

Some sailors aboard the *Sequoia* wept openly, this being the last place that President Roosevelt had been seen alive. Others stood in a near-catatonic state, witnesses to this great disaster, unable to move or react: and, for that matter, unable to comprehend:

November 20, 1939. Roosevelt, most assuredly, was dead.

PART SEVEN

Thanksgiving-Christmas
1939

FORTY-FOUR

The newspapers called the explosion aboard the *Sequoia* a "horrible accident," but no actual explanation was ever attributed. The Hearst newspapers, which had never in Roosevelt's political lifetime been members of his fan club, hinted broadly at some evil, foreign conspiracy, and the tabloids likened the blast to the one which sunk the United States warship *Maine* in Havana Harbor in 1898. But those with a long memory recalled that no evidence was ever offered as to culpability in that blast, either.

At the FBI in Washington, stronger words than "conspiracy" were used. To the American public, however, jittery enough over the course of world events, nothing was ever stated to confirm that a German spy had planted a bomb against the vacationing President's yacht. The body of Stephen Fowler was returned to Bala Cynwyd, Pennsylvania, for burial in the family churchyard. The official cause of death was listed as a motor vehicle accident.

* * *

In the days that followed, as Peter Whiteside recovered in an Alexandria hospital, Dick Wheeler was kept under arrest at an army guardhouse at Fort Meade. This, for the safety of everyone as well as for the convenience of his interrogators from the FBI, many of whom he knew personally.

To them, and to the world at large, Dick Wheeler had little to say. A week passed. Then he said that under certain conditions he would speak to Bill Cochrane—and him in only one session. It was Frank Lerrick who conveyed this to Cochrane. The latter said what the hell, he was getting out of town anyway. Why not invest an afternoon in it? Lerrick asked Cochrane to keep his FBI shield for a few days into the next month.

Fort Meade was a sorry place on a gray December morning, made even more somber by the presence of truckloads of quaking new Army recruits. Cochrane drove there alone. Along the way, he was reminded of the trip to see Mauer, and he could only hope that the German, reunited with his family and now in Toronto, could find some peace. Cochrane used his FBI identification at the gates. Two MP's in Army khaki and white helmets saluted him smartly after checking his name off a list. His visit was more official than even he had thought. The Bureau was still playing games.

"The guardhouse is along that route, sir," one of the MP's told him, giving a nod to an asphalt driveway which veered to the left—the opposite direction of the bomb disposal unit.

But Cochrane could have picked out the guardhouse

with his eyes closed. It was a big, dark granite bunker dating from the grimmest days of the WPA, and when his car reached it there was another team of sentries. The Hudson was to remain outside the inner fence, but he was cleared for admission.

Cochrane found Dick Wheeler on a cot in a six-by-twelve cell. The walls were concrete on two sides and barred on the other two. Wheeler was hunched into a corner, a bottle of Coca-Cola in his hand, staring off into the distant space across his tiny cell.

"Hello, Dick," Cochrane said.

Wheeler turned and a smile flashed. Cochrane had a sense of visiting a terminally ill friend in a hospital. There was an ice bag by the cot and Cochrane could see by the large bruise across the side of Wheeler's forehead that Burns and Allen had performed a bit of their act.

A sergeant unlocked the cell. Wheeler stood as Cochrane was admitted. "I'm sorry I can't offer you more gracious surroundings," Wheeler began. "We're not very long on comfort here."

Cochrane sat down on a straight-backed wooden chair and Wheeler sank back onto the bed. "They even took my goddamned pipe. They had some insane idea that I might fashion a shiv out of it. Imagine."

A hundred reactions hit Cochrane at once. First, there were the charges against Wheeler. Second, there was the depth to which Bureau activities had been compromised since 1936. Cochrane envisioned the days when he had fled Munich with a Luger tucked into his coat and a Gestapo shield in a sweat-soaked palm. His anger flared. Then, just as quickly, there was little point in rage. Before him was Dick Wheeler. Big Dick.

The Bear. And they used to throw junction boxes and catch crooks together in Kansas City.

"They told me you wanted to see me," Cochrane said. "Instead of a lawyer."

"Oh, I'll see a lawyer eventually," Wheeler answered. "But I'd rather see a friendly face right now." Cochrane realized that he must have remained impassive, because Wheeler studied him for a moment and quickly added, "You are a friendly face, aren't you?"

"As friendly as you're going to be seeing," Cochrane allowed.

Wheeler laughed very slightly and seemed to be looking for his pipe out of force of habit, then stopped when he remembered. Cochrane smiled very uneasily.

"They"—meaning the inquisitors who had spent two days "talking" to him—"seem to think I'm some sort of Nazi," Wheeler explained. "I was hoping maybe you would explain things to them."

"Only if you explain them to me first."

"You don't understand?" Wheeler was surpised.

Cochrane gave a mild shake of the head.

"Doesn't anyone in this country see what's coming?" Wheeler snapped angrily. "We're about to embark on a second world war. And you know what? We're on the wrong side."

Thereupon Wheeler launched an account of himself and his politics, harking all the way back, Cochrane suddenly realized, to an impoverished boyhood in the Ozark hills of rural Missouri. The real enemy of America, Wheeler maintained, was the subversion of what he called "America's national spirit." "This is a God-fearing, white Protestant country," Wheeler explained without remorse or hesitation. "And may it always remain so."

But Wheeler had lived forty-two years, he reminded Cochrane, and wasn't happy with what he had seen over the last ten. "A tidal wave of immigrants . . . a rise of home-grown leftist politics . . . a flood of Jewish rabble into the country . . . it all takes its toll on the American fabric. Do you understand what I'm saying?"

Cochrane felt a sinking feeling in his stomach, but did admit to being familiar with Wheeler's point of view. It wasn't unpopular in these insular days.

"Roosevelt is responsible for much of it," Wheeler maintained. "He made left-wing politics acceptable during the Depression. Roosevelt embarked us on the road to socialism. First step to making us all Red."

And now, Wheeler postulated, there was in the offing an alliance with Russia. The Bolshevik demons. Told by Dick Wheeler in a soft midwestern drawl, it all *did* sound very frightening. Stalin was the incarnation of the crimson Marxist devil, sculpted moustache, pointed tail, cloven feet, and all. America was about to go to war against the industrious blond-haired Germans, with Satan as our sidekick.

"Does it make any sense to you?" Wheeler asked, seeming to want an honest answer. Then he forged ahead, not waiting.

"Compare the two systems," Wheeler explained. "Look at Germany in 1920. Weak. Impotent. Poor. Now look at what Hitler has done. Pride is restored. The Left has been vanquished. And a powerful Wehrmacht rules Europe."

"For today," Cochrane allowed.

"Now look at Western Europe. And look, if you

wish, at America. Socialism crept in during this decade and what has it brought us? Second-class world status, a tidal wave of filthy immigrants, twelve million unemployed, and a legion of Communists who wish to destroy every institution we have. Do I make my case clear?" Wheeler sipped the remainder from his bottle of Coca-Cola and waited.

"And so for this Roosevelt was to be killed?" Cochrane asked.

No, Wheeler answered, shifting his position on the cot. It was not quite that simple.

His own sympathies, Wheeler explained, were never so much pro-Hitler as they were pro-America. Early on in his FBI career he made a conscious decision. He would do what he could to keep America away from any entanglement with the Communists. If that meant helping the America First Committee, the German-American Bund, the Campfire Girls, or the Nazis themselves, which it gradually and inevitably did, well then, so be it.

"Siegfried started to work independently," Wheeler said, "and Fritz Duquaine was the key link. Fowler brought his services to Duquaine early on; his rightist pro-American editorials caught everyone's attention, including theirs. He insisted upon anonymity and to some degree he maintained it. But from the very outset, Duquaine knew who Fowler was. Didn't take him very seriously at first, then suddenly realized how brilliantly efficient he was."

"And you did nothing to stop him?"

"Since he was potentially harming an Anglo-American-Russian alliance, no, I didn't." He paused and elaborated, "I'd been in contact with Fritz

Duquaine, myself. I helped him stay a step ahead of everyone on this end."

"And the death of Roosevelt?"

"Fowler's grand design, I imagine. But you see," he added hesitantly, "as war approaches, *some* grave radical step must be taken. If it's the death of a President . . . well, we've survived that before, haven't we?"

Cochrane nodded without conviction.

"My goal," Wheeler concluded pensively, "was to save America for white Christians. That's what I told those morons this afternoon. That's what they failed to understand. Kept asking me instead about Bund networks in Wisconsin. God!"

"I'll see if I can straighten them out."

"*Would* you?" At least a quarter minute passed. It was an uneasy lapse of time, and when it ended, Wheeler's tones were considerably sadder. "I know what's in store for me, after all," he said. "Know what I mean?"

He seemed to want an answer, so Cochrane gave him an honest one. "You'll be tried for treason. Probably be executed."

"And you know what?" Wheeler asked. "I consider myself a patriot." He was suddenly adamant: "The real *physical* enemy is the Soviet Union, Bill. As long as you live, don't ever forget that."

Then the gears seemed to shift and Dick Wheeler began to ramble. He talked again of the penury of his own boyhood in the Ozarks and how his family, honest working people, never took a handout from the government, never needed the writings of Marx, always sent their males into the armed forces, and worked their way from lean to prosperous times. Why, Wheeler wanted to know, couldn't everyone do that?

From there Wheeler returned to his politics. Cochrane found himself listening politely but turning a deaf ear to it. There was no point in discussing it, challenging it, or even prolonging it. Afterward, certain phrases stayed with Cochrane:

Roosevelt will have all of us—white, yellow, and colored—communized and intermarried. By the year 2000, we will all be niggers. . . .

I hate the Jews very deeply. Every boatload of them that arrives in New York should be turned back out to sea and set on fire. . . .

To safeguard the Republic from Bolshevism, presidential elections might someday need to be canceled; a strong Christian leader from the military could then guide the country indefinitely. . . .

And, to round things out as Bill Cochrane grew weary:

Unionized labor should be outlawed. . . .

The Bill of Rights should be suspended. Summary executions of known criminals by police squads could be held in public places. . . .

The monstrosity of all this, weighing in on Bill Cochrane as the afternoon died, helped prompt him to his feet. Cochrane promised that he would attempt to make clear Dick Wheeler's point of view to the inquisitors. Wheeler said he was grateful.

"They have such sledgehammer personalities, Hoover's people," Wheeler said. "You're about the only one to whom I can make an intellectual appeal."

"I'm honored."

Wheeler cocked his head in a diffident manner.

"Something else," he said.

Cochrane asked what.

"You fed the German naval code to Lanny Slotkin intentionally, didn't you?" Wheeler asked. "The proper additive and all."

Cochrane nodded. "You figured if I slipped a trap through the FBI," he answered, "it would have come through Bobby Martin or Hope Ming. Or even Roddy Schwarzkopf or Liz Pfeiffer. So I figured Lanny was the surest way of showing you the bait."

"Point." Wheeler grimaced.

Cochrane felt his anger rise very slightly. "Well, *someone* was going to take the bait from within the FBI," he said. "My contact in Berlin was murdered before my arrival. I was under surveillance the entire time. Otto Mauer and his family escaped only because they were both ingenious and lucky. And someone, *someone*, tipped Siegfried as to the name and address of who was closing in on him. How else does a bomb magically arrive under my bed?"

For the first time, Wheeler appeared unnerved by the whole conversation. But he looked without remorse at the younger man.

"Well, nothing personal you understand, Bill," he said. "But you'd become a nuisance. Something had to be done."

"But why was I selected in the first place?"

"Not *my* goddamned idea!" Wheeler snapped, rummaging again for the missing pipe. "I argued long and hard for someone else. But you were the only choice—experience against Gestapo in Germany, veteran Bureau, background in explosives in the U.S. Army. Roosevelt handpicked you, himself, in case you never knew."

Which brought Cochrane to attention. "No. I didn't know."

Wheeler's eyebrows arched. "Final point?" he asked. Cochrane waited.

"Word reaches me," Wheeler said, "that you're having it on with Stephen Fowler's widow. Any truth to that?"

"We're seeing each other," Cochrane admitted after a suitable pause.

Wheeler considered it and then gave Cochrane a schoolboy grin that had a conspiratorial leer to it. Then Wheeler laughed. "Do one other thing for me. On your way out see if the soldier boys who are guarding me will slip me another bottle or two of Coke. I'm dying of thirst."

Cochrane said he would. He rapped on the cell door for a guard while Wheeler added a request for a newspaper.

"They're nice young men, these soldiers," Wheeler said in closing. "It's a fucking national obscenity that they're all going to be sent off to be slaughtered in Europe. It's Stalin who's the real enemy. Don't forget."

Cochrane called it a day, said good-bye, and left.

On the drive back to Washington, Cochrane realized how much the afternoon had depressed him. There had been a morose, condemned air to his entire meeting with Dick Wheeler. He wondered very deeply, weighing the entire intrigue involving Wheeler and Fowler, whether anything had been gained by anyone. Like a war itself, there seemed nothing but waste and destruction everywhere one looked.

Cochrane drove directly to the Shoreham, anxious to redeem the day in any way possible. He arrived toward 8 P.M.

Laura, when she came downstairs to meet Bill Cochrane, took his breath away. She was in a slim, tailored dark blue gown that featured the most interesting neckline that he had seen in ten years. Or maybe that was simply because it was beautiful Laura in that gown and the day had otherwise been so beastly.

The Shoreham dining room was grand and ornate, patterned after the great hotel dining rooms of England and the Continent. The room was a sea of white tablecloths and floral arrangements beneath a high-beamed ceiling. Waiters and captains in black formal attire scurried from party to party. The room was busy. Washington scuttlebutt and policy was bandied from diner to diner. Men were in dark suits and their female companions wore their finest gowns and jewelry. Earlier that week, Soviet Russia had attacked tiny Finland.

As the maître d' showed them to their table, the piano player in the corner sang "Anything Goes." Laura and Bill sat and looked at each other for a moment.

"Hell of a day," he said. And as he spoke, he realized one of the things that had brought him through the day was the prospect of seeing her this evening. "Do you mind if we don't talk about it?"

"I'd prefer we didn't. Want a better subject?"

"I could use one," he answered.

"One of your Bureau errand boys," she said archly, "came by the hotel today. Brought me an airline ticket

571

to Havana. Imagine that. Institutionalized immorality."

"It happens in the best of democracies," he joked. He cleared his throat. "I thought we might get away for a few days. If you're interested."

"When would we leave?"

"Monday of next week," he said. "Ever been to Havana?"

She shook her head. "I hear it's romantic."

"You hear correctly," he said.

A waiter brought a menu and took orders for drinks. Bill Cochrane thought of all he had to put in order. His house. His office. His nongovernment career. His life.

"I suppose I should be making some other travel plans soon, too," she said at length.

"Back to England?"

Laura nodded. "I have to face the facts. I'm at loose ends here. Further, there must be something in England I can do to help. My country's at war."

She heard an echo from long ago: *For England.* But she didn't repeat it. Nor did she need to elaborate. Bill Cochrane understood.

"You'll certainly be welcome to visit me any time," she said. "I want you to, of course."

"Of course." He was nodding unconvincingly as their drinks arrived. His and hers: a good stiff bourbon and a dry sherry.

"You don't look terribly enthused," she said.

"Well," he said, looking downward for a second, then meeting her soft brown eyes with his, "your scenario isn't exactly the same as mine."

"It's not?"

"I thought maybe," he began, "that I should talk you

into staying on a bit in the United States—"

And she was thinking, not saying, *Oh, Peter Whiteside! What a schemer you've made me! What an outstanding subversive!*

"I'm sure"—Cochrane continuing—"you could find a job in Washington. Travel's dangerous these days, and, uh . . ." For the first time since he had known her, he groped for words. He looked away, then boldly back at her.

"Damn it, Laura!" he said. "It's very simple. I'm not *letting* you leave."

The next evening they found an informal little French bistro in Georgetown called Chez Lucien. The owner, Lucien himself, was from Normandy and practically embraced Bill Cochrane as a long-lost brother when Cochrane spoke fluent French to him.

A bottle of the best Margaux appeared, compliments of the house, and the waiter, Julien, also from Normandy, directed the attention of Bill and Laura to the roast duck, which is what they ordered.

Crepes suzette, made specially by Lucien with a startling flourish of liqueur and flame that nearly singed the ceiling, followed the duck. An Armagnac from 1897 completed the memorable evening. Or so it seemed.

Emerging from the restaurant past ten, full and satisfied, they walked back to Twenty-sixth Street, only to find a jeep of the United States Army Military Police, a black Plymouth belonging to the FBI, and a D.C. police car all lining the curb. Half a dozen armed men stepped from various vehicles.

"William Cochrane?" an MP sergeant asked.

"Yes?"

"We have orders to take you to Fort Meade."

"Now?" Cochrane asked, more conscious than ever that Laura was on his arm.

"Yes, sir. Now."

"Am I under arrest?"

"No, sir," the soldier said.

"But you have 'orders'?"

"We're to ask nicely, sir, then bring you anyway, sir."

Laura looked at him in disbelief. Then someone in a suit spoke from an unmarked Plymouth. The man held up something that looked very familiar to Bill Cochrane.

"Bureau business, Mr. Cochrane," the agent said. "Assistant Director Lerrick sent us."

"Naturally," said Cochrane with a groan. "Can we drop the lady back at the Shoreham on the way?"

"Not a chance!" said Laura. "I'm coming with you."

Bill and Laura stepped into the back of the Plymouth and the green and white D.C. police car led the way, it's lights flashing but with no siren. Halfway there he began to get the idea. Something had happened. And fifteen minutes later, after a harrowing fast ride across slick Maryland highways, Cochrane knew what it was as Laura waited outside the army guardhouse.

The MP's checked Wheeler twice an hour, they said, and it never occurred to them how quickly a man could bleed to death. From somewhere he'd obtained a Coca-Cola bottle—strictly against regulations—and he had shattered it against the cement walls of his cell. He'd sharpened the big round shard that came off the heel of the bottle. Then he had set it to both wrists as well as his throat and ankles.

Dick Wheeler's body lay on the floor of the cell in a pool of blood that was immense. Cochrane gagged when he saw it, wanted to throw up, didn't, and turned with undue vehemence upon Frank Lerrick, who stood with him.

"So what's this? Something for my memory scrapbook?" Cochrane demanded. "What'd you bring me here for? You fired me, you know. Or did you forget?"

"Well, uh, he killed himself."

"So it appears."

"Well, uh, why?"

"*Why?* You're Hoover's goddamned handpicked detective. You find out why."

"Cochrane," Frank Lerrick said, "you were the last one he talked to. In your own way, you were the only one in the Bureau who he, uh, had any respect for. What did he say to you yesterday afternoon?"

"He said he was deeply depressed. He said we were going into the war on the wrong side. He said we'd end up fighting the Russians by 1955." Cochrane paused. "He also specifically said that you and Hoover were a pair of feather-brained assholes."

Lerrick was obviously disappointed. "That's *all?*"

"From his point of view, that was quite enough. He also wanted to know if he'd be executed for treason. He said he thought he would be. I told him he was probably right."

Lerrick's anger flashed. "What'd you tell him *that* for?"

"Because that was the truth. And he knew it long before I told him."

Bill Cochrane took a final look at the dead man on the floor. For a moment he winced at the pain that Wheeler must have known before dying and for another moment he felt sorry for him. Then he gave Frank Lerrick a final sour look. "I'll be out of the Twenty-sixth Street house by noon tomorrow," he said. "Not a minute earlier." Then he departed.

With him went the lesson he had learned so well years ago at the National Police Academy, then under Wheeler's own command in Kansas City.

In this line of work . . .

In Cochrane's career, Dick Wheeler had always been the coincidence, but Cochrane had never seen it. Chicago and Kansas City, then Berlin and Washington. Always it had been Dick Wheeler, giving the silent orders, pulling the unseen strings.

When the Gestapo had known ahead of time of Cochrane's arrival, he hadn't seen the coincidence. When Siegfried somehow had learned who was on his trail, and where that "who" lived, Cochrane had only begun to sense the coincidence.

Now Wheeler was dead of his own hand and Bill Cochrane was off the Bureau. At last, coincidence had been eliminated.

FORTY-FIVE

There were two other ghosts to lay to rest.

Cochrane flew to Atlanta on Saturday morning, and early on a chilly afternoon found himself walking through the tall grass of a hillside cemetery at Stone Mountain. Not far from a memorial to the Confederate Civil War dead, Bill Cochrane came to a granite marker of another tragedy: a smaller tragedy, perhaps, but one of equal intensity.

The tombstone read:

Heather Powers Cochrane
1912–1933

He leaned forward and laid a modest bouquet across the grave. Inadvertently, the flowers reminded him of the bouquet she'd thrown as a young girl in a white wedding gown on the afternoon of their marriage.

Funny about life, he thought to himself. Had Heather not died, he would never have applied to the FBI. And he would never have met Laura. Bill

577

Cochrane was only occasionally a religious man, and the grand designs of life—what was meant to be, what was not meant to be—perplexed him endlessly.

"I'm getting remarried, Heather," he said softly, as if as a confession. "The second half of my life has begun. I've chosen the woman I want to spend it with."

For more than half a minute he stood in silence, thinking not praying, observing, putting things in order. He looked at the burial plot on the peaceful Georgia hillside. His eyes focused on the bouquet he had just placed. Life's absurdities and contradictions came toward him in a final rush.

Flowers, he thought, for weddings.

Flowers. For funerals.

Flowers, he could not help but recall from the insane hours in Code Breaking with the Bluebirds. Flowers like Siegfried's, planted in a homicidal pattern across the northeastern United States.

He turned and was gone.

He took the next available flight to Philadelphia. From there it was just a short hop on the Reading Railroad out to Bala Cynwyd, where Bill Cochrane called upon the family of the late Stephen Fowler. Cochrane found what had been overlooked for too long.

Walter Fowler, Stephen's father, still shared his bereavement with his family. But he agreed to speak with Bill Cochrane. Neither mentioned the circumstances of Stephen's death. It barely mattered now. Only the death itself was significant.

Walter Fowler was a tall handsome man in his seventies, and from a certain angle struck an image of his departed son. Fowler spoke of Stephen's life and, in doing so, shed the light that Cochrane sought.

"We lost just about everything during the Depression," Walter Fowler recalled at length. "In January of 1929 I was worth more than a million dollars. By the end of October, I was worth a few hundred. It was that fast. The family rallied, of course. Our business didn't go under. The railroads still had to use tracks. But we learned how quickly the enemies could destroy you if they wanted to."

"Sorry," Bill Cochrane said. "What enemies? I'm not following."

A strange cast came over Walter Fowler's eyes. "Wars and depressions come from the same source," he explained succinctly. "There isn't one that isn't inspired, fomented, and promoted by the great international banking combines. And these, of course, are entirely controlled by Jews. Have you ever read a pamphlet by Henry Ford called *The International Jew?*"

"No, sir. I haven't."

"I'll find you a copy. You should read it."

"Uh huh."

And on it went for another hour until Stephen Fowler made sense. Cochrane then excused himself, saying he wished to catch the 7:23 express from Thirtieth Street Station to Washington.

So inevitably, in a perverse sort of way, all the recent events created their own scheme of logic.

Cochrane sat in the window of the Transworld DC-3 as it lifted off the runway of National Airport on Monday morning. The woman who sat next to him was always nervous when flying; she had been in aircraft only twice before in her life. She fidgeted her hands and Cochrane placed his hand on hers.

Stephen Fowler remained something of a cipher, but Cochrane now understood enough to close his own mental books. The only son in a distinguished, wealthy family, Stephen Fowler made his peace with fascism early in life. Probably at Princeton, Cochrane reckoned. Among the elite, among the other moneyed sons of Nassau, and among the eating clubs and playing fields of the upper class. The Depression came and threatened to take all this from Stephen Fowler and those like him. Fowler reacted to Roosevelt's democratic-socialism with some -isms of his own.

Fascism. Fanaticism. Deism. It was not, as Reverend Fowler himself might have remarked, like St. Paul falling off a horse. The force of Paul's conversion was said to propel him from saddle to roadside, where he sat basking in his new faith. With Fowler it had to have been a longer process, prompted by what the young minister perceived to be the forces of evil in the world. Jews. Leftists. Moderates. Atheists. Democrats. At Princeton he openly opposed all of them. Only later did he develop his cover. By that time he had been contacted. Summoned to grace, as it were. The network of Fritz Duquaine was in the business of talent spotting, and Stephen Fowler was talent pure and simple. Thus followed the months of brooding, then the striking swing leftward to cover the man within.

And what about the church? Cochrane thought to himself. *And what about his marriage?*

More cover? Or true love?

Cochrane weighed it carefully. Surely Fowler must

have believed at least somewhat. Surely there was a time in Fowler's life when he believed in a divine Christian God. Cochrane wanted to believe that this aspect of the man represented the one shred of decency in Laura's husband. But how could Christianity have been reconciled to murder and Hitlerism?

Similarly with his marriage: Could any man have Laura's love bestowed on him and remain impassive? Then Cochrane thought of the knife that had once been held at her throat, the steel point to her jugular. He shuddered, grew angry, and looked out the window of the DC-3.

His boyhood flashed before him. He saw stretched out beneath him the Blue Ridge Mountains of Virginia, and as he peered very carefully he could see the Rivanna River. He turned excitedly to the woman next to him.

"Look, look," he said to Laura, taking her hand and showing her. "That's Virginia. That's where I grew up."

She unbuckled the seat belt and rose slightly, leaning forward toward the window and looking down. Even in December, blue mountains capped with white, the land was extraordinarily beautiful.

There was ice on the Rivanna. Cochrane could see it. But then, in a quick flash, time spiraled and he saw himself barefoot and in dungarees some thirty years earlier, pitching stones into the river, watching the circles form in the water, and his own father was standing beside him.

The vision faded and was replaced by ones of the College of William and Mary, his first wife, and his lonely first days at the Police Academy.

Then white clouds suddenly covered Virginia and

inevitably Cochrane saw in them the billows of cottony smoke that were always present from Dick Wheeler's pipe.

Wheeler's fascism had been on a more sophisticated level than Reverend Fowler's, Cochrane decided. That perplexed him, because Fowler seemed the more sophisticated man. But where Fowler had rejoiced in Hitlerism, the late Dick Wheeler had wrapped himself in stars and stripes. "A patriot," as he had termed himself in the final hours before his suicide. Where Fowler was a disguised monster of international terrorism and totalitarianism, Dick Wheeler was nothing more than a dark mirror held up to the American psyche: racism and lynching, isolationism and gun-wielding violence. Roosevelt had betrayed *Americanism,* Wheeler had concluded, and that, like horse theft in the Old West, was a transgression worthy of hanging.

Where Cochrane had grown up there had been a man in Charlottesville named Jim Horsely. Jim Horsely was a deputy sheriff and owned a candy store. By day he tipped his hat to ladies in the street and gave penny candies to the children who flocked to his store. By night, he was the most notorious Ku Klux Klansman in Albemarle County. After his own death, the stories surfaced: Jim Horsely had personally been responsible for the deaths of at least a dozen colored people over the last two decades. Cochrane as a teenager had been struck with that realization.

There had been two Jim Horselys, just as now there had been two Dick Wheelers. And two Stephen Fowlers.

"You're very quiet," Laura said as the DC-3 banked

582

to the southeast.

He turned to her. "I'm sorry. Just thinking. And I'm very tired."

She nodded. So was she. Physically and spiritually drained. They were nearing Havana two hours later when she spoke again.

"Do you think Stephen believed in God?" she asked.

"In his way, yes. I think he did."

"If there *is* a God," she continued, "I hope He's merciful."

"We all do," Bill Cochrane said.

She was silent again for many minutes, then bravely asked. "What about me? Do you think Stephen ever loved me?"

He replaced his hand on hers. "I know I do," was his only answer.

Then the airplane began its descent for Havana.

As almost all Americans know, almost five and a half years later, at 3:35 in the afternoon of April 12, 1945, the thirty-second President of the United States died of a sudden cerebral hemorrhage. When stricken, he was having his portrait painted at the Little White House in Warm Springs.

The explosion on the presidential yacht in November of 1939 took no fatalities at all. But it might have changed history, had it not been for a quirk of events.

Mrs. Roosevelt disliked ocean voyages of any sort in November. At the last moment, she decided to stay behind in Washington for the weekend, appear at a pair of political functions for her husband, and travel to Warm Springs by train the following Monday.

The President himself, on the night of the explosion erupted mysteriously off the hull of the *Sequoia,* was safely on the forward port of the vessel—as far from the explosion as possible—in the ship's reading room. His insomnia had kicked up again; or, more accurately, it had never abated.

Someone from the FBI had sent him a copy of a naval volume entitled *The Fighting Liners of the Great War,* published in London and not yet available in the United States. Roosevelt had been transfixed by the notion of the great ocean liners again becoming troop ships. He was halfway through the book when the explosion rocked the *Sequoia.*

Mike Reilly, the head of the President's Secret Service detail, was the first to locate the President. Bursting into the reading room in his pajamas and bearing a handgun, Reilly was stunned to see Franklin Delano Roosevelt calm and engrossed in his book. Finally at sea, in fact, the President looked better than he had in weeks. His face was fresh, his body relaxed, and his eyes twinkled.

"Now, Mike," asked the President, looking up with a sly grin, "I know the world is at war, but unless we are several thousand miles off course, we are a long way from a battle zone. So what the blazes was that?"

For a moment Reilly could not bring himself to speak. "A, er, boiler malfunction, I'm told, Mr. President," Reilly answered at length. "Possibly a serious one."

Roosevelt nodded. "Michael, this is a fascinating volume," he added. "You must find out who at the FBI sent it to me."

"Yes, of course, Mr. President." Reilly stared at the

Commander in Chief and awkwardly nestled his revolver to his pajama pocket. He wondered at just what point the President would have to be told that his bedchambers had been destroyed and that two PT vessels were about to evacuate the *Sequoia*. Finally, when Reilly did not move, Roosevelt looked up again.

"Are you *all right,* sir?" Reilly pressed, still staring.

"*I'm* just *splendid,* Michael," Roosevelt answered with a huge grin and a laugh. "How are *you?*"

"I'm okay, sir." Reilly answered. "Thank you."

Then the President returned to his reading. As everyone knew, Franklin Delano Roosevelt's fascination with naval matters was one of the paramount concerns of his life.

PART EIGHT

Cambridge, Massachusetts
May
1984

FORTY-SIX

On the wall of Memorial Hall, the hour, minute, and second hand of the clock came together at the twelve. Dr. Cochrane had run ten minutes past his time. But few students had complained.

He looked to his left and the Englishwoman with the gray hair smiled and motioned to her watch. Suddenly Bill Cochrane was aware of the time. He apologized to the class. They were in a forgiving mood.

Over the last two hours Bill Cochrane had told them about what might have been. With Roosevelt dead or disabled on the presidential yacht, the 1940 election might have been between Wendell Willkie, the bright young star of the Republicans, and John Nance Garner, who had split the Democratic Party by wresting the nomination away from Henry Wallace.

Willkie, the internationalist, had defeated Garner. The Republicans had gone into office. Lend-Lease had happened anyway, only it had come several months later and only in time to repel an invasion of Great Britain.

"The English are people of great tenacity," Cochrane had stressed in his lecture, "as are the American people. Politics of the extreme come and go in both nations. What you must remember is that both peoples will always rally at a point of moderation. Great leaders are important, but never forget—in a democracy the great leaders are allowed to lead only because they are elected."

Hitler had asked his Japanese allies to refrain from attacking Pearl Harbor until England could be defeated. When the R.A.F. and British Navy refused to buckle, Japan attacked anyway on February 21, 1942. A Sunday morning, naturally. America entered the war. It ended by January of 1946. By that time, Thomas Dewey was the President of the United States, having assumed office when an overweight, chain-smoking Willkie suffered his fatal heart attack in 1944.

"The United Nations happened anyway, as did the atomic bomb," Dr. Cochrane theorized. "These, like the war, were events set in motion, more than the actions of a single man. Harry Truman never left the United States Senate and MacArthur never became President because of his dispute with President Dewey over Korea in 1951. Eisenhower became President the next year—running as a Democrat, he defeated Senator Taft—and the McCarthy era happened anyway. Again, events were set in motion. American history always drifts toward the center course, no matter who the personalities involved."

Dr. Cochrane then wrapped up. He told the old joke that had made its rounds of the Harvard Faculty Club since the 1970s: A woman falls into a coma in 1954, and comes out of it in 1980. "How is Senator Taft?" she asks. "Senator Taft is dead," she is told. "How is Senator McCarthy?" she next asks. "Senator McCarthy died," she is told. "Well, then," she inquires at last, "how is President Eisenhower?" "President Eisenhower is dead," she is informed. To this she finally reacts in horror. "Oh, my God!" she cries. "That means Nixon is President!"

The class erupted in laughter. Bill Cochrane, at the spot of his yearly triumph, closed his notebook, held a hand aloft, and waved. The class stood appreciatively and applauded, as was the custom on the last day of lectures.

Some started to file toward the exits but others stayed in place and applauded for several minutes. Bill Cochrane stepped away from the lectern, slightly embarrassed by the outpouring of approval, and Laura came to him. He tried to wave a final time to the class, to dismiss them and send them on to their next sessions.

And gradually the applause did begin to die. But Bill Cochrane was distracted again, because he caught something in Laura's eyes, something he'd seen so many times over the decades, something he'd seen so long ago; pride, strength, integrity, and tenacity. All the things he'd fallen in love with within this woman, in addition to the woman herself: all the things that had made a successful marriage endure forty-three years.

The applause was distant and then neither of them heard it at all. They were somewhere else, remembering.

"You absolute ham," she said to him. "You *should* have been an actor."

"I was, you know," he teased her. "Many years ago.

In Provincetown, Massachusetts. Eugene O'Neill used to come see us."

"Of course, dear," she said. "And I was a spy."

They both laughed. He took Laura's hand and they walked toward the exit at the right of the lectern. He gave the class a final wave and did in fact savor the moment, as she had always accused him.

"Next year," he said aloud. "That's it until next year."

There would always, Bill and Laura Cochrane believed, be a next year.